The Dragon of Illenwell

Testament of Wielders: Book One

Philip Brice

THE DRAGON OF ILLENWELL
TESTAMENT OF WIELDERS: BOOK ONE

iUniverse books may be ordered through booksellers or by contacting:

iUniverse
1663 Liberty Drive
Bloomington, IN 47403
www.iuniverse.com
844-349-9409

ISBN: 978-1-6632-3429-2 (sc)
ISBN: 978-1-6632-5175-6 (hc)
ISBN: 978-1-6632-3428-5 (e)

Library of Congress Control Number: 2022911576

Print information available on the last page.

iUniverse rev. date: 03/15/2023

For my son, Kyle, who couldn't find a dragon
book that he liked, so, I wrote him one.

Love,
Dad

There is no remembrance of the men of old; nor of those to come will there be any remembrance among those who come after them.

—Ecclesiastes 1:11

Acknowledgements

There are many that I wish to thank and there are many more that I could not possibly thank enough.

God, from whom all inspiration comes including those testaments that aid our wielder to success.

To iUniverse including Traci, Maggie and the editorial team for whom I could not have had this book completed.

The Sawmillers, Sam and Melissa. They read this from infancy and encouraged me all the way. Melissa, write that novel!

The neighborhood boys and especially John Joseph Noble who helped me create some of these characters.

The magnificent artwork of Vladimir and his patience to help me understand the cover design.

My awesome and rather large Italian family that adapted me and never stopped believing in me, thanks ever so much and their lovely daughter that married me for better or worse and for our three children, Kyle, Haley and Nolan who helped to inspire me the most with this book.

Olivia Marie Luevano! Welcome to the family and THANK YOU!

Finally, and equally important, thanks Mom, Dad and Oz for all your love and support.

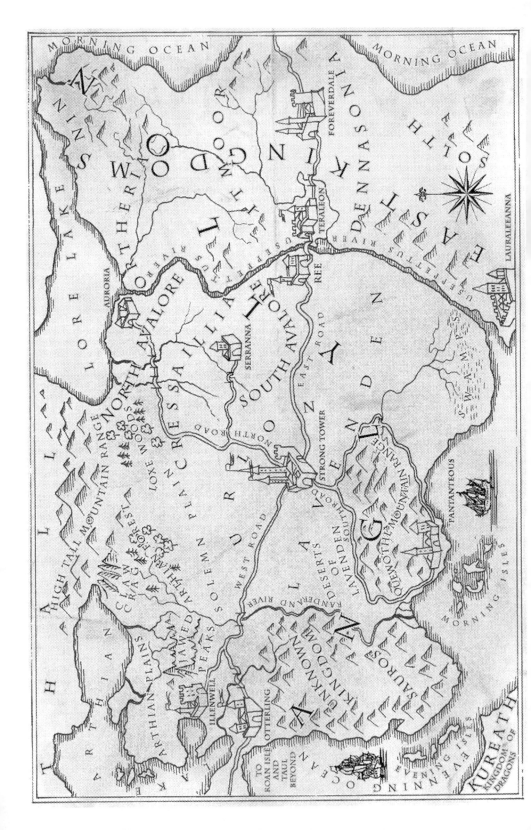

Jubilee Date 18, After Founding 9085

For those who find and can translate and interpret these testaments, blessing be upon you from our Divine Giver. For only He truly knows when these will be found and/or can be even translated or salvaged?

You now hold in your grasp the testaments of Anglyllon and the stories of our age, some nine thousand seasons now.

Testamentors were skilled at their craft. Sources ranged from creditable to eyewitness accounts—from actual events told by those who knew them well to the stories handed down through oral traditions.

They came from actual wielders and apprentices to lords and ladies who ran our kingdoms.

Zoarians, our watcher brothers from the skies, observing us and sharing with us their observations and wisdom.

Here is but one of the many countless deeds of our wielders. Our dates were added to the beginnings in order that one may place them in some chronological order, depending on what, if any, should survive.

Unfortunately, testamentors can be a bit biased (to downright opinionated), so try not to read too much into them.

Some testaments are from anonymous authors—either simply unknown or those who wish to remain unknown or long forgotten.

Many are from those who cleverly and, with great stealth, hid away, while others yet are survivors themselves.

Perhaps you can take our successes and failures to better understand your past and where your future lies.

Still yet perhaps, just maybe, burn these all, along with our past and write your own future.

Chapter 1

The wielder pressed his white windbred on. It was a magnificent beast, sturdy, agile, and just as determined as its owner. Four strong legs swiftly devoured the road. The windbred was as relentless as its owner, and both focused down the East Road and could see nothing but their goal. Muscles tone and taxed to the point of exhaustion as they collapsed the amount of time between them and their destination. The wielder's sword of gold, a distinguished symbol of achievement, bounced with the rhythm of the charging windbred. As he rode low to the beast's neck, he could smell the sweat and perspiration from the heat of the mid sun, coupled by that of the long ride.

They moved as one, breathed as one, thought as one, and ached as one—through the brightest part of the suns and the darkest of nights and everything that came in between. Both rested when needed and ate on the move, for even at this moment, the wielder's mind had already arrived at their destination. But it, unfortunately, would take several more suns to make Strong Tower. And that disturbed him immensely, for he knew that, even now, the kingdom was held together by a thin strand of hope, hope that would now be shadowed behind the eyes of a concerned lady. Her lord and an entire kingdom, not to mention the rest of the country, were forced to wait patiently for their anticipated arrival.

Although, in his mind, there would be no safety on this job, he was at least grateful that his rugged companion could outride whatever distractions would come their way. After all, they had just left the settlement of Ree on the shore of the Useppettus River and would not stop until it intersected with the other three roads in the middle of Strong Tower, some four or five suns away. But for now, this part of the country was thick with forests, and that kept the rider ever more mindful as they cut through the kingdom of South Avalore, where he really expected nothing at all. However, to the direct south was yet another story, for it invited endless possibilities for distractions.

Even though Lord Krhan would say it was part of his kingdom of Lavenden, it was completely open to the development of future kingdoms and sparsely inhabited by small villages and small clusters of tight-knit families who rather relished in their own private affairs, far from lords, orbs, and other such politics. For now, that didn't concern the rider as much as the distractions, so they drove on, each keeping a mindful eye to the thick forest on either side. For leaving this part of the country could not come soon enough.

The windbred momentarily stumbled under the wielder's weight, forcing him to lose his concentration.

"Steady boy," The wielder spoke to his true companion as he reached out and patted the windbred's sweaty head. "I know you need a break. But we can't, my best friend; they needed us there promptly."

But they both understood who really needed him. And it burned impatiently within him, and he tried desperately to bury the thoughts. "One wielder, one sword," he cursed. "What in twilight's end are these Zoarians working at?" He cursed again, and his windbred grunted loudly as if it agreed. There are now too many kingdoms and more coming. He cursed and kicked his loyal companion on.

Perhaps, in the earlier seasons of Anglyllon's founding, this worked. But not now! Too much travel, more corruption. We need one body, one kingdom with all the orbs. Unified Anglyllon. The wielder's exhausted mind screamed for relief. *Will someone listen before I'm dead?* His mind shouted toward his windberd, about the only living thing that understood him right at that moment.

Well, he changed his direction of thought to calm himself down, *at least she is listening to our call for unification*. He continued to address his windbred as he spoke of the lady, but that only transported him to their last departing some four seasons past now. He remembered it all too clearly. The soft rain and cooler evening had just begun to announce the beginning of the harvest season. He held her close to him as they stood on the tall east wall overlooking the road and what lay beyond. Her touch and smell immediately tortured his mind. That moment, like so many moments before, had allowed them to reminisce about what could have been, what should have been, what almost was. And what really was.

That very same moment had plagued him like so many before and had upset him all the same. But that last time was more so than any other departing, just with the remembrance of that embrace and that kiss. It wasn't a farewell kiss or a soft impression upon his lips, not a see-you-soon smack. It wasn't a casual good luck brush across the cheek. Rather, it was the burning, lustful, starving kind of kiss that left the lasting scar of yearning upon his very being. Perhaps that was her plan—he cursed—a plan hard and cruel. Make him never forget his decision, his choosing if you will. True to his word, the wielder had yet to have chosen a woman. If he couldn't have her, he wanted no one else. But he knew all too well that was a futile thought. Soon, he would have to find a bearer of a son to the sword—one who would carry on the testament of alliances and the unification of the orbs if he should fail his testament.

She wanted that position. *No!* The wielder cursed. She had fought for that position—eager to birth the next wielder. But he knew their paths tore them in different directions, and if they would have shared their vows and just stayed true to their union it would have most assuredly driven them both to their ultimate demise. He had to be strong for both their sakes and that of Anglyllon, which at this very moment hung in a fragile state, much like crossing thin ice. It could collapse at any moment, but he could not help to shake his thoughts of her and what she had looked like the last moment before he left. That golden hair with then just the faintest hint of silver beginning to reveal itself as it twisted its way through her soft long curls. Her alluring eyes of hazel always seemed to hide such deceitful acts of crime, where wrinkles sprouted from their corners to blemish a perfect face of gentle smooth cream and her body. *Stop!* His mind screamed at the very thought of her pleasure. The wielder suppressed the images. There were more pressing issues at hand to occupy his mind. But he could only image how she would greet him when he finally arrived. He went over each possibility in his mind, and it helped ease the long, arduous travel, as it grew ever more taxing with each passing sun.

The windbred continued, already sensing its rider was heading off into a different train of thought. Both were exhausted but equally tenacious in achieving their goal. There was a quick jerk, momentarily startling the windbred, as a sudden shift from a sleepy rider's weight almost threw the rider to one side of the road. Instantly, both recovered. Jolted back into alertness, they continued their plight.

There has been far too much traveling. The wielder gave his trustful companion a quick pat of assurance, while his other hand grasped the reign tightly. He was ever grateful that his windbred stayed faithful and true.

The East Kingdoms remained in turmoil, and that was where, regrettably, he would have to leave them, for now, there in the hands of his apprentice. Immediately responding to this latest job, he and his windbred would need to travel west to Strong Tower and aid the lord as fast as possible. For Lord Baylor had fought the good fight to unify. But the issue was not so much that no one wanted the orbs in one place; it was more like, which kingdom should they rest in? And he was all too aware of the opposition that opposed Urlon and its magnificent city of Strong Tower as the recipient. He couldn't help the fact that he was closest to her and the lord, which easily prompted many to see the favoritism. But that truly was not the case. The fact remained that Urlon was almost dead center of Anglyllon. Where better than all the known orbs to be? Where safer than surrounded by the other kingdoms? It was a sound argument to those in favor. But that, unfortunately, was just a handful of kingdoms.

Ahead, the wielder could now visualize the first sign of Urlon's border, two tall markers on opposite sides of the wide road that marked the distance to Strong Tower. He would be grateful to leave the East Kingdoms for a time and get a chance to dry out. The wet season had come—and did it rain. Pour was the more appropriate description. The wielder anticipated the milder season of Urlon, not to mention the more spacious and clear plains that made up most of the kingdom. However, the wielder gave no sign of relief yet, at best a little more than halfway to their goal. He urged the windbred on, for there was still no security once past the border.

Even now, the wielder was surprised by the ultimate silence of his journey and, quite frankly, a little disappointed in the opposition—not one diversion or intervention, not even one distraction. In fact, quite disappointingly, not one came forward offering their services to become the next apprentice. But of course, where this job was about to take him, he knew no one with even half a mind would follow him—not into the Mountain of Illenwell to face that dragon. Besides, the real challenge came after the recovery if there was to be one. After all, one would have a better chance getting the orb from the wielder than that dragon.

With that thought in mind, the wielder had already anticipated his adversaries' next move. Why should we get roasted while trying to retrieve that orb? Why not wait for our esteemed wielder to recover that orb for us, for the kingdom of Urlon was worth the wait. All Anglyllon marveled at Urlon, being one of the larger and wealthier kingdoms under the sun. Its borders stretched across endless fields of lush green grass. Orchards of fruit bearing trees kept a fair portion of the townsfolk working hard during the productive part of the season. Most, if not all, produced there was dispersed throughout the countless opportunities that went toward the creation of the country's favorite drink, *lade*. As for the rest of the kingdom, it attracted some, if not all, the finest Anglyllon had to offer in merchants, scholars, and scientists. Builders, blacksmiths, and crafters of every trade converged upon the kingdom in hopes of adding their own mark upon the kingdom as well.

The buildings and dwellings were advanced for this time of Anglyllon's season. Significant architecture and design had no equal throughout the rest of the country. Travelers and visitors flooded the four roads that led them to the midst of the square. There, the largest structure and the reason for this city's name, Strong Tower, stood as a testimony of the human spirit. It could be easily seen from all directions and had become a symbol of assurance, of justice, and of promising hope.

However, it also attracted all those who envied it. Its owner could do much to change the kingdoms forever, not to mention the quest for unification. The wielder cursed as he urged his windbred on. *It must have taken several seasons to forge such a plan as this. Clever, calculating, and persuasive this individual or organized group must be. Scrutinize them all,* the wielder thought. *Take the orb out of its kingdom! Who tricked the lord into that? What in the name of the great Zoarians was he thinking? And now what of Urlon? Why, the kingdom's people could easily handle Lord Krhan if he was involved in this. But what of Sauros?* Most, if not everyone, had had little tolerance of those lizards since long before the Saurotillian wars. And just the thought of them sending an emissary to the hall. *Well, I'll bet they'll not make it. And they have every right to be there. For at this moment, whoever recovers that orb will rightfully own the kingdom of Urlon. That's the law. That's the way of things for now anyway.* The wielder cursed, for he could just spit over this sudden and recent disrespect of responsibility. He regrettably urged his windbred on harder.

As they continued to own the road, the wielder's mind dug through the depths of his conscious, searching for the possible clues that would confront him while on this next job. There were already several suspects, and the first was the most obvious one—Lord Krhan, for who was just savvy and lowly enough to try and pull off this massive job. But the second person, the wielder couldn't quite place a reason for. He knew Lord Laiaden, and although at first the dragon had come as a threat and a nuisance, oddly enough, over the course of the seasons, both he and Illenwell had begun to see the significance and beauty of having such an animal around. Why, almost immediately, Sauros had ceased its constant attacks upon Illenwell. And soon, no one would risk traveling there. But he would not rule out the conceivable thought that Krhan had involved Laiaden in this plot to some degree or another. And what had been promised in the sale of this idea? For the wielder understood Laiaden to be a radical recluse who, quite possibly, had sold his personality to the kingdom of Illenwell for the sole purpose of keeping it isolate, safe from outside influences, which made his job of trying to unify the kingdoms that much harder. *So, what or who tempted Laiaden into meeting with Baylor?* He probed the possibilities. *But that doesn't make sense? He would not jeopardize his port so. Then again, it wouldn't surprise me if Lord Laiaden were not up to this.*

And with that, Nolan was struck with a terrible thought that he now would have two orbs and kingdoms in peril. Oh, he could just *spit!*

And what of Lord Krhan? Why, that little deceitful dragon parading around as a lord. I'm quite sure that crafty lord has already pounced upon this opportunity. In fact, it wouldn't surprise me at all if he didn't conjure up this plot just to throw me right to the dragon to see what I could come up with? In fact, nothing would surprise me. But I guess I had this coming to me all these seasons of avoiding the inevitable. So, it's either me or that dragon, but Anglyllon can't have both. And with his Lady Tonelia now smack in the middle, best get there, and yester sun wasn't soon enough. They are just so reckless that I could spit! He cursed.

The wielder had contemplated for so long that, when he finally returned his attention back to the road, they were well past the border and on into Urlon. Again, this brought him no relief as of yet, but it did convey to him that, soon, the forests would grow thinner until they melted into the plains that were not far off and would be a clear indicator that they were nearer the city itself. Soon, he would see signs of dwellings, as crop growers would be out attending their ankle-high spices and other profitable greens. From there, he would have a better view of oncoming riders. And just as he thought of nourishment, his stomach abruptly reminded him of the emptiness, and with his arms and back aching and by now his windbred as well, it was time for a quick rest.

But like all things, the sense of urgency kept pecking away at him like woodpecker to tree, relentlessly hammering away until it finds a meal. And with it, one more awful thought plagued him as it surfaced to the forefront of his mind—like dread. What would she have to say to him for being so elusive all these past seasons? Why, the last time he'd seen Strong Tower had been a better part of four seasons. But her face was there all the same, fresh as the air and like the celebration during the start of Jubilee Season. He knew she would be wiser and older, but Tonelia all the same.

The wielder cursed again for his absence, but at this moment, they needed to stop. He searched for a spot to rest and soon got his answer. For far off in the horizon, he spied the majestic flight of a Zoarian as it soared toward him. An occasional updraft made the bird jerk a little, and then it recovered. The wielder had always admired the warm blending of gold, brown, and slightly tanned color of the advisors but just about always dreaded the meetings. And again, the topic would be more of the same. Urlon; its orb and the lord; the counsel; and how, like every other time, it was imperative that he arrive. Not, that he didn't get a little annoyed or anything; after all, he was just one wielder.

He brought the windbred to a quick halt in a clearing just off the road. Then he dismounted and walked his ride to the nearest tree. The Zoarian came in low and circled once. It had already spied the same clearing with those sharp eyes and motioned its body into a smooth landing on its extended talons and then quickly tucked in its wings. The wielder made his way over to an already old friend, which easily towered over him, and gave it an appropriate bow.

"What news do you have for the moment, mighty Vestron?" Nolan requested impatiently.

"Hail, mighty wielder of the golden sword," the Zoarian returned the greeting. Although they had only talked suns before, it was always the custom to return acknowledgements to each other. Vestron continued, "Lord Baylor's brother has come to his aid, and at this very moment, they make a painfully slow return to Strong Tower."

"I see," the wielder said. "Then I still have time."

"Time?" The advisory blinked at him. "I am afraid, as always, that you do not."

Here it comes, the wielder thought and then responded quite sarcastically, "Well you can carry me there."

But the tall birdman was not amused one bit, given that Zoarians' bone structure for flight could not easily handle an adult male.

"After all, I'm just one wielder." He stated the obvious, a slight bitterness in his tone. "I could just spit at their carelessness!"

"We understand your plight, and truly we are sympathetic to your cause, but we are only here to advise you and direct you toward one possible solution," the great Zoarian said.

"But I need a solution, and I need one now," Nolan fumed.

"And a solution that demands you and your kind make a decision and stand with it," the Zoarian responded calmly.

"Why is it that you don't just come out and say what road I must go?" Nolan blurted out irritably. "Aren't you the ones with all the knowledge?"

"Well, yes," Vestron said in defense, "but your species won't learn if we lead you."

The great bird observed the wielder becoming more frustrated than before. *"How would your kind learn if not allowed to experience what logically or naturally follows a decision?"*

"Well," Nolan responded sarcastically, "you'd be keeping us from making a terrible mistake in our decision."

"Then you would blame us for thinking for you." Vestron smirked back.

"Fine," the wielder replied, unsatisfied. "But I don't need to remind you that, back there, my uncle is just barely hanging onto Itmoore," he stated bluntly.

"We understand, Nolan," Vestron said sympathetically. "And we will continue to keep you apprised of that situation. However, the loss of Urlon would be far greater."

Nolan understood that better than anyone, so for the moment and the avoidance of argument, he thought better of continuing this debate. There was a far more pressing task to be dealt with, so he changed his thoughts and moved to the objective at hand. "Now what of Strong Tower?" He was most insistent on getting the report.

"You are anxious to see her again?" Vestron was blunt and was not referring to the kingdom.

"Well, yes, it's been a while," he stated regrettably.

"Understandable," the advisory said. "Now"—Vestron changed his tone— "Aquila has arrived and is at this very moment our only contact for Strong Tower, and he has sent me to inform you that Lord Krhan is due to arrive shortly."

Nolan cursed, for he was anxious to arrive ahead of him. "How soon?" He hoped for time yet to make it.

"I am afraid this sun," Vestron replied.

"I could just spit!" He cursed.

Vestron gave Nolan a moment to collect himself.

"What of Lord Laiaden, then?" he asked knowing, all too well that there was nothing he could do about anything for the moment except get the report.

"I am afraid that all of my brothers and sisters in flight view the mountain as volatile and completely hostile for the moment since the dragon's emergence," he responded, sounding very apologetic.

"Understandable," the wielder replied, knowing all too well that even Zoarians flew the opposite direction of dragons.

"But earlier reports confirmed that twenty-one warriors accompanied the Lord of Illenwell through Jawed Peaks just north of the mountain," Vestron added.

"Twenty-one," the wielder clarified.

"Twenty-one to be exact, and fifty with Lord Baylor." Vestron anticipated the wielder's next question.

"Small parties … treaty," he spoke softly to himself.

"Sounds like it," the Zoarian offered, hearing the wielder clearly enough.

"With Laiaden … But why?" the wielder questioned the advisory. "Why is he risking his orb and kingdom?" Nolan spat.

"If you weren't informed, and we weren't informed?" He returned an inquisitive look.

"Well, someone's up to something." The wielder rubbed the rough shadow of his chin.

"Perhaps you were correct on our previous meeting," Vestron reminded Nolan, "that a lord cooked up an irresistible dish."

Nolan knew it all too well. And he cursed himself for thinking it true. "Saurotillian patrols?" he inquired further.

"Again, I regret to inform the great wielder that none of my brothers or sisters has flown south of the mountain either," Vestron apologized again.

"Besides the obvious," Nolan inquired his advisory, "what advice do you suggest?"

"Well for the moment," Vestron started, "Altorcules is holding the Zoarian council, and they are storming through the past seasons and recalling when the orbs have been in this state before. However, there has never been a dragon involved. So, for now, make for Strong Tower quicker than light and then on to Illenwell for further investigation. Be on guard and ever mindful of all that you encounter," he sternly advised.

Nolan already agreed with the stated obvious. "Then I'll rest momentarily and get back to the road," the wielder said. "Return to Aquila and inform Strong Tower that I will do my best to be there by the third sun."

Vestron bowed in reply. But as the warrior turned away, the Zoarian interrupted him, "Wielder, before we depart, there is one more concern to report."

"Yes?"

"One of the Zoarians had a confirmed sighting that I think would interest you."

"Go on."

"An animal controller was sighted near the Mountain of Illenwell," Vestron said.

"A Taulian," the wielder responded but had no need to question a Zoarian's outstanding eyesight. "When?"

"Several suns ago before the attack."

"How did that Taulian slip into that mountain without Illenwell's knowledge?" Nolan asked directly.

"Apparently down through Claw Crag and straight for the mountain," Vestron answered.

"Why, that doesn't surprise me. It has always been believed that Taul sent that dragon over here to spy on us." The wielder spoke his thoughts.

"Yes, but why?" Vestron inquired.

The wielder responded, "Some have suggested to me that Taul sends their young animal controllers in training over here periodically to study our animals and learn to control them, but we do not know or understand the length or extent of their power or why they are even interested in us and our kingdoms." They paused a moment to reflect. "But why send the dragon to interfere with that small meeting?" the wielder asked further.

"Perhaps out of curiosity?" the Zoarian offered.

"Well, it's something," the wielder said, "and that something concerns me."

"And that greatly concerns us as well, since an orb is involved," Vestron replied.

Upon that, Nolan returned the Zoarian a glance of disgust, as they both understood what Lord Baylor had just done to jeopardize it all.

"Perhaps, Nolan," Vestron continued, "someone has read your testament of unification and is assisting it along?"

"Perhaps … but what would a Taulian want with an orb or unified Anglyllon?" Nolan paused and was distracted by another thought. "Perhaps it's not Laiaden, Krhan or a Taulian at all that we need to concern ourselves with?"

Vestron studied the wielder closely. "Then whom should we be concerned with?"

"Perhaps a visit to that tongue-flicking sun brain from Sauros and what he and his horde of lizard companions are up to and what they will foolishly do when they catch scent of Urlon's loss?"

"If they aren't the ones who are initially responsible for this," the Zoarian questioned.

The two of them remained reflective in thought for a moment and then realized that their time was shorter than they had expected and quickly parted ways, both on route to find answers.

Nolan watched the magnificent Zoarian stretch out its wings, catch the wind and was gone in a rush. It soon mastered the blue sky and was gone from sight.

As Nolan returned to his windbred deep in thoughts on why the Zoarians had established wielders in the first place some eight-thousand seasons now. With some fifty-seven wielders by now which had their names forever scribed to the testaments. Most of them from either two dominant families, the Hammer and the Vonika line. Splattered with a few mixed wielders that came and went. Each with their own unique and sometimes different agenda and often, mixed with their own opinions on how the sword of gold should be wielded. He got it, he understood it. There had to be a third party. A neutral, unbiased person. But that was never easy nor was it accomplished. And regrettably, this job would prove that point.

But for Nolan and his line of Hammers, his father, like his father before him, the wielder traits would be continued through the Hammer line. To find the good in everyone, a heart to forgive the worst and a mind to forget all the bad. Plus, a soul to never loose faith. He would hold true to his personal commitment to not fail himself, his father, the Zoarians nor the kingdoms and their precious orbs. And the lady that he loved and so admired. But this job, would most assuredly tax his ability to negotiate, find a compromise and establish some sort of peace. Let alone retrieve an orb from a dragon. However, the reports were soon to be in. Both Urlon and Illenwell would be under siege, Sauros would be on the move and to the south, in the shipping lanes, two more vessels would meet their fate to a dragon and one of those would be commanded by Lord Krhan's son, Logar. And soon he would comfort an unseen assailant with a deeper motive.

He could just spit!

Chapter 2

P.D. 96, A.F. 8130

Settled in the northwest corner of Anglyllon and residing in the shadows, the mountainous range of Jawed Peaks was the port of Illenwell. It was an isolated haven for most of the countries less respectable inhabitants. There were only two ways in: the road that cut directly between the mountain range—which passed dangerously close to the dragon and bordered north of Sauros or the preferred way, the port—which was the only way the kingdom could practice its living, trading with the island of Roan and Lord Krhan. Now, it had not always been that way. Nolan was pretty accurate with his perception regarding Lord Laiaden and his plans for Illenwell, but it hadn't always been so. His anger vented more toward the Zoarians for their refusal to send the wielder upon the dragon's first appearance, which had come, oddly enough, at the start of the Saurotillian wars. The wars had begun to escalate in the south between Lord Lavenden and Sauros, leaving the Zoarians to make a command decision that the wielder was needed where the orbs were in grave danger. And while the dragon had left most the of the port of Illenwell devastated, Lord Laiaden couldn't really fault the wielder for not coming to their aid as the Saurotillian war began in the south with Lord Krhan and his kingdom at stake. Still, the lord considered Nolan more a puppet in the talons of the Zoarians than an actual wielder. Torn by loyalty, devotion and later, love.

So, in an effort to appease the Lord of Illenwell, the Zoarians had sent a very skilled troll to his kingdom. Being one that was extremely creative with metal, the giant was quickly able to bring the port back to life—in fact, better than ever. But now, that could all change instantly. For at this moment, it was greatly compromised, despite what anyone else thought. Up until recently, the talk of a massive treaty between Urlon and Illenwell was not in Laiaden's best interest. However, the loss of lives, expensive ships, and supplies for not only himself, but Lavenden as well, forced a rather reclusive lord to rethink the future of his kingdom. The last dragon attack near the Evening Isles and just south of Sauros had left both kingdoms to quickly ponder different alternatives to their business practices. And although Lord Krhan had somewhat of a relationship with Lord Baylor, it was not so for Laiaden, which prompted the lords to meet. And that would mean Lord Baylor would need to travel closer to Illenwell and bring his orb as proof.

Which now left Laiaden in a quandary of what to do with his orb? Especially when traveling so close to the dragon and the north boarder of Sauros that Lord Vax kept heavily guarded with small bands of Saurotillian centurions. That meant that the meeting had to be as secretive as possible, and it also meant that next to no one knew of the meeting. So now what happened? How did a dragon, who for several seasons now, had rested quietly in the depths of the mountain just happen to be out on a flight and find the two lords out in the open? And furthermore, one of which was conveniently in possession of his orb?

These thoughts plagued a tall and battered lord as he quickly ascended the steps to a huge wooden structure that expanded out into the harbor that was not only his home but also the kingdom's hall—much like that of Urlon's, and every other hall for that matter. But this morning, it was empty, for the kingdom of Illenwell was not as bustling or as robust as other kingdoms. For Illenwell, it was about the harbor. Each pier had a set of guards and, at any given time of sun, a swing leader, one of many who would know what goods went where. Each pier would buy, sell, trade, and collect from dawn until dusk. Then the busy port would shut down, and everyone would head off to the drinking inns for *lade* and the vast selection of food, camaraderie, physical desires, and all sorts of gambling. Empty boats awaiting the next morning's supplies to fill their bellies would watch, as bloated ships would stroll out of the harbor and then cast off to their destinations.

As for Illenwell's major contribution to Anglyllon, well, it was wood. Here grew the biggest and strongest trees, like none the rest of the kingdoms had ever seen. Even the vast forests of North Avalore could not boast of such timber. And it was that very same supply that had built the hall for the second time since it was last burnt to the ground but now reinforced with a metal frame thanks to the troll.

The lord burst through the double doors and quickly snatched a large pourer of *lade* that was stationed in the middle of a long, plain wooden table. He filled a cup and gulped down several mouthfuls before his aide came urgently to his side, spitting out deeply concerned words. "Lord Laiaden, I just received the news and take it that the plan failed?"

"Miserably," the lord did not take his eyes off the next gulp of *lade*. "That blasted dragon interrupted everything!"

"But how?" Tobus fumbled. "And why?"

"I don't know!" Laiaden barked irritably.

"I see," Tobus replied, showing no signs of hurt feelings. The thin and timid person glanced nervously about as he franticly searched for the right words to say. "Shall I have Ott go and see the dragon?"

"What and annoy the beast further?" Laiaden glanced at him. "That troll won't be of any use. He'll just get himself killed, and then we'll be out a perfectly good metal maker" He paused for another gulp. "Our more immediate concern is to find out what or who drove that blasted beast from the mountain in the first place and how it knew to come to us," he snapped.

"Well, begging the lord's pardon," Tobus began uncertainly, "shouldn't you immediately dispatch a small emissary to Strong Tower?"

Laiaden treated him to a rather annoyed look.

Tobus pleaded, "To inform them that it was not your intention to have the dragon attack."

"Why? They would know I had no control over a dragon!" Laiaden burst out with anger.

"Yes, my lord," Tobus replied rather regrettably, "but there are others that do."

The lord paused from his drinking and continued to study his aide. And just what was he driving at?

"Why, that would mean a Taulian, my lord," Tobus spoke uneasily his little eyes jerking about like an anxious hen, not knowing what to do next.

"I know that would mean a Taulian," Laiaden spat in mockery. Then refilled his cup and downed it again, but his nerves remained unsatisfied.

"But, my lord, there's been no sightings of any Taulian in the port," the aide said, mystified. "And none have reported into the pier guards for some time."

Laiaden froze from his next gulp for just a second, long enough to drive his stare right through his aide. And he knew it. "Since when does a Taulian knock on my door or anyone's, for that fact, just to announce their arrival?"

"Oh, you're right," the aide agreed, almost sorry he'd mentioned it, his small eyes fleeing about the room, not wishing to make further eye contact with an already irate lord.

Laiaden returned to his drinking and allowed his mind to quickly shift through all the next possible courses of action, for clearly his aide was of little assistance.

"What of Lord Baylor and the orb?" Tobus timidly interrupted his thoughts.

"We never got that far." The lord shook his head and spoke in a more solemn tone. "The dragon hit us at the foot of the last mountain in the forest, just north of the road."

"Oh." A small audible tone leaked from the aid's mouth.

"Then it flew east," Laiaden said, eyes fixed in a trance.

Tobus could visibly see the lord recount the moment through his mind's eye. "Did anyone else make it?" Tobus asked, further knowing all too well who had accompanied the lord on this mission, and it sort of struck him as funny. Those who had gone were clearly the not to be trusted type, and Tobus had thought for sure that Laiaden would not survive the meeting. But to his surprise, when a lone warrior had shown up this past sun to the hall and had delivered Tobus the report, he just could not believe that the dragon had been there to interfere. He'd quickly paid the warrior for his silence and sped him on his way. But apparently, it was not enough to keep his tongue, for even Lord Laiaden found the tension throughout his port thicker than the fog that rolled in after dark.

"Well by the looks of my kingdom," Laiaden said, controlling his anger, "some of the warriors must have survived?" He knew that most had survived and he had paid them all handsomely to keep quiet.

"Why, yes," Tobus agreed with the obvious. "The town's been scurrying around like a mound of disturbed ants now that you mention it."

"We'll need to spread the word immediately through the port that the situation is under control for now," he instructed.

"At once." Tobus bowed in acknowledgement.

Just then, doors flew opened and their attention turned to the arrival of Laiaden's lead warrior Slomak, who hurriedly entered through the swinging doors. He was a large and well-armed man, who also showed several visible signs of a struggle but did not appear to Tobus to be as shaken as the lord was from their brief encounter with the dragon just suns before. They both had returned together, for Slomak had never left the lord's side through the entire ordeal. He had just come from securing the windbreds, but by the apparent look on his brow, there was more news yet to come.

"Orders?" the warrior asked, reaching the lord's side.

Laiaden poured another cup and turned to address them. "No one, and I mean no one, is to travel near that mountain except for the patrols you are going to immediately double—no wait, triple. And for the sake of Zoarians, keep them quiet!" he ordered Slomak. "If I know Lord Vax, and I do—all too well—that arrogant sunbaked brain has already caught the scent of this. And I wouldn't put it past him to recklessly send his entire armada up here!" he ranted.

"At once, but my lord—"

"Tobus," the lord interrupted Slomak's next words, "spread the word and find out who knows what around this cornstalk full of ears. I want answers, and I want them before the wielder gets here. Is that understood?"

The aide nodded in response and departed, bolting past the lead warrior, who regarded him as insignificant, and the aide knew it.

"Tobus," the lord called out, "one last thing."

"Yes, my lord." The aide turned in his tracks.

"Send for our ghost. We'll need him at once."

Tobus understood the lord's request and turned to continue his orders with a slight detour of the utmost importance.

Both men awaited Tobus to leave, before they continued their private conversation.

"You will get him involved?" Slomak inquired at the mention of the ghost and momentarily distracted from his report. "He might disturb it," he added warningly.

"He will go in, see that the orb is there, and then do his job," the lord said pointedly.

"Do you know what that could mean?" the lead spoke, impatiently but now clearly distracted by a flood of new thoughts.

Laiaden spied him over the rim of his cup as he drew the last drop.

"Yes," Laiaden said as he filled his cup again. Still deep in reflective thought, he stepped up and out to the wooden balcony that overlooked the harbor, with Slomak dead on his heels.

"Urlon at your doorstep," the lead prompted from just over his shoulder.

Slomak's hot breath lofted across the lord's shoulder, and he could easily smell the musky scent. But he kept his eye over the harbor and did not look back as he responded. "I wouldn't lie to you or myself, but Strong Tower is near my grasp." The lord curled his long empty fingers.

"It will bring the wielder this time," Slomak added.

Laiaden turned and stared at his lead. The lord could easily read his face, as he controlled his thoughts for the moment but was clearly in need of releasing his hidden words. "Yes, it will bring the wielder and you know what to do from there?" The lord stared at him deeply.

"Yes, Lord Laiaden," Slomak replied understandingly.

But the lord could see from his facial expressions that he had something more urgent to say. "Oh, I see," the lord said, "you need reimbursement for taking care of the warriors after we were attacked. I'll have Tobus—"

"No!" Slomak interrupted him irritably.

"No? Then what?" Laiaden asked impatiently. "Is there something more, lead?"

"Yes," Slomak regained his train of thought but then momentarily hesitated. "It might be a tad late to block off the mountain."

"What?" The lord scrutinized him as he immediately remembered his orders to secure the mountain.

Slomak continued, hesitantly, "I regret to inform you that a small band of Saurotillians have recently entered the mountain before we were able to intercept them."

The lord's eyes glared, "*Vax!*" he hissed, sending his cup across the room.

Chapter 3

P.D. 97, A.F. 8130

By now, the large Saurotillian leader named Vlognar, followed closely by his little party of unfaithful loyalists, were deep within the Mountain of Illenwell, and they knew exactly where the tunnels would lead them. But the very thought of his actions haunted him every step of the way. Had he sent the right centurion back to Lord Vax for the report? Was Thar trustworthy? Then again, were any of them to be trusted? He looked over his shoulders and spied the little band of misfits. They hovered just behind, and already there were clear signs of indignant behavior and treachery. He could easily spot it behind their beady little red eyes. Sure, they encouraged him on, but which one of them would try to throw him first to the dragon as a clear distraction while the others went for the orb?

Wait! Vlognar stopped in his tracks.

The others came to a noisy halt just behind him with rattling armor. He cursed under his breath. *What orb*? Vlognar had a momentary flash of brilliance. Although they'd witnessed the dragon attack and had seen the lord fall, had he brought the orb? The orb of Urlon, the orb of Strong Tower, did he have it with him? What if he was wrong? Perhaps that was the reason for the strong feelings he sensed from his loyalists. What if the dragon had not taken the orb? What if there was no orb? Then what? He had to risk it. After all, the orb of Urlon was worth the sacrifice of some untrustworthy loyalists.

He chuckled quietly in amusement to himself. Then he heard a whisper from over his shoulder.

"What is he waiting for?" hissed a centurion.

"For you idiots to stop clanging your armor," Vlognar snapped.

A low growl emerged from the black depths.

The band froze. Tense, slender muscles gripped swords and spears tightly in large reptilian talons. Red eyes scanned the tunnel ahead, for they had exceptional sight and needed no torches to see. After a long impatient wait for the darkness to be still again, the patrol cautiously moved on through the winding tunnel until, coming close to their destination, they gathered in a small huddle.

The dark silence was broken by the occasional noise of metal, clanking, and banging against cavern walls as the clumsy, awkward, and rather large lizards tried to negotiate the narrow pathway. This was followed by the sounds of hissing as they spat at each other in annoyance. Their entrance was near the cavern of the dragon, and their plan was to split up from here. After all, they knew every inch of Jawed Peaks and the caves and endless tunnels that ran far below the land. They negotiated every dark way with ease.

Vlognar pointed his talon, and the small band broke apart and went their chosen paths. Hunched and cramped in the small narrow passageways, the small group broke away, and their armor repeatedly banged into rocks, and they hit and hissed at each other with disgust. Fortunately for them, they had seen no one else since their arrival shortly after the dragon's attack. That gave them the advantage of being the first to see what the dragon was so interested in. And hopefully, if it was, what they suspected it to be, then they would be the first to retrieve the orb. After all, why would a dragon attack them, its own kind? For countless seasons, they had all been the same blood—cold.

Within a few minutes, the small band of Saurotillians moved slowly down a tunnel, and ahead of them was a narrow opening to the back of the dragon's chamber.

"If it is what we seek, what will you do with the orb?" A centurion quietly flapped its forked tongue into Vlognar's small ear.

"Use it to smash in your skull to keep you ever silent!" he retorted.

"And Vax's as well?" the centurion inquired, brushing off the threat.

The leader then turned and brought the group to a halt. "I am conjuring special plans for him." He produced a large reptilian grin.

"You should not have sent back Thar to report," another lizard whispered defiantly.

"It wouldn't matter." Vlognar chuckled. "Soon I will have the orb. It will take a few suns' ride for him to get there." The leader reassured the others.

"He'll send an armada," a third centurion added.

"I have informed Thar to alert the loyalists when *I* return with the orb." Vlognar snickered. "Then all opposition will be removed." He chuckled.

"When *we* return with the orb," the first centurion corrected.

Vlognar's talon found his handle, but before he could strike the centurion dead, "This plan of yours better work!" the third one interrupted, referring to the other band of Saurotillians that had departed some time ago.

"Locnod will not fail." Vlognar hissed in defiance. "They will rush the dragon, and we will go for the orb."

"They shall not survive," the first centurion candidly pointed out.

"Well, sacrifices must be made. And I'm willing to sacrifice them," Vlognar hissed back. "Now prepare yourselves."

And with that, they eagerly awaited Locnod's signal as they crept quickly into place. None of them had any idea of what the signal was to be.

On the other side of the dragon's cavern, Locnod and his small company of Saurotillians arrived at the large opening of the cavern. They crept along the wall to a large opening, where Locnod cautiously peered around the corner for a better look.

There in the dark lay the long white beast. It appeared to be just lying there admiring its new addition. Its long tail twitched nervously about like a cat that had spied something small and cute to chase. The rest of its sleek body stretched out across the hard, cold floor. Ribs rose and fell with the rhythm of its deep breathing. Mounds of gold, silver, and other countless pieces of wealth were piled up against the cavern wall. Some of it was fused together from the dragon's hot breath. Various loose objects littered the floor about the cavern.

But none of that attracted Locnod like the beautiful, cylindrical crystal-clear ball that glowed with flashes of red reflections from the various small fires that burned throughout the dragon's cavern. It laid nestled high on a ledge near the back wall and just above the treasure, nicely displayed for its owner to keep an eye on its most prize possession. From there, the orb of Urlon defiantly mocked them all.

Quietly, Locnod surveyed the surroundings. He eyed the objective and saw it would be difficult for Vlognar to reach it, but his scheming was interrupted. One of his impatient cohorts poked him in the side with a drawn sword.

"What do you see?' Lax whispered from the side of his pointed snout.

"The dragon sleeps on the floor," the irritated centurion lied while he was quickly conjuring up his thoughtful demise of Vlognar. *After all, why should he rule us?* Locnod thought craftily. *I am by far much smarter than he is.* Locnod chuckled silently to himself. "Our destiny rests high in the nest. It will be difficult to fetch," he continued.

"It will be our deaths to challenge that dragon," Lax protested.

"This is not a good plan," another one added.

"Fools," Locnod hissed back at them. "I know that. However, Vlognar does not know our plan." He snickered back as his shoulders jerked up and down in amusement.

The centurions stared blankly back at him and then looked at each other. Purple tongues flickered about confusedly.

Then, all at once, the little band of thieves understood. "Clever. We shall serve our new lord without question." Lax bowed his head to Locnod in submission.

But the leader only snapped his pointed snout at Lax. "Fools, I neither want nor need no kingdom. And if you don't stop hissing the only thing that you'll be serving is yourselves to that dragon."

Blank and confused stares overtook the centurions again, and Locnod could not help but notice.

Looking perturbed, Locnod snapped at them again. "The wielder will arrive within due time. Think what Vax and Sauros will do when we return with his head, the orb, and all the kingdoms in disarray. Why should we risk our scales when the wielder will know how to retrieve that orb?" He glared at them.

They all nodded their snouts in agreement.

"But Vlognar awaits our attack," Lax snapped back, interrupting Locnod's perfect little plan.

"We will return and inform him that the dragon is alert and ready to attack us if we enter. Best wait for it to fall asleep." Locnod explained his plan impatiently.

"Ah," said Lax, "then while we wait, we overtake and slay our leader."

Their devious chuckling was immediately interrupted by a low audible growl, followed by movement as a large object shuffled about the cavern. Sounds of loose metal and a single object bounced off into the blackness, reverberating through the cavern.

The little band of subordinates froze. Purple tongues nervously lashed about in the darkness.

On the opposite side of the cavern, Vlognar's awaiting party also heard the commotions. They continued in silence now, crouched down on all fours, talons digging into the cave's soft dirt while their tongues flickered about nervously with all their senses alert, ready, and tense for blood.

Vlognar's long, slender, muscle-toned tail twitched in the awful silence. Directly behind him, the other three centurions waited impatiently as well.

Their purple tongues slithered out between their small slits on their lower lips like forked worms protruding from their sheltered homes to violently shake about and then disappear again.

"What if Locnod has a different objective than yours?" the Saurotillian next to Vlognar hissed out in the darkness.

"Then I will personally feed him to the dragon myself," Vlognar retorted without looking back to the centurion.

"And what if the *scaleless* one, Laiaden, sends in that slow-thinking metal weaver to take out the dragon?" The third centurion referred to the troll.

An irritated Vlognar turned. "Nothing will be here except the wielder. So, if you don't shut your snouts, I will slay you all and finish this job in silence!" he hissed back in annoyance.

The other three stood there with their snouts closed, and not a tongue moved. Once Vlognar was assured that he had cooperation, he turned his attention back to the dragon's cavern. The stillness lasted for only a moment.

"But we must be prepared if Locnod should change your plan," the middle Saurotillian chimed in.

"Bet he is on his way back here right now to inform us that the plan is off," the third one offered.

Vlognar whirled about on his talons, and this time he meant silence!

Quiet, Locnod motioned the others with his talon. The small band waited for further noise. The dragon stirred again. They remained still waiting their opportunity.

For a long time, the reptiles stood quietly with their backs against the cold cave wall. Their tongues flicked the air for smells, tastes, and any other information they could gather. But all was quiet and black.

After a fashion, the impatient lizards looked to Locnod and motioned with their long pointy snouts for him to peer around the corner and have another look. He stared back at them in disgust and then slowly stretched his long neck around the corner and peered out. His glimpse showed only a huge roll of black teeth. The jaw snapped around his neck, and he was immediately jerked away.

The other three centurions mistakenly thought Locnod had seized the opportunity, and with swords ready, they came barreling around the corner and into the cavern. But instead of encountering a sleeping beast, they found one standing on all fours with a struggling Saurotillian pounding his fists against a white jaw. The dragon jerked its head about and flung the headless body across the cavern and roared back in defiance. The warriors charged the beast, swinging aimlessly. The dragon spat fire and clawed the air with its front talons. Wings spread wide, they flapped about, and the cavern burst into shouts of screams and flashes of red, hot light.

Vlognar and his warriors watched Locnod's body hit the ground and slide past.

"That's the signal!" he cried. And with that, the warriors charged into the cavern. Coming around the nest, they stopped dead in their tracks as the dragon incinerated the last of Locnod's warriors to the ground and then stamped on their burning carcasses.

"*Attack!*" cried Vlognar.

The startled dragon came about and confronted the unexpected new threat.

While the centurions charged the bewildered dragon in an attempt for a diversion, Vlognar spied his objective at the top of the nest. He sprang upon the pile and quickly began to negotiate the massive mound of treasure beneath his claws. He cursed, for the loot hindered his advancement toward his reward by being too unstable and loose under his talons, and he slipped and fell several times. Cursing, Vlognar knew that he had precious little time. And he was right. Behind came the screams of agony and the bursts of fireballs as the small band of centurions were flung, burned, and mauled until none survived except one. That one had just reached the ledge and was about to grab the trophy when, suddenly, the entire nest jumped beneath him as if it were struck by an enormous quake. Dead silence rushed over Vlognar like a wave of intense heat followed closely by the heavy foul smell of death as it penetrated his sensitive nostrils. Turning about slowly, he came face-to-face with the defender.

Vlognar sliced the air with his large, long sword. "Back. I'm your master!" He sliced again. "My sword can cut through even the thickest Tyrannattor's hide." He threatened his attacker.

The dragon recoiled its head at Vlognar's rough retort, and a deep, long snarl filled the cavern.

For a brief time, it eyed the sword as it sliced the air. The dragon stood there growling from the side of its mouth at the annoying nuisance. Its long, pointed, lipless snout was filled with exposed black teeth that outlined the entire jaw up and down in a jagged menacing grin. It sneered at the defiant Saurotillian while, up near the skull, black lifeless eyes poised, ready to strike. Vlognar watched the hot saliva ooze down the dragon's grin; a large glop fell upon the treasure, fusing the spot with a sizzling sound followed by a swirling puff of gray smoke.

Vlognar kept the sword between them and frantically searched for an escape. The cavern glowed with burning bodies and small fires from the dragon's spit. He found himself in a most precarious position, and his only aid had been laid about in smoldering pieces scattered around before him. He cut the dragon's breath with his long sword again and shouted, "Back! I'm your master."

The dragon ignored his command and did not flinch, but Vlognar did. The treasure floor beneath him shifted under his weight and sent him tumbling down the nest. His weapon bounced off into the darkness, and the dragon lifted its right front leg out of the way as the lizard tumbled past.

Vlognar hit the floor with a thud. The noise of his armor bounced off the cavern walls. But before he could spring to his feet, the jaws grabbed him, and he found himself sailing through the black empty space. Below him, as if in slow motion, he watched the various fires burn the bodies of his dead loyalists, and then came the fast-approaching cavern wall. Vlognar hit it hard and then tumbled to the floor. Again, the cavern exploded in a thunderous crash of clanging metal.

This time, Vlognar was not so quick to get up. His legs were broken, along with his right arm. He could only watch the approaching dragon as it bounced across the cavern towards him. Like a puppy with a stuffed toy, it fell upon Vlognar and tossed him all around its happy home.

Finally, with broken bones and large cuts bleeding from just about everywhere on his exposed reptilian body, Vlognar came to rest at the foot of the large treasure bed. With one eye swollen shut and the other barely open, he peered up at the orb and helplessly reached out a bloody talon to grasp the fleeting image of power.

The dragon curled up next to him and began tearing off scraps of what was left of his metal armor to expose the tasty scaly flesh beneath. A quick burst of fire roasted the meal.

After its snack was finished, it inspected its nest and adjoining cavern for any further surprises. When it was satisfied with its search, it returned to the nest. Up to the top it climbed and eyed its new prize. This little gem was much different than any other glittering toy it had in its collection; the dragon sat and studied it. Totally unaware of its great significances and importance to the outside world, the dragon did not realize it had just inherited a kingdom and that the intrusions were far from over.

But somewhere in a nearby cavern, the intrusion was coming. For a figure in a long white robe had watched the entire scene of mayhem unfold through the white dragon's eyes.

Standing next to the figure was a massive black dragon. It curled its lips and snarled.

"Patience, my pet," the figure reached up and patted the large jaw. "We must test the orbs and then the wielder, when he arrives."

Her pet responded in a low, audible growl, while, from under the white hood, the figure smirked and contemplated.

Chapter 4

Testament of Wielders
Harvest Period
Date 96 of 119
After Founding 8131 seasons

> *This account is of the arrival of one, Nolan*
> *Hammer, wielder of the golden sword, at*
> *Strong Tower of the kingdom of Urlon. As*
> *recorded by testamentor Merrith LoneRiver.*

P.D. 84, A.F. 8130

Three suns later, as the wielder had said, he and his windbred came up over a large hill. There before them stood the unmistakable giant tower, reaching up to the sky like a long white finger, surrounded by the entire city as it sprawled across the green pastures. A glorious sky of blue illuminated the late afternoon and was accompanied by scattered puffs of carefree rolling white clouds. But the entire lavish exhibition failed the wielder's attention as he concentrated on the east gate and the job that awaited him within. He sat upon his windbred; his eyes fixed to the massive tower. Anticipation of seeing her again was driving his heart to pound deep in his chest. His mind could envision the greeting he would receive from her—if it would be a greeting at all.

The huge double wooden and metal doors were flung outward and caught his attention. He watched as through the massive opening came what the wielder speculated to be near a thousand warriors upon windbreds flooding out of the east wall like a giant swarm of ants. Nolan watched the long line engulf the road ahead of him. He decided to wait patiently while the massive shape approached him.

"Hail, wielder of the golden sword," a young warrior of sandy blonde hair and goatee shouted as he neared.

"Greetings, young Golar, but I'll need no escort," he said.

"Unfortunately," the young warrior responded, "no escort will be given. We are to ride east on a special request from our new lead warrior, Tholin."

At the mention of this name, Nolan was curious. "And what mission is that?"

The young man's face burst into a smile. "He knew you'd ask that, so I'm to inform you that he will fill you in on the matter after you arrive."

"And Lord Krhan?" Nolan asked. "Is he in the hall?"

"Since I'm the lead for the east wall, I am unable to answer that. But from the sounds of it, that dragon is here and has made himself at home already."

"Very well," the wielder should have known better. "Then I hope you are successful." He wished them well.

"You as well," Golar bowed, "you're going to need it where you're headed."

"And you're right, that dragon has got nothing on the one in that hall." The wielder made light of the situation.

Golar and his warriors let out a laugh, and then both departed. Nolan allowed the rest to pass before he took control of the road and steered his windbred to the doors.

The road watchers, one high above each door, waved in recognition to the wielder and then sounded their horns. The chords lifted above the city and echoed down the square to prepare for the wielder's arrival. Guards in the watchtowers stationed along the road shouted to the city folk below. They jumped and moved quickly out of the way of the familiar rider. Most cheered, while others looked on in awe. They cleared the road as best they could. Straight ahead, the warrior aimed for his target. The massive hall and the towering structure of the Lord's court loomed just ahead. More horns resounded his arrival.

The warrior brought his windbred to a halt in front of the east stairs. A paige ran swiftly down the stairs and grabbed his reins as the mighty wielder flew off his saddle in eager anticipation of what lay ahead. He gave the youth a quick pat on the shoulder with a nod of appreciation, and then up the granite steps and through the two huge bay doors, he disappeared.

The massive hall was one large open room, for it was constructed at the very bottom of the Strong Tower itself. Standing in the middle of the court, one could see all four doors to each road. There were balconies everywhere that were accessible from the nearby buildings but heavily guarded. The hall itself was filled with chairs and tables. Groups of warriors and advisors talked or quarreled among themselves about plans that needed immediate attention. Various paintings adorned the walls. Flags and banners of different kingdoms hung from poles affixed to large marble pillars.

Magnificent painted glass and huge open windows allowed the hall to be filled with fresh air. An occasional warm breeze upset the tapestries as it blew through the court. One would hardly believe that, on such a beautiful sun, the shadow of darkness was already settling in this fair kingdom. The black tarnished fingers of greed and deceit were planted and germinating in the mind of a man.

Lord Krhan Hearthol, from Pantanteous, the large city of the Lavenden Kingdom, had come to claim Urlon. He had already dispatched his finest warriors to fetch the orb, and all were quite aware that it would be a difficult task to undergo. Unfortunately, the lord realized he had precious little time. Although he knew most of the other kingdoms were undergoing their own internal battles and would not, at this moment, consider the vulnerability of Urlon, there was one other kingdom that had already jumped into action.

For now, Urlon's hope lay with the wielder's ability, and they all knew of his unquestionable reputation. The kingdom's lady also relied on the wielder's great prowess; she stood patiently and confidently by while her aides kept her informed of the daily progress. One of those was Aquila, the Zoarian, who had been first to deliver the news of the dragon's attack. The wielder would report directly to him and the lady, and then Aquila would return to the Zoarian council, which resided somewhere high in an undisclosed part of the mountains and keep them apprised of the situation. Now, those who had been in the court when the advisory arrived kept their composure for now. Aquila was very thorough with his report. The attack on Lord Baylor and his warriors by the white dragon was very descriptive. For now, all Urlon awaited apprehensively for the arrival of the wielder and the course of his next action, which would, ultimately, take him to the mountain and, perhaps, the easier part of his job.

Finally, the suns of waiting had ended, as, with a crash, the hall doors burst open to reveal the wielder. Everyone's attention was quickly diverted to his arrival, followed by dead silence. The wielder's eyes immediately spied the large, golden white, brown bird towering over the entire assembly and, standing right next to him, his objective.

But last he remembered; her smile was as alluring as her eyes. Even from the distance across the crowded hall, he could see them filled with a vast mixture of concern, stress, desperation, and anticipation, which immediately ebbed into relief as their eyes locked. "Nolan," her voiced boomed over the large, crowded hall.

The wielder never noticed the great parting of people as he made his way toward her. He focused on only her as he rushed through the opening. He did not mean to be rude to his fellow companions, but there was work to be done. His path was set. No one dared cross it or block it. The other warriors, some of whom owed him their very lives, stood erect and quiet to give reverence to a legendary warrior. With his left hand resting on his sword handle and shoulders swinging with the quick motion of his step, he came to her without hesitation and with an undeniable purpose.

"Yes, Lady Tonelia," he responded as he drove up the steps to greet her. His concerned look of mixed emotions searched her eyes, and he indicated to her that he was not happy.

They both stood there momentarily in silence as if they were the only ones in the entire hall. And to make things even more complicated, neither was sure which to do first—kiss, hug, or should he just break her jaw for being so reckless and careless with their responsibility?

Body language screamed for physical contact, but it was Nolan who broke the desire first. "I apologize to this court for my delay." He never took his eyes off hers as he addressed the court in a serious businesslike tone. "The ride was long and hard, and I needed to gather more facts from the attentive Zoarians."

"And they are?" A man interrupted them as he discarded a handful of parchments and then swung his feet from the table and casually approach Nolan, who recognized the voice of his antagonist.

"Why would a dragon have any interest in an orb?" Nolan uttered in annoyance, for he had so wanted to be here before him. There was much he needed to discuss in private with the lady before he could confront this dragon.

"Well, we'll know soon enough," Krhan replied. "It took you many suns to get here. Why I, myself only just arrived a few suns ago." He paused with a smile between his flaming, well-groomed red beard, and mustache. "But fear not, for you arrived at the most opportune moment. I'm sure that my warriors will arrive soon with the orb safely in their care," he continued most assuredly.

Nolan smirked back. "Your warriors arrived, I'll wager, right into the belly of that dragon." There was a pause from the hall. "Or one of them will come to claim this land."

The lord's expression changed upon the possibility. After all, it could be true. The harsh reality that he'd ordered his finest to their fate did not sit well, and that may have led to a new leader.

He raised an eyebrow at Nolan. "Really," he retorted. "What fact do you base *that* on?" He turned to address the hall, which remained silent. "We know so little of dragons. Why, this one could have been a friendly fire-breather." He scanned the crowd. "And as far as questioning the loyalty of my finest," he turned back to the wielder, "it's unquestionable."

Krhan had a point, Nolan thought. The dragon of Illenwell hid away. The only other encounters had been in the shipping lane. And oddly enough, more attacks happened to the ships trading from Illenwell to Lavenden, which brought his suspicion closer to either Lord Krhan, Lord Laiaden or possibly both. "Then best hope they return with that orb," Nolan said, wishing the best and hopefully keeping him from going after that orb.

Lord Krhan stood there studying the wielder.

"Lady Tonelia." Nolan started to address an already fearful court. "We are all aware of the grave situation this kingdom has fallen into, and I will pledge to correct that as soon as possible. But I'll need to inquire further into this matter so as to better formulate a plan of action." He spoke with assurance in an effort to calm the hall. "For I do not have all the critical details as of yet on how and why that dragon would have attacked the good lord. Furthermore, what were Lord Baylor and Lord Laiaden doing meeting without the presence of a wielder?" He turned to question Tonelia.

"Nor will you." Krhan interrupted the lady before she had a chance to respond. Annoyed by the interruptions, Nolan watched Tonelia fight the urge to break eye contact with him and direct her attention toward Krhan. But she was keeping her urge to destroy the annoying lord well. And Nolan was pleased with her restraint and professional composure.

"My apologies, Lady Tonelia." Lord Krhan bowed curtly, wearing a smirk, and then continued. "I assure you that, when my warriors return safely with the orb, I will take possession of this kingdom and make a smooth transition of this court." He bowed again with a gesture toward Aquila. "I express my gratitude that you are here, Nolan Hammer, along with a Zoarian to oversee the proper proceedings and to assure everyone present that my possession of the orb will be a lawful and just one." He paused with that crafty smile and acknowledged the court. "My warriors have most likely recovered the stolen orb as we speak, and are already on their way here," he finished with a touch of arrogance.

"You understand," Aquila, the Zoarian, addressed the court, "that if he is truthful in his words, the kingdom is his." He addressed both Tonelia and Nolan.

There was a moment of silence as Nolan gathered himself. He also caught the concerned eye of Tonelia. Nolan could not ignore her pleading body language as it nervously exhibited its yearning. She was upset and doing the best job of controlling her emotions. He longed to run to her side and comfort her in this moment of uncertainty. Even though she was quite capable of handling this dragon, Nolan knew she would have rather faced the one at Illenwell. He also hoped she was not planning a defensive against Krhan. Once alone, he would have to probe her further for her true intentions.

The wielder turned to the tall Zoarian. "We understand." Nolan acknowledged the advisory. "But the orb has not yet been recovered."

"And you base that fact on?" Krhan almost charged the platform for an immediate answer.

"The Zoarian never acknowledged that it was recovered," he responded calmly. "There is always a Zoarian nearby to keep us informed on where that orb has gotten off to." Nolan reassured Tonelia and the court that there was yet still hope. "Or have you forgotten your business partner?" He eyed Krhan. "Lord Laiaden will not have anyone break in there and disturb that beast and risk his kingdom be roasted."

Krhan scoffed at the answer. "Nolan, Nolan, Zoarians are the intelligent ones here, and not one of them will fly anywhere near that mountain." He paused. "Lest you forget, they're afraid of dragons." Krhan smiled at Aquila. "As for the orb, they're resourceful warriors, and I of course can repay any debt to 'my business partner' for this gracious oversight." Krhan smiled like the crooked dragon he was.

The wielder spat back in Aquila's defense. "And what about the warriors you just sent to their deaths; don't you think they may have feared dragons as well?"

Krhan took a step toward Nolan until their noses almost met, "Oh … and you do not?" He challenged the wielder. There was a long moment of tension between them.

Nolan spun on his heels in the direction of Tonelia. "I am prepared to face any and all challenges to uphold the rightful heirs to the orbs." He reaffirmed his testament.

"Looks like you will get your chance." Krhan smirked and strolled away.

Nolan could see by Krhan's expression that he was done for the moment, so he seized the opportunity to question the lady without further interruptions. "First, any word on our lord?"

She did not answer him, but her eyes were heavy with concern.

Nolan glanced quickly up to Aquila, who returned the same concern. "Second, why were the two lords meeting?"

"A treaty," Tonelia finally spoke.

"And that purpose?" the wielder continued.

"Between us, Illenwell"—she paused apprehensively— "and Lavenden," she added apprehensively.

The wielder turned to address Krhan "Then why weren't you there?"

"Lady Tonelia," the lord addressed her as he looked over Nolan's shoulder, "kindly inform the inquiring wielder why I was not invited to that next meeting."

"The next meeting," Nolan blurted out. "Why, how many have we had?"

But the lady remained silent, and for the first time, her eyes were fixed on Krhan.

By the lack of response from either of them, Nolan was not sure if this was the first that Krhan had heard of this. Or perhaps there was more to this then he had yet to discover? In any event, someone was up to something.

"Lady Tonelia?" he asked for her explanation without taking his eyes of the dragon Krhan.

"Why, Lord Krhan." She volleyed the question on. "I believe you were pitching this treaty more than we were with Laiaden many meetings ago. After all, you're already trading with Illenwell." Nolan caught those alluring hazel eyes as they loomed in on their prey.

"All right," Nolan interrupted, a little annoyed. "Where were you going with this?"

Krhan sighed and then addressed the wielder. "As you are by now quite aware, more and more of our ships are being attack by dragons from Kureath. Best look to trading up the river of Randerend."

"Naturally," Nolan agreed, "and that would mean a treaty with Urlon and—"

"Yes, yes," Krhan interrupted before Nolan could finish his thought. "But Lord Laiaden and I seemed to have come to a more immediate impasse before involving him." Both Nolan and Tonelia exchanged glances of understanding that Krhan was speaking of Lord Vax of Sauros.

"Compensation of course." The wielder knew.

"Yes, yes, and the dragon, which Lord Laiaden assured me he would have under control by then." Krhan kept a blazing stare toward Tonelia. "And we're all painfully aware on where that river borders?"

The wielder stepped in between Krhan and Tonelia. "So cut out the middle reptile and have the orb tossed to the wind and see who can jump the highest?" Nolan suggested, trying to bait the deceiver.

"I did no such thing!" the lord blared back in defense.

"Prove it!" Nolan challenged.

"*No, you,*" Krhan retaliated. "After all, you're the great wielder!"

"*No,*" Tonelia burst in. "It's not like that at all Nolan."

"What's it like then?" The wielder checked his anger.

"It's more," she hesitated. "Like someone's …?" Suddenly, she bit her lip and stopped dead in her thoughts. Tonelia's eyes raced back and forth from Nolan to Krhan as she desperately searched for the right words, but strangely, she was at a loss.

"Out with it." Nolan took an impatient step towards her.

Krhan swooped in as well.

Tonelia defiantly held her ground while her mind raced for words. All eyes fell upon her, and the hall grew deathly quiet. She'd finally resolved to answer when the horns blasted, saving her with instant relief. The entire hall was startled.

"*The lord returns,*" a warrior from the west door shouted.

The court immediately exploded into a frenzy of commotion and preparation.

Both Tonelia and Nolan turned to despair as they quickly assimilated the announcement.

Nolan bolted toward the doors, fighting his way through the crowd, while Krhan uncharacteristically and leisurely strolled down the steps. All the while he kept a wary eye upon the lady. She gave Krhan a quick glance and then ran for the doors.

As they reached the doors, two large warriors burst through, aiding a badly injured man. His long gray hair and beard were stained in blood. A scarlet-soaked headband dressed a serious wound that covered most of the features of the kingdom's lord.

Chapter 5

P.D. 84, A.F. 8130

News arrived in the kingdom of Lavenden that the wielder was enroute to Urlon and Lord Krhan had made it there first. But the earlier morning only found the big trading vessel *Ocean Dominator* leaving the port of Pantanteous and bound for Illenwell. Its hall was full, packed with much-needed trade.

Several lost vessels from both ports, Pantanteous and Illenwell, had already taken their toll on trade and industries. And now that the treaty was lost, new directions needed to quickly present themselves to the situation before all was lost, again.

The sun, like a large bright ball of heat, hung in the east and slowly worked its way across the blue waters south of Lavenden and the port of Pantanteous.

Small clouds and flocks of birds floated and flowed across the blue sky. Various ocean life skimmed the water's surface and a few, leaped through the passing waves. Their scaly skins shimmered in the sparkling waters.

Warm, inviting, and full of optimism, winds filled the sails of both the arriving and departing ships, while salty spray breezes filled the air.

One such ship, a massive and well-constructed vessel that had seen many such profitable trips, slowly crept out past the harbors and peers.

On board the large vessel was a strong crew of one hundred. All were fighting sailors, the toughest of the personally handpicked warriors to accompany the ship and master.

Bound for Illenwell, ready and eager, the vessel moved out towards the Morning Isles and just below Sauros and through the most dangerous part, the Evening Isles and Kureath, the land of dragons just south—and, unfortunately, where most of the attacks from dragons took place. Get through there unharmed, and the ship could easily make the port of Illenwell, and then one more pass through the dangerous channel without an attack would get them home safely.

Sails bloated and bugled by the strong winds boasted of their prowess, while thick, sturdy masts held their own against the forces of the ocean.

The deck below bustled with life as crew scurried about their daily activities.

"Lord, Master." A well statured warrior/sailor climbed the stairs to the wheel and addressed the captain of the ship.

"Keep her straight and true." Logar Hearthol patted Tolo, his trusted driver of the large wheel, and then turned his attention to the approaching sailor.

Romar was a force all by himself. Bulging arms and chest. Legs like tree trunks. Twice the size of anyone on board. And feared nothing. Not even a dragon. During the Saurotillian wars he faced and defeated many a centurion and their tanks, the Tyrannattors, alone and single handedly. But surprisingly to all, he was far from arrogant and was even known by most as a gentle giant. He was also respectful—especially to Lord, Master Logar Hearthol. But today would be different. Something or someone crawled about his mind like a tiny, annoying little worm, and he appeared, to Logar anyway, just a bit aggravated and disgruntled about some issue or issues.

"The crew armed and ready?" Logar addressed him.

"Ay." He nodded and grabbed the hilt of his large sword. "But you mark this statement to be true." He looked out over the waters. "There will not be a dragon in sight."

Logar was hopeful but not optimistic. He too felt the weight of his own sword.

Romar scanned the well-armed warrior/sailors as they went about their assigned duties without protest. But still, to Romar, many of these were his closest companions, and he wished no harm to come to any of them. However, with concern, he needed to ask, "How many ships now have been lost to the dragons?" Romar moved over to the starboard and watched the port of Pantanteous slowly shrink away.

Despite the news and growing concerns of the ill-fated attack on Lord Baylor and the loss of the kingdom's orb, ships continued to arrive daily from the east ports of Lauraleeanna, Teraleon and further up the Useppettus River to Lord Toranden's kingdom of North Avalore and Auroria. This date was no exception, and they all sailed into the waiting harbor and anticipated news of a kingdom in an auction state.

Master Logar came to his side and leaned over the rail himself. "More than my father cared to lose." He spat over the side and answered the troubled warrior.

"We heard tell of nine." Romar turned and leaned his back against the rail. "Nine big ones, and expensive." He paused. "And all the crew and cargo," he added.

Logar nodded. "Most of the crews anyways. The few that survived were later rescued. But Lord Laiaden has lost his share as well," Logar pointed out in appeasement.

A murderous look came over Romar's face upon the mention of Lord Laiaden. "Hear tell that one or two of *his* ships had a stinking animal controller on board." He spat over the side again in disgust.

"True." Logar nodded. "I can't deny the fact that, yes, one or two of those Taulians sailed down here upon Laiaden's ships and took control of the dragons from attacking the vessels that they were on."

Romar looked ever more disgusted and spat again. "Wondering who is really driving this treaty?"

Logar remained silent but kept his comments to himself.

When Romar's patience was spent awaiting the lord to reply, he spoke his mind. "What makes them so special?" He referred to Lord Laiaden.

"It was a private matter between my father and Lord Laiaden." It was all Logar was going to offer in response.

"Private!" Romar grunted. "Private like that incident up north with Lord Baylor?"

"Now that's a completely different situation," Logar pointed out.

"How different?" Romar spat. "And just as foolish."

Logar only nodded in agreement.

"All the same," Romar grumbled, "a dragon attack, and I wager Lord Baylor lost his orb and the kingdom of Urlon with it."

"Yes," Logar responded. "And now an auction state."

"Sure, it is." Romar said. "And our lord ran up there to retrieve it along with that kingdom."

Logar need not respond to the fact.

Romar continued, "And I have heard that your brother, Lantor, was sent immediately to that mountain where the dragon may have taken the orb back to."

Again, Logar remained silent, but he did respect the big man's thoughts.

Almost attempting to get Logar to talk, Romar continued, "Bet he got a Taulian to control that white dragon of Illenwell and offered him a pretty gem for it."

Logar, again, remained composed and only smirked over to Romar.

"Oh, I wager that pretty Lady Tonelia's not happy." Romar continued with the jabs.

Logar took a deep breath of the fresh, salty ocean air.

"The wielder will be on his way," Romar said.

Logar pushed away from the rail. "I'm sure he is already there." Then he walked over to Tolo to check on the course. Turning toward his cabin door, he disappeared through it, leaving Romar to his wicked thoughts about just what was really happening up north.

The rest of the day remained calm and steady, but the crew, despite their fearless nature, grew ever more apprehensive, for they knew all too well that just ahead was Kureath.

The next day arrived with clear blue skies above and deep blue waters that brought wave after wave smashing into the bow. To the starboard side, the kingdom of Lavenden just hung in one's sight—a shadowy outline now fading into the point of Sauros and Sauros Prime to the north.

To the port side, the Morning Isles pushed their way up out of the waters—all barren and protruding points. There were some smaller islands. But these were devoid of any life and vegetation. Most of the isles resembled some gigantic creature's teeth, stretching up and pointing toward the sky. They arose from the ocean in various heights. Some had small caves and were jagged. But none offered anything habitable.

Logar was at the wheel while the crew continued their tasks. Each remained alert and weary as the approaching channel of Kureath crept into view.

Romar appeared from a doorway after just finishing his morning meal and rounds of the ship. He walked up the stairs and took his place next to Logar when he eyed Sauros.

"That will be the immediate defeat of that treaty." He nodded toward the shores of the Saurotillian Lord Vax.

Logar glanced over and said, "The wielder can handle them."

Romar spat in disgust. "No one can handle that useless kind."

"Nevertheless," Logar insisted, "they have a kingdom and an orb and a river that we will need for this treaty." He stated the oblivious.

"That river needs no treaty." Romar sneered. "It's free."

"Nonetheless, my big friend," Logar argued, "it will need to be made safe from centurion attacks."

"And you think our brave Nolan Hammer will be able to negotiate with that tongue flicker of a lord of theirs?" Romar responded in a deep, poison tone.

"He will get through," Logar replied optimistically, for he was a good friend of Nolan, and he respected the wielder. Many, including himself, would trust their confidence to the wielder.

Romar waved him off in disgust. "Your shortsightedness of this great wielder lies in his weakness for that lady."

Logar remained calm but could not get a handle on what was eating Romar and his sudden turn in attitude. He was about to inquire when an interruption came from high above.

"A ship!" The lookout pointed down from his nest.

Logar had been steering the ship all morning, while Tolo had taken a break for some food and *lade*. Romar went erect and alert at the news.

Both looked off toward the same direction and caught the glimpse of the tiny sails as they came into sight.

Logar gave Romar an inquisitive glance. "Tolo!" Logar shouted. "Hurry, come take the wheel."

Tolo appeared and ran up the stairs and grabbed the wheel, while Logar and Romar moved toward the bow. Soon they were accompanied by the gathering sailors as they, too, caught the sails of a fast-approaching ship.

"Illenwell's," Romar remarked.

Logar nodded. "She made it passed Kureath."

"With a Taulian no doubt." Romar spat over the side.

"Perhaps?" Logar squinted to catch a glimpse of the ship's markings.

"*Dragon!*" The lookout shouted madly and jumped about the nest pointing. "*Dragon!*"

All eyes fell on the red object as it came up from the port side of the approaching ship.

"Arm yourselves!" Logar commanded the sailors. "Get ready. We can't afford to lose these vessels."

Sailors immediately scrambled for their arms. And the deck quickly broke out into a frenzy of rushing bodies. Dragon fear had not yet grabbed them, and they were far from allowing it to settle in.

"*To the ship!*" Logar shouted back to Tolo.

He responded and quickly turned the wheel, and the ship changed course at the command.

"Bring that dragon to me." Romar eagerly anticipated the battle.

"We will, my big friend," Logar said. "But first, let the cannons do their trick."

Aboard the *Ocean Dominator* were the latest weapons—four large, spring-loaded cannons. Plans had been brought from the Zoarians and given to the troll, Opp, who lived in the mountains of Qeuwothl of Lavenden and north of Pantanteous. An excellent troll, Opp's skill was wood making, carving, and designs. Building and aiding Lord Krhan and the kingdom, the troll remained an elusive but most productive being.

When the dragon attacks had begun, cries were made to the wielder and Zoarians, but finding a peaceful resolution was far from their control and ability. So, the Zoarians had come up with plans for the cannons to aid the ships protection.

The design was simple. The cannon could shoot a large iron made netting that would hopefully entangle the wings and bring the dragon crashing down into the water.

With any luck, the ship could run while the dragon fought to free itself. However, this was theory and had not yet been tested.

Logar would now have that chance. But much like his father, an arrogant air about him would blind side his vision, and this would once again be their downfall.

Both Logar and Romar watched as the large red dragon swept around the fleeing ship. It then hovered off the starboard side of the ship as if it was studying her.

"*Ah!*" Romar hit the rail with his fist, and it vibrated violently. "You mark my word, they have a Taulian aboard!"

"No," Logar quickly disagreed. "I don't believe so."

They were well out of range of hearing anything from the other ship. But by the looks of what was happening, it was not going to be good. And with that, the dragon sprayed the entire deck with one continuous sweep of fire. From stern to bow, the ship ignited and erupted into a huge red ball, and black smoke rose from the inferno and drifted with the breeze toward the south shores of Sauros.

Watching in horror, the crew of *Ocean Dominator* sailed quickly toward the tragedy, completely helpless to aid.

Logar watched the ship burn and rock then slowly dip to its port and sink.

The dragon floated there in victory and then spied the approaching vessel and turned to greet her as well.

"Steady." Logar addressed the bow cannon operator.

He nodded in confidence but never took his eyes from the dragon.

It rushed across the waters and roared in defiance.

"Steady." Logar again said. "You got this. Aim for the head and wait for the distance. It will try to turn, and we should catch one of the wings."

The dragon roared and quickly approached the stern. All hands braced and prayed.

The distance collapsed, and the operator released the lever, and the net came springing forth with a great force. It immediately fanned and opened but the startled dragon countered by quickly tucking its wings about its body. It completely ignored the passing net. And then, straight like an arrow, it dove down into the waters just off the stern.

All rushed over to peer over the side as the dragon disappeared under a rush of foaming white water.

Logar did not need to shout an order, for the cannon was already being quickly reloaded.

"*Stand ready!*" Logar shouted to the other three cannons. "*Mind the ports!*"

The warriors broke apart and quickly covered the ship's sides. Shields, spears, and swords awaited the beast's return. But all remained deathly silent and calm.

"Where the…," Romar sneered under his breath.

"*There!*" the lookout shouted and pointed off the port side.

All hands watched as the red dragon emerged several yards south of the ship. It rose high above the water and just hovered there, wings beating in a steady rhythm.

Black eyes scrutinized the ship from a safe distance. It coolly flapped about, calculating its next offensive.

"*Blast!*" Romar smashed his fist into the rail. "It's sizing us up!" He spat.

"Good," Logar responded rather calmly. "Perhaps it understands our defense and is thinking twice about another foolish attack."

But with that said, the dragon tucked its wings in again and shot down into the ocean like a long spear.

"He's coming up on us!" Logar shouted.

The dragon's head and long neck suddenly appeared over the starboard side, and before the cannon and operator could react, black teeth sunk in, and both the operator and cannon were torn from the side and flung out to the waters, the operator screaming all the way.

The bow cannon fired again since he had the cleanness shot, but the dragon had already disappeared, and the net went flying off into the water, harmlessly.

"He is going for the cannons!" Romar rushed to the port cannon.

Logar was still at the bow when the dragon erupted from the starboard side again and leaped onto the deck in the middle of the ship. The vessel rocked under the violent thud of the dragon's weight as it came bearing down, taking out the middle mast and sending the lookout screaming over the side.

"*Attack!*" Romar shouted, and immediately the armed warriors fell upon the large red target.

It bellowed in defiance and swung its long tail around the stern side of the ship, taking out the mast, cannon, and wheel, along with several warriors. Everything and everyone in its path were swept over the side in a crash of screams and splashes.

The dragon fired away, and the blast consumed the other fast approaching warriors.

Logar anticipated the beast's next move and, with all his speed and strength, rushed across the deck and, with all his body weight, hit Romar like a boulder, and the two went overboard just as the dragon sprayed the port cannon and those warriors with death.

Seeing that the vessel was lost, the remaining warriors dove for the water. The dragon roared again and then faced down and released another long blast of flames. The deck exploded in fire, and black smoke rose high into the blue sky.

Logar and Romar emerged from the waters and watched the ship buckle in the middle, accompanied by the loud sickening crack of lumber. The bow and stern rose from the water as the middle of the ship sank. The dragon burst upward like a phoenix from the ashes and roared triumphantly.

It rose, turned, and hovered above the carnage. Then it began its death dives, scooping up warriors for a well-deserved meal.

Logar and Romar were soon joined by another survivor, Tolo, who also managed to flee the doomed ship as well. The trio watched in horror as their comrades were either consumed, dead, or drowning.

When the dragon had finished, it bellowed again and then flew away towards Kureath, soon disappearing without even giving the trio so much as a look.

Now desperately clinging to debris, the trio watched the *Ocean Dominator*, crushed, smashed, and sinking before them. The stern slowly slipped away under the waves. Each watched the bow bob about useless in the waters to finally roll over and sink.

Logar circled about in the water and eyed the Morning Isles for refuge. They would still be a distance. That was when he caught sight of something big—something black high in one of the distant points. But a wave suddenly crashed about him and lifted him up and over.

When he regained himself, the point was out of sight, and he lost his objective. He second-guessed himself and brushed it aside. Survival became the important factor here, not imaginary illusions brought about by a traumatizing event.

"Which way?" Tolo said between waves and warm, salty ocean water from his mouth.

"Gather what you can." Logar referenced the floating debris as they bobbed about. "And make for Sauros Prime."

"Not there." Romar sneered. But what choice had they?

The trio bobbed about, but without handy alternatives, they reluctantly swam about and pulled together whatever was floating. Then they kicked off and, with any luck, would make shore by late evening—if they should survive the creatures of the watery depth.

Logar had been correct and his eyesight keen. High above and well out of sight, the entire ordeal was witnessed by a large black dragon. Its golden eyes watched the survivors swim slowly north. It growled.

"Patience, my pet." A slender hand reached up and rubbed its chin. "Let us watch and see what happens next," the white-robed figure suggested.

Chapter 6

P.D. 94, A.F. 8130

Twilight slowly consumed the port of Illenwell. Ghostly red tentacles stretched out from the fading sun in a fleeting attempt to drag away the ships as they gently bobbed about in the calm waters of a still port. While on shore, the harbor's people hurried about to their destinations, whether their dwellings or drinking places; they could not help glancing nervously up toward the ominous mountain range that represented their kingdom and their fate. But the only response was an eerie grimace of eminent doom.

Long before the port's founding, sailors would often view the angle of Jawed Peaks, which resembled the lower jaw of a large dog or, worse yet, a dragon. What appeared to be the incisors were, in fact, a group of smaller and shorter mountains that ran between the two more-pointed canines of the peaks. The taller one was nearer the port and, so, named the Mountain of Illenwell. The smaller twin sat more to the north and was less ominous. This is how it had been since the beginning of seasons' time. And to add more foreboding to Jawed Peaks, deep, long, and winding endless black tunnels carved throughout the range had supported, for many seasons, the likes of Saurotillians and other assorted creatures that favored the black darkness. All these even before the arrival of the dragon.

Sauros found the secrets an advantage point for ambushing the port. But they would have to share the darkness with other quiet and deadly creatures that lurked in the cracks.

It was also reported that, in the seasons of the dreaded Vorgoloth, trolls would come and mine the mountain for its precious stones—which was, ironically where Ott, the troll, had left his pile of metals and where, for the moment, the dragon found safety. The Vorgoloth traveled freely throughout the tunnels feasting on Saurotillians and other lost souls who foolishly came to steal the troll horde of treasure. This clever creature of seasons past was feared by all, especially Nolan, who had been forced during the Saurotillian wars too confront and defeat the creature.

So, for now the dragon had arrived and destroyed the unfortunate port just at the start of the Saurotillian wars and made its home there in the darkness. It had arrived in the height of Lord Laiaden's rule and would most likely remain long after his departure. The port continued to grow and rebuild its mighty harbor, and the folks kept an ever-watchful eye toward the mountain. The troll, Ott, who the Zoarian council had sent, could do little to hinder the beast. But he could work magic with his brawny hands and soon found a new talent by helping the city rebuild.

As news arrived of the dragon's attack and the orb of Urlon within its grasp, the folks looked up to the mountain in fear that someone would disturb the despicable thief. The tunnels and passageways were, indeed, at this very moment crawling with *would be treasure hunters* and those aspiring to be lords. Foolish as that might be, they came in as quietly as possible and thought of nothing else but retrieving the priceless orb of Urlon, no matter what the price and despite Lord Laiaden's recent orders.

Others were attracted, too, but for a different purpose. One of these made his way slowly and patiently through the blackness. The tunnels went forever on as he cautiously made his way through them with as little light as possible. Fortunately for him, some of the tunnels Ott had thoughtfully installed either held mounted torches or large basins of huge burning fires as the troll dug here and there carting debris or frames to other parts of the caves for storage. It was amusing, for the metal he thought inadequate to use as sturdy building material he discarded in the spacious cavern where the dragon preferred to be. For this, thieves were grateful at one point in the seasons or another, for if one could get past the troll, the Vorgoloth, and the Saurotillians, one could be a rich thief with a sack full of wealth.

The dark figure smirked at the thoughts of the cavern and what lay ahead. But after all, Illenwell wouldn't want to lose its most valuable thief, "the Ghost" as the lord called him. Laiaden was counting on him—not to fetch the orb or to anger the dragon. On the contrary, he was there to keep things quiet as it were—to make sure that *everything* remained in place.

And that took a lot of money; time; and, of course, resourcefulness on his part. After all, there were a few brave orb hunters who had made their way in here for the lost item. The Ghost was familiar with the mountain since Lord Laiaden had hired him many times before to look out for things up here. He was able to offer his services in guiding the orb seekers passage to the cavern. Of course, they reached their destination.

Let's see, the Ghost thought to himself. *The first thief ran into a large spider that took him for an evening meal. Or was it a morning meal? One can never tell what time of sun it is while traveling around under the mountain. Another fell down a large fissure. Poor thief accidently lost his footing. Or was that after being mysteriously pushed? No bumped.* He smiled to himself.

The third one had insisted on a partnership. But later, a dagger had come between them. And all too sadly, he'd had to dissolve that arrangement.

Oh, that reminded him, *clean the blade of the bloodstains.* After all, Lord Laiaden had forbidden any of the thieves from coming in here and disturbing its most excellent resident, the dragon, from its slumber. The Ghost was just carrying out orders from the Lord. How generous of him. He thought nothing of his own sacrifice but only of the safety of Illenwell, his home. The Ghost would be greatly rewarded for this unselfish act of heroism.

But he did so want to see the orb. And perhaps touch it. "OK," he said to himself, "it is worth a lot!"

Up ahead, The Ghost would have his chance. This part of the cavern and joining tunnels glowed and flickered with the smoldering remains of the arrogant Saurotillians, and a distant growl stopped him in his steps.

His palms began to sweat, and a bead of perspiration dragged slowly down from the corner of his right eye. He cursed his pounding heart as it beat from his chest like it was trying to send a clear signal to the dragon—a feeble attempt to attract it to its next meal like a dinner bell. He moved to one side of the tunnel and disappeared into the shadow. He looked out over the few smoldering bodies and could make out the reptilian skulls. Their bones were black, and armor melted, sagging in some places, while what was left of their limp bodies lay about the area, displaying the carnage of the battle. Spears, swords, and one or two helmets mingled amongst the debris as a clear indicator of their uselessness against dragon hide.

Arrogant tongue flickers, The Ghost thought to himself. *They assumed they could just come here and take the orb.*

The Ghost, known to a few as Thoan, looked ahead and spied the large opening to a nearby cavern and, once again, heard the soft growl of a contented creature. He was intrigued, for he had yet to see the beast up close. He first thought the better of it, but standing there, he decided to chance it and see this magnificent creature up close—but not too close. Who was he fooling? he jested to himself, for no one else was around. Ahead, the cavern and the orb of Urlon, right there for the taking. Why, he knew in a moment that, if he was with anyone else, they would not have walked away either. What a mocking he would receive if he thought the better of it and turned right around. *Right here. Do it now. Walk away.*

Still, the intrigue got the better of him despite what instincts and wisdom screamed at him from within his head. He stood there in the darkness and let wisdom and foolishness slug it out in his brain until finally he made a decision and broke the two apart. For the first time ever, it dawned upon him that he had yet to see an orb. Neither Thoan, nor anyone else for that fact, in Illenwell other than Lord Laiaden had ever seen their orb. Laiaden kept it hidden and safe somewhere in the massive wooden hall. Now both were before him, the guardian, and the prize. Best take a quick peek and see how valuable the thing I'm supposed to be guarding is. He kept to the shadows and inched his way toward the large opening of the cavern just ahead.

Thoan cursed to himself for missing the show as he slipped past the remains. The smell of burnt lizard penetrated his nostrils, and his eyes began to tear from the stench of smoke. By the looks of the remains, it had been a sun or so ago. Now, Thoan had no idea that he was early for a second showing that was shortly in the making. And as he stood there surveying the remains, he had a thought of his own mortality. *It's a pity the old friends he had come to known throughout the seasons might say, old Thoan went to his demise in the forgotten blackness as he pursued his foolish attempt to guard the orb. He could hear the drinking stories.*

"What happen to what's his name?" one would ask.

"I think he settled down and found a partner," another would add.

"No, no, I think the dragon got him," would comment another.

"Perhaps he found his fortune after all," yet still another would say.

"Yes, the long drinking and eating at twilight's end." They would all laugh and bring their cups full of *lade* up high, splashing about.

"To Lord Thoan," they would cheer. "He bravely got the orb, fooled the dragon, and kept our port safe."

No! He stopped in the dark. *I want no orb or kingdom. I do not desire these things. I wish to retain my anonymity, to not attract attention. The shadows are where I work the best. This is my life and my home. After all, it pays the debts.*

Again, he thought the better of his curiosity and told himself to turn away.

You want to see it. His conscience mocked him. Daring him, like a great tempter, his pounding heart continued to ring like a dinner bell.

Enough! he screamed in his head.

Taking control, he slid into the dragon's cavern and stopped dead in his tracks. The white beast lay dead ahead, its body sprawled upon the cold cavern floor. The long neck stretched before Thoan as his eyes followed it to the head, and there, with its eyes slit so fine he could barely make out the blackness of its pupils, the pointed jaw rested a few yards from him. He could smell the musty, dank breath. Thoan stood deep in the shadows, sure the dragon had neither seen nor smelled him. For how could he be smelled? The cavern reeked of smoldering lizard flesh. Small fires burned what was left and gave the surroundings a deep glow of dark red as the images softly flickered upon the walls. He spied more large basins, but they looked as if they had not supported fires in many a season. Thoan searched the cavern and the mound of treasure piled behind the dragon, stretched out across the floor and up toward one side of the far cavern. And there, quite by coincidence, was the orb of Urlon. The dragon motioned and shifted its weight. Thoan remained poised and still, but the dragon made no further movement other than steady long breaths of a deep, raspy sound. Its lengthy tail tapered off into the darkness.

Thoan returned his attention to the orb and pondered the strange circumstances that had brought it here. No one in Illenwell had heard of any reason for Laiaden to meet with Baylor. Had the dragon conjured this deceit? Thoan smirked and then decided to leave while the leaving was good. But suddenly, the dragon's long tooth-filled snout lifted off the floor and turned toward him. Thoan, still frozen in place, shot a command to his heart to cease pounding. But it ignored him, so he stood with muscles tense, fighting every urge to bolt.

You will never make it, his mind screamed at his legs. But to his surprise, the dragon's head wrapped up and over its body and, for a long moment, seemed to be pleased with its trophy still resting on the ledge above the treasure. Thoan made his move and cautiously slipped around the same corner from which he'd come. Still keeping to the shadows, he followed the smoldering centurion bodies back down the tunnel.

Once there, Thoan broke out into the middle of the next tunnel and made a quick dash, putting some distance between him and his objective.

With his curiosity fed, he decided on a safer route away and, while he was at it, to have a peek at what the troll was up to.

Sometime later, Thoan followed several different tunnels and marked each accordingly with special symbols to create a map that only he could understand. Specific markings were for the dragon, while others would mark the troll, just as soon as he found the big lurking cow. For Thoan had never entered the true mouth of the mountain that faced the southwest part toward the port but, rather, had come through a smaller, narrower crack near the west side of the mountain. Ott worked near the main entrance and kept it cluttered with a vast array of metal frames and other projects that kept him preoccupied. But all the same, Thoan neither needed nor desired any interference from that troll. Besides, the shadows were where he worked the best. After all, he was the Ghost.

And as he strolled down a rather dark tunnel, he could faintly hear the muffled sounds of a disturbance. Thoan froze as the distant sound of shuffling feet became clearer. He looked to both sides and found a crack. Squirming into the nook, he moved back as far as possible. A small animal squealed, ran over his feet, and disappeared somewhere further to the back of the nook. He didn't flinch but waited patiently as the shuffling feet grew nearer, along with muffled sounds of heavy breathing. He could barely make out several warriors as they passed him by. They wore no body armor, but he could make out the outline of full shields in the dark light—most likely built of wood. They passed by quickly with one torch leading while the final warrior held another. He gave them a few moments to make their way down the tunnel and then slipped out and followed behind the last warrior, well out of sight.

Thoan followed them for some time as they moved in and out of passageways and tunnels until they came to a halt and dropped to a squat. Thoan pondered at how the warriors knew their way and what guided them on their way. He stood there in the dark shadows and listened closely to the whispers as the warriors' voices broke through the quiet.

"We'll wait here while Orun moves ahead and scouts out the dragon," one whispered.

Thoan took him for the leader and waited patiently until he could get an accurate count of their numbers, since the group had split, making it more difficult to formulate a plan for their quick and untimely demise.

"What are the lord's instructions?" one of the warriors whispered.

"To wait patiently," the voice broke through the blackness.

"And what of her?" another warrior whispered in concern.

Thoan's ears perked at the mention of a female.

"Now that's a concern, for she is to bring the wielder here," the lead warrior's voice responded.

"Like that'll happen," one scoffed in a whisper.

"It will," the lead retorted.

"And how can you be so sure?" a deep voice inquired.

"I know the wielder, and he can't resist a challenge," the leader whispered with assurance.

"Yes, but what if he doesn't want anyone along?" one warrior spoke, sounding unconvinced.

"Yeah," the deeper voice chimed in. "I've heard she's not to be trusted."

"No, she can be," the lead hissed.

"That wielder wouldn't come here and face that dragon," another answered under his breath. "Nolan's too wise for that. He wouldn't get himself roasted for an orb."

"No," the lead whispered, "he is a wielder and a warrior of testament, and that's what this plan depends on in order for it to work."

"It's much more than the testament," the deeper voice whispered. "It's her that he loves and would do anything for her, including traveling to Roan and Taul beyond if she bid him to."

"Let's hope that our lord's plan goes accordingly."

No one spoke further, while tension and uneasiness overtook the blackness.

Thoan stood in the dark shadows, for he could not see the warriors well with only their two torches. But he suspected that it would take Orun sometime before he returned—*if he returns at all*. He smiled. This would be a good time to make that happen. However, he was blind and was not sure of the location or direction or the number of warriors that had accompanied Orun. So, he would have to wait it out.

Occasionally, he could hear them stir and then whisper. He strained his ears to hear, but they were too low for him to make out any of the words. His legs were numbing and his patience as well. His mind began to drift, and several times, he had to fight back the yawns of sleep. At one time, his stomach protested its emptiness, so he slipped his hand into his sack and felt for the muffins he'd brought. They were wrapped in moist towels and still tasted slightly fresh. He had dried fish, fruits, and vegetables. He also had some small sticks of dried flare meat, but unfortunately, he had mistakenly brought a spicier kind and shied from those due to a lack of drink. Besides, there was only a small supply, and soon he would have to leave to replenish the goods. As for the spicier meat, he would consume those later over a tall cup filled with *lade* back in Illenwell. For now, he nibbled away and took in a drink of what little *lade* that he had left. That too would soon run dry. He kept ever cautious of his surroundings— picking up every sound he could hear. If something did come, he would be in trouble, as would his uninvited guests.

Chapter 7

The daily affairs at Strong Tower had been long and informative, but the night would be agonizing and sleepless. The physicians rushed Lord Baylor to the infirmary and bid the wielder time to allow the lord to recover. He protested under the circumstances. However, the lady interceded promising she would meet Nolan later and sending both him and Lord Baylor's brother Lord Toranden to Nolan's room. There, the two were brought all they would need to make the evening more bearable. Nolan's guest room was well furnished with a bed, couches, a long wooden table, and chairs connected to a spacious balcony, high in the tower, which overlooked the west side of the city. This was Nolan's favorite room when he came to visit, which was not often, and the view this evening was twilight as it overtook the kingdom. Nolan was anxious to get Toranden alone and find out what the brother knew of this treaty and the dragon incident, which perplexed him the most. As they entered their quarters, the wielder leapt upon him for details.

"All right, Lord." Nolan fired off a succession of questions. "What's with this treaty and dragon? Why was your brother out there with his orb?"

"Hold." The lord displayed an open palm to his interrogator. "I was called along to flank and nothing more. And from our distance, there was no Lord Laiaden, no Sauros, just the dragon." He grabbed a nearby cup, filled it, and offered it to the wielder.

Under normal circumstances, Nolan would have hoped for his sweeter cup of *lade*, but that was furthest from his thoughts. Besides, the staff had already anticipated his needs. He accepted the drink but was still lost in a rush of thoughts. Toranden filled his own cup and then spied the food that was spread across the long wooden table.

"How long did you wait?" he asked the lord.

"Almost two full sun cycles for Lord Laiaden," he responded. "The third morning, we spied smoke bellowing out of the forest near the last range of Jawed Peaks."

"Lord Laiaden?" Nolan inquired.

But Toranden only answered with a quick blank glance and a slight shoulder shrug. "Best ask him when you get there," the lord offered. "For I'm sure by now he's doing all he can do to keep whatever and whoever out of that mountain in fear of provoking the beast any further." He paused. "And he is most likely trying to figure out what to do with you." He pointed at the wielder.

Nolan stood a few moments in reflection and then gave the lord a strange look. "Tell me, could Lord Laiaden have used an animal controller? Why would he have jeopardized his own orb and why look to Urlon?" Now he was really perplexed.

"Again," Toranden spoke, "you'll need to ask him directly. I've never met the lord. But from what I understand, he loves that pet dragon, and they have exploited it to bring seclusion to their hearty port." He chuckled. "Great for security, I might add." Toranden downed his cup and went back for fourths. But Nolan had lost count.

"Bribe … negotiations … extortion … what?" the wielder pondered to the lord, who shrugged his shoulders and drank some more.

Nolan could easily see that there would be no further answers from Toranden, and they were clearly left out of this plot. He strolled to the railing and swirled his half cup of *lade* around. Too busy to eat and too tired to drink, which brought a smile to his face, since he *always* made time to drink and eat with an old friend. But under the circumstances, this evening, he better keep his mind focused on the moment and waited for

Tonelia to arrive with word. So, he decided for a more casual conversation with the lord.

"He'll be fine you know." Nolan attempted to reassure Toranden as he scanned the peaceful city far below.

Toranden glance at Nolan. "They'll both be fine."

Nolan understood. They both knew his mind was completely on Tonelia. "Besides"—the lord laughed— "he's got a rock head." He sucked down another cup of *lade*. "Remember the blow he took from Tonelia during the war?" He refilled his cup.

Nolan chuckled. "Hey, the stone head ran right into her back."

"Well, you'd mistake him for a Saurotillian yourself if you had your back to him," Toranden said, stuffing a chunk of meat into his mouth. And with that, they both broke into smiles as if anyone could mistake a person for one of those nine-foot-tall, cold-blooded tongue flicking Saurotillians.

"How's Auroria coming along?" the concerned wielder asked as he moved toward the table and surveyed the pickings.

Toranden swallowed his food. "Cold." And he was not referring to the current season.

Nolan understood. He took a cut of meat and rolled it unto some bread. "Thalls?"

The lord nodded back in response.

The wielder understood all too well that the little hairy, black humanlike animals normally only invaded North Avalore during the harvest part of the season when the snow arrived. But to have sightings and periodic encounters during the hotter part of the production season typically meant the hunting packs were hungrier than usual.

"Mostly near Claw Crag and the Arthian Forest," Toranden explained. "So, if you have to return that way, please stay alert, and I will get word to the patrols to be on their best." He added this stern warning.

"Where I'm going," Nolan raised his eyebrows, "Thalls are the least of my challenges." He walked past the lord and poured a bit more *lade* in his cup and ate his sandwich.

"Yes, after all, you'll have to meet Lord Laiaden." Toranden did not need to remind him again.

Nolan glanced down at his cup and then looked to the aging lord. "It wouldn't have made a bit of difference you know."

Toranden stopped everything he was doing—from his jaw crushing his food to his thoughts—and gave the wielder a direct stare. "Yes, it would have," the lord offered back after catching Nolan's intention.

The wielder cocked his head.

The lord smiled in response. "We'd all be at twilight's end after the dragon has finished us and be having more than just this *lade*." He lifted his cup in praise of the afterlife.

They cheered, and two metal cups broke the quiet night with a slight clang. The old friends were content to drink the time away, for at that moment, all was out of their control.

But it was short-lived, for as the two stood there in thought, both were distracted by the approach of a rather stout and muscular young warrior, who came through the doorway and out toward the balcony.

"Ah," Toranden perked up, "our nightly report."

The wielder stared at the handsome youth as he approached them both. Stunning blue eyes under a soft crop of sandy blond hair, a small nose, and solid jaw molded into a muscular neck while square and sturdy shoulders confidently approached them.

"Nolan," the lord said, starting the introduction, "I don't believe you've met Urlon's new lead warrior."

"No, I hadn't the opportunity to meet him yet, but Golar had mentioned him and that you were sending him east."

"That's correct," Tholin responded rather rudely.

Almost immediately. the wielder was overwhelmed by the gaze of arrogance and the body language that boasted of self-esteem and confidence. He had never, in his entire career, been more offended by the introduction of anyone until now. "And that mission would be?" Nolan shrugged it off for the moment but felt agitated.

"The lady will fill you in later." Tholin sounded cross.

"And a real piece of work," the lord interrupted, already sensing the growing hostility. "Tholin of the Awuer family, this is the great wielder, Nolan Hammer."

"Yes, I recognize the golden sword," he responded indignantly.

Nolan glanced to the lord for a reprimand, but oddly, none was forth coming. The young warrior returned a quick nod to Nolan and continued, "Warriors"—Nolan watched the youth's stern jaw fight to restrain himself as he was forced to address them—"the lady sent me here to inform you that she should arrive shortly, and I am to report to *you*, since you *are* the acting superiors, that the city is secure for the evening." He spoke with an indignant subtlety, and it clearly sounded to Nolan as if this youth didn't have to answer to anyone.

Nolan gave Toranden a couple more glances but got the distinct feeling from the lord's expression and lack of response that he was more tolerant of the youth than Nolan was going to be. Or perhaps the *lade* that the lord had been consuming all evening had finally paralyzed his mind.

"I'm also here to make sure that all your *needs* are met." Tholin didn't ask for their wishes and Nolan couldn't help but feel that he and the lord should be waiting on him, rather than vice versa. The youth was cocky at best. It made the wielder quite uncomfortable just standing in his presence.

"No," a relaxed lord answered for both. "The *wielder* and I are fine." Toranden's emphasis on Nolan's rank causally instructed the youth in respect.

Nolan was just about to lose his patient when in walked Tholin's savior.

The young warrior quickly noticed he had lost their attention as their eyes followed the figure that approached him from behind. He spun on his heels. "Lady Tonelia," the youth said, transforming into a respectful warrior. Nolan caught the game but would let it go for now.

"Toranden," Tonelia said with her eyes affixed to Nolan's, as they had been since she had entered the balcony. "Will you please spell me for a time and go and sit with your brother while I speak to Nolan?" She asked pleasantly but was clearly exhausted from the daily events. And even though Nolan had not taken his eyes from her, he couldn't help but notice the young warrior had never taken his admiring eyes off her either, and his persona begged for her attention.

"Yes," the lord responded, breaking Nolan's concentration, "take all the time you need." And with that, he bowed to the wielder and bid Tholin an uneventful evening and then made for the doorway and disappeared.

There was a moment of uneasiness between the three of them. And without facing the lead warrior, "You may also be excused," she ordered politely.

"Yes, my lady," he replied with a clear undertone of offense as if the wielder should have been excused instead. But the youth stayed composed and gave Nolan a quick jerk of his head. Then he, accompanied by his arrogance, left the room.

Nolan scrutinized the warrior with one watchful eye while the other studied Tonelia as she waited for the youth to leave. As soon as she heard the unmistakable click of the door locking, she dove into Nolan, and hungry lips devoured his. His cup bounced across the balcony, quickly discarded by a hand that needed no further distractions as it probed every inch of her lustful desires. Arms, hands, and fingers flew across each other in a single effort to consume it all. And just at the point when all dignity was about to be abandoned, Nolan's hands grasped her quivering waist and pried them apart until they stood there at arm's length. He watched her passion slowly subside as the moment of seduction appeased her yearning for the time. Nolan's barrel chest rose as it filled with life-giving oxygen nearly splitting his tight-fitting shirt in two.

"I couldn't wait for you to arrive." She sounded exasperated.

"What on Zoarian's name are you two up to?" He lashed out at her.

"I know." She pleaded.

"You know?" He mucked. "You didn't need to place your partner into harm and jeopardize not only your kingdom but Anglyllon as well." He crocked. "I was so disgusted I spit over the news the Zoarian had brought!"

"I know it was foolish," she continued to plead. "We greatly jeopardized everything by not being respectful enough to the orb's value."

"Value," he said. "They are more valuable than you'll ever understand." He grabbed her arms tightly. "Not to mention the incredibly bad timing of this—I'm leaving my uncle, his orb, and my family's kingdom in dire need!"

"I apologize for this, Nolan. I really do. But Urlon is more valuable than its orb." She tried to break free, but he was strong.

"For starters, they represent accomplishment and common sense." He stared deep into her eyes. "Second, this is the way it has been ever since the Zoarians brought them into existence some eight thousand seasons ago to help us organize and establish ourselves from among the other countries, especially Taul, for whom oppression is their way of dealing with their country."

"Yes, I understand." And you're right. Our orb is extremely valuable. And I should"—she paused for a moment— "understand how what is valuable to Baylor is also what's important to me." She was genuinely hurt, and he could see it in her eyes. "But I need to understand what else makes them so valuable?" She eyed him.

He reluctantly released his grip and took a few steps away from her to calm his temper. "As you can't share with me certain secrets in fear that it might bring me harm, please than respect my secrets, for they also could do much damage to not only you but also the rest of the kingdoms." He paused. "It is also a wielder's duty to keep the Zoarians' image in their best interest." For the first time, he turned away from her.

"What secrets?" She came up behind him. "What of the orbs?"

"Secrets." He spun on his heels. "Secrets like why you sent Golar east and about that meeting with Laiaden?" he fired off accusingly. "How about explaining to me why a valuable kingdom is in an auction state?" he finished bluntly.

He gave her a moment to collect her thoughts. After a few minutes, she spoke. "There is much to explain and little time to do it in."

He agreed.

"You, by now, no doubt see that I'm exhausted. And with the arrival of Krhan—"

"Yes, I tried to make—"

"No need," she interrupted him from his apology, "I took care of the matter. "Why, sometimes I think that he is the son of a Saurotillian." She smirked.

"Krhan?" He jested with her.

"Yes, Krhan," she confirmed as she strolled past him and out toward the railing. "Why, sometimes I think his father was a Saurotillian." She smiled while Nolan followed her. "But he's a good lord, and despite the past, Lavenden has flourished. I that you should concentrate on more likely suspects to our immediate peril," she offered as she reached the railing in the humid evening air and surveyed the quiet city far below.

"And which suspects should that be?" he asked, puzzled by her logic.

Their eyes locked and both committed the moment to memory.

"I should apologize for that." She struggled for words to describe her behavior, which Nolan thought uncharacteristic of her, for she was never without something to express.

"What, about Krhan?" he asked.

"Yes, that wasn't fair of me."

"Why, I think that it was. He is the highest on the list with the most to gain."

"No," she defended. "He caught our vulnerability and exploited it. And upon his arrival, I chastised him for it."

"And how did he respond?"

"Arrogantly as always." She smiled.

He loved to see her smile. It made him feel rested and reassured.

"Any way," she went on. "The lord is safe for now, and you are here." She turned away and gazed back out over her city.

"Baylor will be fine," he agreed. They were never good with their feelings, but Nolan tried. "But it is I who must apologize for the seasons since I've been here last." He let his regret color his voice. "It makes it hard when we're apart for this long."

"I apologize that you return under these circumstances." She spoke softly.

"Well, let's try not to make a habit of misplacing your orb every time you need to see me" Nolan offered.

She forced a sincere smile.

"I'm here. What's on your mind?" He continued in a more business tone.

"I don't know where to begin." She smiled.

"Perhaps with what you were going to offer at the hall just before Lord Baylor arrived," he suggested.

"That's a hard road to negotiate." She turned to a more serious tone.

"Try me." Nolan straightened.

"Look, what brought you here?"

Nolan did not understand and gave her a blank stare while waiting for her to explain further.

"Well, did you ever stop to consider that the Zoarians play a bigger part in our destinies than we do?" She observed his reaction.

"Go on," he encouraged her.

"Why do you think they study us so?" she inquired. "And their insights. If they have been in our place before, then why not show us the way out?" She drove for answers on which he could only speculate.

"How do they then control a dragon?" he served back.

"We're not absolutely certain they don't interact with the Taulians just because they say they don't." Tonelia spoke her thought. "How do we know if they can control a dragon or not?" She paused. "Why, I often feel they control us." She dared him to argue.

"If Taul controlled dragons, they would have turned on the Zoarians," Nolan stated.

"Not if they control everything." Tonelia turned her focus back to the Zoarians. "I sometimes get the impression that they only inform us of what they feel concerns us," she said by way of further explanation.

Nolan smiled, for she was determined to win her cause. So, he tried a new diversion. "So, you got Krhan under control then?" He changed the subject from her interrogating questions focused on proving the Zoarians' guilt in all things.

"Absolutely," she turned to face him. "He knows that, if he makes one flinch toward my border, all he'll inherit is a pile of smoldering cinders. Why, at this very moment, my warriors are poised at their stations throughout the city and await my orders."

"And this doesn't make you a bit nervous?" he responded causally.

"No," she said. "The warfare and bloodshed have long been abandoned seasons ago, as lords discovered the expense and time consumed in not only taking the orb but rebuilding the kingdom. Not to mention the resources and people. And for what? Just to have someone else turn around and destroy it and take it from you?" She paused for breath. "You saw the seasons that it took Baylor and I to rebuild this, and we're still no closer to its completion." The lady spoke a little flustered. "Krhan always said political warfare is much more ingenious, don't you think, Nolan?" She changed her tone of voice.

"And where is he staying?" He avoided her question.

"Why?"

"I will need to see him before I leave."

"I took care of him." She directed him to stay out of that business.

He did not respond but only studied her intently.

"Especially after watching what he did during the Saurotillian wars," Tonelia reminded him. "Perhaps on second thought, we should keep a watchful eye on him?" She quickly changed her mind.

Nolan went erect and responded defensively, "You'd better, since I'm not the one who turned him away." Nolan spoke his thought, meaning that she should be more suspicious of Krhan's motives.

"I was willing to give up everything for you," she reminded him.

"Then after the war, why didn't you return to him?" His touch of jealousy sprang to life.

"For personal reasons. And besides that, you turned it all away!" She volleyed the excuse back.

"That is not what I am here for." He wanted to find immediate harmony between them before things got out of hand, but he had already guessed her thoughts.

"A wielder, Nolan!" She smashed the railing with her fist in frustration. "Just think about all the orbs under Strong Tower"—she paused— "you, me, and everything. Everyone knows how selfishly you hang onto that sword."

"Selfish?" He pointed to himself. "How about your selfish reasons?" He took a step forward and drove his face into hers. "I saw the sparkle in your eyes." Nolan pointed his finger at her. "When I first mentioned the word *unification* and Urlon as the ideal location, you leapt at that opportunity. Leaving Krhan to eat sand from the talons of Sauros during a war that he would have lost."

"You're wrong, Nolan." Her eyes blazed. "We will never live to see that sun. And do you want to know why?" Tonelia cut him apart with her stare. "Oh, the people are in great favor of this unification of ours, this testament of yours, and they don't dispute Urlon as the perfect location for the orbs either." She paused. "What they have an issue with is that you and I are too close and that we may have schemed this entire affair right from the beginning."

"What are you driving at?" He calmed to give her space, for as quickly as their tempers flared, so, too, did their compassion flow for each other. So, when she sensed that she would get no further fight from him, she reluctantly backed off and placed a soft and gentle hand to his rough face. "Nolan." She smiled lovingly. "You are getting older, and you have not taken a partner yet."

He removed himself from her touch and returned his stare back to the city. She was right. He would never take a partner, and that would jeopardize all that he was trying to accomplish.

"I have an apprentice," he said, hoping that would appease her.

She broke into a radiate laugh. "And just where is your apprentice?"

Nolan paused, reluctant to answer. "I needed to leave him behind."

"Well, there's an issue," she said. "Just how many or not so many apprentices have you trained?"

But Nolan refused to catch her eye. And the lack of a response said it all. For it was true; he had taken on very few apprentices. It wasn't that he didn't welcome them or was bothered or impatient with any of them, but the simple fact was that he had yet to find one as skilled as Tonelia.

"In any event," she said, her tone soothing, "you'll need to keep the sword in the Hammer family, just as Strong Tower needs the orbs. But at the same time, we are going to have to allow the seasons to bury our reputations and the rumors. Perhaps through several seasons of wielders," she suggested.

"And is that what you sent Golar to bring back? An heir to the orb?" He searched her expression for the response.

"He goes to have our ally fulfill a vow. And that, I'm afraid, is a discussion we will need to have *after* you have spoken with Baylor tomorrow." She smiled. "Now, if you will forgive me, it has been a long several suns, and now that you're here, I might be able to give my shorter than usual temper some much-needed rest."

She treated him to a long and passionate kiss on the lips and then turned to leave him to his thoughts.

"Tonelia." His voice begged her to stay. "You understand why we could never have been?"

She kept her back to him.

"You wanted me to do something I felt wasn't in me." He pleaded for her forgiveness, but none was needed. "Just as I understood what drove you. And had we taken that path, we both would have regretted it." He finished, wanting her to be in his arms. But she just stood there, apprehensive with her back still to him.

"Nolan," she spoke, still without turning, "you were correct, and it took me several seasons to understand that." And with that, she walked away.

He watched her cross the balcony and the room, and then, through the doorway, she disappeared. Long after she was gone and her image burned squarely into his mind, Nolan continued to study the empty doorway and was lost in deep thought. For some odd reason, just for a moment and a brief one at that, he couldn't help but suspect her or Baylor or both. He told himself to scrutinize all. And that meant *all*. Turning, he leaned out against the railing and scanned the peaceful city below, searching for reasons that would find them guilty. He guessed he would get a clearer picture after speaking with Baylor if the lord would be conscious by morning.

"No drinking." He frowned and made his way to the table, pouring a big helping of *lade*. He grabbed some more meat and bread for a meal, eating heartily.

He filled his cup several more times and then walked out to the balcony again, following the long rolls of dark towers and buildings that ran the length of the streets with his gaze. Some were still under construction, while others were completed. There were a few spacious holes where buildings would later appear. He continued up the west street until he came to the wall just off in the distance, but they offered up no responses. *So many people,* he thought, *so much to be concerned about. All this could change on a single mistake. Worst of all, his mistake. Speaking of which, where was he? Krhan.* Since no one in town really knew him and his little band of cohorts, why, they could be staying anywhere.

He was so disgusted that he was about to spit but then realized he would be wasting the only good taste—that of *Iade*, and her lips which was his only comfort for now.

"I hope that this little campaign of yours isn't some cover for revenge against either Tonelia or Nolan ... or both?" Stith Hackmoore interrogated the lord.

But Krhan only scrutinized his fine lead warrior briefly and then dismissed the statement with a fiendish grin from beneath his fire-red mustache. "We all knew full well what the stakes would be." He responded clearly and decisively so there was no misunderstanding between them. And by the reaction from his lead, he could tell that his point was digested, for the long scar across Stith's face almost straightened as he frowned beneath his thick black mustache.

"Yes, but what about our compromised financial situation?" A timid voice spoke as if out of place. "Lantor could easily compromise our position with Illenwell if Lord Laiaden should hear of this." His voice was concerned.

Krhan rolled up the parchments he was trying to study and tossed them back onto the table, never taking his eyes from Stith. It was apparent that his little entourage was getting a bit nervous over the pending outcome, and this concerned him.

After all, Dorzak, though a timid individual, was not so when it came to the financial state of Lavenden and the overstuffed profits that came in seasonally from Illenwell and those of Urlon.

Plaim, Dorzak's partner, was an even more insecure coward. But with regards to the financial future of Pantanteous, these two transformed into greedy, selfish little dragons—especially, when it came to the possibilities of even the smallest of losses that they would incur. Let alone the major ones.

So, without question, Krhan knew he had to sell the idea that, in the end, they would have a bigger purse if the risk paid off. And of course, that was the sell. And that's what he did best—sell.

"Gentlemen." Krhan turned his attention to Dorzak, who surprisingly held his ground. But the lord could read Dorzak's body language as the little boney fingers ran nervously over the financial parchment clutched to his chest—the very same ones that he and Plaim had been pouring over for quite some time. "The lady Tonelia and Nolan have long entertained this unification. After all, it, along with that golden sword, has been part of the Hammer heritage for countless seasons. And I, myself, knowing the Hammer testaments, have also taken it into considerable consideration." Krhan paused for just a moment. "But there are a few drawbacks."

"Like?" Stith prompted.

"Pulling the orb from Sauros, for one," Krhan stated. "And quite possibly Illenwell, for another. Not to mention the east kingdoms would fancy their separation from us by way of a large river." He paused and smiled. "However,"—he changed to a more positive tone— "look at the overall outcome. Families could be whole again, and no longer would our lords have to hide their heirs, thus completely eliminating the seasons of kidnapping, extortion, and ransom." He sounded quite sympathetic. "I know," he patted Dorzak's thin cheek, and the smack reverberated around the room. "Money, you little dragon." Krhan wore a crooked smile. "But there's more than that."

"Like what?" Plaim surprisingly spoke, his words more a timid whisper than anything forceful.

"Like the testaments," Krhan announced.

"You want to be remembered for the unification?" Dorzak questioned.

"That's reserved for the wielder," Stith interrupted while he filled his glass with more *lade* from the table.

"Is it?" Krhan questioned.

There was a moment of silence from everyone on the balcony.

"Nolan is humble and really wants none of this." Krhan spoke casually. "His only goals are to perform his job, keep the orbs straight, and secure and train an heir."

"What are you saying? He struggles to unify," Stith stated.

"Does he?" Krhan looked perplexed by his lead's statement.

"You want to accomplish it, don't you?" the lead retorted. "How?" He encouraged the lord to share the treachery.

"Tonelia has already started the how." Krhan smiled.

"By what means, my lord?" The timid Dorzak glanced back and forth between Plaim and Stith, nervously awaiting the cost of this prize.

"Well, that's for Bathros to report. And if I know Tonelia, which I will know shortly," Krhan added in a positive tone, "then her so-called 'ally' from the east will need an escort." He finished with a boast about his plan.

"Ah, that's where Bathros got off to," Plaim chimed in with more confidence—not knowing that he and Dorzak were not party to those plans and a few others. Lord Krhan had intentionally left them out since it was not of any financial concern.

"And is there an escort for Nolan?" the timid Dorzak asked, demonstrating his insecurity once again.

"Well," Krhan thought out loud. "Best share that with you both as well. It seems the appropriate time."

"Time," Dorzak screeched. "Is this a monetary escort?" He feared more loss, glancing back to Plaim.

"No"—Krhan smiled— "more like an investment in time." He patted Dorzak's face again.

"But it could be a loss?" Plaim timidly responded back.

"I have no doubt about Orego and Andellynn's abilities," a deep voice interrupted their discussions to add an opinion, "or those of Lantor and Bathros." The speaker treated Krhan to an acknowledging nod of agreement as he stepped out the deep, dark shadows from where he had been sitting on the edge of the balcony. Oriff Klinesfail had been rather enjoying the humid air and the fine view of a now sleeping Strong Tower under a black night.

Oriff had also been secretly entertaining his own dark ambitions. He had been surveying the long stretch of meadows just south of the tower. That would be the location of his future dwelling, along with his next family. He smirked at the dream.

"The wielder doesn't need, nor does he desire any escort from either Orego or Lantor. Or any lady warrior for that matter," the timid financial advisor Plaim squawked at Oriff as he strolled past him.

Oriff brushed him off and headed for the table and poured himself more *lade*.

Stith gave him some room and watched Dorzak's eyes wander toward Plaim, who looked to Stith, like he also was just as insignificant and was desperately trying to find shelter. Had it not been for Krhan, both he and Dorzak would be off in some locked room smacking their lips over all the new profits that were about to be had.

"Yes," Stith said, "but he wouldn't refuse an escort from Andellynn." He glanced toward Oriff for his approval, and both exchanged devious smiles.

But their quiet conversation was about to come to end, for an exhausted but still alert Lady of Urlon entered the room. She ignored the two warriors and made straight for Krhan.

"Tholin said you needed to see me," she said, arms crossed and clearly belligerent.

"Why yes," Lord Krhan morphed into a warm and placating human being. "Gentlemen, would you please?" He motioned politely for a few moments alone with his guest. Or rather, it was Lady Tonelia who needed one second with her guest, and that was all he was about to receive.

The two warriors bowed in respect, but Dorzak and Plaim only addressed her with quick nods and minimum eye contact. Then the four disappeared off the balcony and searched for safer havens to hide in.

"Now that we're alone." Krhan grinned pleasantly.

Though it's closer to a Saurotillian grin than that of a human, Tonelia thought to herself.

"News of Baylor?" He opened on a more personal note, but genuinely he was concerned.

"At this hour," she responded, slightly perturbed, "I should say not."

Krhan strolled to the table and found a glass and then the pourer of *lade*. "Drink?" he offered.

"No, it's late." Her response was polite, but she could not hide the undertones of irritation. "Soon I must go and relieve Toranden. So, what are we to say?" She insisted as she folded her arms under her full bustline and caught his eyes capturing the image.

"Yes, talk," his eyes darted up to meet hers. "Ally to the east, is it?"

"None of your business," she snapped. "Good night." She moved toward the door, giving a clear signal to change the subject, or she would leave him there without answers in the darkness.

"Just a moment," he stepped in front of her. "Sauros then." Krhan suggested another option.

With her escape blocked, all she could do was faintly smile back and listen.

"Or will you burn this down, too, so that your heir to the orb will return to find a smoldering heap of inheritance?" He probed for answers.

She treated him to a more provocative smile and whispered seductively. "Nice try."

When Krhan was convinced, he had her attention, since he knew her all too well, he strolled out toward the railing, taking an occasional sip or two of that fine *lade* he and his men were provided. "These are wonderful accommodations." He tried to sound flattering and appreciative, but it came out as a jabbing insult.

"You can, unfortunately, stay until Nolan recovers that orb." She spat back, a mockery of politeness. "We are now considered an auction state, no thanks to you, I might add."

Krhan all too well understood the meaning of an auction, the Zoarian phrase for a kingdom without an orb. They idly waited by until the wielder or someone else came forth, claiming the orb, and then began the lengthy process of finding the new heir worthy to run the kingdom—unless that was, a lord had recovered it. And that was precisely what Krhan was hoping for.

"I apologize." Krhan looked over his shoulder toward her. "But did I hear your accusation correctly?"

"Yes, you did."

"My dear lady." Krhan's attempt to sound remorseful failed. "I wasn't the one who traveled to Illenwell with my orb."

"No!" she erupted. "But you pulled us into this wild treaty." She paused as she stepped into his face. "Why?"

Lord Krhan kept his stance and rather enjoyed his closeness to her. "We can easily remedy that," he offered as he took another sip of *lade*, waiting for her curiosity to pull her in further.

After a moment, her voice cut the humid air. "What of them?" She almost wished that she hadn't asked. "Are they part of the remedy?"

"Why, we both knew Lord Vax would send an emissary."

"And what of it?" She sneered, waiting for him to get to the point.

"Well, for starters,"—he offered her a crooked smile— "they most likely have sent several centurions into that mountain as well."

Her response was cold. "And they shouldn't have needed to send any in the first place." Tonelia's hot breath blasted the dragon's face.

The lord's eyes twinkled with a sparkle as he took in the sweet smell of her. "Tonelia, that's why I dispatched my finest to fetch back the orb first."

"For your gain," she sneered.

"Tonelia, my dear." He smiled crookedly. "It would be the only fair payment."

"We can handle this," she snapped.

"Your so-called 'handle this' was far away to the east." Sarcasm colored his words as he mocked her. "Why, I'm surprised he made it here so quickly. Not to mention, he must now travel over to Illenwell."

"I'm sure that Lord Laiaden will do all in his power to help aid not only our kingdom, but he would also owe it to aid Nolan as well, as should you." She glared at him.

"In any event," Krhan said, shrugging off her accusations, "your kingdom reacted too slowly."

"We don't have spies everywhere like some lords." She scoffed back.

Krhan remained silent and simply took another drink. "Well," he said, referring to Sauros, "that's one emissary we will not have to worry about."

"Yes, one that I would guess Lord Vax had nothing to do with?" she responded, accurate in her guess. "So, what of it?"

"Well, as I already informed you and the wielder in the hall this sun, after hearing of your unfortunate accident, I immediately sent some of my finest to their peril, I might add, to safeguard the orb for you and Lord Baylor. You understand, until the wielder could arrive."

"That's funny." She smirked. "I'm pretty sure that Aquila and everyone else in that hall this very afternoon heard you clearly state that, when your warriors return with the orb, you will make a smooth transition of this kingdom."

"Well," he grinned, "in a roundabout way … yes."

Tonelia stood her ground, waiting for him to correct his answer.

"It was a formality"—he gestured with his arms waving— "an appeasement for the Zoarian council." He paused to study her.

But she continued with a high eyebrow and crossed arms.

"I have every intention to leave you and Baylor in control. To help kick off the unification."

"Oh, I apologize." Tonelia garnered his meaning and changed into an understanding, almost sarcastic little girl. "All that compassion and concern for our kingdom and Anglyllon. Forgive me, for none of us noticed it at first!" Her demeanor transformed into a nasty creature as she unfolded her arms and stepped into Krhan's face. "But is this not the same concerned lord who pulled our entire kingdom into a one-sided war with the Saurotillians? And when it was all over, Urlon lay in ruins. Not to mention Illenwell laid to waste under a dragon because the wielder was pulled several directions and ended up disappearing on us." She raged.

"Tonelia, Tonelia." Krhan tried for an apology. "I've since learned. And I want only to make up for these past seasons." He sounded pleading enough. "I can help with Laiaden and the East Kingdoms."

"But of course," she retorted, "with Urlon's orb under your control."

"Naturally."

Tonelia smiled. "I expected nothing less."

"Excellent," he rejoiced.

"But what of Laiaden, Ott, and oh … the dragon," she reminded him.

"We're all working together." Krhan smiled. "We wouldn't want anything to interfere with the future kingdom of all the orbs and the wielder's undying testament toward unification."

It stung, but she got the idea. "Now what are you selling?" she changed her tone to a serious one.

Krhan continued his charm. "More like a proposal."

"What are you driving at? It's late!" she snapped.

"More of a united front," he proposed.

"Is that it then?"

"Why, yes, that is."

Tonelia chuckled—a laugh that turned into a snarling thall. "We all understand the vendetta you have for those forked-tongue sunbathers. And mind you, we all feel the same. But again, I reminded you that you have already dragged us into one bloody war that cost us many fine warriors so I needn't remind you of what happened between …" Tonelia stopped, for she could not, as much as she wanted to, reopen scarred wounds in either of them. She still needed to find respect for Krhan and keep him safe, right where she wanted him, which was there in Lavenden. But she also needed for him to understand that, if one season the unification came, they would all have to place aside their indifferences for the betterment of Anglyllon. And that included Sauros as well.

"What of Nolan?" She changed the conversation.

"What of the wielder?"

"You, out of all lords, owe him your respect."

Krhan stood silent for a moment and then quickly came to realize that she was right. "You have my word as a lord that I will not lift a finger against this kingdom until my men return with the orb."

"There you go again, glowing in arrogance. Why you're worse than a Saurotillian," Tonelia blurted out.

Krhan stood there and sipped his *lade*. He waited with a smug expression for her to continue—confident she would be pulled along. But when he began to see a drag in the line, he knew it was time to cut her loose. "I hold nothing personal against you or Baylor for what transcribed after that war," he said quietly. "And I do owe a kingdom's debt. But I would rather feel safe if that orb—"

"Were in your hands rather than those talons of Vax?" Tonelia interrupted him. "They have every right to more orbs, including the one that they possess." She eyed him sternly.

"That's the wielder talking"—he turned from her glare—"about the only human who visits them," he said with disgust.

"Then they'll be more welcomed here then you are." And with that, she spun on her feet and returned to her lord's side for the rest of the evening, leaving Lord Krhan to ponder the outcome of their scheming.

He sipped his *lade* leisurely, all the while glowing from within at his cleverness. And as he did, he pondered the outcome and was certain he knew from where he stood as he overlooked the sleeping city of Strong Tower.

Chapter 8

P.D. 83, A.F. 8130

Nolan awoke to a hazy, humid overcast sun, as if Sauros had crept in and hoarded it all. Nevertheless, it was another busy sun not only for the hall but for the city as well. And although the townsfolk continued about their affairs, there still appeared to be a mounting apprehension that cut through the swelling gray clouds. If Nolan could guess correctly that unshakable feeling was the advancement of Lord Vax's emissary, which was, by now, on its way.

Sweat poured from the wielder as he came alive from his slumbering state. Too much *lade* and too little restraint found him stretched out over a couch near the back wall of the room. The humidity surrounded and engulfed him as anything resembling a cool breeze evaded him, as it had since last night.

He cursed to himself for having overslept and rubbed his head to alertness. Springing from the couch if an effort to bring himself alive, he made for the railing of the balcony where, only hours before, he had stood with Tonelia. She immediately came to mind.

He was still caught in an endless tide of emotions. His burning desire to be in her presence was fighting with a yearning to knock her senseless over her careless actions that had lost the orb. It was like a scale within him on which some malicious creature kept upsetting the balance of love and hate. One moment, it snatched a weight from one side; and while the other hand was not watching, it tossed another weight back on. *Frustrating!*

However, that was Tonelia, and she knew Nolan all too well. She knew there was nothing she could do that would ever prompt him to one sun resort to the physical and just haul off and kill her.

He rubbed the aching welt in the back of his neck where he had slept wrong and peered into the thick haze to spy the sun for some clue of the time. It was a strange sky, he thought, fitting for the sun. Darker gray clouds skirted under those of lighter gray color. So entranced by the oddness was he, he did not notice Toranden as he appeared in the doorway and bellowed to the wielder.

"Come. My brother is up, and the hall awaits Tonelia," he informed Nolan.

Yeah, and so does Krhan. Nolan grimaced at the thought. "Has Aquila arrived?" Nolan inquired as he passed the table and grabbed a big piece of fruit.

"Yes, and all too soon, I'm afraid, those tongue flickers from Lord Vax," he responded, less enthused.

"A little too soon for them yet." Nolan tried to sum up a calculation for that but not until he got some real food and hot *lade* in him. "To Baylor then," Nolan instructed.

The two warriors made their way through the halls and a couple of walkways across the busy streets below, passing several of Strong Tower's staff. Most the wielder knew on a first-name basis, and nods were exchanged, along with brief smiles of reassurance. Yet during the walk, Nolan cursed to himself, for he hoped that this job wouldn't prove to be his last, and perhaps the brief signs of confidence he shared with the passing people were an unnecessary precaution. However, the tower emanated the same confidence that both its lord and lady had, and that was one of utter trust in his abilities.

The two men arrived near a large room, just located off the main living quarters for Baylor and Tonelia. She was nowhere in sight, but that did not mean she was not still sitting with her partner. Nolan was fearful, but from what he could ascertain from Toranden's unspoken thoughts and actions, his brother must be in better shape than they had hoped. And that was a good sign.

"I'll accompany the lady to court while you have a spell with my brother," Toranden said. "Then come down afterward, for Tonelia will need to see you off."

Nolan nodded in response and then added, "Find out where my windbred will be and wait for me there."

Toranden nodded his understanding and then opened the door to the spacious room.

Tonelia looked around and found Nolan immediately. He gave her a glance and then went to Baylor leaving Toranden in the doorway.

The lord was wrapped in the bed like a giant feast for some spider, and although it appeared cozy and inviting, it was clearly the wrong ambiance of a setting. His head was wrapped with new white linens, just slightly stained with the faint appearance of a dark red blotch. His exposed right arm was bent and wrapped, and two wood posts held his lower arm and hand firm. The left arm appeared untouched. He had been shaved, and to Nolan, he didn't appear to be alert. But Tonelia conveyed with her eyes that he was awake and just resting.

She leaned over and gave Baylor a kiss on the check and then stood and moved over to Nolan and brushed his cheek as well. "He's awake." She spoke softly, placing a gentle but very concerned hand to his chest. "But he'll be out again shortly, so be brief with your questions," she instructed.

"I'll come to the hall when I have finished." Nolan smiled and gave Toranden a nod.

Then Toranden took the lady by the arm, and just momentarily, she gave them both, Nolan and Baylor, a quick glance and forced a small smile before departing to the hall and Krhan.

"Nolan." A weary voice broke his gaze from Tonelia as he watched her and Toranden leave the room and secure the door.

"Yes, Baylor." Nolan turned his full attention to the bandaged ghost of a man who lay before him.

The lord painfully tried to motion Nolan to the chair next to him, and the wielder clearly captured the signal. He moved around the bed until he resumed Tonelia's spot. The chair was still warm of her presence and smelled of her sweat since the room was no cooler than the outside.

"Thank you for coming," he rasped. "I know that had to be difficult." The lord understood the wielder's plight—to leave the east kingdoms in near bloodshed.

"Too many orbs and kingdoms," Nolan said remorsefully. "But how can I be everywhere?"

"We all understand, Nolan." The lord tried to be reassuring. "Your uncle, Lord Thaylor, how is the old dragon?"

"He struggles daily with his health I'm afraid," Nolan said with deep concern.

"Has he an heir to Itmoore." Baylor inquired.

"Yes," Nolan said assuredly.

"Good," Baylor said, "but you should have stayed." He coughed. "I understand the threat from Lord Vendoff."

"But I owe you so much," Nolan protested. "I left my apprentice to watch over my uncle and left Lord Vendoff a stern warning. He'll be in good hands," He assured Baylor of his uncle's safety.

Baylor gave a slight nod in response.

"The other kingdoms there do not see Lord Vendoff's concerns. Or a sweeping invasion," Nolan added. "Besides, your orb is gone, and quite possibly Lord Laiaden's as well." Nolan spoke with much concern. "So, it's the least I can do for both of you."

Baylor squinted at the awful truth that he'd just inadvertently plunged his kingdom into peril.

"Can you please explain to me—what in Zoarian's name were you and Tonelia thinking of when you traveled over to Illenwell with your orb?" he asked patiently, keeping his composure.

"We thought it safe," rasped the lord. "My brother was there." He tried to make it sound reassuring.

"Great." Nolan grinned. "And you both could be drinking at twilight's end, leaving Tonelia here to burn down your kingdom."

"OK it was more like her and Krhan's idea than mine." Baylor shamefully admitted.

"Krhan?" Nolan knew better.

"Yes, he came and counseled with us both." Baylor spoke quietly.

"A possible treaty with Lord Laiaden?" The wielder dug for the truth.

"We sent a small emissary to ship out of Pantanteous and make the trade route between there and Illenwell." He stopped to swallow and then continued. "Several trips in, one of the returning ships was attacked by a dragon as it rounded near the southern border of Sauros." He coughed. "It wasn't even close to Kureath." He spat. "How do the dragons know when the ships come along?" He looked worriedly into Nolan's eyes.

But he had no answers. "The reports are true then?"

"After a few suns, the crippled ship limped into port," the lord went on. "Only two emissaries survived and return with their report."

"So, a treaty up the river as Tonelia informed me," Nolan said. "Then why did you fail to treat me to an invitation?"

The lord painfully squeezed out a chuckle, but his face grimaced. "You are by far the busiest wielder of our time. We only thought to give you a break and possibly prove that we could gain alliances without your aid and the Zoarians' intervention." He took a shallow breath. "Tonelia and I are quite aware of the toll you are receiving over there, and we did not want to impose upon you anymore than we have too." He coughed painfully.

Nolan leaned back and reflected on the validity of his lord's words. True he had been busy. But this was Tonelia, and he would have done everything within his control to provide them with aid. It greatly concerned him that they would just treacherously step out like this and try to accomplish this kind of goal without him.

"Did she feel she owed something to Krhan?" Nolan asked Baylor a direct question. The lord studied the wielder, and they both understood the meaning.

"No, it would be a good alliance for us all," Baylor assured him.

"And what were you planning on doing with Lord Vax?" Nolan probed, but the obvious was coming.

"Ah." The lord chuckled painfully again. "That's where you were to come in."

Nolan attempted to look amused but had expected it all the same.

"Looks as if you'll be early for that meeting?" Baylor offered a smile.

Nolan turned to a more serious tone, "Tell me, why didn't Krhan accompany you to Illenwell?"

Baylor squinted in pain and tried to adjust himself under the covers. But that proved futile, and he lay discontented where he was. Then he said in a much softer tone, "We thought it too risky, too close to Sauros."

But to Nolan, that sounded all too convincing of an excuse.

"And you were nowhere near the mountain?" Nolan asked.

The lord smiled and coughed. "We were just north of the West Road and in plain sight of all. Why, we could see an ambush from Sauros long before those tongue flickers would even think to call it an ambush." He coughed at the joke to himself.

"And what of the actual attack with the dragon?" Nolan inquired.

Baylor closed his eyes and left Nolan in holding for a moment or two and then spoke as clearly as his dry throat would allow. "The dragon came fast. We were wide open. It hit us hard. Like lightning." He kept his eyes closed as he recalled the events. "Screaming and ordering and utter chaos." He sounded helpless. He opened his swollen and remorseful eyes and turned them upon Nolan. "Just about all the accompaniment ..." But he trailed off in near tears.

Nolan reached out a sympathetic hand and placed it upon the lord's shoulder, understanding all too well their sacrifice.

"*No!*" The lord scuffed as instant reflexes caused the lord to flinch from the wielder's touch. The pain shot through his shoulder and neck. But it was not as painful as the loss of his warriors—and the orb with it. "Entirely my foolish fault for those lost," he added sadly.

"Don't be so hard, lord," Nolan offered his counsel. "We are warriors and know our places." He paused. "They defended the kingdom, the lord, and the orb to the best of their abilities."

"*Blast!*" The lord spit and then coughed more violently than ever. "I had the orb until that dragon cut across my mount and threw me to the ground." Cough. "Just me." Cough. "I should have died." He coughed so uncontrollably that Nolan leapt to his feet and searched the room until he spied what he needed. A large pourer of water and several metal cups surrounded it. He quickly filled the cup and brought it to the lord, who had momentarily fought his coughs and brought control to his breathing. The wielder placed his hand gently under the lord's head. His hair was drenched with sweat. Nolan supported the lord's head while he sipped from his cup. Just then, several of the lord's attendants had heard his discomfort and rushed through the doors, displaying concerned looks.

Baylor gave them a reassuring eye that he was fine and bid them one moment more with Nolan. They bowed in acknowledgement and then left the room and remained patiently just outside the door.

"Rest for now, my lord," he instructed. "And fear not, for I don't know what's going on around here yet?" Nolan asked this last as a question. "But I am fairly certain that Laiaden doesn't want your orb. and his dragon will keep it safe until I arrive and have words with him about this incident." He went on. "Or perhaps that's what someone is counting on?" he said reflectively. "In any event, the job has started, and I will need to see it through, no matter what the cost."

"Nolan," the now exhausted lord said in a soft voice, "before you depart, I just wanted to say that, in the unforeseeable event that you …" He trailed again.

Nolan moved nearer to the lord's face, in fact so close he could feel the lord's hot breath brush across the rough hairs of a yet-to-be-shaved face.

"Oh, what I'm trying to say past these feeble lips of mine are"—he paused for another breath—"that I hold nothing against you. You are the most patient and forgiving individual I have ever met." He breathed deeply again. "And I even though you let her go, and she willingly gave herself to me, I still need to share her love with you." He peered deeply into Nolan's eyes for an understanding of what he was trying to say. And when the lord was sure the wielder understood his meaning, he continued, "With that said, please listen to her, for she has a good plan." He smiled briefly and then drifted off.

Now, Nolan was not sure what the lord meant, but it was too late to continue, for the lord was gone for now—back into a long, deep, and healing sleep.

"Rest well, my dear old friend," Nolan whispered with deep concern.

He pondered the friendship and loyalty. It was not in the old lord to hold grudges or seek revenge. Yet still, Nolan could not shake that uneasy thought of someone being up to something; and with that, he could just spit. More puzzled than ever, he left the lord's side and walked to the doors and opened the left one slowly. The attendants nodded to the wielder and quietly returned to the room, while Nolan went off to get Tonelia and see about a good plan.

After leaving Lord Baylor to rest, Nolan made straight for the hall to find Tonelia. He was anxious to talk to her one last time before departing. But he knew he was not fooling himself; he just needed to be near her perhaps for the last time. She would be as encouraging and uplifting as she could be. But unfortunately, she would be standoffish and short-tempered as well. She could stand her ground and make her case yet be as fragile as cake and crumble to the touch, alluring and mysterious and then plain and as clear as a cloudless sky.

Nolan cursed, for Baylor was by far a better man than he could ever have been. Even though the lord sounded sincere enough, Nolan still questioned the deeper ulterior motives. This alliance with the three, well four possible lords—that is, if Vax could be negotiable—would certainly be a welcome step toward unification for the kingdoms of Anglyllon and a welcome start to his testament. Scrutinize them all, Nolan said to himself repeatedly, for Lord Baylor's patience was that of time as it dried up even the largest of lakes, just waiting for the right moment to cast the wielder to his fate, no doubt. And this pending job could be just that moment. For with his having shown not one ounce of jealousy or even the faintest thought of revenge, Nolan couldn't help not rule out Baylor's quiet attempt to rid himself of the wielder rival to his love's attention. And what better demise than the dragon who stole his orb and called out the wielder. Illenwell's pet as the murder weapon—what a great cover.

Who would suspect Lord Baylor?

What price for Laiaden's involvement though?

After all, his would be the biggest piece. Nolan knew all too well how he and his kingdom adored that dragon. Well, Nolan thought, it could be the last time if he did not make it past the dragon, let alone Laiaden. The road over to Illenwell would be crawling with distractions. This he was not looking forward to. But he had to accomplish his job no matter what. The protection of orbs, kingdoms, ladies, and lords—and of course even if that meant Sauros as well—was his testament, like his fathers before him and the Hammer line of wielders before them both.

Nolan came to the hall. It was more crowded than usual. The current events had filled its occupancy with impatiently awaiting business folk, who either feared for the worst or those few who wanted change. In any event, they were about to get their wish. Another group that was rather new to the hall was a small handful of testamentors, who just could not wait to start scribbling on their parchments about one of the most anticipated wielder jobs to have come along in some time—not that the East Kingdom was not a job. But Nolan spied one or two faces that he recognized—from either Itmoore or Dennasonia? Whichever the case, they had followed him over. Nolan amused himself as he thought about the testamentors as they trailed just behind him, hoping some terrible demise would fall upon him while on the way here. Just think—be the first testamentor to witness the great Nolan being tricked, defeated, or just plain ambushed. And what if Tonelia had had some murderer show up here in his place, displaying the golden sword? Strong Tower would fall. And how convenient for Krhan to be here and help her up again? And what of the Zoarians had he fallen? Well, it had happened in past seasons, not to mention how his line had lost the sword to deceit. But that was another testament—one he hoped was long forgotten and destroyed.

The city still needed to attend to its daily affairs. And there, of course, huddled near the platform Tonelia and Toranden addressing several concerned merchants, while Aquila stood idly by. Lord Krhan and his small band of emissaries huddled around a table just in front of the platform and continued devouring stacks of parchments. Nolan knew them all—Stith; Oriff; and the two little cowards, Dorzak and his companion Plaim.

Nolan shrugged them off and would allow Tonelia to take care of them—possibly by keeping them close and housing them in one of the nearby adjoining buildings, if not somewhere here in Strong Tower itself.

He shifted his attention back to the platform and caught Tonelia's eyes. And then Toranden captured the scene and interceded for the lady, and she bid Aquila, the merchants, and the lord a pardon as she rushed off the platform and drew toward him. The wielder gave the Zoarian a respectful nod, and Aquila did likewise and understood all too well Nolan's impatience to be off.

Nolan greeted the lady and took her by the arm and the two flew out through the west doors. Nolan surmised it must by now be midsun or slightly after, for only the dark still mingled with lighter gray skies, offering no clue. The road was filled with merchants. There was no relief from the humid, stale air in the cramped road as shouts and street sounds filled the scene with yet promise as vendors continued their business. This encouraged Nolan, and he was sure Tonelia felt the same.

"Tholin awaits us with your windbred at the west wall," she informed him.

But at the mention of Tholin, Nolan immediately had his reservations, "Tholin, you say?"

"Yes," she responded, "and he's trustworthy, despite your first impression of him."

"Well, Toranden seemed to handle him just fine," he added with some comfort as the two pushed their way through the street nearly shoulder to shoulder.

"As he should." She glanced at him briefly as they began to negotiate the crowded main street that would take them to the west wall. "He came from Auroria, and he is of excellent sword," she added, her tone complimentary.

"That's fine." He shrugged it off but did not catch Tonelia's intention.

"One I think you should consider for an apprentice?" she baited.

"All right, so everyone here is quite aware I arrived unaccompanied," he blurted out. "There's a good reason."

"You left him in Itmoore to watch your uncle," she answered understandingly as they continued through the busy street.

"He doesn't know the west," Nolan said in defense. "Besides, if I were to take on an apprentice, and I'm not," he added definitively, "I would for certain interview one who knows this area. However, time dictates that we are behind, so no interviews. Besides, you and I both know I'm going to get into some kind of trouble on this job." Nolan stated the obvious.

"Well, I don't agree," Tonelia retorted. "And as your hiring lady, I think it best that you reconsider, Nolan." She spoke rather authoritatively with a controlled yet demanding tone.

"I will not, under these circumstances, take on an apprentice," Nolan replied rather candidly back. "Where you're hiring me to go, I'd rather do this job alone."

"You want all the glory on this one, don't you?" She did not mean an abrasive attack at all; in fact, he understood her perfectly. She liked, no, wanted, all the attention from just him. And what better way to show his affection then by going the distance alone?

"It's not that," he caught himself talking out loud.

"I understand, Nolan." Tonelia knew his thought but humored him instead. "Safer if you just go in."

"Much," Nolan agreed. "Tonelia, my main concern is facing an enemy I have never met before." He meant the dragon as he pleaded his case to her.

"But my concern, Nolan"—Tonelia stopped and addressed him—"is who's going to watch your back in there?"

"But you can't see anyone's back in there," Nolan retorted.

"Precisely," she bellowed back.

Nolan stood there with a rush of responses that cost him, for she turned on her heels, and within in an instant, she faded away in a crowded, busy road. Most of the folks had easily recognized both the lady and wielder and understood that they were on the most urgent of mission as their plight took them down the street.

Nolan drove through the folks, who either stepped aside or jumped from their paths. And after a moment of quick negotiations, he came to her side with a completely new approach. "Did you sleep?" *Stupid question*, he thought.

"Yes, a little."

She was clearly hiding her exhaustion. And this brought great concern to Nolan, who was almost, at that moment, swept away by a large man who was carrying several huge barrels and had not noticed the wielder at all as he bid the lady acknowledgement.

"Leave the affairs to Toranden and go get some rest after I depart," he ordered her sternly. But he felt the tension.

"I will not rest until you return with our orb." She resisted his order, keeping her eye contact as she walked rather hurriedly.

"Yeah, and that's just what Krhan is counting on. With the lord already down, all he must do is remove you as well," Nolan insisted, "Toranden will hold the tower for a sun or two. He knows his brother's affairs." He flung his authority at her.

"Fine," she retorted.

It surprised him a little that she would give up so easily. But under the circumstances, her condition was appearing to get the best of her, and the dark marks below her worried eyes said more than enough.

Nolan was satisfied for the moment. Or maybe she was just appeasing him for the moment. But in any event, he continued, "You know, I'm proud of you," he complimented her. "You're doing a pretty good job keeping your composure."

"Well, I had a one-on-one talk with myself." She forced a smile as they continued. "This is our fault and only our fault. We were in control, and we lost it. These folks, this kingdom, in fact all Anglyllon awaits the outcome." She spoke the brutal reality of it all. "We thought we were safe. After all, we had Toranden to the north. It was our borders."

"And speaking of Toranden," he said, "I hope we haven't overlooked the possibility of an attack on Auroria and Lady Phyllanna?"

"From whom would that be?" She darted those alluring eyes toward him.

"From anyone," Nolan retorted back. "Take us completely out of our way and then hit North Avalore."

Tonelia treated him to an intriguing eye. "Like what … Thalls?" she said, almost sounding amused, as if they could think on their own.

Suddenly, with that said and without warning, the lady stopped dead in her tracks, and Nolan caught those alluring hazel eyes display the most shocking revelation—as if deep in her subconscious, and that possible plan of hers that Baylor had mentioned could be suddenly compromised beyond all repairs.

"What?" Nolan spoke hastily as he halted with her.

But she only stood briefly there for a moment. Then she shook her head and brushed past his shoulder in an attempt to continue, in hopes the wielder would shrug it off as well.

But Nolan caught her left arm. "Tonelia, I need to know what's going on." He gave her a demanding look. "On the way here, Vestron reported a Taulian in the kingdom of Illenwell." He spoke directly at her, and by her look she wasn't happy with that news.

"Wait until we are in the wall." She pleaded for him to practice his patience—a request he was reluctant to grant.

But the wall lay just ahead, and by his observance of her, she was not going to treat him to her plan, not just yet anyway. So, Nolan went for a new direction, "Now what of your ally and how soon will he or she make Strong Tower?" he asked, trying to ascertain the gender and status as they continued.

"Not now," she responded again, searching the crowd with her eyes. "Wait until we make the seclusion of the West Wall."

"Of course," he said. "I understand the secrecy."

"Do you?" She stopped dead in her tracks and returned him a long hard look.

Nolan stood there, lost for a moment, and waited to hear her accusations and knew that he deserved every bit of them.

"Why, when was the last time that you have been here?" she started to question. "I lost count at when the last season was."

"Yes, I know," he replied sympathetically as he got this kicked back into his teeth. "And I apologize ... With the east kingdoms—"

"No, Nolan," she interrupted, "you visit Sauros often."

"Spying, are we?"

"No, Nolan, common knowledge."

"Oh, I see," he sounded sarcastic.

"What?"

"Krhan knows when I travel through Lavenden."

"Why do you avoid us?"

"I don't avoid," he snapped, knowing all too well the reason. "Just busy."

"Too busy," she said bluntly.

Nolan stood there again, but this time he spoke. "It's not that."

"Then what?" she studied him deeply.

"I just don't want to interfere," he snapped at her. Then he spun on his heels and bolted for the wall.

This time, it was Tonelia who rushed after his rather fast clip through the last of the main street.

A moment later, Tonelia found Nolan, who just stood there staring out the open double doors of the west wall and found the sun was just about to fall behind the plains as they stretched out before them. He could just spit, for he had slept longer than he should have. He couldn't help but see that the fading sun was taking the time with it and revealing the punishing reality that he was already falling behind.

"Come," she said softly, totally understanding his concern. She took Nolan's hand, leading him through a small wooden door that would take them to the guards' quarters and kitchen and, just beyond, to where she'd ordered Tholin to wait with the wielder's windbred.

Neither Nolan or Tonelia caught the inconspicuous figure of a warrior as he stepped out from the crowded street and watched them enter the doorway to the west wall and then, as silently as he'd come, faded again.

Sometime later, that same inconspicuous figure of a warrior made his way back to the tower and spied his objective, which was occupying three tables near the now deserted platform. The sun was fading fast, giving way to long shadows that crept in and misplaced the occupants. Where just minutes before had been a noisy and crowded hall was now a sudden decrescendo to desolation. Lord Toranden, just moments ago, had concluded all business for the sun, and the hall was almost empty except a few stragglers who remained clinging to the north and east doorways and one or two tables where business folk collected themselves for departure.

A lone testamentor lingered in the far corner, and the figure could just discern his scratching marker as it left its testament upon the parchment. Lord Toranden had excused himself and left to check on his brother, while Aquila had departed soon after Tonelia and Nolan. He would make for the council and report the daily affairs to the waiting Zoarians. Meanwhile the figure of a warrior found Lord Krhan deep in parchments that were mostly laws in nature, while to the table to his right, Oriff and Stith studied the city and building structures, along with the wall design for its apparent strengths and weakness, while Dorzak and Plaim sat at a table to the lord's left and digested parchments of business and finances of course. All was free to their eyes, since now the kingdom was an auction state, leaving all to be studied, digested, and scrutinized. And that, unfortunately, allowed the private matters of the kingdom to be seized upon. The entire kingdom was split opened and exposed to a devious little dragon from the south. And that's where the figure came to and paused.

"Yes?" A voice floated above the parchment.

"Excuse the interruption, Lord Krhan," he spoke reverently as he watched green eyes scan the lengthy roll of words.

Krhan folded the parchment and smiled at his warrior, Illon. He was a handsome youth but not quite good with a sword yet. But he had grown to maturity within these walls and knew the kingdom well. And some time ago, he'd been purchased easily by a prying lord.

"Lady Tonelia and the wielder have entered the west wall, sir," he reported. "But I dare not follow," he added rather timidly. "There would be no shadows for me to hide about in."

"Understandable," Stith interrupted as he and Oriff moved to Krhan's side. After their inspection of the drawings and mappings, they confirmed the youth's knowledge of the city.

"Hmmm." The lord sounded slightly despaired. "That would be regrettable."

"How so?" Oriff's deep voice broke in.

"For that is where Tonelia will break invaluable information with him, and she knows those walls are narrow and free of obstructions." Krhan threw the parchment to the table.

"An heir to the orb?" Stith inquired, observing everyone move about, slightly restless at the mention of such a notion.

"What do you think that they are up to?" Stith drove on.

"Well, that's what makes things so damn interesting." Krhan studied his lead. "Keeps us guessing, wouldn't you say?"

"Enough of these games," Oriff spat. "We will never have a greater opportunity as this one to inherit an entire kingdom like this." He glanced around at the small circle. "Especially this one, Urlon." He displayed a mighty fist as he shook it at them.

"That's if she doesn't burn it down with us still in it, my impatient brother," Stith amused.

Lord Krhan just smiled nonchalantly as he remained partially in reflective thought. "Nolan will leave shortly to attend to his destiny."

Krhan spoke with that slightly devious undertone. "We'll be wielder free"—he paused as he teased his red mustache—"free for us to overtake Strong Tower."

"That'll be an undertaking." Oriff looked at Krhan.

"Nonsense," Krhan spoke up. "I've been pouring over the laws while Dorzak and Plaim the finances." He turned to the two small men at the other table. "Now, have you found what we were searching for?" he addressed them.

"And that would be?" Oriff intervened.

Dorzak stood and pushed his chair away and then grabbed a large armful of parchments he'd put aside. Then treated he his lord to a small smile of accomplishment. "That would be, my dear Oriff, most, if not all, the wealthy here within Strong Tower's walls."

"Excellent!" Krhan chirped. "That will leave me to start working on Toranden and to round up the more prominent of Strong Tower and pitch them the opportunity of a season."

"Carve up Urlon like a pig," Stith said

"Nonsense," again Krhan corrected. "Keep it whole and intact with me lording."

"And Lavenden?" Stith questioned. "Who would take over there?" Not that he wanted it.

"Two great kingdoms whole as one." Krhan smiled.

"And who wouldn't want a piece of that profit, my lord?" Stith responded.

"Not without the orb." Oriff's voiced collapsed the sudden talk of victory.

"A technicality." Krhan waved him off.

"A very physical technicality," Oriff blatantly pointed out.

"Our brother is correct." Now Dorzak had interceded into the small circle, leaving Plaim buried in parchments. "The Zoarians will never accept your taking the kingdom without the physical orb in your possession." He began to display his superior knowledge of history and laws.

"Ah." Krhan stood from his chair, pointing his finger in the air. "You forget," he said rather triumphantly, "that I'm a reigning lord with a large and successful kingdom, and I have an orb."

"Your point?" Stith interjected.

"Point is," Lord Krhan reuttered, "that I possess experience in not only obtaining an orb but also sustaining one with prosperity." He finished triumphantly.

"The orb of Lavenden," Dorzak pointed out, "not Urlon."

"Lest you forget," Krhan corrected, "that I sent the finest to retrieve the orb, and they most likely already have accomplished their objective. And soon, some of the best will … detain the wielder." This last bit he said rather politely.

Dorzak was still not sold and spoke his thoughts. "One is unable to take a kingdom on presumption." He scoffed at his lord's arrogance.

"Your point?" Krhan said, rather irritably.

"Lord," Dorzak reuttered, "lest you forget our history." He paused for a moment to grab their attention. "In Anglyllon's earlier seasons, say around 2141 After Founding or so, the Zoarians had just about had enough of our ancestors killing and destroying one another for their orbs. So, they brought about the utter and complete destruction of Polarium to display their absolute displeasure toward our inhumane actions against each other."

"That's a myth with no basis." Oriff scoffed. "And besides, what right do they have to tell us how to live?"

"No," Krhan intervened, "it's fact. Any Zoarian will tell you that the kingdom was completed annihilated as an example. And once we accept an orb, we also accept the consequences of our power."

"It's a political tactic of power to keep us controlled," Stith added.

"And why not?" Dorzak retorted, for he wasn't as timid as he was around strangers. "We brought this upon ourselves," he explained. "The Zoarians are correct in their observation of our society—"

"And that is?" Oriff interrupted.

"We are still immature, even after all these seasons." Plaim spoke for the first time. But immediately after spying everyone staring back at him, his face disappeared again behind a large pile of parchments that shook rather nervously between his hands.

"And until we can prove our humane side to them," Dorzak finished, "we will have to work with them."

Krhan could instantly tell by the small circle of frowning expressions that no one liked the history lesson any more than he did. For if it was a proven one and Polarium had been made the example of Zoarian power, they could risk losing Lavenden and their lives with a repeat performance.

"Now," Krhan said, cheerfully changing the flow, "we'll continue on the plan."

"Which is?" Stith asked almost regrettably.

"To sell the plan." Krhan smiled.

"Oh, not this again." Oriff, the fighting warrior, wanted war not to talk.

"Yes, unification," the lord said authoritatively.

"And just how is this different than the wielder's testament, may we ask?" Stith inquired.

"His is riddled with conspiracy," the lord said. "His closeness to Tonelia not only ruins his credibility but also jeopardizes his very family testament." He spoke with a clear tone of contempt. "He can't sell the unification to most of Anglyllon."

"He is correct." Dorzak confirmed his lord's statement. "This will not be a majority vote; all kingdoms must agree."

"And yours will sell?" Stith asked.

Krhan's crafty smile always left Stith regretting the asking. "His lacks—the financial aspects of this great undertaking," he stated, adding, "So, while our lady keeps our wielder preoccupied, I think I'll slip away and make a sales call."

Chapter 9

P.D. 91, A.F. 8130

The blistering sun had risen over the long stretch of mountains that enclosed the large kingdom of Sauros, and the temperature rose to well over a hundred degrees. The land was sparse and sandy, and small, tough little bushes darted the uneven landscape of rocks and cracks. Gorges of all shapes, sizes, and depths carved their remembrances across the hostile environment. Where once, eons ago, water had rushed and feasted upon the loose ground and carried it off to lower levels of the terrain, the place was now replaced by deathly quiet unhealed scars of time.

The world here was not as devoid of life as one would have come to believe. For all sorts of strange and exotic creatures flourished under the cloudless, relentless sun that showed no mercy. Cold nights of moonlit skies brought out the rest of the living side of life that would venture forth to struggle for existence. Among the few for who enjoyed the brutal sun were the Saurotillians. They dwelled deep within the large range of mountains that ran the breath of the south shore. And there were sheer cliffs that overlooked the sea that divided Anglyllon from the dragon land of Kureath—the very channel where the dragons were attacking the shipping lines and the reason for quick action between Illenwell and Lavenden before more profits could be jeopardized. The vast caverns, unlike those of Jawed Peaks were filled daily with the fresh breeze that blew in from the southern currents and offered the Saurotillians a refreshing coolness after a long hot bout under the beating sun.

By now it was midmorning, and the reptiles were gorging themselves on the giant ball of burning life. Most, if not all, had already shed their armor and mesh so every ounce of their being could drink in the heat.

Arid heat kept them working and productive. If they weren't pounding out metal for shields and swords, they were crafting spears and helmets and breastplates. The females of the species nourished, instructed, and closely guarded their young, while others of the adolescence ran, frolicked, and fought among themselves. Theirs was a life of survival. No different than anyone else. But it had not always been that way, and one wielder had been shown the truth but was sworn to never reveal it, since those of Anglyllon would never accept it as truth anyway, or worse, try to capitalize upon it.

So, for now, the Sauros population grew slowly and painfully. Their numbers had taken a great toll during the last war over Lavenden, and even though they had failed in their attempt to procure the orb, they had, however, succeeded in carving a large dent into Anglyllon's population as well. The loss had mostly been in warriors, which greatly concerned the wielder, who'd unwillingly sacrificed his time to work with the then Sauros leader and bring an end to the long war—which, by the way, he suspected Krhan to have started. But much like with this present job, he could not yet prove that.

Now, some forty-three seasons later, and nine Sauros lords later, Nolan could only imagine what the present lord was up to—or, in reality, down to. For the lord lay upon his belly completely nude, his arms and legs sprawled out over the large boulder of glorious heat. His reptilian head rested comfortably upon a small lift on the boulder that almost resembled a pillow. The small aperture just below his snout slowly exposed the long purple tongue as it slithered out like a snake from its hole in the ground and then jerked up and down a few times, gathering up needed information before retreating again back under the lip.

The lord's accompaniment of ten centurions stood idly by, clutching long spears that extended far above their heads. One stood alone and held a long staff. Fixed to the end was the orb of Sauros, and it twinkled and sparkled like the rays of light that penetrated its very depth. The distinctive pattern that was engraved within the orb cast brilliant displays upon the harsh landscape. But its flare was lost, as the centurions discontentedly eyed their ruthless lord just baking away and wondered how many more seasons he would last.

Vax had been the swiftest and strongest Saurotillian leader yet. He was cunning and sleek, and the last several attempts to usurp him from the orb had proved fatal, for he killed mercilessly. Now, with eyes half slits like a drunkard slumbering away, he did not fool the centurions; they knew all too well how alert their pious lord was. And the only reason he continued to rule was that no other Saurotillian had yet been able to sneak up upon him, until this moment that is. But he would once again quickly squelch that attempt.

The approaching centurion could just make out the pupils of his lord as they came to life and conveyed a look of annoyance. For this was one of those who'd tried to foolishly usurp him, but this centurion thought himself above suspicion, foolish as that may be.

"Lord Vax," hissed the centurion hesitantly as he bowed before him.

The lizard lord lifted his reptilian head and flicked his tongue. He knew the foul smell of his centurion Thar.

"You disturbed me," hissed Vax. "Why?"

"To the north," Thar reported, "the dragon struck."

"So?" he responded indifferently, trying to enjoy the sun's hot gift.

"So, it was the scaleless lord of Strong Tower," Thar hissed back impatiently.

Vax's beady little black pupils homed in on the centurion and bid him to continue.

"He was near the border with a large army, perhaps a surprise attack on Illenwell." And with that, his shoulders jerked up and down with a giggle. "He got a surprise," he added for his own amusement, "Illenwell's dragon." He snickered.

"Well, that will teach them to disturb it." Vax chuckled along.

"But they did not, my lord. It just flew in from the mountain," Thar pointed out.

Vax looked perplexed for a moment and changed the tone to a more serious one. "What were they up to?"

"They appeared to be waiting," Thar answered.

Vax blinked and paused for a moment in thought. "What would they want with Laiaden?"

"Worse yet," Thar intervened, "that scaleless traitor Krhan."

Both sneered in disgust at the mere mention of his name. For that lord was always up to some sort of mischievous treaty.

"What he cost us," Thar hissed.

"Yes, his season will come to an end all too quickly." Vax growled from the back of his throat. "But inform me." He changed the subject. "Why did not Vlognar attack and finish them?" The lord spat.

"We were but a small patrol party," he answered almost apologetically, adding, "and they had not crossed our border. By the time we could call for reinforcements, the attack was over, and another bigger army emerged from the woods to aid them."

"Most likely his scaleless partner from the north." The lord jeered. "This is an unexpected surprise." Vax continued his calculations. "What wager do you want to accept that the foolish ones without scales brought their priceless orb?" he questioned Thar. "Perhaps a treaty right in front of our snouts," he hissed at Thar, who just sheepishly smirked at the thought, knowing all too well that Vlognar had gone for what they had hoped to be the orb.

"Their lord could not have done such a thing." He tried to convince Vax otherwise and to waste no further thought to it—as all the while, Vlognar worked his treacherous plan of rebellion. "That would leave his kingdom for the taking." Thar suggested that this conversation should end.

"Precisely," Vax smirked. "What choice had he?"

Thar kept from smirking in triumph over his having fooled the lord. "You would have thought that, after all these seasons, they would have dropped that way of thinking." Thar suggested further that there was no orb present.

"Old habits are traits," the lord hissed. "The scaleless ones still fear that they could be lured away from their precious orbs and kingdoms—perhaps to fall victim to schemes, incantations, and other devices brought about by those who want possession of said objects."

"Orders to Vlognar?" The impatient lizard waited. However, he never heard the reply. A giant blade removed his head. His body flopped lifelessly to the rocky ground with a thud, spilling hot red blood upon the dry sandy ground.

Vuroc then came and stood over the dead lizard and eyed Vax as he wiped his blade.

"Vlognar thinks me foolish." He addressed his lead centurion. "The orb is lost to Baylor and ours to retrieve," he boasted to Vuroc who had only arrived earlier with the news of a meeting between Laiaden and Baylor. And that would mean orbs. "Find Vlognar's loyalists and do the same," Vax ordered.

The centurion bowed his pointy snout and went on his quest.

"Klax," the lizard lord summoned as he lifted his muscular bulk from the burning rock. "You heard the tale?" He questioned the approaching Saurotillian.

Klax had been standing off to the side and had heard the entire conversation. He also knew that Vax could not trust him but that would not stop the lord from sending him upon his next appointed mission. "Yes, very wise, your most awesomeness. Vlognar could never be trusted," Klax stated.

"And you are any better?" the lord hissed back.

Klax returned him a glance of indifference since Saurotillians were not bred with much in the feeling department. "Fear not, my lord. Vlognar and his brothers lay in the dragon's belly. And you will undoubtedly gain the most prized orb in all of Anglyllon," Klax announced.

"I'll send you to Strong Tower, while I formulate a plan," Vax ordered.

"But we will not make it there before the wielder," Klax protested, thinking that they could do much damage if they would only attack Urlon now. *What is the lord thinking?* he thought to himself.

"The wielder will have come and gone by the time you reach Strong Tower." Vax hissed impatiently. "Your job will be to keep Krhan occupied so he doesn't trick Baylor into something foolish."

"As for the wielder?" Klax retorted back.

"Leave him to me," Vax hissed.

"What does the Warner see?" Klax jerked his head for advice from a tall, dark figure hiding just out of sight and far behind the centurion guard.

"Yes," Vax responded, clearly perturbed at the mention of the most annoying addition to their clan, one he'd protested. But then again, it was part of the negotiations between his former lord and the wielder. So, with great reluctance he turned to summon the ghostly statue.

A very tall and skinny humanoid glided from out of the shadows, fully cloaked, and they could not see his face. His arms were folded and disappeared into his sleeves just below his chest. Klax watched the slender figure as he effortlessly floated across the sandy ground toward them. His cloak dragged upon the ground, completely covering the fluent motion of his two slender legs. He stopped just shy of both of them and produced a large, shining crystal that he clutched in his white, long, bony left hand with four lengthy fingers, each with six knuckles.

"Tell us, Warner," the lord ordered. "Have you not heard the tale?"

The head of the cloak clearly nodded in response.

"Quickly, then, tell us your warnings," the lord replied in a tone that clearly conveyed his humor at accepting none of this as serious.

The extremely tall humanoid was nearly the height of a Saurotillian, if not quite by an inch or two. And though he had his freedom—won by the wielder—he accepted a time of servitude in order to aid the wielder and maintain a collar around the Saurotillians, of which they were clearly unaware of Nolan's true intention. So, he instructed or rather warned, as his given name from the Saurotillians most appropriately suited him, "the orb is not lost." A voice emerged from the shadowy hood that covered the Warner's facial features. It was a rather unusual tone, not human at all, more of a smooth liquid and harmonious sound as it drifted out over the air. "The kingdom is safe, and the wielder has been summoned," the unseen face informed them. "Take no action. The matter will be resolved immediately. Aid him, and you will be rewarded. You have been warned." He finished his advice to them. His long fingers closed around the pulsating crystal as it and his hands once again disappeared into the folds of his cloak.

Both the Lord and Klax eyed the Warner and then glanced at each other indifferently.

"Oh, we'll aid the wielder." Vax chuckled, his shoulders bouncing up and down in amusement.

"Wait for the wielder?" Klax hissed questioningly. "What makes you think he will come to you?"

"Because we'll have something he'll need."

They locked their beady little red eyes for several moments and then chuckled deviously long into the hot afternoon.

Chapter 10

P.D. 83, A.F. 8130

Like the rest of Strong Tower, the walls were a marvelous feat of engineering unto themselves. Wide, high, and each interconnecting, though they were not all straight, nor did they box the city in like a huge square, they did, however, support a unity and structural comprehension that was unique to all Anglyllon, as they engulfed the entire city. And this was where it became an issue. The walls were built long before Baylor and Tonelia had become heirs to the kingdom, and both knew they would have to be eventually dismantled, for they hindered the growth of the city. Nolan; Baylor; and, of course, Tonelia had already purposed the unification of the orbs to this kingdom and would have to prove its open eagerness to allow the entire land of Anglyllon free reign within its city. This immediately caught the attention of not only young aspiring builders and designers but also of veterans—all of whom could not wait to jump upon yet another anticipated project. The walls must go. But unfortunately, that proved to be a bigger obstacle for the wielder's testament, for there were those who thought the walls should remain. And unfortunately for Nolan and the kingdom's rulers, those individuals were in places of financial strength and were very prominent among the daily activities in the hall and the kingdom's outlook overall. However, there were many who wished for change, and most feared that too long overdue. And with the unification still on the wielder's testament list, it could be seasons until anything really started to transpire.

For now, the hallways, small rooms and walkways would be home to the guards. And higher up, a long, straight pathway permitted two people a quiet glimpse of a calm meadow landscape as they hurried to the

113

wielder's departure spot. There would be a set of stairs that would descend to the kitchen area and then a walkway to his windbred. But before they would reach it, Nolan made his move to stop her and, with seclusion accomplished, pressure her into an attempt to have her divulge any and all remaining information he would need to accomplish this pending job.

"All right." Nolan grasped her under the arm and rather roughly swung her to the railing. "Let's continue this conversation." He made himself clear and blurted out impatiently, "Baylor spoke of a plan."

"What do you know already?" she inquired.

"Besides the obvious, I need to know why Tholin sent Golar and his warriors east and what is the plan?"

"All right then. We sent for an ally to fulfill a need," Tonelia answered.

"An ally or an heir or both?" He inquired.

"I need to … be careful here." She hesitated.

"Why?"

"Because of your position and what it may compromise."

"What's that got to do with it?"

"Everything," she resounded.

There was a long moment of silence as each of them stared at one another. Then Nolan, reluctantly, eased his grip and allowed her some room to explain.

"Nolan," she said calmly, "you know for a fact that just about every lord and lady has some sort of heir or heirs."

He easily agreed to that.

"But where they are and how many?" she went on. "That's never been privileged information to you or the Zoarians."

"For the understandable reason," he responded, "but that, I feel and so do the Zoarians, should no longer be a practiced custom."

"And we agree," she said. "However, seasons still dictate otherwise—especially here at Urlon."

"I would attend to agree with you," he said, "had this not been Urlon, which is by far one of the safest to have raised your heir or heirs, whichever the case maybe," he stated plainly.

"Not so," she disagreed.

"Why, not so?" he inquired back. "You and Baylor are respected and admired. Why, look at what you have accomplished just here in Strong Tower alone," he complimented. "You brought back this kingdom from almost utter destruction after the Saurotillian wars." He paused. "It was devastated." He watched her stand and slightly fidget nervously as if there was more to this that he was not grasping. So, he decided that he would not get any heir information from her and changed back to the immediate concern. "So, I need to understand exactly what I am in for and what is going on to the east."

"All right, Nolan," she spoke up. "We have allied with a very strong and committed warrior."

"Yes," he answered with nervous anticipation. "But what part of the east?"

She answered with a question. "What do the Zoarians tell you of Ree?"

"Ree?" he was puzzled.

"Go on," Tonelia said, giving him time to think it out.

He collected his thoughts as he studied her features for clues to her motives and then continued. "The Zoarians inform me of a young warrior lady of excellent sword and quite the negotiator—or perhaps a little too persuasive for their likes, so I've heard."

"Good," she responded favorably.

"But there is quite the speculation," he continued, "since Ree sprang up between the borders of South Avalore and Lavenden. How will this wannabe lady bargain for land from either Lord Asperoan's South Avalore or, worse yet, Krhan, who I've heard she completely despises. This leaves me to question whether or not Ree can become a powerful kingdom any time in the near seasons to come."

"Nolan"—she grinned at him— "not unless she had a very strong ally … or two … perhaps three?"

"You and Toranden of course." The obvious. "But Krhan?" he turned from her and looked out over the west plains as night engulfed the last of Urlon.

Tonelia reached his side and brought her hand up to touch his shoulder, and Nolan melted in response. The small hairs on his arms straightened and tingled with dire expectations of touching more of her, leaving his mind to slap his conscience with that regrettable, but necessary, choice that they had painfully made all those seasons back. But he kept his stare to the west and his desires in check in hopes of an interruption. He knew none would come; she'd brought him this way for a reason. Perhaps she had many reasons, but for the most obvious one, it was intimate.

"In return for aiding us in a time of great need," she spoke softly near his ear, "such as in this case, the three lords have agreed, once you and the Zoarians approve that is, to aid her in establishing Ree as a new kingdom and the right of an orb."

Nolan digested the thought; her warm breath almost drove him to his knees as he struggled to concentrate.

He turned and stared at her for a moment or two. Their lips were close. "Part of your plan?" He hesitated. "So, just how long has everyone been working on this plan?"

Tonelia did not move from her spot next to him. "Longer than you think, Nolan. And it didn't include the dragon, I might add." She pointed a finger at him.

"Of course," he smirked. "Lord Laiaden most likely had that under control."

"Why yes," she said. "Laiaden did give his word that we would meet on our kingdom."

"All right." Nolan put the plan together in his head. "Lord Asperoan has agreed to help your lady warrior and Baylor and you, respectfully. But what of Lord Krhan?"

"I'll see to him regarding this matter when the time presents itself," she said confidently. "I'm sure that, after I present the facts, he will consent."

Nolan was not completely satisfied with the explanation. However, he knew Tonelia, and he was not going to get any more information from those alluring hazel eyes that hid innocent crimes. So, he probed westward. "All right, why didn't Lord Laiaden just travel here instead?"

"Well, we felt safer meeting him closer to Illenwell," she responded, "especially with Toranden just to the north."

Nolan listened.

"That way, Laiaden was not too far out of reach from his port."

"Besides me, none of you have ever met the lord." He inquired, "So was he bringing his orb for identification or were you going to trust a stranger?"

"He said he would bring what we would need," she answered.

"But why was I not informed?" He turned to confront her. "I could have assisted here."

This time. she moved just an inch or two away. "Well, if you weren't so busy with the east kingdom." She sounded suddenly just a bit hostile.

He stood erect and became defensive once more. "That is my uncle, my land, and my kingdom."

"Yes, we see how you jump for them." Now she was animate. "You're supposed to be neutral."

He wanted no argument when they were just so close again, but he knew all too well why she drove a wedge between them. It was always the physical contact, and they knew it.

"Well, there was peace here until …" He instantly let his words trail off, not wanting to cause more of an issue, for he could sense her quick turn to aggression, usually a sign of her hiding some deeper issue or trouble.

"No, Nolan." Tonelia took a few steps away from him and then turned on her heels. "That's not it at all."

"Then what is it?" He hated when she could not be open with him.

"Remember last night when I mentioned that you should be looking for suspects other than Krhan?" She was visibly apprehensive, and Nolan watched her twist her hands together while her mind wrestled with an internal dilemma. "Well," she finally broke. "I think that it is them."

"It's who?"

"It's the Zoarians!" she blurted out, rather impatient with him.

"That again." He groaned as if he should have seen this. "And they are responsible for you meeting with Laiaden and losing the orb to a dragon that just happened to come by?" he said a little too convincingly. "This job is proving to be all too coincidental for my likings and, apparently, the Zoarians'." He did not mean to mock her, but it just came out that way, and he saw the sudden red in those alluring hazel eyes that hid seemingly innocent crimes. And this was clearly one on them. But he continued, "The Zoarians have also informed me of not knowing anything going on between you, Krhan, and Laiaden either. So why is that?"

"Look, Nolan." She composed herself. "I need you to completely understand my inner most gut feeling regarding those Zoarians."

"And that would be?"

"It is imperative that you keep this to yourself." Her eyes darted back and forth as she studied his. "Sacred as our love for each other."

"My word," he assured her with a soft smile.

"No one and I mean no one"—she defiantly eyed him—"knows how I feel about those Zoarians." She kept constant eye contact with his. "Not even Baylor or Toranden or the hall or—" She paused.

He wanted to hear heirs, but no such luck.

"No one," she said definitively. "For if the Zoarians would even suspect this, why, I could easily damage not only our relationship with them but also everything that Baylor and I have accomplished here."

"I get it," he answered, but respectfully as not to hurt her feelings.

"I feel manipulated by them," she said definitively. "Do you understand me?

"I believe that I do."

"But do you agree?" She paused. "Manipulated."

"I understand where your position is on this," he answered understandingly. "But I don't follow the manipulation part." He thought for a moment. "Come to think of it, I have not heard this from any other lord. And I, for one, would have heard someone else suggest it. But for now, everyone else seems content with the Zoarians. After all, they have always seemed fair in their thoughts and actions," he said, defending them.

"Of course, you don't see anything," she retorted back. "They keep you close and are always feeding you advice but never the right answer."

"That's because there is no right answer, Tonelia," he blurted out. "They keep me informed when orbs could be jeopardized, which is exactly what just happened here." He pointed a finger to the ground. His muscle bulged and, with it, nearly his forehead vein.

"And that is exactly why we kept them out," she said.

Nolan was hurt. "Because you didn't want me to know either?"

He saw her sudden reaction to his comment. "Yes and no." She pivoted to recover.

"Well, which is it?" he asked.

"It's because you would have intervened during the progress."

"How would I have accomplished that?"

"You would have stopped us from seeing Lord Laiaden."

"But why would I do that?" Nolan asked. "I would have most certainly gotten Baylor and Laiaden together. And in far safer place, I might add."

"You still don't understand," Tonelia responded with a long pause.

"Go on."

She hesitated and then said very tenderly, "I—no, we—want," she paused.

Nolan hung on waiting.

"Nolan, you deserve a life," she said.

He was touched. "I have a life."

"Do you, really?" she was quick to point out the fact that he does not and that was clearly obvious that he needed to settle down and produce an heir to the sword. Of which Nolan was not willing to admit too.

"Yes, I do," he said in defense, but he did not what to change the mood or the subject.

But she was just as determined to go somewhere else. "You travel more than any wielder before you, including your father," she candidly pointed out.

And Nolan knew how right she was.

"Your father raised you, and you're one of the finest wielders there've been," she added with confidence. "But Anglyllon, as a whole, needs to show you how much we care and give back, with much gratitude I might add, your life."

Nolan was not sure where she was heading with this. Nor did he grasp the whole gratitude part. He felt more comfortable with arguing over Zoarians than with digging up old bones and, quite possibly more, regrets. After all, if the kingdoms, as a whole, wanted to really show their appreciation, they would stop their petty little indifferences to each other, the continual practice of some seasons' old custom of hiding off their young, their political mind games and give him and every other wielder to come many restful seasons. But who was he fouling?

Tonelia reached for him again, a tender hand, a reassuring hand supported by a soft smile. "Nolan." She brought him back to reality. "What do you dream of if you could make it so?" she asked honestly what would have become of them if they had decided differently. "What would have been of us?"

He smiled warmly and touched her soft face. She slid into place under his strong arm, and together they turned and observed the quiet plains as they reminisced of dreams gone by. Tonelia lovingly wrapped her arms about his waist where he stood leaning against a stone rail high above the city and its immediate concerns. The night allowed the stars to shine, and an almost full moon lit the field and treated them to a moment of peace. Some small passing clouds idly strolled by, adding to the ambiance of a beautiful and calm evening. Various clusters of far-off farmhouses glowed with their burning fires as they prepared their evening meals. Barrels of smoke arose from their chimneys and grew to the sky and fanned out to nothingness. Tonelia was swept with passion and clung on tightly to his waist.

"A small but comfortable dwelling in the field over there,' he pointed.

She snuggled and lost herself in the images.

"There would be smoke from our chimney from the cooking area. Our children play safe and sound after we have united these kingdoms. Our oldest wields the golden sword that, hopefully, he will never have to use. And a little mischievous girl, just like her mother," he said amusedly, "would be off tormenting somebody."

"Hey." She poked him in the side. "And just how many do we have?" she asked.

"I lost count after eleven." He grinned sheepishly at her.

"Oh, we were busy."

"We hunt and fish together, and our suns, for the most part, are relaxing," he continued.

"There are still suns," she added, "dragons, Saurotillians, and new challenges that the seasons will bring." She sounded dismayed.

"Yes, but few and far between, I hope?" he said softly.

"Then, you must settle down and train the next wielder." She broke the whole mood. "Your past apprentices are not strong enough," she added as she stepped away from him.

"Not now." He groaned.

"Yes, now." She said insistently.

"Is this what this is all about?"

"Yes, Nolan this is exactly what this about!" She flared.

"Heir to the sword?" He searched her. "Did you lure me up here just to open that wound of regret again?" He pressed her for the truth.

"No, Nolan," she said in defense. "I brought you this way so that you might come this way a bit more often." She now was hurt, and he knew it.

"Look, this is not a good time to discuss regrets or heirs to orbs or swords," Nolan said. "I have not the time to partner or even think of a real heir to the sword." He continued with his excuses. "You have a kingdom in an auction with a slimly reptile down in the hall at this very moment, who is arrogantly spouting off about taking control of this kingdom—not to mention, any sun now, an emissary from Sauros about to arrive claiming their victory."

"Nolan Hammer." Tonelia interrupted his little show. "There is never a good time to do anything." She paused to get his attention. "You must make the time. That is the way."

"I know." He stared back at her for some time. "Wielders know their time," he answered regrettably. He turned from her and once again, longingly looked out over the peaceful land. "Mine is coming. This body is feeling the seasons of wear. So, let's continue this story after I finish this job," he asked politely, "under less stressful circumstances and a clearer head?"

"Your time is already past," she said bluntly, and he know it. "Ninety-one seasons now?" she asked.

"Ninety," he corrected.

"And how many of those have you been a wielder?"

But he did not answer her.

"Too many, as far as I'm concerned," she said.

He sighed and knew not to argue any further.

"So, I'll make a deal with you, wielder of the golden sword, if you will return a favor?"

He hesitated. "A favor?"

"Yes."

"Well, Baylor said that you have a plan."

"Evening," came the disturbing voice from beyond the shadows.

Lord Toranden grumbled to himself as he immediately smelled the annoying fragrance of smoke, followed by the unmistakable sound of his voice, for he had just entered his dark quarters and made his way out to the balcony for a quick breather. Evening was wearing on, for there was much that had to be completed after Tonelia left with Nolan and he dismissed the hall. With a quick check on his brother, there were still a few more tasks that he needed to accomplish and then off to bed.

"Oh, why are you still here?" Toranden made the question sound as annoyed as possible as he made a hasty retreat from the balcony.

"You forget, lord, that I was invited." The figure inhaled, the embers from his smoke momentarily illuminating his facial features with a ghostly shade of dark red.

"And who would have done such a foolish thing?" Toranden searched for the hot pot of boiling water he had requested from one of his room aids, for he desperately needed to make a quick cup of herbal brew to help revitalize himself, and the last thing he needed was this unwanted intrusion.

"You know all too well who invited me," the voice went on. "But that's not important. What matters is why I am here." The figured sheepishly smiled, and Toranden could easily sense the foreshadow of some treachery.

"You are suspected of causing all this, you know?" Toranden candidly pointed out. "Best leave, *now*," he added with a clear sense of urgency.

The voice chuckled. "And why would I want to leave so soon?"

"Oh, I don't know," Toranden responded sarcastically. "Maybe because all of Urlon will skin you alive and most of Anglyllon as well, should any of them catch you outside the security of this tower?"

"Don't you wish that you could be so popular?" The intruder shrugged off the warning while exhaling a long trail of smoke.

"The only thing I want right now is my bed." He warned the phantom again to leave.

"Please explain," the voice said, while completely ignoring Toranden's plea. "Why would I have caused all this?"

"Oh, I don't know, Krhan. Why don't you tell me?" He burst into the shadow and hovered just above the Lord of Lavenden.

But Krhan only smiled back amusedly. He took in a long inhale and motioned that he would stand up.

Reluctantly, Toranden moved away and watched Krhan stand and step away leisurely, strolling out farther onto the balcony, "tell me. Where would I find the wielder and our fine lady this very evening?"

"Being respectful, which is more than I can say about you." He turned back to find that pot, or any other heavy object would do to rid him of this annoyance.

"I don't need to tell you of their relationship," Krhan said. "But it does concern me." He tried to rattle an old jealousy.

"What are you getting at?" Toranden said as he found the pot and poured the hot water into a large cup and dropped in a handful of herbs. He also needed something for his pounding head and an immediate remedy to the ailment standing by the railing. Maybe an accidental push would relieve his headache?

"You know," Krhan went on, "they might be in on this."

"Might be in on what?

"Oh, don't you see?"

"See?"

"This could be against your brother?"

"My bro— Get on with it!" Toranden bellowed in annoyance.

"Remove him from the triangle." Krhan spun on his heels, wearing that continual sheepish smile.

"Oh, great Zoarian," Toranden screeched, "what triangle?" Exhaustion was getting the better of him.

"Well, certainly not the treaty between the three of us."

"Look." Toranden turned and eyed Krhan. "Those two worked out their differences many seasons ago." He was referring to the war and Nolan and Baylor and their obvious affections towards Tonelia.

"Are you sure?"

"Positive." Moaned Toranden.

But by Krhan's expression, Toranden could tell he did not buy it. "Is this what this late-night intrusion is all about? A love quarrel?" Toranden blurted out.

"Perhaps." Krhan was unsure.

"Look, if I give you some reassurance, will you please leave?" he pleaded. "And I mean like Urlon and go home to work out your own affairs. Or are you so bored that you needed to stir up some commotion, for I must be popular?" Toranden sarcastically fired off.

"What sort of reassurance?" Krhan looked serious.

"Oh, like trust for one." Toranden said. "This is Nolan that we are talking about. Remember, the one who's helped save your kingdom and everyone else as well for I don't know how many seasons now?"

"Oh, I trust he is in good hands, or should I dare say arms, at this very moment," he whimsically stated.

Toranden held his anger and stepped threateningly toward Krhan. "They are meeting in private to discuss confidential information that will help our wielder form a better course of action."

"There's action, I wager," Krhan said amusedly.

Toranden's fists clenched. "Whatever you're selling—"

"Look." Krhan spoke candidly. "You need to assist here."

"Assist?"

"Why, yes."

"And just what am I supposed to assist you with?"

Krhan looked appalled, as if Toranden should know this answer. "With your reputation of course."

"Now what are you pitching?"

"Why, we are going to need to salvage your reputation." He tried for sincerity.

"Oh, good Zoarian." Exhaustion was overwhelming. "Salvage what reputation?"

"Well," Krhan went on, "there are rumors around the hall where we sit."

"Like what?"

"Oh, that quite possibly you were there to ambush the good Lord Laiaden."

"I was there to do no such thing!" He bellowed in defense.

"That's not what I hear from some of your business partners."

"We were there to make sure of no ambushes," he clearly stated, "especially, from you." He pointed an accusing finger into Krhan's face.

"From me?" He smiled innocently.

"Yes, from you," Toranden blasted. "I don't need to remind you of your last clever move with Sauros that nearly cost this country everything."

Krhan smiled like a lizard. "Nolan nor the Zoarians could prove anything of my involvement with Sauros during those wars. They acted of their own accord, and I apologized many times over for even the slightest hint of my involvement."

"Yes." Toranden stepped into Krhan's face. "But when they do prove your hand was in control of that huge mess, I hope that I'm there to see you fall."

"Hope away." Krhan smiled, brushing the lord off with a wave of his hand. "But the facts remain."

"And those are?" He was hoping to get a confession, but Krhan changed the subject back to his sale.

"The facts are that Laiaden doesn't have the biggest or best warriors," Krhan started as he stepped away, cupping his hands behind his back, his smoke recently discarded. "In fact, he is about the only kingdom with very few good warriors. And why should he?" He paused. "Sauros doesn't attack anymore, and in fact about the only threat they have comes from the Thalls. But he certainly does his best to protect that mountain from them so that they just don't go blindly entering it. Why, the commotion those Thalls would create." He grinned, and Toranden despised it immensely.

"What windbred are you riding now?" Toranden asked annoyingly.

"Getting back to your reputation of course," he candidly said.

"What?"

"Like I said before, I'll clear this whole matter away for you, if you just return the favor."

"There is no favor!" Toranden was close to murder. "And you are a fine one to talk reputation, Lord!"

"I make them profits." He kept his cool. "They forget and forgive everything when their pocket purses are overflowing."

"It's extortion and skullduggery, and I wouldn't have it." Toranden sneered.

"Exactly," Krhan boomed triumphantly. "That's why I'm here to aid you. Clear your good name."

"There is no reputation to salvage here. But there is a close on this deal. *Good night!*" And Toranden motioned for the doors.

"Now, just a moment." Krhan waved a hand about.

"What?" Toranden spun around.

"Now, please, Lord," Krhan said politely. "Allow us to be patient with one another."

Toranden sighed. He realized there would be no end to this pitch unless Krhan was allowed to continue his sell. So might as well amuse him. Then kill him. "Go on."

"First," Krhan started.

"Here it comes." Toranden rolled his eyes.

"A favor in return for clearing your good name," he stated his terms of agreement.

"What?" There was a long pause.

"We'll help establish the first of the kingdoms toward unification," Krhan pronounced his proclamation.

Toranden stood there for a moment while the word rattled about his head. Then he roared in laughter; it was so loud that it could have woken all Anglyllon. He laughed so hard that his sides hurt. "I knew that you were born half Saurotillian," he roared. "You think just as half-sunbaked as they do!" He grasped his aching side and belly roared until it absolutely hurt him to no end. But as soon as he could catch his breath, he spied Krhan just standing there, serious. Toranden composed himself and finally calmed. "And when your man returns with the orb and you take full collection of this kingdom, so she informs me, then I suppose you think you can wrestle me into some kind of negotiation for my orb as well?"

"Precisely," Krhan beamed. "But remember, I'm not the one who hurt your kingdom or your reputation. You did that on your own." He pointed a finger at him.

"What?"

"Your reputation," Krhan clarified.

"Oh, not that again." Toranden groaned.

"Yes, but I will clear it for you."

"Oh, good Zoarian," Toranden boomed in frustration, since by now he had abandoned all hope of salvaging this evening. "What could they possibly be talking about down there in the hall?"

"Well," Krhan started, "there are those who will break trade with you if they suspect the slightest hostility, you may have had against Lord Laiaden?"

"There's only one person I harbor hostility against in this kingdom." Toranden glared into Krhan's eyes.

"See how you treat a business partner, an ally who is just trying to help," Krhan said with a slightly hurt tone.

"All I see is a half scaly sales lizard with fried brains."

"Hostility," Krhan retorted.

Toranden cursed and took a moment to calm. "What else?" He waved Krhan off.

"I can't say I blame them for talking," he went on, "for if I were in your kingdom, I would have most likely tried the same thing."

"And that is?"

"Well, remove the dragon, and Illenwell's profits look extremely attractive, not to mention the expansion of your territory?"

"What?"

"Look, I just want the facts on what your brother offered you so that I understand the bargaining power I'm up against."

"There was no offer. There is no need for an offer. I'm his brother!" Toranden flew off into a rage.

Krhan remained unemotional for a time and studied Toranden. Then suddenly, his faced beamed as a thought struck him. "Why of course." He presented that crooked smile again. "Right before me the whole time."

Toranden was lost not only in exhaustion but also as to Krhan's selling.

"Why, he didn't offer you anything," Krhan whispered. "But she did."

"Now look here." Toranden was red. "There was no offer from Tonelia or from my brother or from anyone."

"Of course, there was." He smiled. "I see the plan now, you and several of your finest archers poised just north of the meeting. You really could not hear anything, so let's say there was a sudden commotion, a fight broke out, caused by your brother. But you mistakenly observed it as a surprise attack from Laiaden. You acted swiftly and slay all of Illenwell's party, including Laiaden, who just happened to have brought his orb."

"And just what do you think the Zoarian council will say to that?" Toranden retorted.

"It's in your possession now," he said. "You are worthy. After all, you do run a respectable kingdom already."

"And is that what you think this all boils down to?" Toranden inquired.

"But of course." He grinned. "Leaders," he arrogantly stated.

Toranden remained silent for a long moment. He realized his headache had been replaced with a heartache—and by Nolan's reflections about this country and the people who tried to control it by slippery persuasions and crafty manipulations that drove deep wedges between the kingdoms, keeping unification just ever so out of reach. For if one person could not control all Anglyllon, they would for certainly, in their own selfishness, make sure no one else could darn well control it either. And that did mean Sauros as well. Toranden asked apprehensively, "And what would be the entire plan to that?"

"Well, let's go over the facts about unifying these kingdoms again, shall we."

"Now look." Toranden was animate. "Unification is for Nolan. It's his testament. He can handle it, and he will organize it one of the seasons or another."

"Well, let's just suppose," Krhan painted his plan, "that Nolan's thoughts on how the kingdoms should be run well greatly differ from ours?" He eyed Toranden.

"How so?" he almost regretted asking.

"Let's say … that his is a little … cloudy," he suggested.

"You mean Tonelia," Toranden interjected.

"Why, yes, precisely," Krhan agreed.

"Well, that is exactly why he turned her away," Toranden said, defending the wielder, "so that nothing would cloud his testament and job regarding this undertaking. And you should know exactly how that feels don't you, Krhan?" There was a long uneasy pause between them. "Yes, just before Nolan arrived, there are a few of us who remember your relationship with her." Toranden cut open the wound. "And just perhaps those talks of reputations down there in the hall are really aimed at you?" Toranden moved a little closer to Krhan's expressionless face. "Perhaps, you are behind this chance to get even? You have always been looking for an opportunity to bring both down." He came within a nose of Krhan.

"You are mistaken. My motives are quite different here." He forced a nervous smile.

Toranden got a good smell of nervousness. "Oh, do explain." Toranden did not back away.

"I'm beginning to understand that, if this unification were ever to occur, it would be much easier if all the lords and ladies were on the same plane of thinking." Krhan strolled away from Toranden while speaking his thoughts. "Take for example, Cressaillia's lord, Highlor Logginos. He will enter the collective kingdoms if he is the last to join, and then of course there are others who will oppose it, at all costs, I dare say, even if it means an all-out war."

"That's understandable," Toranden said. "And by what you and Laiaden are facing with the losses due to dragon attacks upon your ships, I could easily see a need to speed along this unification."

"Precisely," Krhan said optimistically.

"However, in order for you two to accomplish this new trade route up the Randerend River, you both will need to remove an obstacle."

"Well, you are correct," Krhan agreed.

"And you are sadly mistaken," Toranden continued. "Laiaden adores that dragon, and I would not ever allow anything to happen to their fine guardian or our esteemed wielder. And just maybe, if he suspected you of any ideas, why, I bet your already compromised reputation would just be damaged all that more."

"Well, there is that" Krhan agreed.

"So, am I to assume that there would be a three-way treaty just as long as Laiaden is assured that there would be no hassle with the dragon?" Toranden asked.

"That is an interesting challenge of course." Krhan visibly squirmed under the question.

"So, what was your plan?" Toranden was direct.

"Plan?" Krhan chirped. "Why, my good lord, I had no plan in this."

"Now look." Toranden now smiled as he watched Krhan become defensive. "If we are to have a partnership, then honesty must be in the foundation."

"Yes, of course." Krhan squirmed further.

"Now, either you're not being forthcoming with pertinent information for the basis of this contract, or you're just blowing smoke around our agreement, offer, and acceptance." Toranden pushed on.

"Well," Krhan said uneasily, "it is late, and I must really be off to meet with my associates." He motioned to leave. "You will pardon me?"

"No, just a moment, your popularship." Toranden blocked Krhan's escape to the doors. "Let's finish our little verbal contract regarding unification."

"No, it's late, and I can plainly see how exhausted that you must be." Krhan struggled for positioning. "After all, you have been here aiding your brother's hall for quite some time now."

"I'm fine," Toranden reassured him. "Let's continue, shall we?"

Krhan was visibly apprehensive, for Toranden had trumped him at his own game.

So now Toranden would finish it. "Now, what was your real motive for this sell tonight? Surely, you didn't think for one second that you could negotiate for my orb, did you?"

Krhan smiled. "Of course not. You are far cleverer than I." He tried for sincerity. "I guess I am still trying for a remediation for an action on the past that caused much suffering, not to mention the great embarrassment I brought upon Lavenden and Anglyllon as a whole."

"*Ah!*" Toranden triumphed. "You admit your guilt in those wars."

"No," Krhan defended. "I mean an embracement in having known of their plans seasons before and not mentioning them to Nolan upon his visits."

"A costly oversight, and embracement does not even begin to describe it," Toranden said bitterly.

"Then let me make amends, an offer to you and your bother for the wrong I committed." Krhan sounded sympathetic.

"I'm listening." Toranden encouraged him.

"The moment my men return with Urlon's orb, I will volunteer my orb as well, and once we have found an agreement, you can join the start of this unification." Krhan paused for a moment to study Toranden's expressions. "For Nolan's sake, of course," he added.

"Oh, and how so?" Toranden wriggled his eyebrows.

"Our four kingdoms will start the unification." He answered back.

Toranden chuckled, "Laiaden will never be in."

Krhan shook his finger at Toranden. "But there is where you are mistaken."

Toranden studied him while waiting for more.

"What if Laiaden were convinced this would work?"

Toranden listened.

"Or perhaps … removed from his position," Krhan said intriguingly.

"What?"

"The kingdom's people could usurp him." Krhan stepped toward Toranden while speaking in a low tone. "And his successor—one who is more, shall we say, representative of the wielder's cause—could come to power as a new lord of Illenwell," he suggested.

Toranden now chuckled. "Never happen."

"Why?" Krhan looked serious.

"You forget," Toranden said. "Look what represents Illenwell. A bunch of thieves and murders, all isolated over there nice and safe like. All sound under a temperamental dragon."

"That's why we need a united front," Krhan protested.

"Why?"

"Well, suppose Vendoff unites the east kingdoms and decides to come this way?" Krhan suggested.

"Nonsense." Toranden scoffed. "Nolan's got it covered."

"Does he?" Krhan retorted. "Thaylor is weak and near his journey to twilight's end."

"Look, what are you getting to?" Toranden asked irritably.

"So … what if all the lords and ladies were related?" Krhan probed. "Wouldn't that help unify?" he added shiftily.

Toranden's full beard broke into a wide grin. "You think that Tonelia, Baylor, and Nolan are somehow strategically positioning relatives into key positions as lords and ladies of our surrounding kingdoms?"

"I didn't think that at all." Krhan said.

"What did you think?"

Krhan paused for a moment. "Well, just her." He said this quietly.

Toranden was amused. "Tonelia?" He laughed. "That's it. I've had enough of your gibberish for one night." With that, Toranden grabbed the lord under his arm and escorted him to the doors.

"Well, I see I will have to take my business elsewhere." Krhan broke from the grasp.

"Yes, back to Lavenden," Toranden said.

"No, Toranden," Krhan said defiantly. "I will stay to see this through."

"Splendid," Toranden bellowed. "I was hoping you would hang around, for I hear the Saurotillian emissary should arrive any sun now, and I'm sure they just can't wait to see you again." And with that said, Toranden opened the door and motioned Krhan outside. Once through the doors, he slammed them in the lord's face.

Toranden stood there and listened intently for the sound of boots as Krhan hastily shuffled off. Then his whole persona changed to an alert and focused one as he gathered his thoughts over a new cup of herbal brew. He felt the anxiety of already being late for his next meeting—no thanks in part be the unwelcomed intrusion. He would give things a moment or two to die down, and then he would slip off quietly.

"Look, you don't have to offer me anything," a male voice echoed down the stairway. "This is just part of my job."

"I know, but it is the least we can do for our mess," a female voice responded through the eerie shadows as two lone figures descended toward the meal area. Wall torches cast eerie shadows of multiple dark figures that danced on the walls like ghostly apparitions, misrepresenting the fact that there were only two individuals.

"Rewards come from the satisfactions of knowing each and every kingdom is at some kind of peace with one another—free enough to establish their own individuality while being prosperous and cooperative with each other." The deeper male voice echoed off the walls. "Besides, each kingdom provides me with a spacious place to stay, plenty of food, and lots of great sweet *lade*. So really, no one needs to bribe me with anything. You know that I would have done anything for you and Baylor."

The two ghostly figures continued their descent.

"I know," responded a kinder feminine voice. "And we are forever grateful for your unconditional willingness to aid us at any cost." The sweeter notes of appreciation now laced the tone. "You have sacrificed greatly for the Zoarian cause and the orbs. Your testament toward unifying these kingdoms will help strengthen our country and even, perhaps, give you a rest. It is the least we could do."

"I would like to hope so," the male voice responded less optimistically. "Our prior conversation informs me otherwise. Quite possibly, neither you nor I will be here to see it through."

"Possibly?" the female voice said. "But at least from twilight's end we'll know that our heirs will complete the task of unification with all the orbs in one location and the kingdoms united." She sounded hopeful.

"So, you and Baylor think this offer will work?" a concerned male voice asked.

"Absolutely. Our ally has been informed and is, at this moment, on her way here," responded a confident voice. "After all, you gave me a decision. Now stand with it."

The two figures stopped midway down the stairway. "I'll stand," the deeper voice said.

"Great!" The word boomed down the stairway.

"You just make sure Urlanna fulfills her part of the plan."

"She's committed."

There was a moment of silence between them. "All right then," he said, "inform Baylor I will accept your most generous offer and your plan."

She lit up like a sunny Jubilee sun.

"Besides," she winked, "it'll keep you close."

And with that, the two finished their descent and headed toward their next destination.

"One last concern, Nolan." She reached out and touched his arm.

They both paused at the bottom of the last step, and Tonelia drew close to him. "The offer is a very private matter," she said plainly.

"I understand." He looked squarely into her eyes.

"Very private," she again clarified. "You understand that, besides you and me, Baylor and our heir are the only ones to know of this offer."

"I said that I understood." He did not mean to be cross, but it just came out that way.

And by her reaction, she was content with it. "Good, for we wouldn't what to jeopardize anything that should transpire during this job."

Nolan nodded in agreement. And with that said, they turned and continued on their way.

The meal area, a large, square open room, was just a small part of the large complex of connected towers and vast living areas where the lord would meet frequently with warriors and other city officials who kept each section of the city protected and in working order. Strong Tower was a significant kingdom, and every side demanded attention. Even though, the past few seasons had been quieter times, the kingdom still needed to be mindful. The Saurotillian wars had been quick and very destructive. Now a season, these walls housed only warriors and guards to occupy and make their home here as they did throughout all the walls. There was a large and well-stocked meal area, which was the direction Tonelia, and Nolan headed toward. There was also a stable and plenty of windbreds, continuing down the next hallway. There, the wielder's windbred had been brought as ordered by Tonelia. It was resting and eating comfortably throughout the evening. The taller towers gave an excellent view of the surrounding fields and small towns and villages where harvesters and other Urlon inhabitants settled to live in the security of the massive shadow of Strong Tower.

As they were discussing the offer, Tonelia and Nolan had entered the main area. A carrier had been dispatched earlier to alert the staff of their arrival. Cooking pots and pans were spread about the tables in preparation for a large meal. Various fruits, vegetables, meats, and breads were scattered about on tables and cooking areas. Unfinished deserts sat on a tray nearby. There was a bottle of sweet *lade* and a pot of harvest brew that was simmering over a small fire. The two were so absorbed by their talk down the steep and narrow stone stairway against the far wall that they never noticed the area was completely void of staff or the disorganized setting that gave the appearance the staff had been ushered away.

Nolan glanced toward the meal area to his left down the open stairs. He immediately stopped Tonelia by shooting his muscular right arm in front of her as he grabbed the handle and drew his sword. The fires glistened and danced off the golden blade. Both quickly surveyed the room. Large torches hung from the ceiling, and other than the sounds of boiling water and simmering pots, the kitchen had an eerie dead silence to it. Without warning, Nolan flung his sword down to the area and it deeply lodged itself into the marble floor with a tremendous clang. The sword's handle violently shook for a few brief moments as it came to rest. She threw a glance at him, but he ignored her as he stared off to the hallway on the opposite side of the room.

"I could feel your arrogance from the other side of Anglyllon." Nolan addressed a hidden figure.

Tonelia directed her attention over to the opposite hallway, where there, just hidden in the shadows, a figure stood, straight and defiant.

"I sent them on an errand so as not to disturb our talk." The shadow spoke in a low but audible tone.

"And I have already anticipated the subject of this conversation," Nolan responded. "So please, Tholin, come join us." Nolan gestured with is hand as they completed the stairway and came to a stop in front of a large wooden table that spanned the length of the meal area. "I'm sure there is plenty of food and kingdom for all."

Tonelia crossed her arms and gave the young warrior a very stern and indignant glare as he stepped out from under the shadow and moved over to the sword with an intoxicated stare that never left the alluring and beckoning summons of the golden object.

Surprisingly, Nolan did not feel the same sense of arrogance and pride as he had during his first encounter with the lad. He could only surmise that Tholin was in the company of the Lady Tonelia, and he had already witnessed that transformation from the young warrior when he was in her presence. This time, it was more controlled and tamer, so Nolan thought it a perfect time to play with the young lead. "Pull it from the stone, and it is yours," Nolan bid, "along with all the other responsibilities it demands," he added. "Do you lust for the respect that it will slave you to?"

He watched the lead's reaction intently.

"Nolan," Tonelia interrupted, "perhaps I should explain."

"No explanation required," he said as he continued to eye the lead. "Come, Tholin. Take your place as the new wielder," he begged. "You would be doing me a great favor." He smiled. "Although I'll miss the traveling from one kingdom to another, with no place to call home— seldom finding refuge or peace; always on the move and running here and there; always on the alert and on the offensive, for the kingdoms expect it; always trying to balance fighting lords and political debates over land and orbs and ownerships. All for what?" He paused. "Perhaps you want to become one of the countless apprentices to accompany me on my jobs? Perhaps once I regain this orb, you'll trick me and leave me for the dragon's fury, if you are clever enough?" Nolan jested with him.

Tonelia had heard enough and moved to interrupt again, clearly not satisfied with where this conversation was headed. But Nolan stopped her with a slight gesture of his own, and she reluctantly received the signal loud and clear.

Nolan never lost his attention, his focus remaining on the youth. Tholin appeared to be listening, but he never took his eyes away from the challenge. Nolan knew exactly what Tholin was feeling. The gold glistened of fire. It beckoned to be touched and manipulated and controlled—so perfectly made that all other swords were frail in comparison to this priceless creation. Just the honor of standing within its presence and examining it so closely was far greater than Tholin had thought or dreamed. Sure, there had been and would be in the future swords of gold. But they would lack the endurance and marksmanship in comparison to this one. He hovered over it, and cautiously he reached out his hand.

Nolan watched him reach for the handle and anticipate the feel. Would it be rough and worn or cold and lifeless? Would it magically transform him into a mighty and powerful wielder? There it was, begging him to grasp it. *Take it!* The sword cried for him.

Then his fingers met the handle. He was surprised at first—not the cold touch of a heartless monster but the warm, soft touch of a sensitive being, longing to be held and mastered and dominated. He studied the ball on the end of the handle. It was a carving of Thriteria, their home world and the lands they knew of and others they did not, for only the Zoarians knew what the entire world looked like. He let his hand feel the raised etchings as they slid down to the handle. A black leather material made up the grasp of the sword, wrapping it ever so perfectly. It did not feel worn or loose. The blade was craved with an exact likeness of a Zoarian. Its wings folded to the sides and its marvelous head turned to one side and looking off to the distance. Its arms crossed its chest, and the legs and talons disappeared into the marble floor. The Zoarian was covered in feathers, each one done in perfect detail. To Tholin's astonishment, the sword showed not one notch or blemish from the countless seasons of battles. This troll was truly gifted—and well beyond any crafter of the season or any other season. His grip found the sword too deep in the marble floor to be moved. There was only one in the room who could release it now. Tholin brought his attention back to the wielder in reverence. He made no further attempt to remove or desire the symbol of respect.

"I heard you, wielder," he responded arrogantly.

"That will be enough, Tholin." Tonelia stepped forward, but Nolan placed a hand on her shoulder.

"Yes, but how's that stomach of yours?" Nolan asked. "It will turn all the same when you need to visit Lord Vax."

Tholin shot him an eye.

"Oh yes," the wielder said back. "That's part of the deal also. They do have an orb, remember?" He watched the lead's reaction. "And they will expect you to jump when summoned."

With that point driven home, the three of them stood there in silence for several moments while pots boiled away at their places. Aroma from the cooking food filled the area as they all maintained their stances, looking at one another.

Nolan continued to control the conversation. "So best check that ego of yours, since the Saurotillians will easily sense it. and trust me, they will not stand for it."

"I don't have an issue here," Tholin retorted.

"Oh, but I believe that you do. Your actions speak it," Nolan said. "And trust me further." He eyed the lead. "The other kingdoms will not tolerate it either. In fact"—Nolan chuckled briefly— "you may just have given Lord Krhan a run for his money."

There was tension, but it was controlled, and Nolan could easily feel it between the lady and the lead. "Explain to me, why did you leave as the lead to Lord Toranden and North Auroria and come here?"

"DoMion retired," Tonelia answered for Tholin.

Nolan looked toward her, a question in his gaze. "But why? He was yet young in seasons."

"He gave us good reason," she answered.

"There's more here." Nolan was not satisfied. "You are surrounded with some of the finest in Anglyllon. Why wasn't one of them appointed?"

She hesitated as she kept her eye on Tholin. Then she answered. "None of them wanted the position, so we needed to interview. Our need was immediate."

"How convenient. Baylor turned to his brother, and he quickly provided Tholin." Now the wielder understood but was still not sure where this would end up.

"Why, yes," she agreed, "best recommendation ever, trustworthy."

"That may be," Nolan rattled back, "but why Urlon for Auroria?" He asked Tholin to explain.

The youth's eyes darted between Tonelia's and Nolan's until they finally came back to rest upon the sword.

Nolan gave the youth a moment more before he interrupted the young warrior's thoughts and continued with his game. "Nothing to explain?"

There was more silence.

"Then let me explain. I think you and Toranden had a little talk recently up there. Perhaps you heard something of this coming meeting with Baylor and Laiaden? And since you craved more glory and knew the wielder would soon be involved, you thought you'd best get here to Urlon."

"That's not it!" Tonelia tried again to interrupt, but Nolan gestured otherwise.

"What an excellent opportunity," Nolan continued. "Get here and give great reason why you should be my apprentice on this job. Pit the wielder against an opponent he can't possibly defeat. While I get burned, grab the orb. And after the dragon does me in, grab the sword on the way out."

"That's not it." The retort came from Tholin this time.

"Perhaps not," Nolan continued. "I think your arrogance got the best of you up there, and Toranden needed to send you a long—here, to Urlon. Let his brother and lady help you work out your own internal issues."

"That's not it." This time, it was Tonelia, but Nolan stopped her again with a quick glance of daggerlike eyes. Tonelia backed away again and Nolan continued, "Frustrations … perhaps." He returned his attention to the warrior. "Something out of your reach from up there in Auroria?"

"Nothing is out of my reach!" Tholin finally snapped arrogantly.

"No?" Nolan mucked. "Perhaps a kingdom and orb you seek?"

Tholin's eyes immediately locked with his own. This time he'd gotten the youth's attention. "Perhaps we have you to thank for losing the orb to Illenwell?"

"You're out of place, Nolan!" Tonelia snapped.

"Why do you keep defending him?" He whirled around to face her.

"Because we gave Toranden our word," she said

"And what word would that be?"

"Training," she responded, "training from you, me, Baylor, and the rest of the fine warriors."

There was a long pause between them. Nolan reluctantly grinned and looked back to Tholin, who just continued to stand and stare at the sword.

"I understand frustration." Nolan spoke easily and with reflection. "You try so hard to lead, and no one follows. And no matter how many times you prove the right path is right there in front of them, people that is, they just stubbornly remain to their courses." He smiled to himself at the very thought of their foolishness. "No matter how off course they may be"—he looked at Tonelia for understanding, of which she approved—"they just blindly go on their way."

Nolan cautiously stepped toward Tholin and his sword. "You understand, Tholin, that people will easily sense what we are made of, and that just aids them along their perilous paths." He took a step closer and caught the youth's eyes. "They blindly go on their way when a leader is arrogant and boastful or condescending, just using people for personal gain."

Tholin listened intently.

"There is nothing wrong with being confident and secure." Nolan complimented the youth. "You are much like us—an achiever, a person of action—and that is something to be proud of. However, gone unchecked, it becomes an issue of pride, which brings me to my father's haunting words of rebuke when I was a young promising wielder just like you." Nolan smiled warmly and fatherly toward Tholin. "Change the way you teach people how to treat you." Nolan gave a moment of silence for his words to sink into the youth. "That still doesn't help matters." He attempted to bring Tholin to ease. "You can lead your windbred to the stall, but if he's not tired, then he's just not tired, and there is nothing more you can do about it." He smiled. "You can only control you."

Nolan continued to study Tholin, who just stood there tall and youthful, his left hand now clutching the top handle of his sword while his other muscular right arm formed the v shape as he closed his fist into his side. A thick neck and hairless face with short, flat blond hair gave the warrior very sharp features. His eyes were small, and it was hard to find their color. His silver and gold warrior armor were colorfully decorated and proved his status among warriors.

Nolan thought it time to get better acquainted with the young warrior and win him to the job at hand.

"Your record is impressive, and you are reported to be the youngest ever to hold this position." He complimented Tholin "Tell me, before you arrived here, where did you train and with who?" Nolan asked.

"I trained with Lord Toranden before I left Auroria for here," he explained.

Nolan found that conveniently suspicious under the given circumstances.

Toranden had not mentioned that to Nolan, so he best fish for answers. "Why would you leave Auroria and just a wonderful kingdom as North Avalore?"

"For a better opportunity," he answered but unconvincingly at best.

"Why was this opportunity any different from that opportunity?" Nolan probed. "A lead's a lead."

"Not true." The youth blazed. "This is Urlon," he said proudly.

"And?" Nolan waited.

"You can go anywhere from here," he said, again proudly.

"I see. Respect," Nolan said.

"No," the youth blurted back.

Now it was Nolan's turn to listening intently.

"Don't you see?" Tholin said enthusiastically. "Lady Tonelia, you and your testament, right here, bring all the orbs to rest in Strong Tower." He pointed his finger to the ground in one swift motion.

Nolan smiled just as enthusiastically as the idea hit him in the head. "Of course, my young brilliant lead." Nolan laughed. "You would be the first lead to be here when that happens." He smacked the youth on his hard, strong shoulder. "Help organize it, aid the wielder," Nolan agreed. "Be part of the testament."

"Absolutely," the youth for the first time sounded relaxed and open with not only the wielder but the lady as well.

"So, you think that you are up for this undertaking, do you?" Nolan inquired.

"I think that he is," Tonelia agreed.

Nolan rubbed his chin while his eyes darted back and forth between the lady and the youth. Both looked optimistic and hopeful, but he still did not feel convinced. "Tell me, Tholin, where were you born and raised? Tell me about your parents."

Tholin looked to the lady for a moment, and Nolan caught her giving the young warrior an encouraging eye to continue, as if they had rehearsed this before.

"Very well," Tholin said. "I was born in Ortheria, in a small village just on the opposite side of Cressaillia."

"Really," Nolan did not sound convinced but urged him on.

"When I was of season, my father shipped me here, to Urlon, to find a craft that I would find suitable."

"What did you try?" Nolan inquired.

"Oh, you know, I was a kid." He squirmed under slight embarrassment. "I failed … a lot."

"So did we all," Nolan sympathized.

"Well, yes," the youth continued, "just until a few seasons back. That's when I met DoMion," he said excitedly.

"And?" Nolan bid him to further explain.

"He introduced me to the sword," he said proudly, "shortly after, the testaments."

"So, you want to be a wielder?"

"No, I do not," he answered harshly.

"Then what?"

"I want to lead."

Nolan continued to listen.

"I began my training here in the city," the youth responded.

"I did some of the training myself, after DoMion had introduced us," Tonelia said.

"Then off to Lord Toranden," Nolan added.

Tholin nodded.

"Have you started a family yet?" Nolan asked.

Tholin shook his head no.

"Good. Neither have I … yet." Nolan treated Tonelia to a secret smile. "But I would like one some season. But again, I digress. Being a wielder leaves very little for a family. However, it will demand one soon. A new wielder will I need to train. And with strategically placed and well-trained apprentices throughout the kingdoms, I could possibly settle down and raise one or two in the security of a good kingdom. But for now, the demand for answers and compromises of Lords awaits my decisions and that of the Zoarian council. So please, take the sword and relieve me or join me as a new apprentice?" Nolan motioned to him.

Moments of silence went by as the anticipated answer was awaited. The boiling pots and crackling of the cooking fires broke the dead stillness as the three stood there.

Tholin smiled and moved past the sword.

"He seeks a kingdom to lead," Tonelia said.

"Yes, that I do," he answered, "but not in blood."

Nolan studied the youth for a moment. "Are we sure he hasn't trained with anyone else?" He directed his question toward the lady.

"I would have almost guessed that he had, after that comment," she answered.

"Only one person in this country was taught in political overtaking," Nolan said suspiciously as he watched Tholin for signs of nervousness. But to his surprise, the youth stayed composed. "Explain to us, Tholin, how did you summon the dragon?" Nolan sought a different direction to take the young sword.

"I didn't."

"Then who?" the lady demanded.

"It was just a happening," Tholin said calmly.

"No. Somebody is behind this." Nolan probed further. "And like everyone else around here, he wants in on the pay."

"You would need a speaker of animals," Tholin suggested.

"There hasn't been one in this kingdom for some time," Tonelia remarked.

"No," Tholin shot back. "The wielder is correct; I have spied an opportunity, and like any eager person, I jumped at the chance." He looked at Nolan with those small and calculating eyes. He then caught Lady Tonelia's glare. "Please, Lady Tonelia, I meant no disrespect for you or Lord Baylor. Urlon lost its Lead warrior, and I knew how to replace him. And I have you, Lord Baylor, and Toranden to thank for that." He continued. "And like any other resourceful warrior I waited patiently and continued about my service."

"So, you've been working your plan all the time," she accused.

"No," he defended, "just my plan to lead."

"We took you in and gave you, our trust." She took her place between Nolan and the youth.

Nolan moved away from the conversation but kept his ears open. It took both hands and straining muscles to pull the blade free. He pointed it at Tholin, who stared defiantly still, his stern jawed locked, and eyeing Nolan back. Admiring his courage, Nolan sheathed his sword.

"Enough of this!" he barked at the two. "I will give you a sporting chance at the orb."

Tonelia shot Nolan a questioning look.

He answered her but kept his eye on Tholin. "The orb is free to anyone who retrieves it, and you know that. The Zoarians allow you and the lord to remain in charge, for that is the legal way," Nolan reminded her. "However, whoever returns with the orb is immediately granted the kingdom. And you understand what that would mean?"

"But" she protested.

"No buts," he snapped back, turning to Tholin. "Now apologize to Lady Tonelia for your rude matter and thank her for all this kingdom has given you. And do it now!" Nolan commanded the young warrior.

"Indeed, Lady, I have wronged you." The young warrior sounded apologetic enough to Nolan. "And I will immediately right myself by pledging to the wielder here any and all that Urlon asks of me, your lead warrior."

"Great," Nolan blurted out. "Now, with that nonsense out of the way, the two of you *sit down* while I get us food." And he promptly, without argument, fetched bowls and utensils and tossed them to the table. With a very large bowl, he scooped several spoonful's of cooked greens and savory meats swimming in thick brown gravy and placed it on the table. Nolan negotiated his chair promptly between them and served each one of them a big helping of nutrition while, surprisingly, Tholin poured sweet *lade* into three cups.

"Now both of you, pay attention," Nolan commanded. "It is imperative that you keep your forces intact and here close to Strong Tower and be prepared to defend her until I return." He glanced back and forth for understanding. "Do I make myself clear?"

Chapter 11

Nolan fled in the later part of night while Urlon was deathly quiet. But he knew all too well that the prying eyes of spies and wannabe apprentices filled the black voids at this very moment—not to mention the testamentors who eagerly waited, all the while trying to anticipate the wielder's next move. Although Nolan appreciated the space that they gave themselves between himself and in many ways do not interfere, they still could become a nuisance, and he had rather hoped that they would be easily discouraged from any endeavor on their part to try and enter the Mountain of Illenwell after him. Since most of the testamentors consisted of the quieter, more studied sorts and not the outgoing reckless types, there were still those foolish few that would interfere in some sort of mischievousness. But for the moment, Nolan felt he could make Illenwell's border with as little followers as possible. They would most likely stay to the hall and inner walls of Strong Tower. And there, hopefully, they would gather, converse, investigate, and detail what they had already heard and found to be true. Some would be off to speculate, while others yet would wait patiently, polishing off various other testaments. But in reality, he hoped that the guardian of Illenwell would be sufficient enough to ensure even the bravest of warriors to give considerable reconsideration to their pursuing apprenticeships, testaments, and heroics for now.

As the west wall faded away behind him, he cursed, for the night was clear without a single cloud. The moon lit the blackness and left even the shadows to bare their secrets. One could easily spot a ground runt scurry across the road. He had wanted to leave immediately but was content to leave shortly after his meeting concluded with both Tonelia and Tholin. There were several tasks that had needed to be attended to in order to progress on this job. He'd left with the lead warrior, Tholin, vivid instructions to safeguard Urlon, along with the complete understanding of his role as lead and the extreme complexities of his responsibility, which meant replacing his ego with maturity. With Tonelia, after he'd dismissed the lead, they'd stolen a few precious moments of passion as she led him down the darker tunnel and out to his windbred. But that brief encounter had only left yet another scar of regret.

They'd both emerged from the tunnel and met Toranden, for he was the only other person Nolan felt he could trust right at the moment. The lord had never failed him in all these past seasons. Toranden had to complete a twofold plan—first, make dead sure his windbred was there and well cared for, since it had ended up in Tholin's care, and that made Nolan extremely nervous. However, to the wielder's relief, his ride appeared in excellent condition. Toranden, in his thoughtful conception, had brought Nolan an extra windbred, for which he was grateful. Second, he explained to the good lord his task that would need to be accomplished—to which he full-heartedly agreed.

Toranden had shared with him the brief meeting that had taken place earlier that evening with Krhan. Nolan had expected as much. So, he tucked it away in his mind and would chew on it later. With the last pieces in place, he'd left them to wait patiently. He vowed to his rides that, by first light, they would walk a spell. Nolan rode the extra windbred while his real companion took up the rear and followed along. But Nolan caught a glance of his favorite windbred as it displayed a slight hint of jealousy from behind his big almond-colored eyes.

The wielder sped through the closer dwellings that stretched out at this point of the road under the close watch of the west wall. This part of the kingdom was, for the most part, occupied by crafters and specialist who worked in and around Strong Tower. In a sun's ride or two, Nolan would be in the midst of the fields of *lade* production. But for now, the dwellings were close together and hugged the road. It was late, and all were asleep, so Nolan had the opportunity to concentrate on all that had transpired in the last few hours. His first concern came in the form of regret. He'd compounded the brief encounter of passion he'd just shared with Tonelia, with the choice he'd just given his commitment to. And he began to really wonder where this would lead. After all, he had no idea what he was in for. Tonelia and Baylor's daughter—just how many heirs did they have? She hadn't given him much to go on, other than she would be awaiting his return—if he would, in fact, return. At that moment, his skin crawled with the very thought of the reality that, in just ten or so suns from now, he would, in fact, be confronting that obstacle somewhere deep in the Mountain of Illenwell. Nolan reminded himself that a visit to Lord Laiaden would have to transpire before entering that place.

Sometime much later, he reached the last of the dwellings, and finally, the fields that endlessly spread out before him. The transition from night to sun was almost translucent, for it had been a bright night. Desertion and stillness continued to surround him. Not one craftsman or eager traveler on their way to Strong Tower passed nor greeted him. So, he remained grateful for now, yet puzzled as he passed the last of the dwellings that still appeared closed and empty however the way was still yet long, and Lord Krhan troubled him the most. The distraction, as he liked to call them, could come at any time, at any place, or in any form, so he would have to be collected, alert, and on constant guard. However, Nolan had a passing thought that perhaps Krhan would forgo the interceptions and would quite possibly concentrate all his efforts on recovering the stolen property, just so Nolan could waste his time making his way to the mountain for nothing other than getting him out of the away and far from Tonelia.

The sun floated over the east land, and Nolan felt the warming rays fall upon his back. In anticipation, his rides neighed for him to fulfill his vow. He brought them to a halt and climbed off the saddle and led the windbreds side by side as he walked the west road for quite a while. He really did enjoy this part of Urlon. It was the great plains of endless fields. No trees or wild growing bushes, just the large dwellings of harvesters, and even those were far and few between. The sun was cheerier and blue as if to say to him, *"All will be well, in Illenwell, Nolan Hammer, wielder of the golden sword and defender of the orbs."* For now, yes. But in the suns to come? What will those bring? More complexity to this job?

Tonelia, the offer, and the rest of the kingdoms weighed heavy upon his mind. And what of his uncle back at Itmoore? He thought of his apprentice, who was now free from his vow. If he would just stay to watch over Thaylor and the rest of the kingdom, Nolan would be forever grateful. For Borth Nivenlos had been not only a childhood friend but, in later seasons and just a bit older than Nolan himself, had become quite a swordsman. But age and some bad knees had taken their toll. And for him, being a wielder would only come out of necessity of true friends. That was where both he and Nolan had agreed before parting ways.

After Nolan had left his uncle, Borth, and Itmoore, he'd vowed not to take an apprentice on this job. He replaced selfishness and pride with concern and caution, for this job was, by far, way out of hand. The mounting complications plagued him the most, and all he needed was the addition of another body to add to the mess. He would need to move as swiftly as possible, for there would be much in the way of dodging, since the west road to Illenwell would be longer than that of the east road. And that left a considerable amount of time for anything to happen and, unfortunately, a great deal of distractions that could fall his way.

He kept his mind on the job and rode on for the rest of the sun. And only two suns later, he found himself approaching the part of the kingdom that had become known as the mass lands. Here, the wealthier harvesters had large and spacious fields for their planting pleasure. Nolan could never understand how such a little green plant no higher than one's ankle could produce so many varieties of *lade*-flavored drinks. His favorite, the sweeter and truer tasting *lade*, was produced from these fields. But there was sour and brewed. And stripped and pounded—whatever that meant. There were varieties aged, young, and old (one season or two, perhaps three, but some argued four was aged enough).

But no matter how it was made, *lade* was still profit and wealth. It was no wonder Urlon was the only grower of the plant. It needed lots of sun and absolutely no shade. No other kingdom could grow it—which now just meant a greater number of would-be owners craving this orb. And that left a bitter feeling within his gut, one that reminded him of his past meeting with the young Tholin and his parting words about leading people to the right path to follow—which only left him disgusted even further with this country. There was here a true lack of gratitude and appreciation for anything anyone did for the country. Nolan could just spit. You could control yourself, but that was about it. He brought the two windbreds to a halt. He swung his legs around and swiftly dismounted from his ride. He landed on the dirty road with a thump in aggravation, stood erect, and placed both his fists into his sides.

Scanning the wealthy fields of the north, he watched the *lade* plants quietly sway back and forth as a gentle breeze descended over the open plain. *Why should I risk myself for this?*

He challenged his inner thoughts. *Because you chose*, came his answer. *You made a decision and made a stand. You made the oath, and when the season came, you made one to the Zoarians.*

He gave a long sigh, and thought of Tonelia, the deep concern in her eyes. He laughed. Would their heir have the same alluring eyes of deceit or, worse yet, her reckless ways? Still, Tonelia had those hazel eyes of alluring innocence that was always hiding some kind of deceitful acts. What in Zoarian's name was she up to now? He could just spit. "Should just let them lose this all." He addressed his windbreds. "See if they learn anything?"

But the more he thought about it, the more he saw how great the impact his selfish act would cause. It would damage his uncle, who was counting on him. Not to mention Tonelia and Baylor, in fact, all Urlon, plus their heirs, depending on how many were hidden, in addition to the heir for whom an offer was accepted. And he knew it would need to be honored. All were waiting patiently on this outcome. What about letting down Urlanna? Here was the perfect opportunity to help establish a new kingdom and, perhaps, another valuable champion to his testament. He sighed. "Take your eyes off yourself," he whispered to his windbred. "Could there be any other way?"

But only a mild and peaceful sun answered him back. Little *lade* plants toiled there in the soil and gave not one thought to this wielder's perplexing situation. He turned and walked south across the road and surveyed the fields there. And while he scanned and thought, his eyes fell upon the grim reminder of deceit and destruction. The frames of a once wealthy and large estate loomed out there over the plains of little green plants. Its skeletal frames were black and charcoal with the trademarks of the short-lived Saurotillian occupation of a war that, for now, seemed to have never happened in this wielder's cycle of seasons. The sight of the remains forced flashbacks and vivid reminders of that war as fleeting images rushed past his inner eye. Tonelia in her earlier and more reckless season, a young, vibrant figure filled with a stubborn passion to right the wrongs. He'd almost lost sight of his testament once his eyes found her. At that precise moment of their meeting had started the internal conflict between what needed to be done and what he needed. It was a relentless struggle between what was greater—Anglyllon's needs or his own selfish desires. The hardest part of being a wielder, his father warned him, would be taking your eyes off yourself, and looking to the needs of others. He could just spit.

That war had also produced two very strong-willed brothers from Auroria, both out to proof their worth. Nolan smiled as he remembered Toranden the older and Baylor the smarter. And as sure as all, as soon as those two saw Tonelia, that was that. In fact, Nolan was not too sure what fight he had gotten involved with. —the Saurotillians or the two big mountain heads who'd started fighting over her. Then throw Lord Krhan into the mess, and that was a war for all to try and forget. But now, with the seasons done and halfway through another cycle, messes were still just messes for him to clean up.

Just like the mess of a war that was, Krhan, Nolan knew all too well, had somehow been behind this mess as well. And now like then, despite his best effort, neither he nor the Zoarians could find the evidence to remove him from Lavenden and revoke his orb and lordship. So Krhan just continued to silently mock them all, and Nolan knew it. But he remained powerless to act and bring justice. Deep within him, he had hopes that the lord was, perhaps, behind this unfortunate job. And just by chance, this would be Nolan's long-awaited moment of retribution should Krhan be involved in the misplacing of this orb.

Standing there for quite a long time, he was able, for once, to just clear his thoughts. Nolan had an obligation to set things right and knew it to be the right thing to be done. He was also too punishingly aware of his age, and though he would not openly admit to it, he would have to make the time to settle down and produce an heir to the sword. He had made that decision, and he would fulfill it. Her argument was sound and just. Turning from the fields, he crawled onto his own windbred and patted its strong neck. Both understood their master's bidding and took off in a light trot. The following late afternoon under a gray and cloudily sun, Nolan found himself reporting to one of the more experienced, wiser, and older of the Zoarians.

"Well, I can plainly see that you decided against a complement of warriors," the tall, splendored bird creature said rhetorically.

But Nolan just stood there and smiled.

"We, the counsel, are also not surprised at this decision."

Again, Nolan just smiled back.

"And I'm sure by the plain fact in front of me that no apprentice has joined you either?"

Nolan nodded.

"Very well then; it's your decision," Aquila carried on. "What do you perceive so far?"

Nolan rubbed the back of his head. "A mess," he mumbled.

"A mess." The Zoarian heard him well enough, for their eyes were not the only exceptional feature about them.

"The east, Illenwell, Baylor, why I have never seen such a mess." He threw his hands about in a chaotic motion. "Why, the Saurotillian wars went smoother than this," he added amusedly.

Aquila stood there with not an expression on his beaked face.

"Why, I can't even hand you my sword and leave this for Borth. That's how bad this is." Nolan laughed. "I certainly wouldn't want that to happen to him anyway." He trailed off.

Aquila shared no sympathy. "You chose the sword. You made a choice and stood with it. And for this, you make us proud."

Nolan thought he heard just a hint of pride.

"We also understand that this comes with great sacrifice and discipline on your part, for which we are extremely grateful. We all too well understand your feelings for the lady."

"You for sure," Nolan said, "but as for the rest of this country …" He trailed off in visible disgust.

"Nolan Hammer," the great Zoarian started with reverence, "if all of Anglyllon were like you, where would we be?"

Nolan grinned and then let out a chuckle. "Drinking lots of *lade*."

"Come now." Aquila ignored his comment, wanting to remain serious. "Report on your private conversations."

Nolan collected his thoughts and would start from what he already knew. "Well, first, there is a treaty."

"Yes, and a plausible one at that," Aquila said.

"Why, don't you think that there is need for such a treaty?" Nolan asked.

"No."

"Good. Neither do I." Nolan offered. "Tonelia and Baylor have an understanding with Krhan. Krhan, of course, has a business dealing with Laiaden. From there, I can now understand the breakdown with Urlon and Illenwell, but it still could be easily remedied since, in a roundabout matter, Illenwell receives *lade* from Urlon through Lavenden's port. But what doesn't make sense is that Lord Laiaden fully understands he is paying more for it to be shipped through Krhan's harbors." Nolan rubbed his head again over the mess.

"Yes," Aquila partly agreed, "Lord Laiaden brought that price upon his kingdom."

"By falling in love with that guardian of theirs," Nolan said.

"Well, it does provide a valuable benefit."

"Yes, but at what cost?"

"So, everything went to risk over a treaty that was already transparent to the three of them?" The Zoarian almost seemed amused at all this. "Everyone just needs to discover a workaround."

"Apparently so." Nolan smiled. "And if Laiaden had really wanted to, he could have had a Taulian remove that dragon."

"True, unless a Taulian had planted that dragon there?"

"Well, in any event," Nolan said, slightly discouraged, "it is there regardless how it got there. And now it quite possibly has the orb."

"What of Tonelia?" Aquila inquired.

"Well, here's our real mess," the wielder started. "She and Baylor have some treaty with a young warrior lady in Ree."

"Yes, Urlanna," Aquila answered.

"She would do anything to assist Urlon for the return favor of helping to finally establish Ree back as a kingdom," Nolan continued.

"So perhaps this is a setup to aid her?" Aquila asked.

"If it is, it was an extremely risky and reckless one on their part," Nolan stated flatly.

"And we at the Zoarian council agree," Aquila said. "Now, what would be the advantages and disadvantages to such an undertaking of developing Ree to its former glory?" The Zoarian pondered.

"Well, of course, the kingdom would be right between Urlon, South Avalore, and yours truly," Nolan suggested.

"Lord Krhan," Aquila added.

"So, what's he get out of the deal?" Nolan pondered.

"Less land," Aquila offered in amusement. And for one brief moment, Nolan was treated to a Zoarian wit.

"That is a fact." He eyed the bird. "But Ree is for right now the only crossover to the East Kingdoms." Nolan spoke his concern.

"So, you are thinking our clever Lord Krhan might be looking east while driving, you, the wielder, west and further out of his way?" the Zoarian asked.

Nolan remained silent in thought for a moment. "Perhaps Lord Vendoff?"

"Krhan and Lord Vendoff?" Aquila seemed intrigued at the very thought.

"No. I feel that he really is just jumping at an unfortunate opportunity," Nolan suggested. "That's his nature."

"However, forced by dragon attacks, he and Lord Laiaden will have to trade up the Randerend River sooner than later," Aquila offered.

"Yes, with Sauros just wagging those slippery tongues at the very thought of all that merchandise flowing to and from." Nolan chuckled.

"But there is a bigger obstacle there," Aquila said what Nolan was already thinking. "And one that just doesn't make sense," he added.

"So, let's talk dragon." Nolan dreaded the thought. "We both know what brought them here to our world, and the only ones who can control them are the Taulians. So where does that leave me?" He asked the Zoarian, hoping this time for strong advisement from the wise ones.

"Nolan, you are by far the most knowledgeable wielder we have had to season," Aquila started. "You have uncovered the deepest secrets to the orbs, Anglyllon's history, and where this could all end."

"Yes, no thanks to the Lord of Sauros," he mumbled, irritated.

"Yes, it's true he unwittingly sent you down there," Aquila stated the facts. "That now, regrettably, places you in a most compromising situation."

"My personal testaments have not been recorded yet," Nolan defended. "So therefore, you and the rest of the Zoarians are the only ones who know of that job."

"And for now, we must keep it that way," Aquila sternly advised.

"Yes, however, when the season is right, they will need to be written," Nolan stated plainly.

"I suppose that you are correct," Aquila said, his tone tinged with regret, "The truth will have to be shared."

"So, for now, where does that leave us?" Nolan sounded frustrated.

"There is only one possible chance," Aquila offered.

"Yeah, find the Taulian."

"Perhaps?" the Zoarian offered.

"But I'm still puzzled by their interference in this treaty and how this Taulian, if one is involved, ever caught wind of this meeting?" Nolan rubbed the back of his head again.

"Perhaps questions for Lord Laiaden?" the Zoarian offered.

"Plenty of them," Nolan said, "including the ones regarding that dragon of theirs and how to deal with it."

"Even your sword will not penetrate the creature's hide," Aquila reminded him.

"Well, that will not happen," Nolan retorted. "Lord Laiaden will have me for sure if I even think about harming that pet of theirs."

"That only leaves you to control its mind."

"Just as the Saurotillians once were able to do," Nolan said.

"Yes, but they are unable to aid you now," Aquila added. "Greed and moral decay are slowly replacing their once gifted being."

"All right," Nolan said, flustered by the Zoarian's lack of advice. "So where does that leave me?" He asked for a straight and honest thought from the Zoarian.

"Nolan Hammer, "Aquila thundered, "after all these cycle seasons of being calm and levelheaded, you still ask of us this kind of question?"

Nolan stood silent and speechless for a moment.

"Opportunities will always present themselves to you," Aquila reminded him.

"Yes, yes," he responded in discontent, waving the tall Zoarian off while he thought up a different approach. "What did you observe back at Strong Tower?" he challenged the Zoarian.

"Other than great anguish and much concern, there seems to have been an undertone of something far more devious."

"Oh, how so?" Nolan perked up.

"The sudden arrival of Lord Krhan for one," Aquila said.

"Yes, regrettably he did arrive there faster than I would have anticipated."

"So, how sure are you that he is just 'jumping upon an unfortunate opportunity,' if I may paraphrase you correctly?" Aquila asked politely.

"Well, I'm not sure of anything," Nolan responded, "other than Tonelia's concern for Baylor and her kingdom."

"And, of course, the wielder." Aquila stared down at Nolan.

"Yes, I know." He sounded just slightly embarrassed. "But I have kept myself in check and disciplined." He defended her honor.

"I didn't say anything to the contrary," Aquila scoffed.

"No, but your actions spoke to me," he accused.

"Nolan, all of Anglyllon understands and knows perfectly well how you feel about each other," Aquila said plainly. "It's no secret."

"And that's exactly what concerns me," Nolan said.

Aquila studied him for a moment or two and then spoke discreetly. "I see. Not Lord Krhan but perhaps Lord Baylor?"

"I didn't rule out anyone," Nolan said. "He gave me his word that there is nothing between us and nothing for me to fear."

"However." The Zoarian bid him to finish his thought.

"A strong treaty between him and Laiaden without Krhan would be a total defeat in Krhan's eyes." Nolan spoke openly.

"Why, that would make good sense." Aquila agreed to the logic.

"Laiaden does have the first contact with most Taulians who come to Anglyllon." Nolan stated.

"Yes," Aquila said, "but so too does Lord Krhan receive, on occasion, an animal controller."

"Laiaden makes more sense," Nolan offered.

Concerned, the Zoarian looked down at Nolan. "Control the dragon and hold the orb for safe keeping until ..." Aquila pointed a talon at Nolan, and there was a long pause between them. "You best take on an apprentice."

"Well, it's a little late to discuss that," Nolan blurted out. "We should have addressed this topic back at Strong Tower."

"I tried," Aquila defended, "but you were a bit preoccupied."

"There you go again." Nolan advised the Zoarian to speak more carefully.

"That's not what I am referring to," the Zoarian defended.

"Then what?" the wielder asked.

"Nolan," Aquila said strongly, "you are about to be flanked on all sides. Yet you go without warriors or apprentice to face a predator like none you've faced before. Where are you going with this?"

"Don't know." He shrugged his shoulders. "But I'll let you know when I arrive."

"The only place you will arrive is twilight's end," the big bird rebuked him. "Now what is your plan for this job?" Aquila demanded an explanation.

Nolan looked up toward the big bird. "You're right, Aquila, I'm about to face a predator I have never met before. So, at this point of the job, I couldn't possibly ask anyone to accompany me down into certain death." He paused. "Besides, I have discovered during my travels that these dragons are, perhaps, far more clever than anyone gives them credit for."

"That is precisely why you need to take on an apprentice," Aquila scolded him.

"And when would you have liked me to have done that?" Nolan blurted out.

"Opportunities will present themselves."

"I'll spit if you remind me of that again." Nolan poked a warning finger up into Aquila's beak.

"Nolan," Aquila said sternly, "you seek my advice, which I now give you; take on apprentice for this job. You will clearly need someone not only to watch your back but also as a companion to exchange opinions with. We will continue to keep you apprised of all the situations until you reach the borders of Illenwell and the Unknown Kingdom. From there, I'm afraid you'll be on your own without an apprentice." Aquila made sure that the wielder was paying attention. "No Zoarian will take a chance near Illenwell. I will send an advisory to you one last time near the abandoned kingdom of Solemn Plain."

"Understood." Nolan nodded but was visibly displeased by this conversation.

"You also should send for your other advisor," Aquila suggested.

"That will be addressed shortly, I'm sure," Nolan said with confidence. "Now, until the next meeting then."

"By Solemn Plain," Aquila reminded him.

Nolan nodded and turned to leave.

"Nolan," Aquila said, interrupting his departure, "whoever set this plan in motion knows you all too well."

Nolan paused and was silent for only a second and then replied, "Well, that could be anyone."

Aquila blinked and stared longingly one last time. Then he spread his magnificent wings and, in one quick and fluent motion, took to the sky.

As Nolan stood there and watched Aquila fly off to present his report to the Zoarian council, he was suddenly struck with the most horrific thought—one that he'd never had since he'd first became wielder. And that was, what if Tonelia was right about their manipulation? Aquila was dead right; Nolan knew more than any other wielder that had come before him. His complete testaments had not yet been written. Only those from afar had been recorded. He knew what the dragons were and why they were here. He understood the orbs and their purpose. What if this whole job was the creation of the Zoarians to bring an end to him as a wielder? To quiet him before others could learn the truth. And what would be so wrong about learning the truth? A Zoarian cover-up. The great Nolan Hammer, wielder of the golden sword, devoured by a dragon and Urlon's orb recovered by Krhan's brave warriors. Or worst yet, a Saurotillian. Take his secret to twilight's end? Was this what this job was all about?

Chapter 12

P.D. 77, A.F. 8130

Thoan sat deep within one of the dark tunnels. His back was propped against the cool wall, and stale, moist air permeated his nostrils, bringing with it the faint smell of decay. He couldn't seem to shake the feeling of death. Nor could he determine where the warriors had gotten off to. It was then that he cursed himself for leaving them. But he'd had little choice. After they had waited awhile, they'd started on their way, and as he tried to follow and mark the way, he'd eventually lost them. He even lost count of the passing suns and nights. Since most of the time was spend deep within this mountain. He divided his time be watching the cavern with the dragon and the orb and the rest of the time searching for the warriors. But somewhere along the way he completely lost track and had to, on occasions, slip back down to Illenwell to replenish supplies and scout the port for any signs of the warriors. And that's when he cursed to himself the most. Perhaps, he hoped that they had found the wits to give up this orb retrieval task. Or worse yet, they were awaiting reinforcements or just like him and everyone else, they were patiently waiting for the wielder's arrival as well.

Unfortunately, with his sustenance starting to dwindle again, he would have to make his way to the cave opening near the west side of the mountain to find the supplies his employer's aid would leave him with every other sun until the job was done. But there, in the darkness with his torch extinguished for now and as his eyes adjusted to the blackness, he could clearly hear the words of both his respected employers now. And if the first were to catch wind of what the second offered, then he, most assuredly, would get a sword full. So, in order to keep his innards intact, he best not stray from the task at hand. Once again, he reran the quick plans over in his head to make absolutely sure of his job—and a simple one at that. But it needed cleverness and patience in order to execute it, plus one of Thoan's specialties, improvisation—since this was not just a clear-cut job like most of them were.

So, there he sat, totally surrounded by a black void and the events of the last couple of suns and the conversations that flooded past his mind in complete succession one after the other.

It had been a somewhat clear morning, well over twenty or so suns ago, as he'd sat on the port near the southern half of Illenwell. He was just near the edge of the last few remaining dwellings, and there, he cast out a long line to the water just to see what the leisure sun would catch. He'd had no idea how big of a catch he was about to receive, for there, out of the corner of his eye and moving toward him was the recognizable shape of his employer's aide, who always knew where to find him. The out-of-breath messenger left his windbred near a tree and made his way out to Thoan; the aide, would be hopping over several large boulders that stretched out to the harbor. And Thoan liked it that way, private like, but just enough visual to catch a glimpse of intrusions, like now for instance.

The message was simple. "Come directly after the last of the drink houses close, this very night!"

Later, when the last *lade* was consumed and the inns began to close, Thoan had found himself silently creeping through the wooden structure of Illenwell's hall and easily avoiding the brighter torch ways. With swift and fluent motions, his long, strong legs quietly guided him along. The ghost, adorned in one of his pitch-black attires complete with hood, floated passed two warrior sentinels and, later, Slomak, who hurriedly rushed by accompanied by several of his lead warriors and was so lost in giving orders that not one of them even noticed the ghost standing there in the thick darkness flashing a rude gesture at them.

When the way became still again, the ghost did not make for the two wooden doors that would lead to Laiaden's hall. Instead, he made for a smaller door near the end of the hall. Stopping, he pushed his ear against the door and listened intently. After a fashion, he gingerly opened the door and slid in. Moments later, a dark figure gracefully and silently flew over the outside railing and stopped sudden as he caught the pair of crossed legs of the lord sitting in his usual chair watching the double doors, he would have expected the ghost to come through.

"Ah, our ghost has arrived." The lord jumped from his reclining chair and immediately poured his late-night guest a cup of *lade* and offered it to him.

Thoan straightened and cursed under his breath. "Clumsy." He entered and accepted the cup. There was no one else among them.

"You arrived unnoticed and promptly on time as always." The lord smiled appreciatively.

Thoan nodded in response.

Laiaden smiled. "Thought that you would not use the door."

Thoan shrugged.

"Excellent approach anyway," he commended. "Now, you no doubt understand why you are here?"

"I got the idea when Tobus found me," Thoan responded with intrigue as he followed the lord back out to the spacious balcony.

"Look out over the port and tell me what you see," the lord bid.

The balcony and hall of Illenwell stretched out over the harbor and gave a marvelous yet serene view of a large city that continued to expand southward. Various vessels of all sizes and shapes slowly hovered out on the water and gently rocked away under a partly cloudy night. And where the clouds permitted, an ominous moon hung over the harbor and moonlight danced and glittered off the softly rolling waters below. The air was warm with that feel of moisture from the ocean breeze, and Thoan let it blow his red and perfectly groomed hair about. "Seclusion," he answered idly.

"And that is exactly why I like you," Laiaden boomed triumphantly, throwing a punch to his arm. "For you are the closest representation to this kingdom of anyone I have met so far." He complimented the ghost again. "Except for me, that is."

"Yes, I know," Thoan responded like he'd heard this before. "But I thought that this incident would not concern me?"

"Ah but it does," Laiaden said.

"That I can now see." He motioned to the lord and went to sip his *lade*, but Laiaden placed his hand over the rim and gently pushed it down.

"Do you remember when the dragon came?" the lord asked as he stepped away.

"Yes, I was just a young warlog then." Thoan referred to a runty little animal that was great for roasting as he looked down at the swirling *lade* that remained untouched.

"Then you no doubt watched this kingdom struggle to pull its dignity back together?"

"I lost most of my family," Thoan said remorsefully. "My mother and I survived and struggled until her death, regrettably, a few seasons after."

"Then I know exactly how you feel about working completely alone." Laiaden sounded sympathetic as he started the pitch. "More like under cover, elusive, ghostlike, you might say."

Thoan listened as he continued to look down at the *lade,* he so much wanted to taste, for this was surely going down the path of the dragon. This he didn't mind, but it would cost double the usual wage.

"Then you'll no doubt understand how imperative this job of yours is going to be?" the lord said.

"I get the picture."

"Do you?"

There was a long uncomfortable pause between them.

"For this time, if you are not successful, you could be the cause of someone losing their family." Laiaden paused until he was sure his point sunk in. "Perhaps, many children would suffer the loss of entire families." He paused again. "Worse yet, families could suffer the unbearable loss of children."

"I said I understood." Thoan sounded a bit annoyed.

"See that you do."

Thoan did not respond. After all, everyone had a right to live.

"But I'm fooling myself." Laiaden smiled. "Success is the only option for you." He continued the compliment, speaking candidly. "Your crafty skill with that sword will be all that stands from our serenity and chaos."

"Does the dragon have orbs?" Thoan pitched to see what his lord's response would be.

"Go in and find out," Laiaden said, "for I am almost sure of it."

"And if they're there?" Thoan inquired.

"Nolan will figure it out," he instructed, clearly avoiding the question.

"You don't want the kingdom of Urlon?" he dared question, and by Laiaden's quick glance, he knew the nerve was hit.

"If you don't like this quiet, serene little corner at twilight's end," the lord said, clearly annoyed, "then by all means, leave."

"It's not that at all," Thoan said, defending himself. "I just thought you would send in that troll to retrieve the orb and then you, yourself, return it to the good Lord of Urlon."

"Ott will not go in for the orb." Laiaden stated. "Nor will he enter the dragon's cavern and further annoy it." Laiaden paused. "He, like the rest of us here in Illenwell rather appreciate our white guardian—for it has added a certain ambiance to our little affair, wouldn't you agree?"

Thoan nodded indifferently, for that ambiance came by way of an enormous price, the almost total destruction of their port.

"Besides, no one wants to disturb the troll while he is working hard," the lord continued. "And that has contributed to our profits nicely here in Illenwell, so we will not jeopardize him!"

"I agree," Thoan said. "We wouldn't want to risk it."

"But there are those here, for whom decrees are only meant to be broken," Laiaden said sharply. "And those are the ones with whom you, my fine keeper of the decrees, will make sure the decree stays enforced." He finished with a grin in Thoan's direction.

"Success is the only option." He lifted his cup to the lord.

"And that's what I'm counting on." But the lord interrupted him again from drinking as he passed Thoan and made for the long wooden table where a pourer of *lade* and cups were placed.

"Then what drove the dragon to that meeting?" Thoan boldly asked with a now slightly parched throat as he followed the lord back inside.

Lord Laiaden remained quiet, in refection for a moment. "I have Slomak working on that now."

"You mean, ripping apart this port in search of an animal controller?" Thoan responded plainly.

"If that be the case?" the lord said.

"If that be the case," Thoan went on, "then what would a Taulian want with an orb?"

"If Slomak is successful with his mission," the lord said, "then we will have an answer."

"And that might be better unanswered," Thoan responded bluntly. He then waited for the offer.

And the lord knew by his expression that the deal was proceeding as planned. So, without further selling, "Triple—*no!* —four times your usual amount." The lord smiled, and then produced a large purse that was hidden from his view. Laiaden tossed it across the table.

And with a quick motion, Thoan's hand snatched it away without spilling one drop of fine *lade* upon one of his best black attires.

"You just make absolutely sure that nothing from Sauros to Solth, from Taul to from here in Illenwell and or from anywhere else gets to that orb, that dragon—nothing," he stated very adamantly. "You are the only line between our existence and extinction should that dragon get really annoyed with constant intrusions."

Thoan could only nod in agreement, all the while feeling the large compensation that nearly broke his fingers.

"And *all* opposition must be handled immediately and appropriately." Laiaden looked to see if his meaning was clear.

Thoan threw him a quick glance of confusion, and the lord understood from his expression that his statement needed further clarification.

"Except that of fine wielder," Laiaden answered. "I'll take care of him."

"I understand," Thoan responded. "I was thinking more on the line of lords."

Laiaden studied him for a moment or two. "What are you getting at?"

"Possibly not giving the orb back to Lord Baylor?" he smirked.

"Then who would you suggest?"

"Perhaps ... Lord Krhan?"

"I would do no such thing." He snapped.

"Well, it's none of my business." Thoan smiled.

Laiaden straightened in defense and Thoan could easily spot the undertone of a much more complex plan that he was not to be party to.

"I already have one dragon in this kingdom," Laiaden said harshly. "I don't want one in the kingdom next door too." He paused. "I like Krhan right where he is, and you are going to make sure that it stays that way. Do I make my pitch here clear?" He stared at Thoan.

Again, Thoan did not need to reply or inquire, for it was not his place. He just nodded in assurance and felt the heavy persuasion in his palm.

"We have an agreement then?" The lord approached Thoan with an outstretched cup.

Finally, Thoan thought and brought his cup to Laiaden's.

"Now, slip away quietly?" Laiaden said.

Thoan nodded one last time. He drained his cup and disappeared.

First, Thoan needed a quick detour and to send off a most urgent message.

Thoan waited all the next sun quietly hidden until the response could come. He busied himself by sharpening his sword and knife and gathered the few personal objects he would clearly need while away in the belly of the mountain. By early evening, the messenger returned with instructions, and so off went Thoan to his next employer.

Later that evening, he crept about in the town's shadow until he came to his next appointment, for he admired his ability to pit one employer against another. After all, it paid the debts.

It was a usual warm night, and a half moon glimmered upon a calm bay. Full ships had left for their destinations while new vessels had emptied their wares. Their sails and crew all tucked away for the night in local drinking dens while the hollow vessels awaited the morning to be filled. To the ports of Roan and Pantanteous some of the ships would speed too. Others would make for Lauraleeanna of Solth and further north to Avalore and Auroria. But while all was quiet for the night, no one saw the stealthy ghost as he made his way among the shadows of the glowing moon. Although he had never met the lord's competition, payment was always proper and plenty for his services. And he had never suspected who he was or where he was from. His path was revealed to him, as well as his future. And it was all coming together nicely.

He slipped down the back deserted streets and silent walkways between the buildings. No windbred, no sound, just the ghost and the moon. He soon found his door with the markings of the rest haven, *"Harbor Spoils."* It was not one of the more popular places you would come to Illenwell for, but it was packed nightly with the usual crowd. And this very night, it would do for a special meeting. He checked the door for the lock. It clicked open. He was expected. After a brief glance to search the deserted street, he slipped in unnoticed.

The door creaked as he gently shut it. Thoan cursed. He then turned and found himself in the large storeroom to the haven, and well stocked it was. Crates, boxes, and bulging sacks were piled everywhere. There were small pathways between them, and the dirty floor showed its well-traveled tracks of employees shifting through various stocks. He allowed his eyes to adjust.

The room was pungent with various food smells. The aroma of drinks and *lade* filled his nose. He stopped briefly here and there through his little trek to the other room for his meeting and grabbed handfuls of vegetables and nuts. He stuffed the items deep within his pack until it bulged. A large sack of dried meat and some smoking leaves he tucked away as well.

Then he spied his objective and made his way over. Thoan gently rapped on an old wooden door and waited for the response. It came as a raspy sound, and with that, he pulled the door open and entered, closing it behind him with a most hideous creaking that made him cringe.

It was a small musty cellar. He had to bend his head as he descended a few stairs as to not hit it on the crossbeam. The floor was dirt. It was blacker than the caves, and it reeked of old stale air. Thoan positioned himself in front of an old, thick dark curtain that hung between him and his boss, and aside from a small burning candle there was no other light.

"I understand your message," the voice crocked irritably, knowing this would cost plenty.

"Most apologies," Thoan politely replied. "But you no doubt have heard of Urlon's dilemma?"

"Most unfortunate," The voice resounded with amusement. "Too sad for her lady."

"They had it coming." Thoan smirked.

"How fortunate for her carelessness." The voice sounded triumphal.

"Laiaden believes the orb is there in the dragon's chamber," Thoan offered.

"Most assuredly it is," the voice rasped again.

"What's it worth to you?" Thoan stated the obvious.

"Let's just say, you'll never have another debt." The voice chuckled.

"I'm to guard it until Nolan shows." Thoan shared his job description.

"Excellent," crocked the voice. "Let him figure out how to get the orb without being burned or infuriating the beast."

"My thoughts exactly," Thoan agreed. "Then let us quickly conclude our business so I can return and await my reward." Thoan referred to the orb.

"Be on guard, for it has most recently become known to me that Nolan may be tricked into bringing an apprentice and one of most excellent sword," the voice informed him.

"Oh," Thoan said whimsically, "a challenge for the orb?"

"The plan grows more complex, does it not?" The voice seemed to mock him.

"Challenges are good." He smirked back as he rubbed his perfectly groomed red bread, totally engrossed in the ever-developing challenges. "It keeps your sword sharp," He whispered to himself.

"You are most excellently optimistic." The voice sounded all too pleased. "Let the wielder fall to the apprentice and finally bring an end to the Hammer line and, with it, his testament. Then three kingdoms will be joined under one solid and strong ruler who will bring wrath to our sworn enemy." The voice sounded extremely diabolical.

"Illenwell will remain intact?" Thoan needed reassurance to this deal.

"Intact it shall be and shall remain," the voice clarified.

"And the dragon?" came his next concern.

"It will continue to provide its service unabated." There came a quiet chuckle.

"Our business then is done?" Thoan asked.

"Yes, of course," the voice hissed. "Look for your first installment, there, under the last stair."

Thoan could not see under the step in the darkness, so he stepped over, reached down, and felt the ground until his fingers found the sack.

"Very well then," Thoan replied, satisfied. "We'll meet again after this job is completed." He did not await a response from the voice and turned and left the cellar. He climbed the stairs and shut the creaky cellar door.

He stood there for a few moments, lost in thought. *Perhaps I should find out more of this apprentice. Why was I not given all the information? How am I expected to execute my orders without critical knowledge of my opponents? The wielder I know. But this apprentice, it intrigues me.*

He opened the door again to return and ask his questions. He peered down the steps into a completely deserted cellar. The curtain was gone, and no other door was present. "What?" he whispered to himself.

Scanning the dark, Thoan was about to enter when his left arm was grabbed, and he was swung around to face a very large man.

"Yeah, what're you up to?" The man's voice boomed at him in the dark.

But before Thoan went for his dagger to finish the intruder, his face came into the light of a nearby torch, and it was the rest haven's owner. He was a rather large and plump man. Messy black, brown, and gray strands of hair tossed about his head. From a rough, unshaven face, small pupils for eyes searched Thoan for answers. An old, long white, and dirty shirt clung tightly around the bulging stomach. And a blue apron with the Haven's insignia on it wrapped around his rolling folds, covered in smears and smudges of colors Thoan would rather not be concerned with.

"Oh, it's you?" the startled owner said as he caught site of Thoan's face. "Apologies." He loosened his grip. "Did you have business back here?" he asked. "Nothing messy, if you know what I mean?" he added. "I always have to pay the help more when there's a mess, if you know what I mean."

"None tonight, owner," Thoan responded with assurance. "But I needed some things." And with that, Thoan found his pouch and pulled two big rocks worth, a small fortune from it, and slipped them into the owner's sweaty palm.

He felt the weight and was pleasantly surprised by the reimbursement. "Why of course," he answered back, "anything at all." He urged Thoan to the stock room.

"Well … just one more," Thoan said.

The haven owner nodded.

"Some of your older *lade*. I couldn't find your good stuff; thought you might have hidden it down there?" Thoan motioned for the door offering a quick excuse to avoid any questions.

"Ah … this way." He pointed, and the two went off to a far corner, and he filled Thoan's sack with several bottles.

"There, you enjoy." Then the two called it a night, and Thoan retreated into Illenwell's shadows.

There, he'd remained until now where he sat in the darkness rethinking his business and what should lie ahead. Thoan checked the stock, and most was good. Nuts, dried meat, vegetables, and one bottle of *lade*; the rest was hidden back at his entrance. Rope, knife, and sword, of course; flint and a bundle of small wood for a quick fire here and there; an extra heavy shirt for the cooler parts of the mountain; and his black gloves, which he now put on. Once all was gathered, he would return to his patrols. He checked the marker that was tucked away in his breast pocket, which he would use on the cave tunnels to mark the way. It was a crude stick made of finely crushed shells, bonded together by wax, which left a clear white marking upon the walls. Since there was no rain in the tunnels, the marks would not easily wash away, and it wasn't like he would be here all that much more. After all, the wielder must be on his way by now. He knew Nolan, and he wouldn't tolerate distractions from his job and would deal with them quickly and efficiently, just as he would now go do with those warriors he had followed before.

Thoan started down one long tunnel and then branched off to ones he had not yet marked. While coming out of one tunnel that emptied into a small cavern, he spied two smaller black holes that drifted off in different directions. Thoan chose one and entered. He followed it for some time until it sharply turned to his left, which is where he about jumped out of his skin as he came face-to-face with two tall and well-armed Saurotillians. They stopped dead in their tracks and flicked their long tongues at him. Both carried large shields and wore helmets. They were in a single file because the tunnel was too narrow for them the walk side by side. And how the troll ever did this was a mystery for Thoan as well. The lizards were also bent over slightly as to not hit their helmets on the cave's ceiling.

At that moment, Thoan had not realized his luck. The tunnel kept the lizards immobile for a moment while Thoan immediately formulated his escape. He could not possibly take on two heavily armed reptiles. They could outrun him and, worse yet, could find him in the dark.

"Quick! Before he retreats!" screamed the one behind the other.

They banged and thudded about as they awkwardly went for their swords.

Thoan turned and jetted down the tunnel. Up ahead, it grew wider, and he sprinted as quickly as he could to put distance between them. The leading Saurotillian caught an obstruction to his head from the ceiling, and it threw him back into the following lizard. They bounced off the walls, and one of them hit the ground, sending the awful sound of clanging metal reverberating down the tunnel.

This might be my luck, Thoan thought, *because I could use a dragon right about now.*

But that was late in coming. Thoan darted down another tunnel, and to his dismay, it doubled back and right into the same two centurions. The Saurotillian who was following the other jumped over his fallen leader and charged Thoan with his long sword poised overhead. The lizard was immediately upon Thoan in about two leaps, and as he brought his sword down, Thoan braced for the strike that never came—for the sword lodged into the low ceiling and stopped dead. Thoan swung hard with his sword and struck the Saurotillian's blocking shield in hopes of knocking it free. But it only bounced off, sparks exploding everywhere.

Thoan saw the beady little eyes from under the metal hood chuckle back at him. Then the lizard's sword came free and finished the swing. Thoan jumped as it hit the rock floor, and more sparks erupted from the force.

The second lizard regained his stance and moved in behind the attacking reptile. Thoan did the best he could do. He blocked, jabbed, and squirmed around the advancing lizards.

"What is taking you so long?" hissed the following lizard.

"I'm playing," the new leader responded with delight.

"Well quit playing and finish the rodent," he bellowed, "before we have to play with that dragon."

"What dragon?" The leader never took his beady red eyes off Thoan, who was growing weaker with every stroke of the lizard's strong swings.

"That one, you foolish, blind fool!" He hit the lizard so hard on the helmet that it fell over his face, temporarily blinding him.

Thoan seized the moment to turn and flee. But as he did, his vision went right down the gapping maw of black teeth. He instantly fell to ground—just as the fire erupted from the dragon's throat. The two Saurotillians drew their shields, and the fire exploded everywhere. Thoan felt the searing heat and rolled to the side of the tunnel and down into a small fissure. His ears rattled with the sound of the roaring dragon. Thoan covered his ears and closed his eyes tightly. He hoped the dragon was too preoccupied with the Saurotillians to have noticed him. His luck was with him, for the dragon took a few steps forward, until Thoan could see its belly. And that's when he seized his second opportunity.

Thoan rolled under the dragon and then crawled toward the hind legs, and out from under the tail he escaped. The tunnel was wider, and to his luck, a few sparsely but well-placed torches lit the area just enough for him to make his escape—which he hoped was somewhere near the dragon's chamber and that orb.

Thoan took off down the tunnel just as the dragon backed out, forced by the two attacking Saurotillians. The dragon caught sight of a fleeing creature and bellowed a resounding roar of defiance that Thoan clearly ignored. But before the dragon could follow, a sword struck its leg, and the dragon's attention was diverted back to the two intruders.

Thoan bolted down the tunnel until the fighting caught his ear. He stopped near a torch to catch his breath and leaned against the cold cavern wall and turned his attention back to the white dragon, which was now fully engaged with the two lizard centurions. He watched the tunnel explode into flashes of red flames. Inside, there was more room for the Saurotillians to move around and attack the dragon. But it made little difference. Thoan watched the white dragon paw an attacker and knock him to the floor. Its pointy snout snapped at the other warrior. The lizard threw up its shield to block, but the dragon's jaw clamped down and ripped it from the lizard's arm. The dragon shook its head violently and sent the shield crashing across the tunnel's wall with echoing effects. The Saurotillian raised his sword to strike, but the dragon swung its head around and grabbed the centurion by the head. The warrior hit the dragon with his sword, and in response, the dragon lifted the warrior and swung him into a nearby wall.

The lifeless body fell to the floor with a crash while the second Saurotillian rushed the slayer. It danced out of the way as he swung his sword, cutting the air and missing his aim completely. As the warrior lost his balance in front of the dragon, the beast's head locked around the waist, and the screaming Saurotillian was covered in a blast of red heat. In another moment, the burning husk was flung up the tunnel and landed just a few feet from where Thoan stood. It struck the ground in an explosion of fire.

Instantly, a terrible thought struck Thoan—worse than a Saurotillian's sword. The dragon's here and some Saurotillians too. But where were those warriors? And finally, who was minding that orb?

Chapter 13

Earlier, and before Thoan could make his way back to the dragon's cavern and check in on the orb, the orb had been minded by a quiet, stealthy group of warriors. Who would soon, inevertantly, disturb the dragon and send it rushing off to be the ghost's unwitting savior from the two Saurotillians.

The stealthy group of warriors had entered through the west tunnel, silently and quickly, as not to be seen by the troll, Ott. Lead Slomak had placed Illenwell guards about the mountain. But guards were sparse and would leave the tunnel unmanned for extended lengths of time. So, all the warriors had needed to do was lie in wait and, one by one, slip in between the watches. And it was not hard to find the tunnel; all they needed to do was follow the guards as Lord Krhan had suggested.

Now, the stealthy, handpicked warriors, some of whom, had arrived in Illenwell some nearly nine days ago from the kingdom of Lavenden, just needed to accomplish their task. They had boarded a cargo ship from the port of Pantanteous. This cargo ship carried a Taulian abroad. Lord Krhan had finally found one and bribed her to secure the ship. This was not an easy task, since Taulians sought power over profit. And monetary gain meant little to them.

This animal controller from Taul was young and had no beast to call her own. So, this venture was more a learning task to see if the youthful Taulian could bring a dragon under control. But all to disappointingly, no dragons had appeared on that trip. And all had arrived safe and sound to the port. Unlike the misfortunate *Ocean Dominator*.

The lead warrior in charge of the mission tried himself to bribe the Taulian into the mountain. But she refused and caught the next cargo ship back to Pantanteous and wished for better luck on a dragon sighting.

While the ship was unloaded, the warriors quietly slipped off and out of sight—up toward the mountain through the forest, following the guards.

It took several attempts in the long and winding tunnels. They'd made frequent hunting trips and trips back to the port for supplies and any sign of their arriving vessel for a quick passage back to Pantanteous with, hopefully, an orb in their possession and a new kingdom for their lord.

Now, once again on a return trip inside the mountain and fumbling about through the dark and winding tunnels, the warriors had grown restless and lost track of time. It had started to appear all too endless, till the group finally discovered the well-lit path that ended near the dragon's cavern. They hugged the wall in the tunnel near the cavern's opening that would lead them into the cavern of the white dragon.

It was there that the low, just barely audible whispers could be heard.

Orun crept over to the lead, and with barely a sound, he mouthed the words, "No use." He shook his head.

The young lad placed a reassuring hand upon Orun's shoulder while the other warriors huddled silently and close together, waiting for further orders.

"That dragon has not moved," Orun whispered further.

"We have time," the young lead, Lantor, whispered back reassuringly.

"But your brother's ship has not yet arrived!" hissed Orun

"And neither has the wielder," Lantor whispered.

"But we most get that orb and get to your brother's ship and get it to your father in Strong Tower," Orun protested in a hissed whisper.

"I understand," Lantor responded. "But we have time."

"How do you know this?" A young warrior near his lead inquired.

"Because Nolan is in the east kingdoms with his uncle. And besides, once he makes Strong Tower, my father and Lady Tonelia will give him plenty of distractions." He wore a deceitful smile.

"Well, I'm not convinced of this," Orun protested further.

"Trust me." Lantor padded the warrior's shoulder. "It will all work out. Now let us go and see what the dragon and our future orb are doing."

Lantor took the lead and the others fell into a silent pursuit, each securing his shield and sword to prevent any clanging that might alert the dragon to their approach.

Lantor cautiously investigated the dragon's cavern and found the beast just lying there near the mound of treasure. The orb, unfortunately, was out of sight. It was high on the ledge around the corner.

"Look at the loot," Orun whispered referencing the large mound of gold, silver, and gems piled high against the back wall.

"Ay," Lantor agreed. "But nothing compared to the wealth of that orb."

"Agreed." Orun nodded.

"And just where is that orb?" a warrior whispered as he scanned the massive cavern.

"Now, that's a good question." Lantor's eyes also dodged about the area.

"Blast!" Orun spat under his breath. "Bet she and the wielder have already been here and gone by the time we found our way here."

Lantor raised his hand to keep him quiet while the dragon stirred for a moment and then settled in again.

"It's here," Lantor whispered. "Otherwise, the dragon would not be."

"Not if they are mixed in with some of those piles," a warrior motioned toward the smoldering ashes of bones and metal.

Lantor shook his head. "Centurions," he clarified. "Notice the skulls."

The group strained through the dim light of the nearby burning basins that Ott kept lit. The long, recognizable snouts of the Saurotillians and hollow black eyes stared back at them ominously, warningly.

"That will be us if we don't make a move," Orun murmured.

Irritated once again, Lantor rose his hand to keep his warriors quiet. "Move back and let us give them more time." He referenced the wielder and, hopefully, their lady warrior.

But just then came a sound from the other side of the cavern. They all froze as a large band of centurions broke into the cavern and rushed the slumbering dragon.

"Saurotillians!" Orun spat. The warriors quickly drew swords.

"*Wait!*" Lantor ordered. "This may be our chance!"

The group remained hidden and watched the chaos unfold.

Three centurions jumped the dragon, swinging large, long thick chains that rattled and brought the cavern to life. In a vain attempt, they tried to swing the chains around the beast's snout. The dragon leaped to its feet as the three straddled the dragon's back and threw the chains about its long neck. The dragon roared in defiance and circled about the cavern, igniting the place with fireballs. The cavern burst into flashes of hot red flames.

From a safe distance, Lantor and the group watched another small party of four centurions rush the side of the treasure, and up the mound they went.

"Now where do you suppose they are going?" Orun asked.

"To safety, if they're smart," a warrior behind him joked.

Lantor did not respond since he now immediately understood.

Despite the dragon's handicap, it caught sight of the Saurotillians moving up the pile, and with a quick move, it swung its tail around and took out the bottom part of the treasure. Objects went flying everywhere and the pile gave way in an avalanche, sending the four Centurions tumbling down to the floor.

There was a small outburst of cheers from Lantor's party, while a few snickered at the clumsiness of the Saurotillians and cleverness of the dragon.

One centurion unfortunately rolled in front of the dragon, and it stepped on the lizard with a front talon. Grabbing the struggling Saurotillian, it flung him over toward Lantor's party, and they watched the centurion hit the floor with a sickening thud and crack. The Saurotillian's lifeless body slid across the floor and hit the wall with a loud crash as its metal armor buckled under the hit.

The dragon swung its head about, and long black teeth sunk into another of the centurions. The lizard beat the dragon's head with his talons and screamed while he was torn from his position. The dragon's head jerked violently back and forth. Then a fireball erupted from its mouth, and the centurion went up in flames. The dragon swung its head, and the burning carcass flew against one of the cavern walls, its body exploding into a flaming flower of red sparks.

One of the fallen centurions scrambled to his feet and began growling out orders. The two remaining on the dragon's back jumped off, while two other surviving centurions ran for a nearby tunnel.

Lantor braced, for this could be the moment!

Those centurions that could escape, ran for the other tunnel, and the dragon quickly took off in pursuit of its fleeing prey.

"Watch my back!" Lantor ordered and ran off into the cavern. He reached the middle and began a frantic circle as he searched the area. Finally, his eyes fell upon the orb. He had known it was there, but as he'd suspected, it had been out of sight from their position.

Quickly, he sprinted up the treasure pile. Noise was no longer an issue, and gems, gold, silver, and other precious objects went flying about from under his stride.

He triumphantly reached the top, and the prize was his.

As he grabbed and secured the orb, a loud, reptilian hiss lifted from the cavern floor, "*You fifthly scaleless one!*"

The startled warriors and Lantor all froze as two centurions appeared from the darkness. They had fooled not only Lantor and his group but also the dragon and had quickly doubled back, leaving the dragon to chase the other centurions.

"That will be ours." The centurion held out an open talon toward Lantor.

"Not this day!" The lead laughed in defiance. He pulled his sword and charged the Saurotillians.

Lantor's warriors came from around the treasure, and the two large centurions hissed and giggled in amusement. "You have ten against us!"

The swords quickly engaged, and the cavern came alive with clanging metal.

"You dare challenge us!" The lead centurion attacked Lantor, Orun, and two other warriors who quickly came to his aid.

"You forget!" Lantor laughed arrogantly. "We are Lavenden warriors and well experienced with your kind!"

But the Centurion was swifter and caught one of the warriors in the midsection, nearly cutting him in half. His body fell to the ground. Innards and blood splashed everywhere.

Lantor caught the other centurion, as he, too, had cleanly sliced a warrior's head from his body and had just driven his sword through another.

Three of his original ten fell quickly.

Orun had also witnessed the slaying and yelled over to Lantor, "*Run!*"

Lantor hesitated; he did not want to leave his warriors. But the fourth fell before him, and the centurion came charging.

Orun rushed the Saurotillian. With full force, he rammed the centurion and knocked it toward the treasure mound: "*Run!*" he shouted again.

Lantor turned and fled the cavern. The two centurions ignored the remaining warriors and fell into pursuit, with the warriors not far behind. But unfortunately, human warriors could not match the stride of a Saurotillian.

Lantor had quickly disappeared down one of the tunnels.

Soon, the cavern died into a silent and deathly still graveyard.

And soon after the stillness had overtaken the once chaotic cavern, a lone warrior found his way into the cavern and frantically searched the area. When he noticed that the orb was missing, he took off down the tunnel.

Somewhere deeper in the dark tunnels, a dragon growled. A black dragon. With deep golden eyes.

A gentle hand reached up and stroked the scaly chin. "There, there my pet," the soothing voice appeased the black beast. "That orb is not going anywhere. Let us be patient, for the wielder will soon arrive."

Chapter 14

P.D. 82, A.F. 8130

Stith Hackmoore stood in the hall of Strong Tower early the next morning. His rough, unshaved face was frozen, poised in a look of disgust as he fixed his dark, piercing brown eyes on the far wall, where several testamentors quietly conversed with one another. Scattered about the rest of the hall were a handful of individual testamentors. Each had a writing utensil in hand, scratching about relentlessly across piles of parchments as they hurriedly transformed thoughts to history. The sound absolutely made his skin crawl.

Without looking up from the parchment that he was absorbed in, Krhan addressed him. "Leave them to their work."

But the lead warrior ignored his lord. "What do you suppose they are scribbling about us?"

"Nothing that concerns us," Krhan said, suggesting he drop the subject.

"But it does." Stith spun on his boots. "I want to make sure they get it right."

Krhan only peered over the top edge of his parchment and scrutinized Stith's disapproval.

"And they will," a timid voice said, stealing the lord's thoughts. "I am, at this very moment, collecting our very words."

"Best be collecting those reports for Lord Krhan," Stith sternly rebuked.

"He is my big friend." Krhan addressed his lead. "Now leave him to do his job," he ordered. "Besides, most if not all their scribbling deals with the wielder."

Stith took a moment to calm. "I apologize, my lord. It's this damn waiting that's got me crawling." His large, gloved hand tightened harder around the handle of his sword, visibly apprehensive for some physical action.

Watching him now, Krhan spoke easily. "Relax, my good friend. All will be fine."

"I should have gone with Orego," he said sounding discontented.

"No, your place is here, with your lord," Krhan reminded him, "keeping me apprised of your respective responsibilities regarding the orb and its successful return."

"Exactly why I should be there," he protested, "should Orego fail."

"And he will not," came a voice from across the hall.

Everyone but Krhan spied the lone warrior and followed him and as he made his way through a maze of tables and chairs, finally coming to a rest near Lord Krhan's side. "The wielder left late last night," he informed them.

"Excellent, Oriff," Krhan said optimistically. "And he left alone?"

"Yes, I have seen to that personally," Oriff smiled sinisterly.

"Good." Krhan understood. "We wouldn't want our valuable wielder to have any distractions—other than ours." He grinned menacingly. "By the way, did you make the stop at the meal room and order our morning's proportions?" Krhan reminded him of one of the most important items among his morning tasks.

"After a tidy sum of persuasion was left with them, I'd say that's one off the list that has been accomplished. They are on their way." He smiled proudly in response to the lord's request.

"Most excellent," Krhan said as he stood up and threw the parchment to the pile of others. "I'm starved and done studying for now," he commented.

But Dorzak and Plaim kept right on devouring word after word until the morning meal would arrive.

"I'm glad that you're starved," Stith said, still discontented with the morning.

"What burrowers got him?" Oriff looked to his lord for an explanation, using an old saying that conjured a nasty little parasite that burrowed through one's flesh, causing irritation, suffering, and pain.

"Everything." Krhan smiled. "He is just outwardly expressing what we are all inwardly feeling," he added cleverly. But he noticed their stares needed a bit more reassuring. "Now look," he started, "we are clearly in control here, and we will be so until our team arrives back here with that orb."

"We're not going to be able to control the wielder," Stith grumbled.

"Right," Krhan agreed, "but we can control his path."

"Andellynn and Orego will see to that," Oriff said, reinforcing the plan.

But Stith was still not satisfied with that reply.

"It's just the waiting game," Krhan said. "So, for now, I suggest we get back to Urlon's business, so we have a handle on what we're about to take control of." He glanced back and forth between his two warriors. Just then, the lord spied the approach he had been waiting for. "Oriff, please save my meal, for I shall return shortly."

Oriff and Stith turned their attention to the arrival of the messenger. Oriff returned Krhan a nod of acknowledgement, and they watched their lord accompany the messenger through the hall and up the stairways, where he eventually disappeared toward the upper parts of the tower. Stith treated Oriff to an ominous stare.

"Now," a resting lord asked, "how did Nolan take the offer?"

Tonelia smiled under puffy, sleepless eyes. "As you would have expected."

"Stubborn as always." He forced a smile, and then Tonelia witnessed the momentary grimace of pain flash across his face, but she could also see the deeper one behind his eyes.

"How will you feel with him so close now?" She leaned out over the bed to him from her chair.

"It's not me I would be concern with." He reached for her hand, and she offered it freely.

Tonelia remained silent, but she returned him a small, warm smile for she knew his thoughts.

"We'll make this work." He tightened his grip with hers. "We'll have to at all costs," he added. Now she forced a bigger smile, but he was not convinced. "Come now, what was discussed?"

Tonelia released his hands and leaned back in her chair. She reran the night's events and closed her irritated eyes. "It's just another job for him." She tried to brush off the conversation.

"He hasn't changed." He chuckled.

"And be thankful for that." Tonelia opened her eyes and stared into his.

Baylor understood all too well what she was driving at and remained calm, even though his head ached, and so did most everything else.

"Well, it is not like we had to make him this offer. He needs to retrieve the orb in any event," she said.

"Yes," Baylor responded apprehensively. "He has had his fair share of bribes and proposals, and this is mostly likely not the first. But we'll make sure it is the last time he gets an offer like this," he said clearly.

"You should rest now," she said. "You were badly wounded, but there is hopefulness from our physicians."

Baylor forced a small smile. "I will in just a bit." His eyes half opened as he studied her face. The worry and concern were clearly visible. But those hazel eyes could not hide the deceitful acts, and this one concerned him the most. He cursed behind his lips for allowing that dragon a good contact with his left shoulder. It had thrown him several feet from his windbred.

While he lay unconscious, the dragon had made quick meals of several of Urlon's finest warriors before wrecking the wagon and dislodging the orb from its protective crate. "Protective crate," he vented under his mustache. "Treaty." He cursed. "How did it know?"

"What?" Tonelia sprung to life after having dozed off.

"Nothing." he smiled. "Go back to sleep."

"I know that this didn't go as planned." She ignored his request and tried for reassurance. "But it was a necessity."

"And you believe that she is ready?" he inquired.

"It's not her who needs to be ready." She eyed him through a sleepy glaze.

Baylor scoffed under his breath. "He'll never make himself ready."

"Well, this time he will have to," Tonelia dismissed the thought.

"Let's just make sure he makes it back with the orb before we get everything ready," Baylor warned. There was a long pause of great concern between them.

"Laiaden will aid where he needs to," Baylor confirmed. "He needs to start rethinking his kingdom's future."

"And this will be a very promising beginning." Tonelia tried for optimism.

"But it will still take many seasons to accomplish," Baylor said from behind closed eyes.

"Many that you'll be around to help with." She returned promising words.

"If Krhan or those Saurotillians don't do me in first," he responded.

"I have them all under control."

"I had no worries about that."

There was a rap at the door. A second later, it swung halfway open, and in stepped Lord Toranden. "We apologize for the intrusion."

"No apology needed for you, Toranden." Tonelia smiled. "You were expected."

"And what of me?" a tall slender lord stepped out from Toranden's shadow and quickly covered ground as he made his way to Baylor's bedside. "How's the good lord?" He tried to sound sympathetic.

"You reptile!" she lashed out. "You weren't summoned here just for a social visit!"

"I'm fine." Baylor raised a hand for peace. "Now we need to clear a few issues here." He addressed Krhan as the lord propped himself up against the pillows.

"Why of course," Krhan responded cheerfully. "And what shall we clear?"

"The air of your foul stench for starters," Toranden said amusedly, taking his place next to Tonelia.

"Why, I'm not the one who smells of Thalls," Krhan retorted whimsically.

"And like you're any better being down wind of Sauros?" Toranden snarled back.

"Enough." Tonelia jumped from her chair and leveraged herself between them.

"Yes," Baylor interceded, "those rather rude tongue flickers need to be part of this conversation," he candidly pointed out.

"Apologies, please," Toranden addressed the lady and Baylor.

"Lord Krhan," Tonelia started, "it is imperative that we understand one another."

"Agreed," he answered.

"Just what where your plans for Lord Vax?" Baylor inquired.

"Well, since you felt the need to leave me out of your eventful meeting with Lord Laiaden," Krhan said, "why should I share my thoughts on dealing with them?"

Tonelia took a few steps toward Krhan. "Lord Baylor and I meant to leave you from that first meeting for good reasons."

"Just as I meant to leave you out of my dealings with Sauros." Krhan grinned back.

"Please." Baylor raised his hand again. "Allow us to continue."

There was a reluctant pause from Krhan, and then he waved it off. "Fine."

"We felt a meeting alone without your presence would aid us in a first comfortable impression with the Lord of Illenwell," Tonelia explained.

"But I know him personally," Krhan protested.

"We know," Tonelia clarified. "And that is precisely what concerns us the most."

"So, we lack trust here?" Krhan replied.

"We lack communication," Tonelia stated. "But you would have been present at the next set of meetings."

"We just didn't want any awkward moments between us," Baylor added.

"Oh, how so?" Krhan asked defensively.

"Well, you could have persuaded him toward different views on this treaty then we would have intended," Baylor responded.

"And that's where you are sadly mistaken," Krhan retorted. "Come now, you take me for one of those sunbaked scale heads. I want nothing less than to see treaties strengthen our kingdoms."

"Yes, and we all understand well enough what that would entail?" Toranden stated the obvious.

"Why, the same thing that our dear wielder wants to accomplish with that testament of his." Krhan chuckled.

"Yes, but to which advantage?" Tonelia inquired.

"Why, to all of our advantages," Krhan bellowed. "Isn't that the testament?" He looked puzzled. "Finally, after some eight thousand seasons, there would be all the orbs, united, under one strong and collective body." Krhan's tone was almost mocking.

"Yes, you agree," Tonelia said, "but just not here, under Urlon."

"No, you're mistaken," Krhan pointed out. "I clearly believe that they should be here. And I am doing everything within my power to hasten the orb's return."

"Oh, I bet you are." Toranden took a step toward Krhan.

"Careful, Lord." Krhan sounded just a bit threatening. "The foul smell of Thalls has clearly clouded your judgment from up there in your cold dark kingdom."

"The two of you," Tonelia pleaded, "for the peace of Lord Baylor."

"Oh, that's all right, my dear," Baylor interrupted. "I rather needed some entertainment right about now. It will distract from the pain." He chuckled and then coughed.

"I know what you're up too." Tonelia stepped into Krhan's face. "But Nolan is on it now and will be back with the orb long before your team ever figures out how to leave that mountain."

"If their still alive at all," Toranden murmured.

"I beg you, lady and lords, for this sudden intrusion," a warrior messenger interrupted them, speaking politely but visibly impatient with news as he'd appeared unnoticed through the open door.

"Yes, continue," Tonelia bid the messenger, never taking her eyes from Krhan's.

However, the rest of the room regarded the messenger with concern of bad news.

"From the southwest border," he said exasperated, "an emissary from Sauros."

"What?" Krhan almost jumped the messenger.

"That is to be expected, Lord," Tonelia said calmly. "Come now, when are they to arrive?" she addressed the warrior.

"Three, maybe four suns from now, Lady," he answered.

Krhan scanned the room and found the others to be just as calm as her. "Please excuse me," he said politely, "but apparently our little chat has come to a break." He bowed in respect and hastily retreated from the room, leaving the occupants to share inquisitive looks with one another.

A short time later, Krhan came flying across the walkways and down the stairways, through the maze of tables and chairs and aimed right for his little band of workers. By now they were eating heartily and were so engrossed in their work that none of them even spied their lord as he descended upon them swiftly like a dragon.

He flew right passed Stith, for he was leaning against the table with a plate and utensil in hand, greedily shoveling portions into his mouth. His back had been to Krhan's approach. "You're just in time for your meal—"

"Not now!" Krhan hissed and waved him off. Everyone else glanced up as Krhan came to a dead stop right in front of his objective. "Your job was to have them distracted!" he spat at the warrior.

Oriff froze. A large lump of food filled his cheek, and he appeared completely off guard with Krhan breathing hot air in his face. He chewed rapidly, swallowed, and placed his plate back onto the table behind him. "I can only distract what I can distract with. I advised you against this from the start." He defended his task, knowing full well what his lord was after.

"Must I remind you all," Krhan snapped, "that this acquisition of securing Urlon—or any other kingdom, for that fact—will only come about by the most disciplined, sharp, and tactful leader surrounded by a competent and strong team diligently working on the same goal." Lord Krhan snarled. "Success isn't just an option; it's the norm for us."

"My Lord Krhan," Oriff said, defending himself, "Urlon will not allow those creatures past the walls."

"That's not entirely true," a timid voice interrupted. "Urlon is in an auction state, and any lord from any kingdom can and will send emissaries to contest the right of the kingdom." Plaim paused, keeping a nervous stare on Krhan. "As long as they procure the orb," he added.

"And that will be us." Krhan grinned. Turning his direction toward Plaim, he walked over and patted his loyal watchdog of knowledge on the cheek.

"Now relax all of you," he spun on his heels and made for the food. "The orb will return here with someone on our team. That I will a sure you." Krhan spoke definitively.

There was a long pause between them all, and Krhan could feel the sense of confidence from the small band.

"Now all we need do is wait while I continue to work out other details to this acquisition." He addressed them all but stared at Stith.

"I should be there," Stith said discontentedly, for the last time.

"They will do their job," Krhan finished sternly.

Several suns later, Nolan had passed through the entire fields of *lade* production and now approached the southern parts of the Arthian Forest. Here, he would have to make a decision and stand with it. Cut up north towards Jawed Peaks near where Lord Baylor had been attacked or head south, toward the mountain range that ran north along the Unknown Kingdom and on to Solemn Plain to meet the last Zoarian. His decision would be directed by what he thought Krhan would most likely attempt to do. So, he decided to break from the west road and head southwest toward the abandoned kingdom and see what would become of that decision.

Feeling that less would occur on that route, he rode through the night until morning and found a good spot to bed down for a while and rest the windbreds. Some good, dried fruits and a salty stick of meat filled his belly. He washed it down with cool water from a nearby spring, although a good long shallow of *lade* he would have preferred. He took care of some personal needs and fell fast asleep between the two windbreds. But all too soon, his personal windbred woke him with a hot, thick, slime-covered tongued, and he was none too happy. But he was just as grateful, for the two guardians had neither seen nor heard much throughout the morning and into the early afternoon.

He packed up his sack and got in a quick bite to eat. Nolan favored his personal windbred, and the three of them continued toward the mountain range of the Unknown Kingdom. They were not far now, and the tops were just about visible through patches of branches and trees.

By late afternoon, he found himself riding through that last of the Arthian Forest that had stretched this far south. Still, there had been no one. This made him ever more suspicious, and he kept alert through his final ride through the trees. Soon, the way would give way to fields and plains once again and then the mountains thereafter. He would have better visibility of advancing warriors or any other distractions.

As he came up a hill, Nolan heard the clear and unmistakable sounds of clanging metal and shouting men. He urged his windbred onward toward the fighting. He soon found himself overlooking a steep slope. There, in a gorge below him came two fighters as they backed away from a warrior demonstrating some of her fine sword control. He grinned as the young lady just missed a slice from one of the men and drove her sword into the other. No sooner did he fall than two more warriors came from the foliage to her left. They showed signs of bleeding. This fight has been awhile, Nolan surmised. He noticed, by their clothing, they were from Lavenden, and that just did not sit well with him. They weren't heavily armed but were well stocked with knifes, spears, and swords. They wore no shields or helmets, but the plain green and black shirts with white pants gave them away. He surmised an ambush from Krhan to distract him even further. So, how had this lady warrior gotten involved?

Nolan's first instinct was to ride on. He was tossed, though, by his conscience—should he stay and either aid the young warrior and then thank her later, or should he be off and leave her to her work? But as he continued to observe the confrontation, the lady warrior jumped upon them, knocking one to the ground and driving the end of her handle into the face of the other bewildered warrior. He groaned and collapsed to the ground. Two more warriors appeared, and the lady warrior became outnumbered. Nolan thought the better of leaving and decided to grant her a hand.

"Don't you dare come down here!" the lady warrior's voice arose over the clanging.

Startled, Nolan remarked back as he dismounted. "Why, I was just going to get a bite to eat."

"See to it!" she barked back, slicing her blade across a warrior's back. As he hit the ground, a warrior jumped over him with a spear in hand thrusting forward in attempt to make her back up.

Nolan found a nice, big white piece of fruit and plucked it from the branch. As he wiped it clean, he leaned against the tree with his left shoulder and continued to observe the swordplay in the gorge beneath him. His windbreds wandered off and found some green leaves to nibble on by a nearby bush.

Nolan watched as the lady warrior was cleverly warding off the warrior with the spear while keeping her distance. Just as Nolan was about to bite into his meal, a warrior came blasting out of nowhere from behind her. With a quick barrel roll, she avoided the attacker from behind and rolled safely under the thrusting spear. However, the poor rushing fool was impaled by accident.

Nolan flinched at the site.

Gulping down some more of his fruit, he watched her break the warriors' spear in two, and pivoting on her left leg she gave the warrior a swift kick with her right. Her boot connected hard between his legs, and the warrior hit the ground with a grunt. Her sword finished him before he could recover.

Nolan was impressed. She was fast, cunning, and agile and well trained with a sword. Most likely the daughter of a lead or head warrior of some kingdom, Nolan thought.

She began to tackle what appeared to be the last surviving warrior. He had two swords and was giving her quite a challenge. They danced about a bit and drove at each other hard, metal clanging and steel flashing as the two circled each other. Nolan recognized this warrior immediately. She managed to lock their swords in the air. Then with one smooth motion, she pulled the dagger from her belt and plunged it deep into his midsection.

Feeling the man's pain, Nolan flinched. She looked up over her shoulder at Nolan. Then she pulled the dagger free and made an impressive spin, releasing the dagger into the air. Nolan heard the grunt from behind him. It was one of Krhan's men who had been sneaking up on him. He sank to his knees clutching the handle. He looked up at Nolan just before he fell off the ledge and hit the gorge floor with a thud.

As she made her way over to the fallen warrior, Nolan could see why she was fighting off Krhan's men. She wore a brown vest jacket over a black leathery body suit that covered her from neck to toe and black boots that came well over her knees. Some money sacks, a dagger, and a few smaller bags hung from her belt. Her sword was what really caught his attention, and it was very impressive—long, slender, and black, almost like her. And what appeared to be an orb on the handle's end. Her hair was braided long and black. Bending down to retrieve her dagger, he caught another glimpse of her lady features, hips that had yet to bare heirs. As she replaced her dagger, he also could not help but notice her full size bulging from her open vest.

"I now understand why you had to ward off Krhan's men." Nolan smirked down at her.

"You're mistaken." She grinned. "You don't understand why they had to ward me off first."

Caught off guard by the response, Nolan said, "All right, you proved yourself. Now, let us get our rides. These woods will be crawling with more of Krhan's warriors." He said starting after his windbreds. As Nolan grabbed the reins he leaned in and spoke softly into his windbred's ear. "Let's discover why she had to do that."

The creature responded with a head nod as if it understood.

"Then ditch her," he whispered.

After negotiating down one of the narrow passageways to the gorge, he got a closer look at Krhan's men. He made his way to one of the fallen who he recognized. He bent down to the body and turned it over. He was unfortunately correct.

"Orego," Nolan said softly and sympathetically.

"I apologize. Did you know him?" the lady warrior asked as she walked her windbred over to Nolan.

"Yes. He was one of Krhan's men who had been very close to him. I mean … he accomplished tasks for Krhan to keeps things quiet, shall we say," Nolan explained as he continued to study the dead man in reverence.

"But if Krhan knew he couldn't stop you, then why send him?" she asked.

Nolan stood and then turned to meet his defender. He was taken back by her smooth facial appearance. Hers wasn't the rough physique he had come to know from most of the lady warriors he encountered. Stunning green eyes sparkled back at him. She had black eyebrows and tanned skin, perhaps of a southern kingdom like Lavenden. But why would she kill Krhan's warriors? Grudge maybe? But this lady could not have come from the kingdom of Lavenden and so close to Krhan. Nolan was intrigued.

But before he could question her origin, she spoke as if she read his thoughts. "An ambush?" she inquired.

"Why, yes," he agreed. "But I am surprised. Orego was good with those." He continued to study the young beauty who stood tall and confident in from of him. Her small and almost pointy nose wrinkled in the sunlight.

"Not this very sun," she responded with a wink. "Fortunate for you, I was just making my way to meet you when I came upon them." She began her story. "They were still riding. I caught one off his ride and then the others turned to charge. I killed one more and injured two before the really good fighting started," she continued with a distinct tone of enthusiasm.

Nolan looked at her with a raised eyebrow.

"What made you think they were coming for me?" Nolan was now intrigued.

She smiled back. "Because I followed them for some time, and last night, I crept over to their camp and heard their plan."

Nolan looked at her with further curiosity.

"Well, I did say I was coming to find you," she repeated herself.

"We saw you emerge from the small orchard, and they knew where to catch you," she continued. "So, I caught up with them … just a little faster than I expected."

Nolan just stood there listening to her with that raised eyebrow.

"Well," she squawked, "it was either kill them for you and save you time or have you kill them and waste time," she argued her point.

"Thanks, but who said I would have finished them off?" Nolan questioned her.

"Because they would have stood in your way," she responded.

"My young warrior, not every response needs that kind of point driven into them," Nolan said, intending to educate her.

"At times, it seems to me that's all men seem to understand." She came back with a glare.

"Men?" he looked puzzled about her remark.

She bobbed her head back in response with a slightly opened mouth and retorted, "Hey, men."

Nolan slammed his mouth shut immediately. *Don't start an argument.* His training quietly reprimanded him as he quickly thought of his training. "Look," he turned to her, "you proved your worth," he changed the subject in a quieter tone. "And I'm grateful for your intervention, but on this job,

I'm not accepting any apprentice." He spoke bluntly and appropriately spun on his heels to leave.

"Yes, but you'll need me along." She was quick.

"Oh, and why?" He kept walking.

"Because where you're headed, you're going to need watching over." She blurted out the obvious.

"And where would that be?" As if all Anglyllon had not already known.

"Well, I need a recommendation from you," she yelled just a bit louder.

"I will have none to give if I don't complete this job." He could hear her now pursuing him.

"You're the best recommendation ever," she blurted out.

"Why?" He suddenly recalled Aquila's advice about taking on an apprentice. "Where could you possibly use my recommendation?"

"Auroria!" she announced.

He stopped dead.

"Please," she pleaded. "Give me a chance to help prove myself?"

He thought the better of this, but she was, after all, saying what he had been thinking about ever since he had left Aquila. Apprehensively, he turned on his boots to face her. "I said no apprentice." Just to see what she would do.

She defiantly approached him, "You'll have to kill me," she said. "That will be your only option for stopping me." She paused for the thought to sink in. "Other than that, I will pursue you," she added amusedly and walked right past him.

Nolan sighed and just knew he should have kept riding on. "So, you want to work for Lord Toranden, do you?" He stood his place.

"Yes," she answered eagerly but kept walking. "He apparently released his former lead so he could take the appointment for Urlon, which leaves me a wonderful opportunity."

"Yes, and he hasn't filled it yet either," Nolan stated.

"Why of course," she shouted back optimistically. "There's not many who will face a pack of Thalls."

"Why north and Thalls?" he questioned back.

This time she stopped and turned. "I've never met a Thall." She smiled at him.

"And you don't want to." He tried for persuasion against that kind of insanity.

"So, what is to be your answer? Will you help me?" She completely ignored his response.

Nolan just stood there for some time and sized her up. "Well, you just did a fine job polishing off some very tough warriors." He tossed her the compliment as he now strolled past.

She nodded in response.

"And you seemed to know how to handle a sword. And by what I could observe, you did a good job in not losing your composure." There was a long pause as he reluctantly continued to study her. "You're not afraid of a little fire, are you?" he finally asked.

"Nothing," she boldly stated.

"Nothing?" He shot her back a glance.

She eagerly shook her head in response.

"Not even pitch-black places and deceiving lords, scales, teeth … death?" He threw out the inevitable.

"Nothing," she said definitively.

"How about a really big and jealous half-crazy woman I left a few kingdoms back?" he jokingly retorted.

"Nothing, but murder will keep me from that appointment," she said sternly.

Nolan could just spit, for standing before him was an individual who just was not about to give up. *Kill her now,* he thought, *before you regret this. For even a good bang to the head wouldn't keep this one down for long.* He stared back into her eyes, and he was instantly confronted by three things he simply could not let go of—a woman warrior with a sword and an aggressive attitude and number one, worst yet, deceptively mysterious.

"Well, you certainly weren't part of my plan," he said to her. Then, with reluctance, he made a decision. "So, what shall I call my new hero and apprentice in training?"

Her face suddenly exploded into a brilliant smile of gleaming white teeth. "Andellynn from Cressaillia."

Chapter 15

P.D. 76, A.F. 8130

Tonelia watched from her balcony on the higher level of Strong Tower the marking of the sixth sun since Nolan's departure. Late afternoon wore on, and so did her thoughts as she leaned against the dry wall, arms folded across her chest clutching a warm shawl that covered her shoulders and left her head exposed. A storm had arrived, and for the last two suns it had pelted the city with a downpour. Her once huge canopy that shaded her from the hot sun now sagged and bulged with large sums of rain that collected. A waterfall had developed at the far end, and the maddening sound of constant water beating the floor still could not penetrate her concentration. Even the relentless flapping of loose canopy ends could not drive her away. As an extra measure, she even had one of her aides bound her blond silver hair into a tight and neatly woven braid just so it would not blow about her face. But no matter what Anglyllon's dark, gray, thick cloud-covered weather could throw at her, it would not deter her from standing her vigilant watch over her kingdom and awaiting news, any news.

Far below, the streets were deserted, as long rivers of water rolled down the inclines along the roads. The people were soaked, and so was pretty much the rest of Strong Tower. In fact, about the only thing the storm had not managed to soak was their spirits. Although, most of Urlon's inhabitants had taken up residents behind Strong Tower's four walls shortly after the Saurotillians wars, most were refugees from the surrounding destroyed kingdoms to the west of near Sauros borders. Without hesitation, Baylor and Tonelia welcomed them in to assist in the rebuilding of the crippled kingdom. And most, if not all, could weather all most anything after that war. This was just another season to make it through. And some, if not most, had their optimism in place that the wielder would pull through yet another job. If not, they knew full well that Lord Baylor would do whatever he could to keep Sauros from taking over the kingdom. Given the choice, they would accept Lord Krhan and his crew over Lord Vax any season.

Far below, a few brave folk and a handful of warriors dashed here and about in hopes of making their destinations before the wind could either strip them of loose articles or turn their garments into waterlogged rags. In either event, they made no attempt to search the high tower for their protector, who, at this very moment, kept them, her lord, and the wielder in the foremost of her thoughts.

She had wondered whether or not Nolan rode through this storm. And if he had, had he still met with Aquila, who she had sent shortly after he had left? And just how many more Zoarians would he seek words with until he reached Illenwell, if any?

What of Krhan and his mischievous cohorts? What distractions had they sent to meet Nolan with? In fact, she became more concerned about their welfare than she was about Nolan's. After all, he could always hold his own.

She watched the clouds violently swirl about. Thunder roared and lightning flashed about, threatening to destroy everything. It clearly reminded her of Nolan and their love, which had seen its fair share of weather—her partner, Baylor, like the helpless clouds caught in a torrential swirl of emotions. How he managed to share her with Nolan she would never understand. But she was grateful that he did.

Then there were their heirs, and what would daughter be in for?

Far below the unmistakable sound of a far-off horn broke her concentration. The horn arose again and made her straighten to catch the direction. It came again, clearly an announcement signal, south.

She stayed close to the dryer walls and made her way to the south end of the balcony. The wind and rain sprayed her as she clung to her shawl and made for the railing for a view. Far below, the horn came once more. She strained to see through patches of low clouds as they flew by uncontrollably. The rain was thick, hard, and heavy. It splattered off roofs and streets relentlessly. On sunny, clear suns, Tonelia could easily observe the four main roads and their corresponding walls and huge double doors. But of all the suns and seasons, the wide and unmistakable south road was particularly washed away and shrouded in a thick blanket of dark gray soup. She concentrated her vision down the road. Near the tower, the south road was completely deserted, and as she continued to follow it south, it disappeared, and both the wall and doors were completely drenched in mist and not visible at all.

She froze against the cold, wet railing, and nothing could be heard other than her heart pounding like the weather. She strained in anticipation of what would appear from the thick soup of mist. Would it be the wielder? Too soon for that. And why the south entrance? Just perhaps by chance he'd encountered Saurotillians coming with the orb. Or worst yet, Lord Krhan's warriors returning triumphantly. What if he'd missed that procession all together, for they had traveled south thinking they would bypass the wielder, who was still enroute to Illenwell. How would the city burn with so much water? She cursed under her lips. What if Nolan was too deep within Illenwell for a Zoarian to reach him? She slammed the wet railing in frustration. The stinging drops of rain assaulted her face and neck.

Far below, the noise of commotion, clanging metal, and the unmistakable clatter of hooves echoing off the road and reverberating off the buildings arose. As she strained to watch, the first signs of movement began to materialize through the gloom. Two windbreds and then a third labored through the pounding rain. The riders struggled to hold their rides straight. Two more emerged to the left, and then three to the right hugged the wide road as they followed next in procession. Tonelia watched them come into view. Rain splattered and crashed upon them. Ominous thunder added to the mix, and soon Tonelia caught the first glimpse of long poles and a ragged flag that wiped about uncontrollably. The group bore the unmistakable markings of a distant kingdom, and soon the emissaries would emerge from the darkness. Tonelia suddenly came to the realization that the warriors were acting as an escort.

Tonelia knew instantly what this kingdom was in for. She pushed away from the balcony and made straight for the hall. Down the stairs and through somewhat crowded corridors, she made her way, almost slipping several times from soaking wet shoes. Workers and visitors bowed as she sped by, treating each with a concerned smile in acknowledgement. She cut across a balcony high above the hall, and she peered down. There was an eerie dead hush from the court below. Thunder cracked and echoed about the hall while a flash of lightning added to the disturbance. She went for the stairs, and down she flew.

A few minutes later, she found herself arriving at the east door and coming into the hall. Out of all suns, the hall had to be filled. Testamentors, warriors, and business folk still came to wait patiently, continue business, and await Urlon's future. Still no message from their wielder and no sighting of Aquila since before the storm came. A large path had been cleared from the south doors all the way to the platform, for no one dared to be in their path. The Saurotillians had taken their position in front of the flat platform. Tholin, surrounded by several other key advisors, looked upon the party of towering lizards with tolerance. For even as the four Sauros representatives stood there, their height allowed them to be at eye level with those standing before them on the platform.

As Tonelia approached, she could easily observe Krhan's defiance; he stood tall and erect, keeping his two warriors from drawing their swords. Plaim and Dorzak still sat at their spots but had placed aside their parchments and watched rather nervously toward the commotion. Tonelia caught Dorzak's stare, and she returned him an unmistakable look of disapproval, for she knew all too well that they were more worried about the profits than anyone else.

She scrambled up the steps just in time to hear the last of the leader

Klax hiss at those on the platform with demands to wait until their warriors came bearing the orb. For unlike Lord Krhan, who started his investigation into the kingdom's affairs, which included everything from Urlon's progress in revenues to their finances, as much as Baylor and Tonelia would tolerate for now, Saurotillians could not even begin to comprehend what was involved. They didn't run their kingdom this way. This opportunity only presented them with more land and space to expand. They kept no records and had no use for money. And that was unfortunate, for in the before seasons when they were at peace with the Unknown Kingdom, their leaders were far wiser and more sophisticated and vastly educated. But as communication died between their species, so did leadership. And the kingdom soon fell into the dictatorship it was now. This would clearly represent a defeat in the internal process of Sauros, and all Anglyllon, including the Zoarians, understood that, within time, Sauros would eventually implode and collapse upon itself, finally bringing this country closer to peace and Nolan's testament for a unity.

Until that happened, the kingdoms would need to deal with Sauros as best they could, including this moment. Tonelia took her place on the platform next to Tholin, who turned ownership over to her, while little reds eyes of the lizards squinted as they all hissed in her direction. Long purple tongues, like snakes from a pit, wiggled at her violently. Saurotillians and their presence were nothing new to this hall. And if the talks continued for Lavenden and Illenwell to move their trade up the river, then they would be seeing more of their kin here at Strong Tower.

Dressed in their heavy armor and their long swords that hung to their sides, they stood erect and balanced on their strong tails. Klax held the flag with the crest of Sauros on it—a world with four swords struck through it—an old, tattered banner at best. It drooped in the dead quiet hall. The others, Daglor; Voth; and an elder lizard, Lorg, leaned on their long spears. Water dripped from their scales, and their armor shimmered of rain droplets as they stood there in their puddles. A trail of water led all the way back to the entrance, where consorts busied themselves mopping up the mess.

There was a conversation already in progress. And Tonelia, like everyone else could not bear their language, with those excruciating long hisses. It sometimes sounded as if none of them would ever finish a sentence. And by the uncomfortable looks from those in the hall, it wasn't a good talk at all. She could only imagine what had been said so far.

"Tonelia, you should have stopped them!" Krhan protested.

"No, Krhan. I stopped you. They are in our kingdom and have every right to be here—lest you forget that we are in an auction state. Now I don't like them anymore than anyone else in this kingdom. But if they retrieve that orb, the Zoarian council will grant them this kingdom," she blared out.

"Before or after you burn it down?" Krhan retorted.

"It wouldn't make any difference," Tonelia snapped.

"Why of course not," he agreed. "They'll have no use for a tower, and I could start fresh."

"You just try me," she volleyed.

Krhan stepped lively into her path, and she stopped suddenly and returned him a clear sign that this was not the appropriate time. "Look, Tonelia." He was quick to the deal. "We'll need to unite right now."

"Unite?"

"Yes, and now."

"You have your nerve." She was clearly hostile. "They're here because of your doing."

"No," he corrected. "That's on you. And right now, that mountain is crawling with centurions," he pointed out. "So, we need to buy our saviors a little more time."

"What's the matter? Afraid they'll beat you to the prize?" Tonelia stared him down.

"You need me." Krhan glared at her. "We need to stand together. All you have is Nolan," he added candidly. "Just in case you haven't notice, there are many kingdoms here that don't share your plan to make Urlon the center of all things. In fact, they feel that your closeness to Nolan and the idea of having unification may be clouding his judgment."

"Oh, like a more suitable kingdom would be yours, perhaps?" Tonelia snapped.

"Anywhere but here." Krhan pointed to the ground and glared back at the Saurotillians.

"We have as much right to the orb and this kingdom as anyone else," Klax said, interrupting their conversation. "Lord Vax has sent his own to retrieve the orb."

Krhan, like the rest of the hall, cringed as the lizard painfully hissed out his words.

"Then they're dead. and the orb shall be no trouble for my men to secure." Krhan smiled. He left Tonelia and strolled over to face the lizards, and it became one of the few times Tonelia welcomed his quick interference.

Krhan watched the little reds eyes peer down at him in utter contempt. Tholin flexed and tensed in preparation for a decisive intervention. Perhaps they would strike Krhan dead, thus quickly and efficiently eliminating an eminent threat. But it was not to be, and the Saurotillians stood their ground and allowed Krhan to continue.

"Oh, Vax thinks that, since you're all kin," Krhan went on, "the dragon will surely just hand over the orb and this fine kingdom to go with it. Why, he probably thinks this was the easiest gift of his life, a rare and golden opportunity at his talons." Krhan laughed with his arms opened wide. "When my men arrive soon with the orb," he continued confidently, "I'm sure they will laugh harder than I will, telling the story of how your warriors begged for the orb, and after the dragon grew bored and hungry, it cooked its dinner and had plenty of leftovers for the next meal." He fired off mockingly, "Say? Where is that big tongue flicker Vax? Why did he send you? Or did he go for the orb personally? Perhaps the dragon would recognize the orb holder and ruler of Sauros and bow to his bidding?" He chuckled at the thought.

"Lucky for you we don't like your meat," Lorg chimed in.

"No. But our tanks do," Daglor stated whimsically.

And with that, the Saurotillians chuckled among themselves. The sound of clanging armor reverberated around the silent hall as it jiggled about their shoulders.

"And while you're chuckling away," Krhan interrupted, "one of your cohorts is most likely, at this very moment, executing a plan to retrieve that orb and take out your beloved ruler." Krhan paused. "And perhaps that new owner doesn't like you either?"

Klax shrugged off the comment. "They have tried and failed for many seasons now."

"You know, I think someone's still a little hurt over a war that he lost," Lorg said antagonistically, interrupting the conversation.

"Don't be too sure he isn't trying to incite another one." Daglor eyed Lady Tonelia.

"Enough of this." She broke their merriment.

"Yes," Klax agreed, "enough. After we have secured Urlon, then we'll concentrate on making Krhan uncomfortable down there in his little safe kingdom." He sneered at the lord while their shoulders once again jiggled in amusement.

"Why, you …" Krhan went for his sword, while Stith and Oriff had already drawn theirs.

"Enough!" Tholin commanded. Around the hall, his warriors drew their own swords. "Not in the presence of our lady, not in this court while I'm in charge. And for the peace of our Lord Baylor, who risked his life for the betterment of us all, I shall not have it!" He drew upon his authority. "Now all of us stand down. And do it now!"

The hall was deafly still, and tension filled every corner. Krhan waved his men off, and after a fashion, when Tholin felt the hall had become manageable again, he gave the signal to his warriors as well.

"You'll have your table," Tonelia said from the platform. "Now take the large one to the south door. And keep it open," she ordered. "Urlon's lead warrior, Tholin, will see to your needs. And will someone fetch Merrith?" She commanded one of the nearby warriors to find the advisor. "Hopefully, the wind will drive you out and take your stench as well."

Lord Krhan watched in disgust as the lizards turned, their claws scratching the hall floor as they moved to claim their table. Those few who had sat there gathered their things and moved to a new table, one that was far to the other side of the hall and one near a door.

Krhan also motioned to his aides to find a more suitable place to claim—the north side of the platform, yet still near the center of the court so he could keep abreast of the affairs. After all, he would soon be taking over—quickly before anything should happen.

"I don't like this one bit." Tholin spoke quietly over Tonelia's shoulder. "Lord Krhan will try everything he can possibly think of to rid this kingdom of Vax's crew."

"Try as he may, your job will be to see that he doesn't"

"He wouldn't be alone in that quest," he pointed out. "I easily spy eyes from certain court members who are already plotting."

"Need I remind you," Tonelia whispered back, "that the Zoarian council will look in favor on our good treatment of those in our kingdom who have come to claim it."

"I understand that" he responded. "Best make it clear to the rest of this hall."

"They understand the consequences of their action, including Lord Krhan."

"Do they?"

"We must make do and give Nolan the time he needs."

"But that will take several passing suns."

"Then suns it will be," she said definitively.

There was a long pause between them as each locked eye and each studied the other.

"Lady Tonelia." A voice broke their private moment. "Merrith, as you requested."

"Thank you," she said to the warrior.

He bowed and moved off while the advisor came through the crowd. Merrith was an elderly man who had seen much in Urlon and Anglyllon. He was thinly built, and except for a few long white hairs that managed to cling to his head, he was almost bald. Long limber arms swayed back, and forth as short, skinny legs bounced his long robe about him. Tonelia did not catch the quick acknowledgement he exchanged with Krhan. Nor did she see how Plaim and Dorzak addressed him as well. For Merrith was, by far, the most respected advisor for not only Urlon but also all Anglyllon. He had an uncanny ability to produce vast amounts of anything from seemingly nothing. That meant *lade*, crops, and building designs and, of course, the financial as well. Countless parchments on all sorts of subjects filled the kingdoms and the financial ones that found their way to Plaim and Dorzak may just have unwittingly contributed to Urlon's demise. Lord Krhan had a special fondness for the man. That was unknown to most among Strong Tower, and the lord was just about to use that knowledge for his personal gain.

Merrith flowed up the stairs and bowed before the lady.

"Please," she addressed him, "we should give you the honor."

"You are most kind," he responded in a quiet and gentle tone. "Now, what may I assist you with?"

"You are, by far, more familiar with each and every kingdom than any of us are," she stated.

"One would believe." He was humble.

"That, unfortunately, includes Sauros," Tonelia said.

"That it does." He flashed a surprisingly polite nod in the direction of the centurions.

But they simply returned him more indignant tongue flickering from their new post near the door.

"Please assist the emissaries from Sauros with their needs until this matter can be quickly resolved," she said. "We will treat them as we always do. Send them to the stables at night and have the warriors catch or buy small animals for them to eat during their feeding time. Permit *no* drinking and eating in the hall. Finally," she ordered, "we'll have them escorted to and from the city for their other personal business."

Merrith nodded.

"I summoned you here since you are the only one, I can trust with this task. Only you will be able to explain things here to our visitors," she said, "in a tongue that only they will be able to understand." She looked to Merrith for a deeper understanding of the message.

He smiled and returned her a quick wink of acknowledgement. "Very well, my lady." He bowed and turned toward the centurions. "Come along then. Let's get started."

He addressed them optimistically as he strolled off toward their table.

"Is this wise?" Tholin, once again concerned, whispered over her shoulder.

"Until Nolan returns with the orb and dismisses them," she quietly responded, "we'll have to deal with them. Besides, if we treat them well, we'll have a better chance at the talks to move that trade up the river to Illenwell," she advised.

"I'll see that they are heavily escorted, everywhere," he added.

"See to it personally." She gave him a quick glance and then left him to inform Baylor of the new developments.

As Tonelia left, she did not acknowledge anyone, and that included Krhan and his small band. They had now retreated to a new location and settled down at a table that had not been occupied. Krhan was watching her bolt past when he spied a soaked warrior searching around the table they had just deserted. He immediately recognized Illon, his messenger. Krhan raised his hand, caught Illon's attention, and waved him over. The warrior was soaked, and his hair was pasted to his head and ringing wet. Water still streaked down his face, and several drops formed on his nose and ears. His sleeves dripped with water leaving another trial for the hall assistants to clean.

"News from the west road." Illon spoke quietly as he reached Krhan's side. The rest of the small band listened intently as the youth shared the report. "I sent a warrior to find Orego as you instructed."

"And?" Krhan inquired.

"He found them," Illon said, "dead."

"What?" Oriff questioned. He and Stith moved in while the other two took their places, laying down their armful of parchments and claiming their chairs while keeping their full attention on the new development.

"Nolan killed them all?" Stith asked, just above a whisper.

"They all knew the price for this objective," Krhan said.

"Nolan would not have done that," Oriff protested. "I know him, and he is better than that."

"But not under these circumstances," Krhan reminded him.

"Please allow me to finish," Illon bid Lord Krhan.

"Yes, of course." Krhan waved a hand, cutting off Oriff and Stith.

"There was a mortally wounded warrior," he went on to explain. "With his last breath, he shared his report."

"And?" Stith interrupted impatiently.

"It wasn't the wielder."

"See, I knew it." Oriff was right.

Krhan raised his hand again, slightly more irritable this time.

"No, my lord, not the wielder," the youth said.

"Then, who?" Stith was impatient.

A moment of hesitation from Illon indicated to Krhan that this would be amusing. "It was her," he answered.

The small group remained silent.

"A worthy death by a dragon or by Saurotillians perhaps, but not a girl warrior who they trusted," Stith protested.

"She is a clever one." Krhan smiled deviously, deep in thought.

"What are you going on about?" Stith fought his anger.

Krhan spun about on his heels and came face to face with Oriff and Stith in a quiet and tight circle. "If you needed to gain someone's trust immediately, what would you have done?"

Tension was thick in the tight circle, and there was a long moment of dead silence as each nervously glanced at each other.

"I wouldn't have killed my own brother," Stith finally retorted. And with a sudden turn, he stormed away, leaving Krhan to ponder the coming circumstances.

The sun wore on, and so did the storm. It raged all the way into the late hours of evening. The hall emptied shortly after all the commotion with the arrival of the Saurotillians. The testamentors would have plenty to scratch about. And for the first time, Krhan agreed with Stith; their scratching became annoying. Merrith instructed the escort to accompany Klax and his centurions to the stables and guard them for the entire evening. There was a moment of disapproval from the escort, but after a fashion and a handsome remediation from the advisors, the warriors accepted their duties more willingly.

Tonelia returned to Baylor, who was now up and eating. He received the news with little thought but inquired often of reports on Nolan, Urlanna from the east, and any other news regarding the arrival of their daughter. However, the weather had squelched any of that, and it only left them to continue through long agonizing suns.

Now, with Strong Tower distracted, a lone figure made his way about the tower and down toward the lower hall, while Stith had disappeared for the rest of the sun to give time to mourn his lost. Oriff stayed with Plaim and Dorzak, for they would most likely call it an early night and go off to find Stith and drag him away to a drinking hall.

The way was well lit, but the lone figure knew just where his destination would take him. He had been there many times before. Down a long hallway, across a few smaller open rooms, and then there, a large solid wooden door, he would find his objective. *I will get him started on yes responses immediately; that will ensure the agreement,* he cleverly thought to himself.

The wooden door came into view, and with it, a smile broke his face. The only thing that would damper his optimism now would be that his objective was still with his order. But it was late for that. Normally these where the hours that he would seek solitude to study and write. He also understood Merrith's soft spots; especially company and good *lade* were always welcomed treats. *He must be there,* he thought.

Upon approaching the door, he placed an ear to the cold wood. He heard the unmistakable sound of faint scratching. *Great news!* He rapped on the door.

"Yes?" came a pleasant response.

"Merrith, my good friend, do you have a moment or two to share some fine *lade* with an old friend?" He raised a pourer and tapped two cups against it.

"Why, yes, yes," came an excited response. "Always make time for *lade* and to hear how things are progressing there in the south."

Krhan's face lit with eager anticipation as he opened the door and slid quietly in.

Chapter 16

P.D. 74, A.F. 8130

Soft, puffy clouds casually floated across a pleasant blue sun as two lone figures approached the last of the forest near the south borders of the Arthian Forest. The warm, sunny moment was almost overshadowed by the looming mountains of the Unknown Kingdom as they towered just ahead. Two rides and an extra windbred had ridden hard and fast since their first initial meeting. There had been little time for conversation since Nolan needed to make up for some lost time. But mostly, he was still preoccupied with thoughts of Tonelia's offer for their daughter, how his uncle was coming along back in Itmoore with his apprentice, and how Urlanna would aid them all. And approaching Illenwell only conjured up a whole new thought of how he would deal with Lord Laiaden or, worse yet, how the lord was going to deal with him upon their arrival—depending on what part of the season they should ever make it? Whatever the outcome, he remained on constant alert for the next distraction—which may come from Sauros or be right there in front of him, he thought as he eyed his newfound savior.

In any event, he felt he had been rude long enough and now returned his attention to Andellynn and just what had really brought this distraction here in the first place. Even though he had been preoccupied with his own concerns, he had kept a watchful eye on his newfound partner and, at that moment, started to collect his arsenal of questions as they slowed to bring their windbreds some much-needed rest.

Various patches of the sun's beams cut through the branches and leaves like spotlights on the warriors as they weaved their way through trees. Their conversation would be more inquiring than idle talk now. Nolan had glanced at Andellynn's sword several times since they'd left, and he'd given not one thought more to his decision to take her along. He'd become too distracted with the artwork and metal carvings that adorned her sword, especially that orb of hers that was smaller than an actual orb and lacked the crest design that signified each kingdom. But most impressive was how the jaw of a black dragon held the orb in place and was cleverly balanced for the sword's weight. The dragon's head and neck made up the rest of the handle. And had the blade not been hidden in its sheath, Nolan would have seen the beautiful shape of the dragon, as it formed the entire length of the blade. Long, black, and slender, it was a perfect fit for the one who wielded it. Black steel was as almost as difficult to forge and was just as strong and enduring as his blade of gold. This led Nolan to ponder his newfound partner. But who had found who? he questioned himself. Still glancing back and forth between her and the sword, he knew at least that she conjured up many more questions. Only trolls had the kind of magic needed to form black steel. So, how had she had this sword made?

"Your sword is a rarity, just as impressive as its owner. How did you come by it if I might ask?"

"Thanks, it's quite a story," she responded enthusiastically.

"And does that story include details on that orb of yours as well?"

"Why, yes it does."

"I am very impressed with how you handle the thrust, since that would bother me and my wrist." He gave the compliment in an attempt to garner an explanation.

"Thanks." She smiled back. "It took some work to get used to, since it is rather large at the end," she explained. "But when you angle it so, I find it much more dangerous."

She amused him. "Well, it should. Only trolls make orbs, and one of them had the special gift of creating this sword." He padded his handle. "I wondered if that very same troll created yours?" He addressed the workmanship. "So, continue, please."

"Well." She batted her greens eyes at him. "It was gift from my father many seasons ago."

"Your father knew some trolls?" This, to Nolan, could have been a possibility.

"Somewhat. It is troll metal and very light to handle," she shared.

"No argument here. I witnessed it in action," Nolan agreed.

Andellynn continued. "The ornament was found while my father was on a mission near Claw Crag. He came upon it near one of the lakes. Said it was on the shore just lying there. Caught his eye as it glimmered there in the high sun. Mistaking it to be an orb, they rushed it back to Lord Toranden. But after further investigation by the Zoarians, they decided it was just an oddity of some kind and returned it to my father. I am not sure of the path it took from there. I only know that, on my fifteenth birth sun, it was presented to me as a priceless token of love and affection. I have been training on it ever since."

Nolan was satisfied for the moment and continued. "So why were you raised in Cressaillia … if your father was an archer in Auroria?" Nolan did not find it odd; he was simply asking.

"Yes, it's true, my father was an archer for Lord Toranden, but he thought it safer for the rest of us to live in the Kingdom of Serranna instead."

"The rest of you," he asked.

"Yes, I come with two brothers, so mind your manners." She glanced at him.

"That I will," he said assuredly.

"So, there is where we lived." She sounded content.

"Makes good sense, your kingdoms border," Nolan added. "I rather like Cressaillia. It's one of the smaller cities of Serranna, is it not?" Nolan knew the right answer.

"Why, yes," she replied. "And what brings you there? That kingdom hasn't seen any trouble there in quite a few seasons." She pondered.

"No," said Nolan, "you're correct. There hasn't been any trouble there in a long season for a matter of fact."

"Good." She grinned back. "Let's leave it that way." She continued to watch the woods ahead.

"What is your father's name? I am most familiar with just about all the warriors in North Avalore and Serranna." Nolan looked over to her.

"Lorse Hodden. But he was killed many seasons back," she added longingly.

"Sorry to hear. I knew of him. He was one of Toranden's finest archers. And I knew of his family." He watched to see if that triggered a response.

"You knew us?" She gave him a look.

"I knew of them," he clarified, "but never actually met any of you."

She seemed relieved and then returned her attention back to the woods.

"What happened?" he inquired.

She reflected for a moment and then went on, "Thall attack in Loxe Woods right near Loxe Pass," she explained. "They fought all night." She continued to look ahead, lost in a distance trance. "He was one of the many who did not come back." Her voice trailed off.

Nolan connected with equal remorse at the lost. Thalls take with them all the dead. "Again, I'm sorry for your loss," he added sympathetically.

She smiled appreciatively as they rode on silently for quite some time, each lost in reflective moments. The trees soon disappeared and gave way to a vast rolling field.

Flowers of different sorts and colors all competed for a traveler's eye. Bugs and small ground-dwelling rodents scattered and scurried away from the approaching intruders, who paid no attention to them. An occasional bee would buzz them with interest until a gentle breeze blew the little annoyance away. The two never admired the lush field of flowers that appeared to bow in reverence, caused by the gentle wind as it rolled across it like a big wave. The next wave followed, but it too went unnoticed.

Nolan saw the sun begin its descent toward the mountains, alerting him their sun was almost complete. Soon, their trail would be the dry rocky road to the mountains. He spoke to his partner some more.

"Whom did you study with? Your style and form are excellent. A few of your moves I have seen before and others that are new."

"It won't matter after I get done learning from the best," she replied, diverting the question.

Clever, thought Nolan.

But before he could get his answer another way, she blindsided him with her own question. "What is your plan for Illenwell, if I might ask?"

Nolan smiled and played along. "I'll have a better sense when we arrive."

"Go on," she inquired.

"Very well then." He paused, "We'll go straight in and attack the dragon."

"Excellent move!" she blurted out. "I'll go for the orb while it chases you around."

"Ah, no that's your job," he retorted whimsically.

"Mine?"

"Well, you're the one wanting apprenticeship." He smiled.

"The things an apprentice has to accomplish around here," she said amusedly. "What else?" she jested. "Cooking?"

"Why, yes, because I'm hungry."

"Before we eat," she broke his thought, "how did Lord Baylor come to lose the orb to the dragon?"

"I didn't say he lost his orb."

"We are going to save Lord Laiaden's orb?" She sounded confused.

"No, not this time." Nolan chuckled and then, after a pause, "Lord Baylor's."

"See, I was right!" She almost jerked her windbred about. "When did that sneaky Illenwell lord steal Baylor's orb?" She gave the wielder both green eyes wide and ready. But before Nolan could respond, "Better yet, how did he accomplish that feat with the dragon and all?" She hungered for gossip.

Nolan just chuckled back again, and said, "Oh … he bribed a Taulian to send that dragon." Then he stopped in anticipation of her response. Surprisingly, none came. She just sat there deep in thought for a moment.

"The dragon of Illenwell," she said quietly. "Sounds like I will get that appointment after all." She smiled. "What do you think the other warriors will say when they hear I helped Nolan Hammer, wielder of the golden sword, tackle a dragon, retrieve an orb, and save a lord and his kingdom— not to mention Toranden's response," she added, savoring the glory.

Nolan almost immediately understood the young apprentice's need to join him. Her father was close to Lord Toranden and could easily have given the command for his daughter to be among the warriors. But that was probably unacceptable for this young inspiring wannabe. So, Nolan now knew she would have to come along in order to gain her respect before the warriors of North Avalore and old Toranden himself. Besides, Nolan knew that any recommendation he would give was as good as his sword of gold and the honor that went with it.

Nolan stared at her as she gleamed, looking up to the sky. A triumphant smile broke upon her face as she visualized herself in the city's court of Auroria, cheered and hailed. For not since many a season had a woman warrior been so treated.

"Ah, so that's why you're along." He interrupted her fantasy. "Did you think this would grant you some kind of glory?"

"Perhaps?" she questioned. "So why aren't we moving faster?" She urged him on.

"Well, my young dark apprentice," he blurted out as he continued to study her, "you do completely understand just who is foolish enough to go in there and steal that orb?"

"We are of course," she fired back.

"That is correct. And I'm just not in any hurry to go rushing right in there at this moment to say hello to some big creature."

"And that is why you are going to need me." She smiled. "I'll be there for your support."

"Yes, but what exactly are your deeper motives here, the orb or the recommendations?" he probed.

"Nolan Hammer!" She immediately pulled her windbred to a stop. "You jabbed, and it hurt." She shot him an extremely hurtful look that took Nolan by surprise. But then her perfect face broke with a warm giggle. "I'm here so those testamentors get it right when they ask me to share my story."

"Ah, the glory," he said.

"No, you're right, the recommendation," she said amusedly.

"Better that recommendation than a sword in our backs." He punched back. "Someone is up to something"—he changed the subject back to a more serious tone— "somewhere, somehow. I hope this is not a trap." He eyed her. "But someone is counting on me and/or us to retrieve that orb." He paused. But who?" he pondered.

Andellynn only responded with an inquisitive move of her eyebrow as she urged her windbred ahead of his.

They rode hard the rest of the sun until the once peaceful field started its gradual change. Within time, small patches of rocks and dry dirt began to creep in along the terrain. As the ride wore on, the patches of grass became the minority, and soon the two riders came to a rest.

Nolan and Andellynn stood there in the middle of nothing. The sun crept down toward the top of the mountain range, and they surveyed the landscape. Before them lay the long ride across the dry, parched ground that would lead them to the mountains that loomed to the west, and just north, the road to Illenwell would pass under the prying eyes of Jawed Peaks.

After a quick bite to eat, attend to personal needs, and give a welcomed rest to the windbreds, the two lone riders cut across the barren way and rode through the night, for it was cooler, and a starry sky aided in their plight. Nothing but the mountains dead ahead came within in their sight. Not even a ground dweller passed them in the glowing night, which passed with little conversation and no signs of opposition. *Very disappointing*, Nolan thought. *But it could be right in plain sight*, he realized as he studied Andellynn. *Or it could be just another clever distraction from what is really going on back at Urlon or further east and back home, where Vendoff is up to his plan.* Nolan tried to keep his head on where they were headed, but what was behind could be a bigger issue.

Before long, the warm sun rose across their backs and Nolan felt it time for a brief break, for he very much wanted to make the river and Solemn Plain where he would, hopefully, meet up with Aquila for one last report before the next nightfall, giving them both a good night's rest. For the climb to the mountains and off to Illenwell would have to be swift in order to elude centurion patrols that monitored these borders constantly. Lord Vax was on the alert for this trade to make progress, and that would mean warriors and goods traveling up and down their river—as if it was Lord Vax's to control.

The river of Randerend ran narrower where he was leading them and shallower, making it easier to cross over and begin the northern track up the side of the rocky mountain range. There were no small cities in this part of the kingdom—too far for the kingdom's warriors to guard against Sauros' attacks. Or worst yet, Thalls, which normally never came this far south.

They looked at one another, and then Nolan took the lead. By evening, as Nolan had hoped, they came to the deserted outskirts of the small kingdom once known as Solemn Plain that snuggled the river's side. Andellynn studied the ruins and the long-burned buildings that now just littered the land like quiet reminders of a war gone wrong. On the other side was the river as it slowly and gently ran south and emptied out next to Lavenden.

"It's deeper than you think." Nolan broke her concentration. "But we will not have to swim it, for just north of here is a crossing we can use."

Andellynn had appeared to hear, but she was clearly preoccupied with distance thoughts. "I have done quite a bit of travel," she responded. "But I've never been this far northwest."

"Despite Sauros and the Unknown Kingdom, the land is very attractive." He looked at Andellynn, who didn't miss the reference to her.

She almost blushed, but dismissed it, for surely their relationship had to be strictly on the job from here on out. But she did, for a moment, fancy the thought that she may have caught Nolan's eye. He watched her dismount, and as he did the same, he thought he caught her watching him as well. *Another night and I'm still alive*, he thought. *Best keep your wits all the same.*

Although Andellynn was his younger, by what he calculated to be forty seasons or so, there were no laws or decrees that kept a wielder from choosing her for a union. Why, it was common knowledge among Anglyllonians that wielders would often choose much younger partners later in their seasons. They would leave a faithful apprentice in charge while they produced and trained the next wielder—if, of course, the next generation showed any sign of willingness to take on the job. For it had been long established that, to force something upon such a young and tender mind, was not always the wisest move to make. He wondered if Andellynn did find the older warrior somewhat attractive. This would make things easier for Tonelia's daughter to accept him. Or was it just a fleeting thought of insecurity on his part? Nolan brushed it off and returned his attention to the moment. There was a charming ruggedness about Andellynn, and he pondered if she felt the same towards him.

He was a bit shorter with streaks of white just above the ears. But that only showed the age of wisdom to her. His shaved faced and hairless arms were smooth looking. Muscles bugled and displayed their every scar and cut. But he had hoped his smile and quick wit would help her get to admire him more. And as he conversed with her and asked questions about her life, he knew that he could quickly show his growing interest in having her for an apprentice. And it was working, why, he knew more of her then she knew of him, and that was the way he needed it to be. But he was in for a unforeseen side of hers that would quickly shine.

"Let's rest here. We'll be safe," Nolan suggested as he pulled his belongs from the windbreds. "We'll cross the river in the morning and take the road along the Unknown Kingdom, and within two full suns, we'll be close to the mountain and the dragon."

"Nolan, I don't want to appear to be rude here, but shouldn't we be getting there as quickly as possible?"

"No hurry." He smiled as he unpacked. "The dragon's got it covered."

"And just who has the dragon covered?" She looked very perplexed. "I mean, aren't you the least bit concerned?"

"How so?" he inquired.

"What if someone should reach the orb before us?"

He chuckled. "Many have reached it by now, one should think."

"And just how will they get it, once they reach it?" she asked.

"Well, we'll ask them after we catch up with them." He smirked.

"Catch up with them." She sounded a bit frantic.

"Maybe it wouldn't hurt them to lose Urlon?" he suggested.

"Nolan," she said anxiously.

"Look, I wouldn't be so concerned," Nolan said causally. "Nobody is going to allow anything to happen to Urlon. They have come to respect what Lord Baylor and Lady Tonelia have accomplished." He smiled at her. "Besides, nobody really wants them to lose all that."

"But how can you be so sure?" she asked, unsettled.

"I'm not sure of anything," he answered, attempting to calm her. "But perhaps, if anything should happen, then perhaps this country will see how important it is that we unify."

"But, Nolan, it's Tonelia." Andellynn knew what that meant to him.

"Perhaps an example would be in order." He studied her hard.

"Is that why in the testaments," Andellynn questioned, "those who have come to claim kingdoms are allowed access to the kingdom's records?"

"It wasn't always so," Nolan replied, "but as the seasons grew on and you lost your orb, in addition you became a public one. The Zoarians initiated that so lords would be more careful and thoughtful about the right they were given—to keep you responsible as it were."

"But what if this was all just a happening?" She pressed on.

"A happening my sword. No one provokes a dragon and drags it out of a mountain where it has been dormant for nearly forty seasons now without good cause."

"And that cause would be?" She inquired.

There was a long uncomfortable silence between them. "That's why we're here," he answered.

"But Urlon, Lord Baylor, Lady Tonelia?" She questioned the cause.

It struck a nerve, and Nolan responded, "At this point in the season, I would almost like to see her lose it for being so reckless." He made sure she understood his point.

"Nolan," she squawked. "How could you?" And she was serious.

"Hard lessons must be learned," he said, intending to educate her.

"And that's going to be a hard one," she reflected.

He did not respond. But deep within, he understood that this loss would mean the end of his testament and, with it, any young wielder from their daughter, which set in discouragement as he pondered the outcome of his choice. Nolan did not need to remind himself of his stand to fix this and certainly not with Andellynn. "Well, just think, my young aspiring apprentice, in just two suns, we'll be introduced to Illenwell's hot head."

"Nolan Hammer"—she whirled about on her heels— "how can you just stand there and insult such a magnificent creature like that dragon?"

"I wasn't referring to the dragon." He chuckled.

"Can't wait." She understood as she turned about and led her windbred off to the river's bank for a drink. Long red fingers of the final sun outstretched over the vast mountain range like a giant spider, which was about to appear from the other side. Andellynn studied the rocky mountain as they climbed up to the darkening night and hid the secret on the other side. Andellynn knew little of the Unknown Kingdom and its history.

In fact, other than wielders, and especially Nolan, most Anglyllonians did not know anything of its rich history before its founding. But it teemed with life—some of which Andellynn could only dream of. Others would cause her to flee, for the sword would be useless. Sauros enjoyed the sunken and enclosed surroundings. It offered security and refuge from the cynical world and its kingdoms. Plenty of hunting and land for the Saurotillians to wander about in and even, on occasion, become lost among. After all, let them get lost. What did Anglyllon folk even care for a Saurotillian? And what gave them distinction to judge and talk about Sauros that way? If, in fact, it wasn't for Nolan's periodical visits, Sauros would have no contact with the outside kingdoms—until the next campaign of course.

Andellynn shifted her attention north and left her thoughts of Sauros. She spied the makings of a long dirt road that rose high and over the rocky terrain.

"That is our course in the morning." Nolan came to her side, bringing two windbreds in tow. "It will take us north to Jawed Peaks."

"Illenwell and Lord Laiaden." she understood but never took her eyes from the road.

"I would very much like to avoid them at all costs," he replied.

"Another delay, perhaps?" She pushed for more details.

"One that I definitely want to avoid," he clarified again.

"But it's inevitable," she said so certainly Nolan just wanted to hit her.

He kept his cool, turned his back to her, and walked away back to the camp he'd started earlier.

She stood there a few more moments and then followed in pursuit.

"What if it's him?" she asked persistently as she came up from behind and then matched his stride.

Nolan confronted her with a questioning look.

"Perhaps, you are mistaken?" she began. "Lord Laiaden doesn't want the orb any more than Lord Baylor wants to lose it ... or the rest of the kingdom of Urlon as well," Andellynn insisted.

Nolan listened.

"Perhaps, he finally wants you to do what needed to be done all those seasons back," she argued.

Nolan was certain he knew not where she was going with this, and Andellynn could tell by his look.

"To finish the job!" she blurted out impatiently.

"What job?" he asked back, bewildered.

"Kill the dragon!" She exploded at him.

There was a long moment of awkwardness as the last of the word echoed off into oblivion.

Nolan studied her for some time, for that thought had had a passing moment several suns ago. But to hear it from a different perspective made him wonder what was really going to happen. "Well, perhaps you're right?"

They turned and slowly walked on. The rocks and sand crunched under their footsteps as Nolan explained his thinking. "Andellynn, I suspect you were no more than a thought for one of your parents when the Saurotillian wars started."

"And you were just starting as a wielder from what I have read of the testaments," she interrupted.

"I was extremely young then and should not have taken that job, so let us leave it at that for now." He made his point and then awaited her acceptance that the conversation was suspended for now.

He then returned his attention to camp, all the time sensing that she was studying him from afar, and that made him quite nervous. He shook off the feeling and returned his thoughts to what would need to be accomplished in the coming suns that would lead him closer to Tonelia's daughter.

They finished setting up their small camp and started a fire. Nolan caught a couple small tallears for the roasting, and Andellynn started to cook the few edible vegetables from the area in a pot with water and began to brew some good herbal harvest. A hot drink could be brewed over a fire and went great with everything, especially Nolan's favorite, tallears—little hairy animals with large upright ears and faster than all. Nolan threw down a large net and tricked a couple into the snare. Skinned and dressed, they were soon ready for the fire.

By then it was late evening, and no moon took the sky—just stars as they twinkled here and there, floating about in the endless blackness of space. The mountains continued their vigilance over the travelers. And Nolan couldn't help noticing Andellynn kept an eye toward them and never seemed to let her guard down either—as if the mountains and the lady warrior were in some sort of a standoff.

"They wouldn't come down that way," Nolan said, reading her thoughts and referring to the Saurotillians "But tomorrow, as we take the road around, we will have to watch our side for ambushes."

"I have seen Saurotillians. And yes, I've slain a few." She informed him proudly of her better past achievements, adding, "Yes, several times."

"Well, that's one training you passed," he said remorsefully.

"I didn't seek them out," she protested, clarifying, "We were attacked, so I understand ambushes."

Nolan did not retort but only understood the circumstances of his young warrior's defense.

"Of course, I foolishly asked my instructor what would happen if I had failed," she quickly added.

Nolan grinned. "Well, I would be with another then, wouldn't I."

She smiled and went back to her meal.

After a quiet meal and the last of the bones were cleaned, Nolan placed more wood in the fire. As the cool air moved in, they huddled closer to the warmth of the fire. Making more harvest to drink, they settled in for the night.

"Wielders are luckier when they raise children." She broke the peaceful night silence. "They don't have to hide them like lords do. After all, who would take a wielder's child for ransom or outright slaughter and bring the wrath of a skilled wielder upon them?" She spoke candidly.

"Oh, don't fool yourself," Nolan objected. "Much worse has happened. We are not above even the lowest of plans. There have been stories of kidnapping the children, if they're young enough, to be raised by someone else and then to cleverly become an apprentice and eventually a wielder."

"Why would anyone go to that trouble?" Perplexed, she asked him back.

"Fame," he answered. "You go about telling the kingdom that the new wielder is your heir, and fame finds you—and, of course, those undesirables who would like to finish you as well." He paused. "No, I think the lords have it right. I don't agree with it, and a united land will end that tradition. But, for now, it's the safest." He finished his drink.

Two lone figures drew blankets about themselves and shifted just a bit closer to the fire.

"I often wondered about myself," she reminisced. "Oh, don't get me wrong, Nolan. I couldn't have been raised any better or with more love than I received. But every child growing up can't help but wonder when they're old enough to hear the stories if they couldn't be one of those."

Nolan listened intently to this new thought from his young, wise warrior.

"To suddenly wake up one sun to the realization that you are someone. And you have been hidden away and referred to as one of those names." She looked at Nolan through a cover of blanket. "You know, flowers of a bush, petals on the wind, windbreds of the plain, and those kinds of names." She chuckled at the references. "Think of the endless and countless ways the lords have hidden their heirs and the numbers they had."

"I'll think better after we get some rest," Nolan said, cutting the conversation short. "We have to travel fast and far across that mountain range."

Andellynn agreed. And with that, they settled in for a long restful sleep beneath a star-filled sky, for the windbreds were not the only ones to keep vigilance again this night.

Thoan awoke to a pounding headache. It was terrific, a constant, persistent throbbing with each heartbeat. He lay there upon his back, sprawled out on the tunnel floor. It was cold, damp, and stunk of decay. He had not realized that his eyes had been wide open for some time since the surroundings were covered in black pitch. He slowly reached out with his left hand and only touched the dirty floor. His right found the surface of a rock-hard wall, cold, damp, and slimy. Something rustled just above his hand, and he heard it clearly shuffle up the wall and fade away deeper into the darkness. Thoan shuddered as something else crawled across his legs. He slowly forced himself to sit up, and his head spun wildly out of control. He groaned and reached for his head and fought back the urge to vomit as his stomach raced signals to his aching head. His hand touched the large egg protrusion on his right side and felt the combination of sticky warm goo and crusty flakes of dry liquid. "Great," he protested there in the dark. "Just how long was I out?" he whispered to another invisible critter as it shuffled past him somewhere out in the blackness.

Regrouping his thoughts on the last moment, Thoan slowly and painfully pulled himself up using the wall. That's when he discovered the large rock that came jetting out and most likely the one, he hadn't seen in his haste. "All right, what was I running for?" He questioned the blackness. No answer. "Thought so," he whispered back.

Behind him, a small glimmer of light started to take shape as he allowed his eyes to readjust. Thoan staggered that way first—down the tunnel and, finally, out into a larger one. There was a torch set high just above the entrance he had just emerged from, and another torch came into view next to an opening just to his right. He followed that tunnel until it came out into a long, narrow cavern. Stepping out cautiously, he peered down the empty space and spied the black, smoldering embers of bones and metal. "Oh dear," he whispered. "I now remember why I was running."

Pulling himself together, Thoan scrambled back the way he'd just come, this time more mindful of the large rock. Just ahead of where the collision had been, Thoan realized that the protruding rock was just out of sight, and he caught himself before he again hit it. Ducking, he took his eyes off the light at the far end of the tunnel and kept a wary eye on his granite adversary, avoiding the monster altogether.

He made his way, cautiously, navigating the rest of the dark tunnel until he came to a halt just short of the opening, and he peeked out. The passageway ran almost straight to the left and made some turns to the right. From the corner of his eye, he caught the unmistakable markings on the opposite wall from where he stood. The dragon's cavern that way, it pointed. "That's what I was rushing to." It all suddenly came back to him, and he hoped it was all going to be in place when he got there.

The ghost dashed, crawled, climbed, and jumped through long mazes and, thankfully, well-lit tunnels. All the time, he kept reminded himself to thank Ott the next that he got to see him, for the torches did their job— even though that wasn't what they were intended for. Ott just needed to see where he was digging and searching the caves. Thoan found all the markings that he had cleverly left behind. To the ordinary thief, they looked like nothing at all, but to the trained ghost, they were everything, including a time saver. For now, everyone else would have been lost from ever reaching the dragon's cavern. Finally, he came to a small tunnel that would lead him straight behind his destination and would come out just near the pile of treasure of Ott's discarded, unusable metals. It was a back way, one Vlognar and his centurions had come through. The ghost had not known that, but the burnt Saurotillian bodies told him he had missed a one-side battle, and he was relieved to see the dragon had been victorious.

Now in the cool darkness, the ghost felt his heart race with anticipation as he took a few moments to catch his breath before entering the cavern. He needed to be extremely cautious, alert, and focus, for he had no idea what to expect. He was not sure how long he had been out or what may or may not have transpired during that time. But he had hoped for the best; that was for sure. Success was the only option, and it would hinge on these next vital moments.

Thoan approached the opening. But even with several moments to catch his breath, he still felt the anxiety of what lay just ahead. The way was dark but not black, and he could just make out the first signs of debris as it littered the floor. Objects of silver and gold and crystals of all sizes glistened by the small, sparse fires that burnt around the cavern, leaving the entire moment under the ominous glow of red. Bodies smoldered and a few flickered with the last signs of flames as they fought to hang on before being squelched by the darkness.

The ghost stepped nervously into the opening. He slid along the wall like a shadow. The air was foul and stunk of rotting flesh. His feet gently and quietly found their footing, ever respectful not to disturb one little pebble, let alone the metals that littered the floor. His eyes adjusted, and he strained to see the ledge where he'd last seen the orb of Urlon. But it was just out of sight and around a corner near the far side of the huge pile of Ott's so-called useless metals. "Damn," he cursed, for he realized he would have to give up his shadow and move out into the middle of the cavern in order to spy the ledge.

Thoan froze. He scanned and scrutinized every inch of the cavern for the dragon or anything else that could easily be lost in the darkness. The large pyres Ott must have used stood there empty and lifeless, abandoned.

A variety of torches lined the cavern walls; three of them were lit near a large opening across the cavern floor. Thoan suspected the worst but was thankful someone had lit them. But by the same thought, that someone could have made things worse not only for the ghost but also for Laiaden and all of Illenwell as well.

He floated ever more apprehensively as he pushed away from the security of the wall and made his way deeper into the cavern, watching the ledge come closer into view. The eerie shadows and the torches barely lit the way, and Thoan thought for sure they might not have been able to light his path all the way up the ledge to spy the orb clearly. He cursed under his breath, for now he was too far out into the open. If he got caught now by the dragon, he would have a difficult time making it back to the small opening he'd just emerged from. Stepping gently and constantly scanning the cavern for any signs of movement, he kept his progress steady and sure. The ledge began to come into view, and he knew it was not deep, just a few inches, so there would be no way the orb would be out of view.

Thoan stopped dead where he was as the disappointment hit him like an arrow. A collection of objects, piled one on top of the other, led to the ledge, and it was dark, hollow, and empty. "Damn!" he cursed under his breath. It wasn't the vision he had hoped for. He was right about the torches, and that meant work. He could only surmise that they'd had the dragon chase someone out while the thief went for the orb. Since he had just met centurions, he could be dealing with more of them. But the last patch hadn't seemed to have been in any hurry to leave the mountain. Nor were they near any exits that he was aware off. So, this most likely meant there were others.

Now, he made for the other entrance where the torches were lit and peered down the adjoining cavern. It was smaller than the dragon's, and it was filled with stalagmites and stalactites. Of various shapes and sizes, they hung from the ceiling and formed their bases along the floor. Thoan spied a clear path between them like a small trail that had naturally formed. Ott had attached torches to various stalagmites, and they were lit, as if someone was lighting the way for him. He cautiously left the dragon's cavern and ventured off down the path. It weaved about until it came to a split. Thoan halted and listened intently, but his pounding and anxious heart was becoming a nuisance. He breathed deeply and then motioned toward the split to his right, when suddenly a faint but unmistakable sound echoed from his left. Frozen and poised, he locked his ears in for more evidence that he was correct.

And there it came again. He was right. The faint sound of a yell was followed by several short metal clangs. Sword fighting. The ghost cursed to himself, *You boneheads, you bring that dragon down upon us!* He sprinted down the left tunnel and on toward what he hoped to be the thieves. And just perhaps, they were either fighting among themselves or, worse yet, with fresh centurions. But all too soon, there would be an annoyed dragon among them.

As he neared, the tunnel began to fill with shouts, yells, and sounds of swords banging and bouncing off several objects. The ghost drew his sword and was prepared to throw himself headlong into the mix and find his objective, which he hoped would be among the fighters. As he came into view of a larger area, there were a dozen or more warriors jumping, stabbing, swinging, and just generally too preoccupied with each other to have noticed the new arrival.

Thoan scanned the commotion until he spied a young warrior who had locked swords with another older and shorter warrior. He was dressed in Lavenden attire—a bright green shirt with white pants—and swinging from his thick belt was a large sack that hung nearly to his knee and had the unmistakable shape of a round solid object hidden away in it. The ghost smiled with the orb thief in his sight. There it was. Now to get it back and return it posthaste—before that dragon could wander back and find it missing.

He lunged toward the two, but before he could arrive, the orb thief pushed off the warrior he'd been battling and sent him tumbling to the ground. Thoan leaped over the warrior while the orb thief had turned and was immediately engaged with a new opponent. Thoan was quick to pounce upon this most fortunate opportunity.

"Not so fast."

Thoan heard a harsh voice interrupt his moment of victory, for the orb thief appeared to have met a more skillful foe. The ghost turned irritably and resumed his defense, and it was a close call, for the sword's swing just missed his left arm. The tall warrior was joined by the shorter one, and Thoan could not recognize their clothing or kingdom. Unlike Lavenden's warriors, they were dressed rather loosely with mismatched clothing, and they were *definitely* not the Illenwell type. They seemed to be rather organized and fought as one. The Illenwell type would have dispensed with the shorter one by now, since the craftier thief always looked out for number one. But no time for fashion or origin. Thoan blocked a swing from the shorter warrior and dodged the thrust from the taller one. By the feel of this, it would have been a great challenge at any other time. But this was not that time, and the orb thief could be cut down shortly and leave the orb for his victor.

As luck would have it, though, Thoan glanced over and saw that the orb thief had been joined by two of his allies. The pair had come to his rescue, and Thoan watched as the thief quickly took advantage of this and bowed out of the fight, making his hasty retreat to a nearby tunnel.

Thoan cursed while blocking a swing and ducked under another. The two attackers were relentless, and Thoan saw no hope of rescue or tackling his opponents. Defending was his only option for the moment. He scanned the surroundings for an instant answer, but none was seen. Three dead bodies and a wounded warrior were scattered about the floor. Several other warriors yelled and shouted back and forth, for they, too, seemed to have their hands full. The orb thief was on his way, and every moment that

Thoan was detained just brought the orb closer to its freedom and the dragon's fury upon his return home.

Suddenly, and as if to answer his hope, the far end of the fighting area erupted into a fireball as the dragon, once again, barreled into view. Two warriors exploded into flames, and yells turned to horrific screams of agony. The dragon roared in defiance, and jaws locked around a helpless warrior. Thoan seized his opportunity while his opponents, guided by their need for the preservation of life, retreated toward the opposite side of the tunnel, leaving him to take off down the passageway after the thief.

The way was lit, but it was unknown to him. After all, he hadn't had the time to find every way around this mountain, but he must have been close to mapping it all by now. There was no sign of the thief, but there was no other way for him to have gone. So, he stayed the path as it weaved up and down. There were several turns, and Thoan was not too concerned with the dark hidden places, since he felt the thief did not think he was being pursued. Escape would be the thief's only thought for now, and he most likely thought it was just moments away. Just up ahead came the faint glow of a new exit, the light growing brighter. But just as he made his way, the thief appeared. He must have gone down a dead end and returned to see if the other way was free. As he turned to come Thoan's way, their eyes met, and he whirled about and ducked into the chamber just ahead.

A few moments later, Thoan charged in after the orb thief, where he was promptly whisked off his feet by two powerful forces. One, cold and hard, tightened around his throat, while the other engulfed his entire sword hand. Thoan struggled about, trying desperately to free his sword with his left hand, and when that became useless, he kicked persistently at his restrainer but to no avail, for his feet just bounced off the heavy armor.

"Look what I caught," the centurion boomed triumphantly, wagging his prize in the air toward his companions.

Through bulging eyes, struggling for air and his feet well above the floor, Thoan glanced about the chamber, which was glowing, with a torch high above a tunnel opening near the other end. There, just above two other centurions, the orb thief was cornered on a ledge and was dodging thrusts from his opponents. Thoan watched in fear as the sack containing his future bounced about uncontrollably, and the orb thief jerked about, swinging at the attackers. He finally reached down to secure the sack just as another swing came under his legs.

"Quit playing and finish the scaleless one!" Thoan's captor ordered over the clanging metal.

"Easy for that one to say," one of the centurions retorted.

The other centurion turned his head and glared back at them. "You quit playing and get—" His snout exploded into a spray of blood, as the orb thief immediately took advantage of his opportunity and sliced it clean off. The wounded lizard wobbled dazed and disorientated. He grabbed his face and stumbled uncontrollably into his partner, knocking him off balance and directly under the orb thief, who thrust his sword and caught the centurion right at the base of the neck. Both fell to the ground.

"*Aaarrggghhhh!*" Thoan's captor howled. And with that, the ghost found himself sailing across the chamber until his back smashed against the wall just above the ledge. The orb thief had leaped out of the way and tumbled down into the other tunnel and disappeared.

The remaining centurion jumped over his falling companions, ignoring Thoan completely as he followed the orb thief down the tunnel. Thoan groaned, slid to the ledge, and then rolled off and hit the two bodies with a thud. The pain was excruciating, but nothing compared to what might happen to all those in Illenwell should that dragon become annoyed. With that motivator in mind, Thoan rolled off the bodies with yet another groan. He struggled to stand as best he could, found his sword, and fell into pursuit.

The tunnel was long, narrow, and went on for what seemed to him an eternity.

Thoan bounced off this wall and tripped over rocks and cursed every way. There was no sight or even a glimpse of either the thief or the Saurotillian. There was no other passageway and no other tunnels he could find as he darted down the long stretch. His side hurt, and his hand ached from the grasp of his sword. He gasped for air as strained leg muscles screamed for rest.

Finally, around a corner, he flew out of the tunnel into a big cavern. He stopped short and spun about in the faint glowing light. One torch was over the tunnel, and there were two more attached to the cavern wall. The ghost was lost, for he had never been here before. He scanned the ground for tracks, but it was hard to make out anything in this light. So, he reached for one of the torches and pulled it free. Thoan pointed the torch toward the ground and started a wide sweep of the area. There, just behind him were the large claw prints of a Saurotillian. Then he spied the unmistakable prints of boots—long strides of a desperately fleeing thief. The tracker followed them through the tunnel and into a passageway.

It was partially lit with sporadic torches, but Thoan held his tight and bolted down the passage. It too was long and weaved about, up, and down until it came to a fork. He used the torch and picked up the tracks. To the left and beyond, he cursed and forced his protesting lungs that drained the cool, dark mountain of damp, stench air. His muscles were begging for rest, but he would not hear of it and sprinted after the thieving orb stealer in hopes of reaching him before that tongue flicker could do him in.

Thoan barreled up a tight incline and then came racing around a sharp corner. Suddenly, his feet struck an immovable object, and he found himself instantly face-first sliding across dirt and rock. Both torch and sword went bouncing off into the darker parts of the tunnel while Thoan found himself facedown and feeling the hurt. He groaned and rolled over unto his back and wiped his face of small hard rocks that found new homes in his cheek, chin, and forehead. Wiping blood and pebbles from his scratches, he regained his footing and found the torch, still burning near the wall's edge.

There, in the way, was the Saurotillian. It was facedown, eyes half shut. Blood from the throat wound said it all, and for a brief moment, he was relieved that the orb thief had been able to bring this one down. By the looks of the footing, the orb thief had made a quick turn and taken advantage of the incline and sharp corner. When the centurion came around, he must not have seen the sword as it struck across his neck. *Dropped him like a boulder*, the ghost thought. *Best be extra cautious as I continue on.* Thoan retrieved his sword and spied the rest of the passage and moved on ahead. *But perhaps the orb thief thinks no one else is pursuing and may have slowed down to catch his breath. I know that I'm dying,* the ghost thought to himself.

Using the torch, he now took heed of his wisdom and walked cautiously down the tunnel while keeping one eye on the tracks and the other straight ahead. Thoan noticed that the stride of his thief had shortened, and by the looks of his left foot, there seemed to be a drag, clearly alerting him that his quarry's left leg or foot may have suffered an injury. Perhaps the weight of the Saurotillian had caught him off guard as the beast had fallen. Thoan made a quick mental note, for this would certainly be an advantage he would need. there was no evidence of blood, though. *This could be a muscle or bone*, he thought to himself.

Thoan pressed on down the long winding passage until he had lost all track of time. He continued the trail, always in hope that the orb thief would be nearby mending his wound. But no such luck. And finally, he followed the tunnel into a smaller cavern and somewhere that he recognized. "Damn," he cursed, for this was near the west side of the mountain, and over there to his left was a short passage that would lead one to a small opening. But there were a couple more tunnels that branched off to his right. All of this area was carved from solid rock, so the tracks ended. Thoan immediately darted to his left and hoped for the best. He would double back to check the other tunnels if need be.

Within a few moments, he emerged at the opening, and his eyes squinted under the sunny sun. He stuck the torch into the ground and swept the area for prints. None but his were present. The ground before him also gave clear evidence, since it had just poured, and the muddy, dirt trail leading off to the woods reveled no tampering. Various pools of rain and wet foliage lay untouched under singing birds. Just down the trail and through green brush, Thoan caught a quick glimpse of a passing warrior—most likely one of Lord Laiaden's just patrolling the mountain's perimeter. That was a relief, but that also meant that the orb thief was still in the mountain and, worse yet, lost.

The ghost turned his attention farther down the valley, where there before him Illenwell stretched across the harbor. Some ships were leaving, while others came. There were quite a few that just silently bobbed about, while others hugged the piers.

Thoan's gaze soon fell upon the huge wooden structure that stood upon massive beams like some giant guardian watching over the port. Lord Laiaden's hall echoed words of solitude and seclusion. After all, Lord Laiaden did admire the ghost for his clear representation of their kingdom. He'd even said so. The lost parents, the orphanage—much like Illenwell and how it attracted the outcast and misfortunate. But here they found new lives and made a secure home for themselves among the harbors. They had Laiaden to guard them and keep the orphans safe and secure, much like the previous lords that had helped to establish this prosperous little hideaway and the characteristics that had come to make Illenwell known throughout Anglyllon.

Thoan sighed and took in the moment. He realized the criticalness of his mission. No more orphans, lost families, and burned homes. For some deep reason, the passion swelled in him to make sure that would not happen again. That dragon, which had become a symbol of security for them all, had to remain calm, content, and secure deep within the mountain. And that rested squarely on his ability to return that orb and wait for Nolan to arrive—as if he was going to be able to fix this mess.

Thoan shrugged at the thought and wondered just how close Nolan could be. The Ghost scanned the peaceful port one last time, for Lord Laiaden understood him better than he had. He smashed his fist against the entrance, snatched up the torch, and disappeared back down the passage to find that orb thief at all costs.

Chapter 17

P.D. 72, A.F. 8130

The distant screech of some large bird broke Andellynn's peaceful rest. The warmth of the rising sun was a welcome relief from the brisk chill of the morning air. But she became more concerned with the uneasy stillness of her surroundings and slowly lifted her head and peeked about. The fire burned nearby as it leisurely consumed a log. Reddish orange flames licked at the bottom of a small pot while herbal harvest slowly boiled away. Just beyond, she spied Nolan's sleeping blankets empty. She promptly sat up and adjusted her sight. A moment later, she threw off the covers and got to her feet. Uneasiness made her extremely nervous. The windbreds remained tied and motionless but none the least bit concerned about their surroundings. That was a relief. But it still left her with only one question.

"Nolan?"

But only the still morning answered her back. She grasped the handle of her sword. It was cold and lifeless, but she paid no attention. Her eyes combed over the open terrain. To the far east and, most likely, near the edge of the forest where they had ridden from, Andellynn could just distinguish the rising smoke of three fires, small campfires of one or two followers perhaps, most likely testamentors. She ignored them with indifference for now and continued her search. Turning west, she allowed her eyes to scan the mountains, and there just across the river and up high on a small cliff, she spied her objective, Nolan. Next to him, on a ledge, she finally got her first look at the impressive sight of a Zoarian. Long darkish yellow legs that were void of any feathers held the creature upright. Wings were affixed to its sides. A beautiful chest was downed in a coat of white that ruffled in the cool morning breeze. The Zoarian was thin and agile looking. Andellynn couldn't tell from the distance, but by the current standards of fitness, this one appeared to be a younger Zoarian at best. The bird's head and beak jerked and twisted about in conversation and by the look of things, they were just rapping up their reports. The Zoarian shook its head at Nolan's last words, and then he waved the bird on, and it took to the sky. The magnificent wingspan of gold and brown feathers found the wind, and it greeted Andellynn with a quick acknowledgement and flew off to the east. *Most likely to Urlon and report there,* Andellynn thought.

Nolan watched the bird, and then his eyes fell upon Andellynn as she stood there. Bouncing down the cliff and to the river's edge, he dove in and swam across the peacefully flowing water. It was cool but comfortable, and he conquered it with great ease, for he so loved the water. It brought back many memories of his Uncle Thaylor and his mom tracking out to Usseppetus River for some cooling off during the hotter production part of the season—such as a sun like now. He emerged on the other side and greeted his young partner as he pulled himself ashore and brushed off his agitation; he did not want to concern her about his present meeting, which once again, had yielded no solid answer as to how he should proceed. And this disgusted him further, so much that he could just spit.

Nolan watched Andellynn approach him and caught her eyes as they instantly darted from his chest to his face. She immediately tried to recover from a faint expression of embarrassment. He was pleased that he was catching her eye. The seasons of being a wielder had started to take their toll, not only on his body but also on his mind, and he'd begun to wonder often if he still had that physique that had so attracted Tonelia during their first encounters while fighting Saurotillians. It would sure help build his confidence when he finished this job, returned the orb, and finally meet a daughter well hidden away by Tonelia.

Andellynn turned and looked back over to the smoke. "Testamentors."

"Most likely," he answered as he too studied the gently rising swirls of gray smoke expand and fade away somewhere high above the far-off trees. "But they'll not follow us much longer."

"Report for the sun?" Andellynn asked the waterlogged Nolan. "Or a bath?" she crossed her arms.

"Well, the Saurotillian emissary reached Strong Tower."

"I'll bet that just thrilled Lord Krhan," she said.

"Not to mention the rest of the court," he added as he rummaged through his sack for a dry shirt.

"Plenty of fun stuff for the testamentors to drool over," Andellynn stated.

"Sorry that I'm missing it." He observed her once again glance away as he caught her staring at him.

"News?" She changed the subject and found their cups.

"News." He did not sound at all himself.

She threw more logs to the fire and poured a hot cup of herbal drink and gave it to Nolan. He gave a nod in thanks and then took a sip. Andellynn fetched a blanket and draped it over him.

He pulled it close and sat near the fire. "It's my uncle, Lord Thaylor."

"Oh, Nolan." She placed a concerning hand to his wet shoulder.

"The old dragon's doing just fine, health wise." He reassured her with a pat to her hand.

"But kingdom wise?" Andellynn was hesitant.

"Well, that's another issue," he spoke solemnly, "one which is concerning. So I hope Tonelia knows what she is doing."

"I'm sure that she does."

"Well, I'm not sure of anything lately."

"You're overwhelmed."

"That's an understatement." He chuckled.

"Why is there more?" she inquired.

"There's more." He paused and took another sip. "Lord Vendoff."

"I know of him." She shined. "He's always stirring up trouble for the East Kingdoms. Some story of an invasion from over the Morning Ocean that will threaten all of Anglyllon."

"Just another way of taking over kingdoms." He waved it off.

"But you did have an apprentice with you, didn't you?" she asked.

"Yes, Borth Nivenlos." He paused. "But I kept him there."

"But why?" she stammered.

"We both agreed that he could better server me and Anglyllon by watching over my uncle."

"Your uncle is the last of your family as I have come to known it." She sounded concerned.

"No, my family is Anglyllon. A lost orb and a kingdom in an auction state takes precedence," Nolan said. "My uncle understood that."

"I'll take it that this isn't the first time?" she asked.

"For me it is. I really haven't ever lost an uncle, a kingdom, and a good apprentice."

"No?" She sounded surprised. "A wielder of your recognition I thought would have been turning away apprentices."

"I have a rather bad reputation for keeping apprentices," he said remorsefully.

"And why's that?" She raised an eyebrow.

He paused for a moment as he studied her face. "I believe in visiting all the kingdoms."

"Oh, I see," she said, "and that means Sauros."

He nodded in agreement as he took another long sip.

"I turned no one away at Strong Tower," he added rather oddly as the thought occurred to him.

"How fortuitous for me." She beamed.

He glanced into her sparkling eyes of overenthusiasm and smiled back. Still working on why she was here.

He finished his brew and stood to change, while Andellynn started on a quick meal. Things remained quiet for the last part of the morning. After eating, they had begun to gather their things when Andellynn glanced over to Nolan.

"Who was your first apprentice?" she asked, trying to help him move on with the approaching sun as it began to warm the air.

Nolan smiled amusedly at her.

"What?" she asked.

"Well, you're not going to believe this." He played her to guess.

"Go on …" She was intrigued.

"All right." He paused. "Thac."

She just stood there for a moment to let the name rattle about her head.

"Andellynn?" the wielder looked at her.

"I heard you!" She snapped. "A Saurotillian."

"Yes." He was concerned about her response wanting desperately to avoid a quarrel.

"And how did the Zoarian council take this?" Her tone turned rather indignant.

Nolan quickly avoided the question with some quick charming wit, "It wasn't them that I was worried about." He said as he threw his belongings over the windbred's back and secured them down. "It was the kingdoms. I was all for it, and so were the Zoarians," Nolan explained.

"I know that I should agree." She said reluctantly. "They have an orb. Why not an apprentice? Or one of the seasons?" She paused.

"A wielder," he answered.

She studied him for a moment.

"Unfortunately, not," he responded to her look.

"And rightly so," she said defiantly. "The kingdoms would not have it!"

"Well, it doesn't matter anyways, now." Nolan said remorsefully.

"Oh?" She appeared startled. "How so?"

"He was killed." Nolan answered her.

"Good!" She said definitively. "As they all should be."

Rather disappointed in her response, Nolan offered a moment of instruction and said, "if you would only get to know them…"

"I have gotten to "know" them." She blurted out. "Or rather they got to know my blade." She grasped the handle and thrusted her sword upwards in a victor's stance and smiled proudly at her past accomplishments.

Disappointed further, he placed his hand over her blade and lowered it to the ground. "We need peace, and you need to get to know them if you are desiring an apprenticeship from me." He spoke sternly.

She broke from him and stepped away, "I don't want to get to know them I want to kill them!" She swung her blade in an angry matter. "I want to kill them on the spot as I have done in my training and while on guard duty." She was strikingly fierce in her tone.

Nolan continued with patience, understanding and tack fullness. "Andellynn, not every conflict needs to be resolved with a blade." He instructed her once again. "I understand your training and duties from down there in Lavenden under Lord Krhan and I clearly understand the culture that you were trained in. But this is not that culture." He pointed down to the ground to clearly represent a different time and place.

"There are many in this country," she spun around to face him with fire in her eyes, "that believe you to be too sympathetic for those tongue flicking scaly ones."

Nolan filled with apprehension and concern as questions began to explode in his mind:

Why was she here?

Who sent this distraction and why?

What are her motives?

Revenge?

The orb?

Fame?

What?

"Andellynn," he rose his hands in a calming gesture. "We must keep our heads if we are to succeed."

She stood there, defiantly for a moment or two longer, then, reluctantly she relaxed and sheathed her sword.

He watched her think through the thoughts, then a compassionate expression came over her, "you really care for them."

"Andellynn," he responded in reverence, "as a wielder and future apprentice, we are to care for all with absolutely no partiality." H stepped towards her.

Still fighting a deep internal conflict, she finally resolved to allow the matter to be buried for now.

She stepped passed Nolan and returned to her windbred.

And as she passed him, he could sense the calming within her for the present. He now understood the lesson learned and would be more attentive to his words and thoughts around her from this moment on.

"How?" She paused "When?"

Nolan understood her questions regarding Thac and answered her remorsefully. "Toward the final battle between Lavenden and Sauros."

"I'm sorry to hear," she said sympathetically. "But how?"

He paused for a moment. "By the sword of Lady Tonelia."

There was a long silence, as Andellynn did not move or say a word. Then she took her eyes from him, and they continued to pack their windbreds. He continued to scrutinize her for signs of a reaction. But she was cool and composed. They buried the ashes of the fire and mounted their rides without further discussion on the topic.

"We need to ride north," Nolan suggested.

As the hot sun pushed off morning into afternoon, Nolan held the lead, while his partner came next with the spare windbred in tow. *She seems to be enjoying this little adventure*, he thought. But he wondered what she thought of the whole mess. While he kept his mind and eye straight ahead and completely ignored the approaching ruins, he could not help noticing that Andellynn continued to scan the burned and hollow buildings that littered this once large kingdom. He wondered what her thoughts were but felt compelled to leave her to them for now. She would talk when ready. Right at this moment, he would rather have the silence in order for him to work out what would happen soon just over the river, and with the first signs of the mountain range just in sight, his hairs began to raise in anticipation of the inevitable.

"Nolan." Her voice broke his concentration.

"Yes." He tried not to be irritable.

"What happen to their orb?" She was referring to Solemn Plain as they continued to ride through the ruins.

Completely thrown by the question, he smiled. "Lost it back to the Zoarians."

"Why didn't the Saurotillians possess it?" she continued to scan the dead black cinders as if in anticipation that someone or something might leap from some hidden spot in a meager attempt to ambush them. But disappointingly, about the only ambushing was the eerie silence of empty buildings.

"When the first attack came," Nolan started, "Lord Ambernol had it dispatched to Urlon for fear it would easily fall into the Saurotillians' claws."

"Apparently he was correct." Andellynn stated the obvious.

"Regrettably so. The kingdom was still young. Many fine warriors perished during that attack." He spoke reverently.

"Does lady Tonelia own this kingdom again?" she inquired.

"No, but it is considered their borders again until someone wants to claim it."

"But who?" she asked.

"Someone with vision," he answered and then pushed his windbred on just a bit faster, leaving her to explore those last few buildings before leaving the last of the ruins. After that, she returned her attention toward a new direction and urged her windbred on with the tow reluctantly trotting along behind.

Sometime later, by early afternoon, Andellynn spied the small, abandoned housing near the river and surrounded by a few sparse trees. She had never seen this place before, but Nolan knew it well. For there, on the river's bank was a pier and a large, flat boat. It was made of wood and rocked back and forth as the gentle waves rolled southward.

Andellynn and Nolan approached the old house. It was surprisingly big. And from what she could observed, it most have been inhabited by several people.

"It was a guard house at one time." Nolan read her thoughts.

"Watching the river or the mountains?" she asked back as they dismounted.

"Both." Nolan replied. "However, it's been long abandoned due to the lack of anything of interest that ever happened here."

Andellynn did not respond as she scanned the immediate area.

"You can't see it anymore." He drew her attention out past the house. "But that is where the west rode ends." He paused. "So, by chance you need to turn around ..." He looked questioningly at her.

She only smiled back, and he understood there would be no going back for now.

They walked down the trail and led the windbreds to the flat boat. Andellynn saw the pulley system that stretched the width of the river. "Does it still work?" she inquired.

Nolan walked out over the boat and tried the thick rope. He jerked and tugged it a few times and then turned to Andellynn, shrugging his shoulders. "Seems sturdy enough. Bring the windbreds on ... slowly."

Andellynn tested the boat and then brought one on and finally the other two. The boat sank a little and wobbled from side to side. One of the windbred's protested slightly. But after the boat settled, so did their mounts.

With security reached, Andellynn freed the boat from the pier, and Nolan started pulling the rope. It wrapped around an old wooden wheel attached to a small wooden structure on the river's edge and then back over the river to a waiting pier and the other part of the pulley. It was built like its counterpart, which, Andellynn found, was surprisingly still intact. The pulley system began to immediately moan as stiff, sturdy lines suddenly bounced and came to life. Wooden wheels squealed as wood rubbed over wood, and old rusty metal parts cranked and awoke a sleepy river with a high-pitched tone. Andellynn tightened her grip on the reins, but the windbreds appeared to be unaffected by both the motion and the annoying noise. They slowly glided across as Nolan pulled the heavy rope through some kind of broad frame that held the ropes to the boat so it would never slip away. Andellynn stood between the windbreds holding the reins fast to keep them calm. They stood in the middle, while Nolan was on the south side of the boat. She watched the clear water flow under them, and she hoped nothing big would mistake them for a meal. However, Nolan had mentioned that this part of the river was shorter but not shallower.

The wheels creaked and moaned from lack of use. But they held as they slowly crossed. Andellynn caught herself watching the mighty wielder as his muscles bugled from the strenuous task of moving them across. But he began to fatigue and wane from fighting the rope. More than halfway across the river, he took a breath and gulped down some water. Sweat poured from his body, and his shirt was drenched under a hot sun. The boat remained still and waited for the wielder to take up the task again.

"Yes." He smiled at her, wiping away the beads of sweat from his forehead. "There were five operators at one time," he said, out of breath. "I'm surprised myself that this thing still works."

"We're just lucky to have a wielder at the rope." She patted the windbreds to reassure them. But it was more for her than them.

With his strength renewed, he took up the rope and gave it the last until they reached the pier. Andellynn secured the boat and negotiated the windbreds off.

Nolan shaded his eyes and took a quick glance toward the sun. It was still high, but all to soon it would start to fade around the mountains that now became their next goal.

They took a quick drink and ate a small meal of dried foods and then started up the mountainside. It was dry and almost lifeless. Small patches of shrubs and small lizards darted here and there. Insects of all shapes and sizes flew or crawled away from the advancing intruders. They chased the sun over the range, and before long, they reached the top. The entire way up, the wielder led the way, and nothing was said for a long time, for the way was narrow and they were forced to climb single file. He looked back on occasions to check on her but never said a word, only showing a small smile of assurance that gave her the answer she sought.

Finally, the top of the mountain range—Andellynn and Nolan took in the mysterious panoramic view of the valley and the ruins before them. The sun made its last warmth be felt. But before long, red rays of fleeting light would be all that would remain. Andellynn had seen different parts of Unknown Kingdom before while on various journeys, and it always looked the same from any angle. Far below them, shrouded in a cloudy mist and the dark shadows of the west mountain range, was the expanse of rubble. She saw crumpled buildings, the likes of which she had never seen before. Vegetation choked, strangled, and grew everywhere. The dying sun illuminated the ghostly scene with slowly faded light. Large and small birds flew and cried far above the decaying monoliths. The rusted steel poles of different heights and shapes bent their jagged edges upward like giant fingers silently poised to snare their unsuspecting prey. Endless roads crossed one another and made perfect squares throughout the valley, weaving in and out of the debris. In the very near distance to the northwest was the huge Mountain of Illenwell, and just a bit further, its smaller twin was faintly visible. Both stood there like dark beckons of doom.

Andellynn shivered for a moment at the sight, and the chill hit her hard. She returned her attention to the valley.

"Who were they?" She brushed off the foreboding feeling.

"Forgotten as the seasons," Nolan responded. "There is no remembrance of those who are forgotten, nor of those to come will there be any remembrance among those who come after them," Nolan quoted.

Andellynn looked at him inquisitively.

"A very old saying with much truth," he went on. "I've been informed that this world is ancient. Countless kingdoms have come and gone. Not a lord is remembered from down there. And despite the best of efforts here, not a lord or wielder shall be remembered during these seasons as well." He gestured.

Andellynn scanned the valley, and to Nolan she appeared to be remorseful for a moment.

"Be fearful of nothing, for a greater hand guides us. It controls all, and we need not worry. Live each sun new. Enjoy one another. Drink in the challenges and celebrate the accomplishments. Relax during turmoil. But be excited at endless opportunities. Love passionately and often." He warmly smiled at her with reassurance.

"But I thought there was none greater than a Zoarian?" she asked.

"No, nothing wiser than a Zoarian," he corrected her. "But I have my doubts about that."

"How so?" she asked.

"Well, they understand the law of life," he answered. "But they're not greater than us just because they can fly or have been here long seasons before us. But there is a greater," he tried to reassure her.

"Did the Zoarians know this kingdom?" she asked, still looking among the ruins.

"They did not," he answered.

"So, what happened here?"

"Well, somewhere along the way, not too different from us, they abandoned worshipping any kind of greater idol and god. But unlike us, they didn't wise up or home up to the fact that we're in control here on this world and need to take responsibility, instead of using the greater gods as excuses." He gestured to the sky, and then he found her eyes again, green and inviting. He so hoped that Tonelia's daughter was every bit as alluring.

"But that is a tough road to ride as well." She broke his concentration.

He was caught off guard and only returned her a blank stare.

"What happened to them?" she inquired.

He knew the answer since he had traveled beneath this kingdom with Thac his apprentice and several other Saurotillians, but he knew to keep it to himself and lead Andellynn where he needed her to go. "They weren't patience or tolerant. And let's leave it at that, shall we?"

"But there is still so much to learn." She sounded impatient.

He smiled in response to her youthful eagerness. "I've been told that the greater one suggests that you stay awake and alert. Never miss a precious moment, for one never knows when the crowning opportunity of gold shall pass by your grasp," Nolan coached.

"And Anglyllon wasn't built in a season, yes, yes," she retorted whimsically.

But before he could respond, a strong wind blew through their hair. And in unison, they both turned to the northwest, where they watched a massive collection of dark clouds begin to roll past the distant loom of mountains and crawl across the valley in their direction. The startled winbreds neighed and jumped about nervously as lightning and thunder announced its approach.

Nolan cursed under his breath, while Andellynn fought to secure her hair.

"Come. There's shelter up the road," he directed her. And with that, the two sped off across the mountain range and ever closer to the Mountain of Illenwell that was now engulfed by a huge, threatening cloud.

They rode north along a rocky but wide path. Just ahead of them, Andellynn saw the first shapes of Jawed Peaks. Woods and hills to the right and the jagged cliffs to the valley below to the left kept them centered on the road. At times, the road weaved in and out of the forest, so they kept an ever-wary eye out for the unexpected. The monstrous black cloud rolled across the north part of the valley, digesting the ruins as it tried to overtake its fleeing prey.

The riders pushed their windbreds faster as the wind grew stronger. Lightning began to illuminate their path with quick brilliant flashes, and then thunder came bursting about them. Nolan hoped to make the shelter in time, but it would be close by the looks of it. The last of the sunlight was burning away rapidly.

The advancing storm and darkness soon gobbled up what was left of twilight, and with it, the terrain changed to all rocks and mountains as Nolan spied the opening of the retreat straight ahead. It was a large cave in one of the first of the small mountains to make up Jawed Peaks. They reached it with in good time, for the sky went completely black and poured its fury.

A short time later, Nolan came into the mouth of the cave and shook the rain from his clothes. The dark, torrential storm outside filled the cave with its constant sound of pounding and cracks of thunder. Lightning occasionally broke the darkness and illuminated the cave's opening, and he wondered for a moment had his un-announcement given Andellynn a stir? Just encase she was expecting Saurotillians to arrive instead.

But he found her busy working the fire. Above it boiled a pot of fresh herbal harvest that began to fill the small cave with its intoxicating aroma. She had removed her vest, and her long black hair swung easily about as she fussed. The first few top buttons to her shirt were undone, and he couldn't help but notice cleavage that glowed by the warmth of the flames. He directed his attention to Tonelia's daughter in hopes of the same. Tonelia's vision clouded his mind, and so did the last embrace they'd shared just before he'd set out on this job. He touched his cheek, completely ignoring the cold and wet surface as he remembered her smell—like fresh lade blossoms on a warm. early production sun.

"Windbreds are safe." Her voice broke his concentration.

"Yes," he answered, realizing it was Andellynn, and returned to the moment.

"I caught our meal." She bent around and showed him a large cave lizard. It was fat, plump, and quite dead. "It never saw me coming." She smiled proudly.

Nolan loosened his wet clothes and moved to the fire to get dry.

Andellynn had removed her sword and belt and left them in a corner. She impaled the lizard on a long stick and placed it over the fire.

"I searched the cave thoroughly ..." Andellynn started to say something as he peeled off his wet shirt just outside the fire's light in the shadows. He could see her staring at him and knew she could just make out the large smooth arms and a nice, huge, hairless chest that formed into a small stomach that did not ripple with muscle but carried a little weight. His soaked pants clung tightly to muscular legs. And his sword of gold shimmered with rain droplets. He stepped into the light of the fire to place his shirt close to the warmth as her eyes darted up to meet his.

"Too much rich food." He smiled, slapping the little fat on his stomach as it jiggled. "Or age." He sighed. But in either case, he was still attracting her, and that was a positive sign.

"That's how I found our meal." She continued with her story while she stole quick glimpses of him. "He'll make good eats."

Nolan almost thought that she smiled at him rather passionately but shook it off. For it brought back memories of when he and Tonelia had found refuge in a large cave near Sauros during the Saurotillian wars. That would be a story best kept hidden in his mind. He smiled in reminisce of that night. But that was seasons ago, and he knew full well that Tonelia thought of that night often as well.

"I see that you found the pile of wood." He glanced at the fire.

"Yes, I did." She threw some small sticks on the hungry flames. "And you left us enough from your last visit."

"No. Others stay here as well," he said, ringing out his soaked shirt and then opening it up toward hot flames. "I thought it would be empty due to current events."

Andellynn nodded in agreement.

"No other passageways in?" He was hoping for no new developments since he'd last visited this cave, no unwanted visitors, and no new tunnels.

"None," she replied as she looked about the cave. "Now, rest while the meal is prepared." She went back to cooking. All the while he caught her studying him from the corner of her eye.

The cave was warming, and so was the food and conversation.

"When do I become an apprentice?" She broke the moment of peace.

Nolan stared back at her with a slightly joking look. "How do you know that you aren't already?"

"Well, that's easy." She laughed. "You haven't given me the oath over the sword."

"And who told you that?" Nolan looked amused.

"The testaments," she said eagerly.

"Testaments," he repeated.

"Why yes, I've read lots of them," she said proudly.

"Great," he announced, "then you already understand what's expected of you."

"Well, yes, and no?" She sounded a bit confused, which was a first from her since they had meant. He rather felt she had a good handle on her direction. But as she sat there watching him, he could clearly see she was hungry for knowledge.

"Well, all right then." He started his explanation with clarity. "All you must accomplish with me in the present, of course, so that I may observe it is anything self-sacrificing."

"Anything," she said most enthusiastically, understanding every word.

Nolan nodded his head in reply. "Anything, as long has it's in front of me, witness sort of thing," he added with a motion of a rolling hand.

Andellynn leaned backed for a moment to reflect. Nolan watched the red glow of the fire bounce on her face, neck, and cleavage.

"Are the testaments meant to be remembrances, so we are not forgotten?" she added.

"One should hope so." His stomach rumbled, and with that she turned the lizard over the fire and poured them both some herbal harvest.

"But as I read the testaments, I still do not understand why a wielder?" she said perplexed.

"Don't misunderstand." She eyed Nolan. "We are all grateful for you." She paid him the compliment and then continued, hesitantly, "Just …"

"Go on."

"Are they to be the voice of Zoarians?" she inquired.

"No."

"Well, that would not make sense, since they do interact with the lords and ladies," she answered herself. "Perhaps a neutral party then." Andellynn perked with her brilliance and gave him a quick glance for assurance.

"Go on." He sipped his drink. It was welcomed and satisfying.

"Because everyone needs someone to be in charge." She smiled.

He smiled back, for that was exactly what he was thinking. "Or someone to blame when things go wrong," he suggested over another sip.

"They do not." She stared at him with those alluring eyes, and she was serious.

He smiled in gratitude and took a sip.

"Then help me understand how you do it." She sat up and treated him with her full attention.

"Understand what?" He placed his cup in a secure spot and grabbed a towel to dry himself.

"How you juggle the decisions." She watched closely.

"How so?" he asked.

"Well, you're here to the west while your home in the east, your uncle is about to lose everything." She was concerned.

He chuckled to himself, for that's what he was thinking. "My young warrior in training, you need to weigh the gains and losses." He understood her concern but was really trying to justify himself internally.

"How so? Itmoore is your home kingdom. It has been in your family for—"

"One thousand nine hundred ninety-eight seasons," he answered.

"That must be hard to turn your back on?"

"I didn't turn my back," he said, defending himself. "Yes, the decisions are most difficult, but you must find the balance. Loose Itmoore, and that's just a small kingdom. Yes, it's a personal loss. But when compared to losing Urlon, especially should it fall into Sauros control, well, that could damage Anglyllon as a whole."

"But if Krhan gains the kingdom?" She looked for an alternative and that's what he had thought of as well.

"It would be well cared for, but she will not let that happen." He spoke of Tonelia and gave Andellynn an assurance.

"And neither will we," she responded boldly.

"See, it is a rewarding job after all," he said encouragingly. "How's the meal looking?" He stared at the lizard as his stomach protested again.

"It needs a bit more waiting, I'm afraid." And with that, her stomach stirred as well.

"More harvest then." He reached his cup out to Andellynn, who promptly refilled it.

"Nolan, I'm sure I don't have to inform you of how divided the land is over your hopes of a united one." She sounded just a bit concerned. "It carries a great deal of merit and would resolve many challenges between the kingdoms. But many questions remain."

Nolan stared into the cup, and swirling steams of hot herbal harvest rose to his senses. "I know. Where would all the orbs go and what do the Zoarians say?" He paused and reflected more. He smirked and looked at her. "You already know that Sauros is in favor."

"Great." She chuckled. "All under Vax's rule or whatever centurion kills him next."

They chuckled at the thought.

"But seriously, Nolan. What if someone or something wanted you out of the way?" She poked the meal and turned it again.

He peered over the rim of his cup and wondered if she was thinking the same thoughts again. "What?" he said hesitantly.

Well, the Hammer line has been a long one," she stated. "Think about it. Your family has had that sword for—"

"We've had it and lost it," he bluntly reminded her.

"I know the testaments and your heritage," Andellynn said plainly. "It's no secret that the first Hammer gained quick favor with the Zoarians, especially with your wisdom."

"What are who driving at?"

"Perhaps you're being set up."

"Why?" he pondered.

"In my brief but vast travels"—she poked the fire— "I've learned there are many who feel a new and different family of wielders should adorn the parchment of testaments." She glanced over to him, and their eyes locked.

He placed his cup down and wished for stronger *lade*. But they had none, and that was perhaps a good thing.

"Because maybe the Hammer line never really wanted unification in the first place." She stared at him.

"Now, that doesn't make sense," he blurted out.

"It's not in the testaments," she said defensively.

He held his tongue while his mind scanned the numerous testaments that, as a boy and even still this season as an experienced wielder, he digested and studied until he knew every fold and crease. It was just common knowledge what his heritage expected. "My father and his father before him all fought for the orbs to be in one location," he corrected her.

"Did they?"

"Yes, they did," he said sternly.

"Perhaps you misunderstood the word *unification*," she said cautiously.

He was not immediately offended and reassured her with a smile that invited her to continue this most unique conversation.

"Unification simply may have meant all the kingdoms joined by a common bond," she offered.

"But aren't they already?" he inquired.

"Survival is one thing, Nolan, but success is another." She paused. "A consolidation of resources, if you prefer some sort of sharing between the kingdoms as opposed to the segregation among them," she proposed.

"And I agree." He was most impressed with his partner's thoughts.

"The kingdoms survive by trading and doing what they need to do in order to grow, but success comes from a common goal."

"And the common goal is to succeed," he stated.

"But not if one kingdom was the last to stand," she pointed out.

"It would succeed then," he said.

"It would struggle to survive, Nolan." She sounded almost correcting. "Look to the Unknown Kingdom for example."

"I could understand that." He continued to agree. "It stood alone, unique, and perhaps it was unable to succeed."

"Perhaps this is what Lord Vendoff understands?"

She offered a new twist that very much intrigued him. "Continue." He sipped his harvest, which was by now cooling.

"Perhaps he doesn't seek all the orbs of the East Kingdoms. Perhaps the common goal is to ward off the impending attack from across the Morning Sea?"

"A united front but each kingdom consolidating instead of uniting the orbs under one lord," he agreed. "But neither the Zoarians nor I see from where he is gathering his evidence," he added candidly. "So, in the Zoarians' eyes, this could be a new thought of taking over the smaller kingdoms."

"Which brings us back to the testaments and wielders," she said.

"And how so?" He was intrigued.

"Someone sees you as a threat."

"Like I haven't heard that before." He waved her off with an amused chuckle.

"And perhaps you weren't listening." She stared at him.

He understood.

"Nolan." It sounded like a plea. "You're trying to change customs, such as these kingdoms, which have been independent since our founding some eight thousand seasons ago. Hiding heirs to the orbs and what it takes to make a kingdom, let alone the responsibility of keeping it. You're not going to be able to just change those thoughts in a few seasons by securing all the orbs in one location, in one kingdom, especially Urlon."

He studied her hard as if his inner thoughts were materializing into solid shape before him. Perhaps for the first time in many seasons, he'd found a person he could bounce his ideas off. For these challenges had plagued him season to season, and perhaps now he would have to finally confront them, make a decision, and stand with it. He had always been highly optimistic, but at this moment, he began to feel just downright excited. Nevertheless, a small battle was already starting to brew deep within his thoughts, one that reminded him of why he'd had so few apprentices during his career. However, he did make a stand with a decision. He could just spit. "I understand," he answered about changing customs.

"Nolan." She reached out and touched his arm. "I'm just saying, what would become of wielders should you and Tonelia achieve your testament?"

He was dead silent without words or action, for this very thought had occurred to him on a daily basis. What would become of a long-standing tradition of wielding should they unite the orbs? Perhaps the wielder would take on new responsibilities? Maybe he was about to change everything old and familiar to something new and different. Change the customs and manners and reinvent an old idea. Create something that would last for seasons to come. Or worse yet, destroy all Anglyllon?

For quite some time, he remained in deep thought, and Andellynn left him to his inner voice. She cut the lizard and offered him some slices. He felt her understand his quietness and that she was not at all put off by his sudden rudeness. After all, she'd shoved the ship out to drift and just wanted to see where the winds would take the ideas.

Nolan nibbled on the tough little hide and sipped away his herbal harvest, all the while staring deep into the red flames of their warm fire. The storm continued its fury. Thunder exploded into the cave and lightning did its finest to illuminate every inch of their small shelter. Thankfully the mouth of the entrance was higher than the road outside, for the rivers of water rushed downhill and spilled out into the ruins far below.

There would be no threat of Saurotillians this night, for they had headed for dryer land, he thought to himself as he now returned his attention back to Andellynn, who was still sitting close and combing out her hair. Who had sent her and why? Was it because he was not listening? Was that why she was here? He scrutinized her closely. Green alluring eyes much like that of Tonelia. Tantalizing young body. Was she there to distract him further? He cursed and could just spit. He had said no apprentice, and he meant it!

"Damn," he said under his breath.

"What?" a startled Andellynn responded.

"Nothing." He brushed it off. "Just what again compelled you to seek me out?"

"I told you." She smiled. "I need an appointment."

"Oh, Lord Toranden and Auroria. I remember now." He sat up and poured a fresh cup.

"So, spill it," she eagerly inquired. "What's the plan?"

"Plan." He rolled to his side and propped himself up on his elbow with his belly more content.

She topped her cup and awaited his response. "Why, yes. You were conversing with a Zoarian only this morning," she said. "The mountain and Port Illenwell are only about a sun's ride."

"Don't be so eager."

He could instantly tell by her stare that she was a little confused. "Didn't the Zoarian give you any advice?" she asked.

He was silent for a moment and rather reluctant to answer, for he was not sure how she would respond. So, he just gave her the truth. "No."

"We have no plan." She looked puzzled.

"On my job," he started, "there could be many distractions, variables, possibilities if you will. I have learned some hard lessons from my past jobs."

"Like what?" she blurted out, eager to learn.

"Let's just say that I have my own vision, my reality"—he chuckled— "of how the job should go."

"And?" She was impatient.

"Stubborn attitudes don't accomplish anything," he said, teaching her.

"What do the Zoarians offer?" she asked.

"Quite a lot actually," he proudly responded.

"Do they?" She did not seem so convinced.

He was puzzled and decided to pursue her thoughts further. "And what, my excellent sword, do you know of Zoarians?"

"Other than catching a glimpse of one this morning," she said honestly, "I've never seen one physically. But what I have heard throughout my travels is another story."

"Like what?"

"I have heard that they're not as wise as one would come to think."

"How so?"

"For one, they never offer solid answers from what I understand," she plainly stated.

"What else?" he wanted her to continue.

"Well, don't you find that frustrating?" she offered.

"Frustrating to the point of what?"

"Perhaps manipulating," she answered.

He straightened immediately upon the word. "Now, where would you have come across a thought like that?" He was sure that only Tonelia thought that way. But honestly, deep down, Andellynn knew his thoughts as well. Best be on guard, for his little warrior was becoming more interesting as the night wore on.

"Well from you," she responded. "You may be calm and weathered by the seasons, but you do have the testament to guide you. Anyone can easily read that. You're also concerned about what information is given to you from the Zoarians and whether they are forthcoming or are they manipulating you for the outcome—learning from your wisdom perhaps."

"I don't recall ever mentioning my thoughts about the Zoarians since we have met."

"No, perhaps you didn't," she said calmly. "But your actions do speak loudly."

He cursed, for she had caught him at the river. "I'll admit that I was slightly agitated by that meeting, but I would have in no way implied that they are manipulating me. So, who would have planted that thought into your pretty little brain? And exactly why are you here?" He kept composed, but he was growing concerned.

"I'm here for the apprentice job and to go no further," she plainly said.

"Are you really?"

"Nolan Hammer," she responded, "I've been traveling all over Anglyllon and studying this sword for almost twenty-five seasons now, and you want me to remember someone once saying that the Zoarians are manipulating thugs." She paused. "Ever since I received this sword, I've trained for this moment."

"And just what moment would that be?" He was apprehensive to hear the answer.

"The position for Lord Toranden and nothing else."

They locked eyes. And within a moment, almost like Tonelia's, her green, alluring eyes suddenly went soft and inviting. "I'm just saying that you shouldn't let anyone, or anything manipulate you, Nolan, especially the Zoarians."

He sipped his harvest and forced himself to relax, for he could not immediately sense that she was up to anything. But he could not shake the feeling that he should have stayed alone on this job. Someone to watch his back there in the black depths of the mountain, he mocked himself. Tonelia and Aquila had both suggested the same thing. All right, what was up? Where was this warrior really from? And after he'd retrieved that orb, would this one really watch his back—perhaps as she drove that black sword through it?

"Nolan." She broke his concentration. "What if you have become too dangerous for the Zoarians?"

"I thought of that," he said softly in contemplation.

"What if they are directing you toward Illenwell and your untimely end?" She leaned toward him, and their eyes met. He could easily tell they were concerned for him.

"Do you know something that makes you dangerous to them?"

He cocked his head and concentrated harder, for perhaps she was onto something.

"I know I shouldn't expect anything in return for my services, but …"
He paused.

"Well, you're the one who turned away every offer ever made to you,"
she replied.

"I don't need anything," he said, defending himself. "All is provided
for my needs. The kingdoms see to that."

"But not all your needs," she pressed.

"Well, yes there are a few," he agreed.

"But on this particular job, you were offered something special." She
continued to stare at him.

"I was." He was now intrigued at what she knew.

"And you made a stand."

"I almost wish I hadn't," he said regretfully, but he was getting more
nervous as to what she knew.

"But if you stop, what will happen to the offer?" She knew his thought
again.

"What offer might we be referring to?" He sat up and leaned toward
her now.

"The one for Tonelia's daughter."

She knew.

He cursed.

"How did you know of that?" he fought to remain calm.

"Relax." She waved him off. "I overheard Krhan's warriors one night
while they were on their way to meet you."

"But none of them could possibly have known." Nolan's concern now
turned to worry—or, worse yet, dread.

"Well, apparently they did."

Nolan jumped to his feet and startled her. "You are absolutely certain
this is what you heard?" He stared down at her.

"Completely," she answered.

"Then there is a spy, or you're right about that manipulation." He cursed and then stormed toward the cave opening.

"Nolan." She called for him, and he stopped. Andellynn sprang to her feet. "You need to trust me." There was a long pause.

"Give me a minute," he responded calmly. Then he continued to the entrance and the raging storm outside.

He reached the opening and cursed the black swirls of thunder and lightning as it poured upon the mountains. "Dorgon, my old friend, I'm so disgusted right now that I could just spit." Cold rain splashed upon his face and the torrential wind pounded against him. But he gave it not a thought. "This is the perfect example of why working alone is better than a team," he tried to yell over the constant noise of rain.

And then, for a long time, he stood there in the entrance. All the while, the raging storm, just the same as his thoughts, fought over mountains, the ruins, and the surrounding terrain. Was there a spy? Or was his new warrior up to something? Could Tonelia be in jeopardy? Or could Krhan be up to more mischief than he had originally thought? This could damage or, worse yet, finish the testament. Nolan would have to see it through. Perhaps Tonelia was being manipulated or unwittingly jeopardizing the entire testament towards unification. But by whom and why? Best make this a quick trip to meet with Laiaden and then off to secure that orb.

Once they had reached the cave, he had begun to formulate a plan to get rid of her and fast. But now, under these new circumstances, best keep Andellynn close at all costs. Not only was she the first apprentice who had really tried to understand him, but she also got it. *But on the other hand, she knows more then she is letting on, and I'd better find out what I'm in for.*

He looked back over his shoulder to find her attending the fire. It was strong and bright. Nolan shrugged his shoulders and returned to his place. Andellynn smiled warmly as she unrolled her blanket for the evening's rest.

"Best keep your sword close," he suggested, "while I take the first watch."

She reached over her head and pulled her black blade close. Once secure, she closed her eyes.

Nolan sat there, with one eye on her and the other on the entrance. It wasn't that he expected anyone or anything. However, after that enlightening conversation, he figured he'd best keep alert from now on. He cursed again and could just spit.

Andellynn was jolted from her sleep by the loud crack of thunder as brilliant explosions of light illuminated their little dark sanctuary. She sat erect and bent her head until she heard the relieving crack from her aching neck. The cave floor had shown no mercy or warmth throughout the rainy storm. Distant thunder once again reverberated throughout the cave. Andellynn looked to the entrance, and it was still late as a dark and stormy night continued its fury. Her eyes adjusted as they fell upon the smoldering embers of their fire. The cave, barely lit by the eerie faint red glow, gave Andellynn that unsecure feeling. More threatening thunder rumbled outside as she began to survey the entire surroundings until her eyes discovered a large, gaping hole that had mysteriously appeared where there was none last night, and she was absolutely certain of that. She sat up and gave the new appearance a bewildered look.

"Nolan." She reached to wake him but only found his empty covers. She peered around and found his sword was missing as well.

She got up and armed herself. Rustling the fire alive again, she searched the small woodpile for just the right stick. She found a heavy one and wrapped some rags that she carried tightly around one end. Putting it to the fire, it was set ablaze, shedding more light on the eerie darkness. The revived fire of life illuminated the cave, giving her plenty of clear vision.

Her first instinct was the windbreds, but the storm appeared to be just as bad as before. The cave entrance appeared to be a waterfall. Nolan would not have left in that, let alone have heard the stir of windbreds over that deafening noise.

She turned her attention toward the new opening and cautiously approached with her torch outstretch. "Nolan?" she called out towards the hole.

Nothing but her pounding heart and empty silence answered her. Drawing her sword and her breath, she went in. The rain and thunder continued to pound outside, and a flash of lighting once again illuminated the empty cave.

With only the security of her torch and a rapidly sweaty palm grasping tightly around the handle of her sword, Andellynn moved nervously down the winding tunnel. Where had it come from? And where was Nolan?

And why didn't he wake me? She cursed. She fought to see just past the glow of the flames, but it was just black. And with each turn, she fought the urge to leap at the unexpected. But so far, just dark, clammy cave walls came within the glow of her light. Andellynn continued her search with her eyes and remained totally alert to the slightest sound or movement. The tunnel never forked. Nor did it expose any other openings; it was as if it was forcing her down this route—mocking her tenaciousness to discover the truth, resolve the mystery, and find the answer. Andellynn cursed, for she knew she had unwittingly trapped herself. She knew she could be reckless at times—such as now and taking on the journey to apprenticeship.

But as Nolan always said, make a decision and stand with it. And so, she did, even to the bitter end and quite possibly the dragon of Illenwell that waited just a head.

Andellynn stopped to rethink her strategy. She waved the torch around the black maw that now had her completely sucked in. She cursed and wanted to turn back. But there it came again; tenaciousness, curiosity, bold foolishness, whatever it was, it called to her, no begged her to take one more step farther into the darkness.

She forged on for some time until, around a corner, came the faint light near the end. Andellynn stopped and studied it. Apprehensively, she pressed on. Tenaciousness. That would be her end. Not much farther was the glow of eerie lights that filled the hallway before her. Cautiously, she approached and looked in. It was a giant cavern, and it immediately drew her in. Her startled moment was replaced by absolute fear, as she locked eyes on the massive throne at the back of the cavern. And the huge multicolored dragon that sat upon it. Its wings spread wide, and its long tail wiped from behind the throne. The large head of horns and white glowing eyes moved on a long, thick neck. With a large grin from its menacing snout full of jagged teeth, it cut her apart like the wielder's sword of gold that could slice anything. It stretched out its right forearm as if it would reach over and grab the young lady warrior, but instead, it pointed one of its long sharp talons at her.

"What do you want?" she yelled back.

But it only pointed at her again.

"What do you want?" she screamed back.

But the dragon just pointed.

"Answer me, or I'll cleave that talon clean off!" she threatened, pointing her sword straight at the defiant dragon.

It angrily stood up and pointed its talon to the far side of the cavern. Following the direction, her eyes fell upon the mound of round spheres.

She did not understand, and the great beast stomped its left leg, and the cavern shook of its fury. Then it pointed again to the spheres.

Andellynn cautiously stepped over for a closer look. And before her were all the orbs gathered from all the kingdoms and kingdoms yet to be founded. She could hear the countless screams of death as the orbs burst with flashes of fire. She drew nearer as if under the orbs' spell. The glow illuminated her face. She watched in shear horror as the individual kingdoms died under the bellows of dragon's fire. Buildings and people burned before her in utter terror and helplessness. She whirled around to the dragon lord and raised her sword high for her impending charge.

The dragon pointed at her again. But this time, she caught the direction and suddenly realized it was the end of her sword and the orb that it contained.

"Come for it!" she yelled back and poised her sword for combat.

The dragon belted an inferno of red death and then grinned at her.

As the cave exploded with its fireball, the massive brilliance illuminated the entire cave. And with it, she caught sight of a long ledge that completely surrounded the entire cavern like a huge balcony; perched like giant birds of prey were countless dragons. They snorted and hissed down at her. Some blew fire, and others screamed. She'd turned to flee when she confronted a familiar figure.

With great relief, she yelled to him, "Nolan, where have you been? Be quick with that sword. We have beasts to slay."

But he just stood there and said nothing.

"Nolan?" she yelled at him again, but she could plainly see he was deep within a trance.

He pointed to her sword as well.

"What is with you?" she screamed, hoping to jar him free from his trap.

"They need your orb," he said plainly.

"Nolan, please, it's me!" she pleaded.

He just stared and pointed.

She looked at him, puzzled. He was not responding.

Nolan moved closer. "Give it to our lord," he ordered her and pointed to the great dragon.

Above her, as response to Nolan, the dragons bellowed and screamed.

"Draw your sword. They're not getting this orb, and we're leaving," she demanded.

"I can't help you, Andellynn," Nolan said as he took another step closer to her.

She stared back at him in confusion and then swung her sword threateningly.

He completely ignored the swing and moved in closer.

"*Nolan Hammer!*" She bellowed and swung twice to cut his path.

But he came all the same.

Andellynn's eyes darted wildly about the cave looking for the escape. There was nothing. Nolan had the tunnel blocked, and the dragon was behind. Above, countless dragons laughed at her.

Her only chance was to move around Nolan and make the tunnel, so she allowed him to advance. But as he came into better view, Andellynn froze. For just below his waist was nothing but exposed black and burned bones. Andellynn's stomach turned, and then she looked into Nolan's pleading eyes.

He continued to move closer to her. "Please. Andellynn, he needs your orb. Make a decision and make a stand." He mocked her. Then he chuckled.

"*No!*" she screamed and turned to face the dragon lord. "What have you done?"

It only replied by fanning its huge wings out over the cavern. That impressive sight was soon hindered by a horde of little, black, hairy humanlike creatures that came pouring around the sides of the dragon's throne. Screaming, they whirled clubs of large white bones and thick heavy tree branches above their heads. They filled the cavern and advanced toward her.

"Thalls." She turned to Nolan again.

This time, he was not alone. Behind him were countless burned zombies, advancing and closing in on her.

"Give our lord the orb," they seemed to be chanting.

"Stop!" she screamed and thrashed her sword at them. Hopeless desperation began to set in, as from behind she heard the coming horde of Thalls.

She stared, pleading with Nolan, but he only responded with, "Make a decision. Make a stand. Give our lord your orb." He grinned.

The circle closed, and Andellynn viciously swung her sword as she whirled around to the closing circle.

"*No!*" she screamed. "*Nooooo!*"

Andellynn shot up from her dream. She was breathing hard, and her hair was wet with sweat. She took control of herself as she looked around. Nolan was still in a restful sleep. His large chest rose and fell, pushing out a small snore of contentment. Andellynn stared off to the entrance of the cave. The weather outside was peaceful and sunny.

After a moment to regain herself, she quietly arose. A gray line of smoke ascended from a dying fire. All was quiet for now. She secured her sword and checked on Nolan again, lying there with his chest slowly rising and falling with each deep breath. She bent down and treated him to a kiss on the check and then smiled and went for the cave's entrance.

Outside, all seemed still and quiet. Blue skies opened to a few passing clouds. A large flock of birds headed west over the mountains. Puddles of rainwater were slowly beginning to evaporate in the midmorning sun. A heavy mist floated in the valley and covered the ruins in a whitish cloud of rolling serenity. More birds screamed and hovered about. Andellynn heard the windbreds rustle from nearby and went down to check on them.

A short time later, Nolan woke to find the cave empty. He rolled out his covers and pulled himself together. No fire was burning. Nor was food or harvest steaming. And no Andellynn. Her sword was gone. *Perhaps she went to take care of her needs*, he thought. *Better check on her and our rides.* He stepped outside, where the sun greeted him, and small clouds slid across a blue sky. He cupped his hands over his eyes and scanned the calm morning and immediately found her tracks as they led off into the direction of the windbreds. He made his way to them. The windbreds were fine but restless. However, nearby. he spied a discomforting discovery—large imprints of some mighty big lizards, several of them. She could not have taken them all.

He cursed under his breath and could just spit. He followed the freshly made tracks of the Tyrannattors as they cut across the muddy road and descended into the Unknown Kingdom, where they disappeared into the thick mist that swirled around towering ruins and wild vegetation.

He immediately knew it would be several suns' travel to Sauros and the court of Vax. That meant more time for someone to get past that dragon. Or perhaps this was part of Vax's plan. *Delay the wielder game again*, he thought.

Tyrannattors were fast, very fast. But if he could go for the windbreds and their belongings, he might have a chance. His thoughts raced as an opportunity had presented itself to him. Now the question was, what to do? He was presented with several choices. Leave her to deal with Sauros. After all, she had dealt with their kind before. Seize this opportunity and make for the Mountain of Illenwell, which loomed just ahead, and spy out the orb and the dragon. Make for port and see Lord Laiaden.

The latter options would leave Andellynn to wrestle many suns with Sauros. And although he knew Vax would not hurt her, she would be trapped there until he worked out any kind of recoveries.

"Make a decision and stand with it!" He cursed out loud.

And that is just what he did.

But the moment he turned back toward the cave, three centurions came racing around the corner of their cave, each riding a very large and hungry Tyrannattor.

Out of shear disgust, he spat. "*Vax!*"

Be on the lookout for *Testament of Wielders*
Book Two: The Wielder's Apprentice

Printed in the United States
by Baker & Taylor Publisher Services